I0612504

The Carson Series

(Books 1 - 4)

By Paul Garvey

Copyright © 2016 Paul Garvey

All rights reserved.

ISBN-10: 1943415021
ISBN-13: 978-1943415021

Each book in the Carson Series is a work of fiction. Any resemblance to actual events or persons, living or dead, is entirely coincidental.

1

The Carson Series

A GHOST IS BORN

Billy Carson

Billy Carson slouched on the steps of Saint Gregory's church with a switchblade in his pocket and an empty flask at his feet. Sweat stains rimmed the outside of his black suit and his face was sharp with stubble. He buried his brother John less than forty-eight hours before, watched the casket get lowered into the hole and stayed there watching until fresh loam covered the stained pine. His eyes found the flask next to his scuffed Bostonians and remained there fixed until a pair of long legs in dark tights walked by and cast a shadow over the hollow tin.

'Excuse me, miss.' He said and watched the pair of legs slow to a stop a safe distance away from him. Billy shielded his eyes from the sun and raised his head. She stopped and was looking at him, but her body language said hurry up.

'You have the time?' he asked.

'You need a doctor or something?' she asked back.

'Doctor? No, the time, that's what I asked.'

'Yeah I know, but you look in rough shape. Carney hospital's down the street. I could get someone to come over for you.'

'You work there?'

She paused. 'None of your business. You want a doc or what?'

'Listen I just want the fucking time.' He said.

She rolled her eyes before looking at her watch. 'It's ten o'clock.' She said then walked away. Billy heard her mutter 'asshole' under her breath, but not that far under.

'Wait' he called 'ten o'clock . . . what day?' He watched her turn briefly. She didn't answer, just turned again and kept walking.

'It's Monday you fucking degenerate.' Billy heard a familiar voice say from behind him. He shifted on the steps and turned towards the door of the church. His head grew light when he moved and he could taste bile or whiskey, or both, rising from his stomach to his throat. He took a moment and swallowed it back down. 'You talk like that inside the church too?' he asked.

'Only in the confessional, I just tack the swearing on at the end of the session, gets me a discount on penance prayers.'

'You're a peach.'

'Yeah and you're a fucking drunk. Look at you Billy.' The man said.

The man was Billy Carson's best friend and current employer, Nick McNulty. A lifelong friend that swore too much and was built like a rhinoceros if a rhino could stand tall on its hind legs. Billy pushed off his elbows and sat up slowly when McNulty approached. 'How'd you find me?'

'You're drinking whiskey on the fucking church steps at ten in the morning . . . on a fucking Monday. You ain't exactly hiding.'

'It's twelve o'clock somewhere.'

'Yeah and it's fucking bed time in Australia, but you don't see me in my pj's like I'm about to hit the sack.'

'They sell 'em that big?'

'Doubt it.' McNulty said and took a seat on the step above Billy.

'Who called? Kathleen?'

'Yeah, your wife called my wife after the Pastor called her.'

'And now here you are.'

'Yeah, here I am. I got chewed out of it just for knowing you. Plus I'm losing customers by the second with that degenerate Blubsy running the shop.'

'Degenerate, you just learn that word or something.'

'No I hear it a lot, especially when your name comes up in conversation.'

'Do yourself a favor and get a thesaurus.'

'What the fuck do I want with a dinosaur?'

'You're fucking with me right?'

McNulty smiled and stood up. 'Come on Billy. You're late for work.'

'You drop me home?'

'I'm not shitting you, you're coming to work. I need you in the warehouse. I got trucks waiting to be loaded. Half the building sites in Boston are probably on extended coffee cause you're standing in the way of some electrician and his co-ax.'

'Kathleen told you not to bring me home huh?'

McNulty nodded. 'You'll get cleaned up at work and

head home tonight. Your boys don't need to see you looking like a shitfaced lounge singer.'

Billy nodded. He stood up and made an attempt to pat the wrinkles from his suit. 'Let's go.' He said.

McNulty led the way around the back of the church to a small parking lot. Billy's head was swimming at first and his legs were rubber, but he felt a little more in control by the time they reached the lot. He slowed his steps when they approached McNulty's mustang. Billy's chest started to ache. The last time he'd seen that car he was driving it with his brother John dying in the seat next to him. His youngest brother, counting his last breaths before his eyes from what everyone said was an overdose, but Billy felt to be more than that. 'John wasn't into drugs' he told himself. 'No way he'd keep that from me.' His other brother, Walter, was there with John when it happened, but he hadn't spoken to Billy once since that night and he'd disappeared after John's funeral.

McNulty stopped walking and stood next to Billy. He looked at the car then back at Billy. Billy figured he'd read his mind and knew what was bothering him.

'Sorry Billy. Haven't had a chance to pick up something else. You want me to knock on the rectory's door and get someone to call a taxi?'

Billy shook his head. 'No, it's okay. I should've expected to see it. Just wasn't ready for it.'

'I know man. Believe me, it'll be in Quincy Quarries within a week or two, once I get my insurance papers lined up.'

Billy nodded. McNulty stepped over and unlocked the doors and they both climbed in. They drove off to McNulty's shop, which was an electric supply store next to the Neponset River. McNulty parked the mustang in a spot behind the shop and went in the back entrance. Billy followed behind him and McNulty led him into the office. He opened a closet in the office and pulled out a brown paper bag and dropped it onto his desk. He reached in again and came out with a pair of work boots and dropped them at Billy's feet. 'Kathleen dropped them off yesterday in case you showed up at some stage. There's toothpaste and deodorant and that shit in there. Why don't you hit the head and take yourself a whore's shower then meet me in the warehouse.'

Billy reached down and picked up the boots. He slid them under his arm, then grabbed the paper bag off the desk. 'Thanks Nick.' He said. Then he left the office and walked off to the bathroom.

He walked out of the bathroom twenty minutes later wearing clean clothes and feeling somewhat fresher than he had before. He kept the paper bag and rolled up his dirty suit and jammed it inside. He left it in the stockroom before heading through to the warehouse. The warehouse looked empty except for Blubsy Donaghue who stood at the other end of the room wielding a heavy push broom with a cloud of dust all around him. He paused then let out an aggressive sneeze. 'Bless you.' Billy yelled out and it echoed off the tall ceilings.

'Oh hey Billy' Blubsy called and started over towards Billy dragging the broom behind him. Blubsy was smiling when he walked over. In fact, he was always smiling. It was that incessant smiling and cheerfulness that drove Billy crazy after a while. 'What's up Blubs?' Billy said.

Blubsy got up close and didn't stop moving. He dropped the broom behind him and startled Billy with a bear hug. The squeezed caught him off guard and he struggled to breathe for a minute. 'Jesus Blubsy, let me go you fucking Ox.'

Blubsy took his arms off Billy and took a step back. 'Sorry Billy. Just . . . I'm sorry to hear . . . you know.'

'I know Blubs and I appreciate it. Thanks buddy.'

'No problem Billy. You'll let me know if you need anything right.'

'You got it. Hey where's Nick?'

'Try the pipe bay. He came out front and told me to scram, but I think I saw him head out there a minute ago.'

Billy ducked under a low doorway on his way out to the back. The pipe bay was behind the warehouse and led to a double gate fence, which they opened when the trucks pulled in for loading. He saw McNulty next to the opened gates stacking a heavy cable reel on top of another. Billy smiled when he saw him, the reels weighed over a hundred pounds alone, but McNulty made them look like empty boxes. Billy's boots scraped over the gravel as he walked and McNulty paused and turned towards him when he heard him approach.

'Feeling any better?' McNulty asked.

'A little. We got trucks coming in?'

McNulty handed him across a couple sheets of paper that outlined the pick-ups. 'You handle this? I have to watch the front desk.'

'Yeah, I'll take care of it.' Billy said and took the papers from McNulty's hands.

McNulty nodded and headed around front through the opened gate. 'I'll check back in a while.' he called out as he walked away.

Billy looked at the truck lists that McNulty handed him

and got to work pulling out what was needed and stacking pallets. He was sweating from the start and even more so when the first truck arrived and he started loading the galvanized pipe onto the bed from the bay. He'd soaked through the fresh clothes in minutes. He knew each of the drivers that showed up. They all small-talked a little, obviously dancing around the topic of Billy's brother. 'In other words, acting awkward so as to not feel awkward.' Billy thought. He couldn't smell any booze, but he knew others did. He'd gone nose deaf and the poison from the last few days came seeping out of his pores. The work was tiring and after an hour his headache came back and he couldn't quench his thirst no matter how much water he sucked down. It did take his thoughts away from his troubles for a time however, which helped his state of mind.

After the last truck left, Billy closed and locked the gates. He sat in the shade on one of the reels and put his feet on another. He took a gallon of water with him and gulped some down before pouring half of it over his head. McNulty came out and sat next to him. He handed him a sub wrapped in wax paper and a beer. Billy put the sub down next to him and cracked open the beer can. 'Thought I was a drunk? Does that make you an enabler?'

McNulty shrugged. 'Maybe it does. Drink it and shut up. It might help with your headache. You might want a few more later if you plan on sleeping tonight. Otherwise you'll be up with the fucking crawlies.'

'Not sure Kathleen will go for that.'

'I can guarantee she won't.'

'I'll head home shortly and talk to her. You can manage here now right?'

'Yeah, go when you're ready.'

'Thanks Nick.'

McNulty stood up and kicked at some gravel at his feet. He stayed facing Billy, but his head was down. 'Billy' he said and looked up 'we haven't talked since the funeral.'

'I know.'

'Yeah . . . well, what's the story man? What are you gonna do here?'

'About John?'

'Yeah, about John. What's your next move? You done going batshit, or do we all have to keep worrying about you?'

Billy paused for a moment. He was embarrassed all of a sudden. He figured the likes of Kathleen and even his sons, young as they were, might be worried about him, but he hadn't really considered many others would. Definitely he couldn't picture McNulty losing sleep worrying about him, but maybe he was wrong.

'I'm not planning to head out on another bender if that's what you're worried about.'

McNulty shook his head. 'Maybe Kathleen's worried about that, and your kids. I'm talking about something a little more high stakes.'

'You mean DiMatteo?'

'No, fucking Big Bird. Of course DiMatteo.'

Billy didn't answer right away. He just sat looking at his hands. Seamus DiMatteo was a hot-headed, violent up-and-comer in Boston's criminal underworld. His mother was Irish and his father Italian. Growing up he split time between D Street projects in South Boston and a former tenement house in the North End. He looked Irish except for his prominent Latin nose, plus he spoke Italian any chance he could get. It was one of his places, a house in Dorchester, where Billy found his brother John just before he died.

'Well?' McNulty asked.

'Nick, there's a difference between what I want to do and what I can do.'

'No fucking shit. I'm asking what are you gonna do?'

'I guess I don't know yet.'

'DiMatteo's connected on both fronts Billy, just remember that. He knows the micks in Southie and the fucking guidos on Hanover Street. It's a no win if you ask me. I mean . . . maybe you don't have kids, a wife, then maybe you take a chance. But you do, so you ask me, you gotta leave it. You keep digging, there's a good chance you don't like what you find. And there's a better chance some dangerous people don't like what you're digging for.'

'If you were me, what then?'

'I ain't, so I guess I don't have to consider that question.'

'Fine, what if it was me then. What if you pulled me out of that house and you knew, in your gut at least, you knew something didn't add up. You know me better than anyone. Never did drugs, never planned to, all of a sudden I'm foaming at the fucking mouth one second and dead as a Kennedy the next.'

'Billy, I ain't got no answers man. You're in a hairy spot, I know that.'

'You sound like you got all the answers.'

'I don't . . . I just don't want you to do something fucking stupid, then I'm left raising your kids, you get me.'

Billy stood up and faced McNulty. The questions irritated him, but only because they were the same he'd asked himself for days since it all happened. He knew

11

what the right thing was. That was easy. The right thing was to leave it. His wife, his boys, they needed him around and McNulty was right. You get caught sticking your nose somewhere others don't want you to see and that could go south quick. He took a deep breath then exhaled slowly.

'I'm gonna leave it Nicky. I can't have that shit coming back on me and the family.'

McNulty's shoulders seemed to drop a few inches as he appeared to relax. 'Good Billy . . . good.'

A loud bang behind McNulty caused both men to turn quickly towards the warehouse entrance just as Blubsy came barreling out the doorway.

'What the fuck Blubs?' McNulty said. 'Nearly shit myself.'

'Sorry Nick' Blubsy said between breaths. He was panting and put his arm on the doorway. He looked over at Billy. 'It's Kathleen, Billy, she called the phone in the office, she sounded upset. Said for you to get home now.'

'What the fuck? She say why Blubs?'

'Not really Billy, something about a couple guys came around your house asking about you, talking tough and shit like that. Said you need to get home quick.'

McNulty looked over at Billy then back at Blubsy, 'Cops?'

'No . . . not cops, she definitely said not cops.'

'Blubs close the shop down.' McNulty said. 'Let's go Billy, I'm coming with you.'

Vinny "Knuckles" Bruxelles

'You order me the soup?' the small fat man asked.

'Yeah the chowder.' Vinny Bruxelles answered.

'The clam or the seafood?'

'Clam. It's better here, the seafood chowder's a thin broth. Clam has the cream and the bacon. You'll like it.'

'Good, thanks Knuckles.'

'No problem'

Seamus DiMatteo reached over to the next table and grabbed a plastic ashtray and dropped it in front of him. He pulled a smoke from his pack and lit it with a match. 'You want a smoke?' he asked Vinny Bruxelles with the lit cigarette between his teeth.

Vinny Bruxelles waved him off. 'Shit'll kill you. Had an uncle kick it from lung cancer before his fiftieth. Not something I want to deal with myself.'

'Your line of work, lung cancer should be lower on your list of shit you're worried about. Murder, mayhem, guns, knives, prison, you know . . . that type of shit should be front and center. Same for me ya know. I ain't gonna worry about having a smoke when I got a much better chance to catch a bullet in the back.'

Vinny Bruxelles nodded. 'I get what you're saying Seamus, but fuck it, why stack the deck against you? Just cause I might die in the street someday don't mean I'm gonna go play in traffic.'

'Suit yourself.' DiMatteo said. A waitress in a blue apron came over and placed his chowder down in front of him along with a few packets of oyster crackers. DiMatteo tried a spoonful then nodded. 'Good call Knuckles. You know your way around this deli.'

'Yeah well, I've been coming here for thirty years.'

DiMatteo tucked a napkin into his shirt and started shoving spoonfuls of chowder into his mouth. Vinny Bruxelles just watched him and sipped his coffee. 'No wonder he's packed the pounds on' he thought, 'Fucking guy needs a shovel.'

'So' DiMatteo said blotting his face with a napkin after he got to the bottom of the soup bowl. 'You get anything for me? Anything on this Carson guy? You know him a long time right? School even?'

'Yeah I know Billy awhile.'

'So, what's the story then? Do we have anything to worry about. This guy gonna climb up my ass looking for answers?'

'Not sure he will. I would've thought that's the cops' job.'

'It is and it isn't. Let's say for anyone else, the cops might be a little more aggressive on their search.'

'And, what, you know people. You get everything squashed?'

'Let's just say the right people know me and those same people are well placed to make sure this goes down as an OD, clear cut.'

'And is it much more than that Seamus? Any other details I should know?'

'Only thing you need to do is talk to me about this Carson character. I heard the other brother took off to Maine or something, I ain't too concerned with him, I seen that pussy around too often. He ain't coming near me.'

'Walter? Yeah, he's the type to run, not confront. I heard the same, that he took off.'

'And the older one, Billy?'

'I'm not sure what you really want to hear on him. He's a good guy, don't bother no one.'

'I heard he was in the life though.'

'Nah . . . Billy, he was a tough kid growing up. Maybe toed the line for a while, but he was never no street guy.'

'He served right?'

'Army, few years. Some peace keeping duty I think, but no real action. Listen, Billy Carson's alright. At most I'd say talk to him and feel him out yourself. He got a family, wife and two kids, probably needs this thing to blow over too. You put his mind at ease, maybe that helps. I could talk to him if you want. Like I said, I know him a little bit.'

'I already got somebody on it.' DiMatteo said.

Vinny Bruxelles leaned back in his chair and stretched his back. He rubbed his hands together and heard his knuckles crack. Early thirties and he already felt chronic pain in his hands. 'It's the decade with Tooth & Nail MC starting to wear on the tendons.' he thought. 'DiMatteo's already put people after Carson, this can't be good.' He knew how guys like DiMatteo worked. They could never wait things out, always jumping to action without thinking the situation through. Sometimes he hated that these were the guys that paid him. He'd stymie the guilt most times, but every so often it'd creep up on him and make him question his life. This was one of those times. Billy Carson wasn't exactly a friend, but he knew him and he thought enough of him to hope there was another way past this.

'What?' DiMatteo asked. 'You got issue with this?'

Vinny Bruxelles shrugged. 'Depends on what this is? You wanna let me in on details.'

'Relax Knuckles. I got a couple guys to peak in on the

wife and kids. Just words for now. Don't worry about it. No need to sit there like you're about to shit yourself.'

'Words right?'

'Yeah, for now.'

'Well if it's done, maybe you gotta think next steps.'

'Why's that? I figured a little fear might force a resolution. Let him know I'm not for playing games.'

'I'd guess it'd speed things up alright.' Vinny Bruxelles said.

'Okay, but . . . I can see you got something to say Knuckles, just fucking come out with it.'

'I really wish you coulda let me have a word first.'

'Listen, don't get soft over this. My line of work, you gotta hit hard and fast. And you gotta hit where it hurts. For some guys it's their pockets. For guys without dough, maybe it's the homestead. Either way, you gotta let people know you can get to 'em, whenever, wherever. What's your problem anyway?'

Vinny Bruxelles shrugged. 'Listen Seamus, you called me in to talk about this. You prefer I take my business elsewhere, that I don't . . . consult on this, then that's fine.'

'Alright alright, calm down Knuckles. I wanna hear what you gotta say. You know I respect your work, you and your gang of thieves.' DiMatteo said and smiled.

Vinny Bruxelles leaned forward and slid his hands across the table. DiMatteo slid back, but not before Bruxelles got hold of his wrist and applied pressure. Vinny Bruxelles watched DiMatteo's face. He could see the young gangster was infuriated, but in too much pain to express it. Vinny Bruxelles said 'You refer to my club as a gang of thieves or anything else that I might find derogatory again and you're no longer gonna need to worry about Billy Carson or the cops or any other fucking thing again. Understand me?' he nodded and waited for DiMatteo to nod in acknowledgement. 'I know you know people and you're connected on a few fronts.' Vinny Bruxelles continued 'but you seem to forget, that Tooth & Nail MC freelances for everybody you know and everybody you don't. Our loyalty is to the club and ourselves. So watch your fucking tongue.'

DiMatteo reached down under the table slowly and Vinny Bruxelles watched him, still holding onto his wrist. DiMatteo's hand came up with a thick brown envelope. He slapped it on the table and slid it across. Through gritted teeth he said, 'I'm ready to rent your loyalty.'

Vinny Bruxelles held onto DiMatteo's wrist a few moments longer then slowly released pressure. Pain was shooting through his own hands, but he consciously refused to rub them in front of DiMatteo. He reached over and picked up the envelope. He opened it and scanned the bills quickly, then stuffed it into his jacket's inside pocket. He watched DiMatteo rub his wrist for a few seconds.

'You want to know what I think Seamus?'

'Yeah, I'm asking?'

'I think you made the wrong move putting guys on Carson's family. You might regret it.'

'Why's that?'

'There might be blowback.'

'I told you the cops aren't gonna be an issue here.'

'I ain't referring to the Police.'

'What then, you think Carson's gonna try something? Come on Knuckles, you said it yourself, he ain't no street guy. What the fuck's he gonna do?'

17

'Maybe he won't, I don't know. I'm just saying, you push some people, they might push back.'

'And you think Billy Carson might be the type of guy to . . . push back. You think that makes me nervous?'

Vinny Bruxelles shrugged. 'I think if you weren't worried about something you would've waited before sending a couple heavies to intimidate this man's wife and kids. All I said is he ain't in the life, don't mean the man won't take exception to being bullied, especially if you're leaning on his family. My guess is we'll find out soon enough.'

DiMatteo smiled. 'I guess we will.'

Vinny Bruxelles slid his chair back and stood up. He watched DiMatteo rub his wrist again. DiMatteo looked angry. 'Good' Vinny Bruxelles thought.

'I'll be in touch shortly' DiMatteo said.

Vinny Bruxelles nodded and pointed at the empty bowl 'Pay for your own fucking soup.' he said then turned and walked out of the restaurant.

Billy Carson

'What did they look like?' Billy Carson asked his wife Kathleen while sitting at the kitchen table full of used coffee mugs and dirty plates.

'I don't know. They looked like guys . . . local, I guess from the way they talked.'

'Come on Kathleen, hair color, eye color, scars, tattoos, what?'

Kathleen's eyes welled up and she dabbed at them with a Kleenex. She made a fist and bit down on her knuckle, obviously fighting back tears.

'Billy.' McNulty said from the doorway. Billy Carson looked over at McNulty. McNulty gave him a slow nod that Billy took to mean 'calm the fuck down.' He took a deep breath and nodded. He knew Kathleen was scared and confused and that badgering her wasn't helping anyone. He was scared and confused himself and full of rage that he was battling to hold back until he had more information, understood more what he was dealing with. He took a step towards Kathleen then knelt down in front of her and put his hand on her knee.

'I'm sorry.' he said in a gentler tone. 'I'm just . . . upset.'

'So am I Billy! Jesus Christ.'

'I know' Billy said and took his hand back. He could feel her recoil when he touched her and didn't blame her one bit. 'What about . . . can you remember what they said? Did they threaten you or the boys, anything like that?'

Kathleen paused for a moment then shook her head slowly. 'Not really. Well, not directly at least. They asked about you, asked where you were, when you'd be home, that type of thing.'

'And you told them all you knew right?'

'Yes, I didn't know who they were or what they wanted at first. I thought maybe cops at first, but no way, they weren't cops. Cops would've said they were cops and showed badges. These guys didn't. Plus they didn't look like cops.'

'Good, that's fine. I'm not hiding Kathleen, no matter who they were. What else did they say?'

'Nothing specific really. Asked if I was alone, asked about the boys. What they said wasn't really what scared me. It was more how they said it. It just felt creepy, like anything they said meant something different than the actual words coming out of their mouths. More like he wanted me to feel threatened without actually threatening me. I know that doesn't sound right. I know it sounds like I'm overreacting, but I don't think I am.'

Billy shook his head. 'I don't think you are either. Something's up Kathleen. They were here to send a message I think.'

'Yeah, but what message is that? I mean, what have you gotten us into?'

'Me? Are you shitting me?'

'What? What else should I expect? Haven't seen you in more than a day, then next thing two creeps show up at my door acting funny and asking questions about you.'

'Doesn't mean I did something to bring them around.'

'Well what then? Jesus Billy, I'm in the dark here, I don't know what to think.'

'I'm not sure of what yet.'

'But you'll find out?'

'I think I have to. I plan to try.'

'Okay . . . well, are you going to leave me here alone

with the boys?'

'I have to go talk to some people and figure this out. My old man's on his way. He'll stay here til I'm back.'

Billy gave Kathleen a kiss on her cheek, it felt cold and forced. Then he went and talked to his sons briefly before leaving again with McNulty. 'What do you think?' Billy asked while climbing into the Mustang.

'Doesn't sit well with me, two fucking dirtbags kicking the tires at your apartment. Doesn't sit well at all.'

'It had to be DiMatteo.'

'I have no doubt. It sure as hell ain't a coincidence.'

'What else have you heard about DiMatteo?'

'Like?'

'Like, how fucking dangerous is the little fat bastard?'

'You've met him?'

'I've seen him before, around Dorchester. I don't know him, never spoke to him.'

'Seems to know you.'

'Seems to intend on getting to know me anyway.'

'I don't like it one bit.'

'Me neither. You know what this means right?'

'You mean about John? My guess is he didn't just take an overdose.'

'If he did, why the fuck would DiMatteo bother trying to antagonize me, or intimidate more likely?'

'My guess is he wouldn't.'

'My guess is the same.'

'Your old man carrying?'

'Didn't say as much, but I know he's got a piece. After everything with John, he's on edge. Withdrawn, like the rest of us, can't believe what happened, not to John. He knows something's up, I can tell. So yeah, I'd say he's carrying.'

'Good. What about you?'

'I don't have a piece. Just this.' Billy said and slid his switchblade to the edge of his pocket so McNulty could see.'

'Well you'll be all set if you want to pick steak out of your teeth.'

'Better than nothing.'

'Find a piece Billy. I can help if you need it.'

'I'll think about it. You think those fucking goons would show up again?'

'I don't know, honestly no fucking idea.'

'I can't risk it. The old man can keep watch for now, but something's gotta give. Maybe I should send them up to the lake til this is settled.'

'Maybe.'

'You don't think it's worth it.'

'I'd say it's worth it. My concern is more how you're gonna settle this.'

'Yeah. Fuck.'

'Talk to the little shit?'

'I guess I'll have to, but . . .'

'You need to cool off a minute first.'

'Why? If the fucking guy's responsible for John. He's fucking dead.'

'And if he is responsible, I one hundred percent agree with that Billy. But, if you fly off the handle and go after this guy, maybe it don't come out so good . . . for you or anybody. You need a second to cool it down, that's all I'm saying.'

Billy nodded. He understood McNulty's point, but his chest was about to explode with pressure.

'You know my uncle that runs the bar?' McNulty asked.

Billy nodded 'yes.'

'He knows some guys.'

'What guys?'

'Old guys. Guys that know the like of DiMatteo.'

'So, what am I supposed to do with that?'

'We talk to my uncle first, then set up a meet with one of these guys. Maybe they can square this.'

'You want me to have a sit-down with some fucking mobster? The like of which probably killed my brother . . . not to mention threatened my family.'

'Hey Billy, do what you want. I'm just telling you, there's ways to handle this. Getting yourself killed ain't the best option. '

'No shit.'

'Then why do you seem so intent on it?'

'I'm not, I'm just angry here Nick.'

'Listen Billy, you find out for sure this fucking half-mick, half-guido sent Johnny packing, I'm right beside you, you hear me. I'll help you anyway I can. All I'm saying is talk to someone first, feel out the situation, then figure it out. No matter what you do from here on in, Johnny ain't coming back.'

Billy paused. He checked the glove box for a pack of cigarettes and managed to find a box with three loose smokes inside. He took one out, put it to his lips and pushed in the car lighter.

'Well?' McNulty asked.

The lighter popped a few seconds later, Billy lit the cigarette, took a haul and blew the smoke out the window. 'Call your Uncle, set up the fucking meeting.' he said.

Vinny "Knuckles" Bruxelles

The meeting with Seamus DiMatteo left grime on Vinny Bruxelles' skin. He'd done a few odd jobs for the man in the past and walked away from most interactions with a similar discomfort. There were plenty of things to loathe about Dimatteo in his opinion. 'Unfortunate that he pays so well.' he thought. Ten minutes on the highway was enough to feel refreshed. The road was empty and he tore through the tarmac, opening up the Harley's engine right from the on-ramp. Tooth & Nail Motorcycle Club's original shop sat in a Boston suburb fifteen minutes south of the city. It was still considered headquarters, though most members spent more time on the road or up in Laconia. The gate was open when Vinny Bruxelles pulled up. He dropped to second gear and cruised onto the grounds. The bike purred to a stop next to a few others outside the shop front. He rested it on it's stand and walked in through the garage door. A couple mechanics nodded when they saw him, he nodded back. The sound of metal tools at work echoed off the shop's high ceilings and the familiar taste of exhaust fumes and engine oil found the back of his throat as he made his way through the garage. He walked to the very back and passed through a wooden door painted black with the Club's patch, a smiling skull with a nail cracked through the crown, stencilled on.

The back room was dim as usual. It had few windows and low drop ceilings stained yellow from decades of cigarette smoke. Vinny Bruxelles was well over six feet and couldn't stand up for long in the room without feeling claustrophobic. He walked by the pool table and up to the bar. They paid one of the mechanic's twenty year old daughter to serve drinks and keep the place clean. She was the only other person in the room when he entered. She was putting glasses away and smiled when she saw Vinny Bruxelles walk up to the bar. He smiled back and leaned on the counter. 'Get you something to drink?' she asked.

'Just a ginger ale with some ice please.'

She nodded and stuck a glass into a bucket of ice for a few cubes then sprayed ginger ale into the glass and slid it in front of him.

'Thanks.' he said. 'Peterson in back?'

'I think I saw him head back there a while ago.'

'Thanks again.' he said. He took his glass of ginger ale and walked into the back of the room towards the small office. He knocked lightly and nudged the door open. He saw Peterson at the desk going through some papers. He walked in and took a seat in front of him.

Peterson nodded 'Knuckles.'

'Pete.' Vinny Bruxelles said back. 'Anything interesting?' he asked and pointed at the stack of paper on the side of the desk.

Peterson shook his head. 'The big stack is bills. The much smaller stack is customer invoices that need to get mailed today.'

'Sounds fun.'

'It's not. I didn't realize getting made VP turned me into the accountant.'

'How's your math skills?'

'They suck, but it don't matter. Accounting ain't math really. It's just counting. The clue's in the name.'

'Learn something new everyday I guess.'

'I guess. What's the word anyway?'

'Just met with DiMatteo. Told you about it before I think. He called me in on something. Just some consulting for now, but might be more.'

'Oh yeah, what's that fucking plastic paddy up to now?'

'Same old tricks from what I can see.'

'What this time?'

'Not a hundred percent on the details yet, but I know there was a local kid overdosed about a week ago. DiMatteo's involved somehow. Well, it went down at his place, but I can tell it's more than that.'

'How can you tell?'

'Well, A. He called me. And B. he's nervous. He's worried people are gonna go digging into the details of what happened to the kid. Particularly nervous about the kid's older brother doing so.'

'Yeah? How nervous?'

'Nervous enough to send some guys around the brother's house, lean on the wife a bit.'

'Downright frightened then is how he sounds.'

'Nah that's just the type of him. Always on edge, prone to overreactions. Not prone to thinking too far ahead.'

'I've heard that before. I know how you feel about him.'

'I know you know.'

'But he pays.' Peterson said and pointed to the stack of bills on the desk.

'I know you know that too. Speaking of which.' Vinny Bruxelles said and pulled out the envelope of cash. He slid it over to Peterson. 'That's for the safe.'

'See Knuckles, he pays.'

'In advance too. See now, that makes me nervous.'

Peterson shrugged. 'Maybe he likes you.'

'He's a sociopath. He don't like no one.'

'Okay loves you then.'

Vinny Bruxelles laughed.

'Why did he call you?' Peterson asked.

'He knows I'm from Dorchester. The kid's brother I mentioned. The one got DiMatteo's feathers up, I know him. DiMatteo must've put it together. Or at least, somebody did and told him.'

'Really? You know the guy?'

'Yeah I do.'

'And?'

'And what?'

'What's he like?'

'He's alright. Same thing I told DiMatteo. Billy Carson ain't a bad guy.'

'What'd DiMatteo say to that?'

'Nothing really. Seems he wanted to hear what I had to say, but it ain't like he waited to hear it. He sent guys to Carson's house before I even talked to him.'

'Sounds rash.'

'That's DiMatteo.'

Peterson nodded. 'What are you hoping for? Honestly.'

'Honestly Pete, I wouldn't mind getting handed a thick envelope with DiMatteo's name on a list.'

'Tread carefully there Knuckles. That brand of talk has broader implications for the Club.'

Vinny Bruxelles nodded. 'Pete, you of all people know I wouldn't act without the vote.'

'You're right, I do know that.'

'Good.'

'So what's next?'

'I'll play it wait and see. He paid me, so he'll call. Just a matter of when and what.'

'Keep me updated.'

'Always do.'

'I know. But hey, when he does get in touch, there's a chance here the "what" could be something you ain't ready to get into.'

'A very good chance if I had to guess. Any suggestions when that happens?'

Peterson took a few seconds to respond. He shuffled the stack of bills again on the desk and straightened them at the corners so that they sat clean one of top of the other. 'That whiskey?' he asked pointing at Vinny Bruxelles' glass.

'Ginger ale.'

'No booze?'

Vinny Bruxelles shook his head. 'Just thirsty.'

'Thirsty.' Peterson said.

'Yeah Pete, even the devil gets thirsty in hell.'

Peterson smiled. 'Listen.' he said. 'You ain't always gonna have the luxury of time . . . for a vote I mean. I know what this Club means to you . . . and I know you ain't the type of guy to make a decision that hurts us without thinking it through. Listen Knuckles, the Club's in some choppy water, we got some bills, we need cash coming in. All that's true, but thinking about it some more right now . . . we start bending our values for the almighty dollar, where does it end?'

'I'm not sure it does end.'

'I tend to agree.'

'Pete, let's see how this plays out. I'll play it close, you know, keep the options open for now.'

'Yeah, okay. Do that. See how it unfolds. You say this Carson guy's alright. You tell me someone's alright, I believe you. I don't want to see Tooth & Nail start jamming up good guys for the sake of a few bucks. Especially when guys like DiMatteo are on the other end.'

'In other words?'

Peterson laughed. 'In other words, if you gotta teach DiMatteo a lesson or two, so be it.'

'Thanks Pete.'

'The fat bastard probably won't pay in advance again, but hey, fuck him if he can't take a joke.

Billy Carson

McNulty's Mustang drove slowly along Carson Beach in South Boston until an open parking spot appeared ahead of a line of cars tightly jammed together on the side of the road. Billy saw the opening first and pointed to the spot. 'Right here Nick.' he said. McNulty slowed to a stop just after the opening then parallel parked along the curb between two cars. McNulty turned the key back and the engine cut out. The radio cut out with it. With the noise in the car gone Billy could hear the sounds coming from the little league field across the street, it was muffled voices with intermittent cheers. Cars continued to whir past and he felt his blood pulsing in his ears. 'Whereabouts? Your uncle say exactly?'

McNulty pointed up ahead 'you see that bench under the stone trellis?'

Billy nodded.

'That's it.'

'Okay. Just wait there for him? How will I know who he is?'

'He'll know you.'

'Is he a fucking ninja or something?'

McNulty shrugged.

'Maybe he reads minds or something.' Billy said.

'Yeah and maybe both, but why don't you knock that shit off before you meet him, else this won't go so well, ya know Billy.'

Billy Nodded, 'Sorry, I'm nervous. That's all.'

'Guy kills people Billy, you should be fucking nervous.'

'Yeah, well, like I said, I am. Your uncle said he's

alright though yeah?'

'He said he'd meet you and hear what you had to say. That's it. They know each other. My uncle asked a favor, so he'll talk to you. That's the extent of it. Try not to piss him off.'

'Thanks.' Billy said. 'Sound advice.' He swung the car door open and slowly put one foot on the curb. He looked over at McNulty and tried to suppress a frown. 'You coming with me?' he asked.

McNulty shook his head. 'I'll stay put. I got eyes on you from here.'

Billy took in a deep breath then exhaled as he got out of the car. He walked slowly over to the bench under the trellis. He took a seat on the splintered wood and looked across Dorchester Bay. He took in another deep breath to try and slow his racing heart and closed his eyes. He heard the noise from the traffic behind him and could still smell exhaust fumes although it mixed with the smell from the sea. He heard seagulls calling in front of him and guessed they were scouring the beach for scraps. If not for the pulsing headache and rapid heartbeat he'd have nearly been at peace sitting there listening to the world move around him as it drowned out his thoughts. He felt a cool breeze on his neck that made him shiver. He opened his eyes and watched a large shadow shift from behind him to his side. He turned quickly towards the figure that appeared next to him and shifted his body away on the bench.

'Relax, it's me.' McNulty said.

'You scared the shit out of me.'

'Why the fuck are you day dreaming?'

'I'm not, I was trying to clear my head.'

'You done?'

'I was close.'

'Sorry.'

'Yeah. I thought you were gonna wait in the car?'

'I got bored.'

'Well we can't have that. What the fuck are you a child?'

'Yeah a real big one. Look alive.' He said and nodded toward the street. 'Here's your man.'

Billy turned towards the street and leaned his elbow on the back of the bench. A long Cadillac was double parked on the street. A tall bald man with a beard stepped out of the passenger seat then reached over and opened the back door. A much older man climbed out. He was thin with silver hair slicked back. He wore a dark suit and dark shades. He walked through the parked cars and stepped up onto the curb. When he did, the sun reflected off his shiny shoes. Billy stood up from the bench when the man approached. McNulty stayed standing next to him. The man motioned for them to sit down, so they did. The man sat on the remaining edge of the bench and looked straight ahead. Billy didn't know whether to look at him or follow his stare out to the sea. He glanced at McNulty for guidance, but McNulty just shrugged. After a while the man spoke. 'You're Billy Carson.'

Billy said 'yes sir'.

'You can call me Mr. Brady.'

'Thank you for meeting with me Mr. Brady. This is Nick McNulty.'

The man turned his head finally to look at Billy. 'I know who he is son. Do you?'

'Of course, I've known Nick my whole life.'

'Do you know what his name means?'

'McNulty . . . no.'

'Tell him what your name means Nick.'

'McNulty means son of the Ulsterman.'

'That's right. Son of the Ulsterman. That means something where I'm from. Me and your uncle go back a long way.'

McNulty and Billy both just nodded, unsure what to say next.

Mr. Brady continued, 'I only say that to you now so you know you're safe. You can speak freely to me here. I'll hear you out and give you any advice I think might be helpful.'

'Okay.' Billy said 'Thank you.'

'So why don't you make it clear for me. You have some problem. Tell me.'

Billy leaned his elbows onto his knees before speaking. Mr. Brady crouched down slightly to indicate he was listening. 'My brother . . . he was . . . he died a few days ago.'

Mr. Brady nodded and took his off his sunglasses. Billy continued. 'I found him and drove him to the hospital, but it was too late. He was gone before we made it there. Everyone seems sure it was an overdose . . .'

'But, you're not so sure?' Mr. Brady asked.

Billy nodded. 'I'm not so sure.'

'Forgive me young man, but this sounds more like a police matter than something I can help with.'

'There's more. I found my brother in Dorchester. It was Seamus DiMatteo's house.'

Mr. Brady slowly sat back upright and put his shades back on. 'You think he's involved, okay. That's not all is it?'

'No. A couple of guys came around my house earlier. I wasn't there. They didn't do anything really, but were asking a lot of questions to my wife . . . made her feel threatened.'

Mr. Brady rubbed his chin for a few seconds. 'Cops?'

Billy shook his head.

'DiMatteo.' Mr. Brady said. Billy knew it wasn't a question. He didn't have evidence to confirm it was DiMatteo, but he knew it was. Mr. Brady appeared to know it too.

Billy asked 'Is there anything you can do for me?'

Mr. Brady tapped the top of his knee caps with his fingertips for a few seconds. 'No.' he said.

Billy exhaled a breath he had been holding and sat upright in the bench. He didn't know what he expected to get from this man, a well-known Irish gangster. He felt foolish for having hope, but it was his family he was talking about, he had to do something. 'Thank you for your time.' Billy said.

All three men stood up. Billy held out his hand. Mr. Brady reached out and shook it. 'I don't owe you any explanation here son.' Mr. Brady said. Billy started to say something to assure the man he was grateful anyway, but Mr. Brady held out his hand to stop him. 'I really do wish I could help you with this. Even in my line of work there's rules. You understand that.'

Billy said 'Yes Mr. Brady.'

'Seamus DiMatteo, he's a young man, a dangerous man. He takes a lot of risks. Many of which many of us don't necessarily agree with. But, he's a man that for one reason or another has some strong and influential supporters. Even if I could have a word with them, I'm afraid it would fall on deaf ears. DiMatteo knows you're skeptical. He makes rash decisions when he feels threatened and in this situation, whether you know it or not, you're a threat to him. Even if I wanted to, I can't advise you to do anything and I definitely won't authorize it.'

'We're talking about my family here Mr. Brady . . . my family. If DiMatteo had a problem with me, why not come after me?'

'I'm sure he will.'

'Then why bother threatening my family.'

'One of two reasons, either he wanted to back you off, which looking at those tense fists of yours right now doesn't seem like it worked. Or two, he enjoys it.'

Billy hadn't realized he'd changed his stance and his fists were clenched. He stretched his hands out and tried to loosen his stance.

'I can see your upset Billy Carson. And I don't blame you. No man hurts or threatens my family. Let me leave you with one thought. A man gets killed, he's made a ghost. Everybody knows that. It's simple. A dead man is a ghost. But, what isn't so obvious is that sometimes a ghost isn't made, instead a ghost is born. A man might do things, take another man's life for instance, and that action spawns two ghosts.'

Billy turned slightly to McNulty. McNulty gave him a blank stare.

Mr. Brady smiled. His smile was not a nice one. He looked like a man that didn't practice it often. 'You're right, maybe it is a little late in the day for being philosophical. Let me put it simply. You go after

DiMatteo, you're going to war with at least half of Boston's underworld. Know that for a certainty son. Good day gentleman.'

Billy watched as Mr. Brady eased his way through the same two parked cars. The tall bald man jumped from the passenger's seat and opened the back door to the Cadillac. Billy took a step towards the curb and yelled out 'What choice do I have?'

Mr. Brady turned towards him and raised his shoulders slightly. 'Sometimes choices are made for you.' He said, then ducked into the car. Billy watched the caddy slowly pull away while a sinking feeling grew in his stomach. Eventually the car disappeared around the bend. It took Billy's short-lived hope for a resolution with it.

Vinny "Knuckles" Bruxelles

The call back from Seamus DiMatteo came sooner than expected. The sun had only just dipped below the horizon when Vinny Bruxelles found himself in a bar in Dorchester known for its affiliation with DiMatteo's crew. There was a private room in the back where DiMatteo gathered together his guys whenever it was necessary. This was one of those times. Vinny Bruxelles looked around the room at the faces as they all watched DiMatteo carry on with his angry rant. Vinny Bruxelles wasn't one of DiMatteo's guys, but he was let in on this meet because he was paid up front, a hired gun. He was the only outsider in the room. The rest looked on DiMatteo with equal amounts of fear and admiration.

There were six guys in total, including DiMatteo, not including himself. Vinny Bruxelles knew by their faces and the way they carried themselves that all five of DiMatteo's men were on his payroll for loyalty mainly and maybe a little brawn. Not one of them appeared to be more than that. Vinny Bruxelles thought it was just like DiMatteo to fill his crew with half-wits that would never challenge him as the group's alpha-male. 'A strong leader enlists strong men, men who can think for themselves, act and react, men who will challenge.' He thought. 'A weak leader chooses puppets.'

Vinny Bruxelles' distaste with DiMatteo grew the longer he stayed in that room. Word had gotten back to DiMatteo that Carson met with a Boss. Questions were being asked and for once DiMatteo wasn't looking for that kind of spotlight. Vinny Bruxelles listened to him describe what he was going to do with Carson once he got his hands on him three times before he decided to get up and get a drink from the bar. Heads turned when the sound of Vinny Bruxelles chair scrapping off the floor echoed through the room. The puppets threw him astonished looks, some even cracked their knuckles and pounded their hands for effect. Vinny Bruxelles had to chew back his laughter at their posturing. DiMatteo stopped his rant and walked closer in his direction.

'You going somewhere Knuckles? I paid you in advance remember.'

Vinny Bruxelles stood up straight and walked closer to DiMatteo. 'I thought I'd get a beer from the bar. That an issue with you?'

'You can get a drink when I'm done talking. I'll even buy one for you, just sit the fuck down til I finish.'

'I think you finished ten minutes ago Seamus, or do you want to go over it again how you're gonna drop Carson off your roof and go bang his wife?' Vinny Bruxelles watched DiMatteo closely. He watched his jaw tighten and his nostrils flare as he took in deep breaths. DiMatteo's anger was obvious. Vinny Bruxelles thought he looked like a spoiled child that just got told 'no' for the first time. He felt the air change in the room and sensed fear and confusion from DiMatteo's men.

DiMatteo got control of his breathing and spoke 'Don't forget whose side you're on here Knuckles. I pay someone to do a job, I expect that job to get done. Reputations depend on that kind of thing.'

'Listen Seamus, you're right, you did pay me to do a job. But unless that job is sitting here and sucking your dick like this band of fucking nitwits, I suggest you get to the fucking point.'

DiMatteo didn't move, but Vinny Bruxelles heard a chair scrape off the floor to his right. A stocky unshaven man kicked his seat back and charged him wildly with his head down and arms out to tackle. Vinny Bruxelles' hands were already in his pockets when he heard the chair scrape off the ground. He looped his fingers through the cold brass holes in his pocket, side-stepped the man's rush and cracked him in the side of the head with the brass knuckles. He heard a loud cracking noise when he struck the man and couldn't help but think of an egg cracking off a counter. The man dropped instantly. Vinny Bruxelles other hand pulled his nine millimeter from his waist and he turned quickly swinging the gun at the group as they all jumped to their feet when the man went down. They were up, but they all froze at the sight of the gun. Vinny Bruxelles had the drop on each of them and they all knew it. He knew it too. One quick move and he was ready to make an example of someone's knee cap.

'Enough!' DiMatteo yelled. 'Knuckles, Jesus Christ, put the fucking gun down.'

'Call your men off first.'

DiMatteo nodded at his guys. Each slowly sat back in their chairs. The one closest to the man on the ground quickly helped his comrade to his chair. Knuckles lowered his gun, but didn't put it away. DiMatteo watched him and shook his head. He pulled a pen slowly from his inside pocket. He leaned on the table and scribbled down a note on a napkin. He stood up when he was done and handed the napkin over to Vinny Bruxelles. Vinny Bruxelles glanced at it and read the sloppy writing quickly, keeping half an eye on the men sitting at the tables.

'It's an address. A motel just over the New Hampshire

border.'

'I see that. What the fuck am I supposed to do with it?'

'Walter Carson. He's been found. He's hiding out in that motel. Room 103. He's alone and probably drunk.'

'Okay.' Vinny Bruxelles said. 'What should I do with him?'

'Shoot him in the fucking head, I don't give a shit.'

Vinny Bruxelles tilted his head and glared at DiMatteo. He felt his hand tense around the gun. 'Ours ain't that type of arrangement. You must have the wrong idea about what we do.'

DiMatteo reached down to the foot of his table and came up with a small black duffel bag. He tossed it to Vinny Bruxelles. Vinny Bruxelles let it drop at his feet. The zip for the bag was open. He used his foot to open the bag more and saw it was overflowing with cash.

'This should straighten out any "wrong idea" I have about our arrangement.'

Vinny Bruxelles picked up the bag. He nodded in agreement.

'Check in at my apartment when you're done. Finish that job and there's another bag and another name and address.'

'Billy?'

'You know him. You can get close and do it quick and quiet.'

'Double this?' Vinny Bruxelles asked pointing to the bag in his hands.

DiMatteo raised his eyebrows and nodded.

Vinny Bruxelles backed out of the room, only putting his gun hand in his pocket at the last second before walking out through the main bar and out to his bike.

He rode north for an hour. The night turned cool on the journey, but the cool air whipping off his skin through his clothes kept him alert. He knew the area just over the New Hampshire border well so he had no problem weaving through the pitch-black roads. He found the motel easily. It was a small place, a one level U-shaped structure with red clapboard siding. He rode into the entrance and pulled up outside Room 103. He made no attempt to hide the bike's noise, not that he'd be able to, the engine roared at any gear. He climbed off the bike and rested the helmet on the seat. He saw lights on at several doorways, including in front of Walter Carson's room. He walked up to the door and saw the curtains move slightly in the front window. He put his ear to the door and knocked loudly. 'Walter, it's Vinny Bruxelles, open up.' He waited a few seconds listening through the door. He wondered if Walter would make a run for it and considered whether to kick the door in. He took a step back for leverage, but heard a latch turn and the door opened a crack. Walter peeked through the opening, the locked safety latch covered part of his face. "Vinny Bruxelles? Knuckles?" he asked.

'Yeah. Can we talk?'

'Who sent you? Billy?'

'Guess again.' Vinny Bruxelles said. He watched Walter tilt his head in confusion. 'DiMatteo.'

When Walter heard the name his eyes widened first, then he moved to close the door. Vinny Bruxelles stuck his boot in the doorway and blocked it from closing then threw his shoulder into the door. The force popped the chain off the wall and flung the door open. Walter stumbled backwards and struggled to regain his footing.

Vinny Bruxelles walked in quickly, hoping the sound wouldn't draw much attention. He shut the door quietly behind him, then turned his attention to Walter. Walter stood frozen in front of a small sofa. 'Sit the fuck down Walter, if I wanted you dead, you wouldn't have heard me drive up. Actually, if I wanted you dead, you already would be.'

Walter appeared to think about it for a few seconds, then slowly took a seat on the sofa. Vinny Bruxelles remained standing. 'Why did DiMatteo send you then? I know who you are . . . what you do.'

'You don't know shit about me kid, so shut the fuck up.' Vinny Bruxelles walked over, grabbed a wooden chair and dragged it away from the small table. He put it right in front of Walter and took a seat. He reached inside his pocket and pulled out two stacks of bills. 'You need to get gone Walter.' He said and put the stacks next to Walter. Walter picked them up and stared at them, but didn't say anything.

'You know where that money came from?' Vinny Bruxelles asked.

Walter looked up at Vinny Bruxelles. 'He paid you to kill me.'

Vinny Bruxelles nodded. He watched Walter's face. It looked more confused than scared.

'What the fuck does DiMatteo want with me?'

'That's why I'm here Walter. That's what the fuck I want to know.'

'Me? How would I know?'

Vinny Bruxelles grew irritated suddenly. 'Listen kid. I don't have time for this shit. DiMatteo handed me a bag full of cash to put a bullet in your fucking head. Then he offered me another one to do the same to your brother. See, the thing is. I know your brother. Knew him in school, always liked him. Always thought he was a good guy. If I didn't know Billy, you'd be in a hole somewhere in the White Mountains right now, you dig? But I do, so you're not. So I ain't gonna kill you and I sure as shit ain't gonna kill him. But the thing is, that puts me in a tight spot seeing as though I was paid to do so by someone who probably has a rolodex full of guys just like me. So let's wrap this thing the fuck up so I can go talk to your brother and sort this out. You were there that night when your brother John kicked it. You had a habit of hanging around with DiMatteo and his fucking douchebag crew. So skip the fucking bullshit and give it to me straight before I change my mind.'

Walter put the cash down on the sofa next to him and rubbed his hands through his hair. Vinny Bruxelles took a deep breath and settled back into the chair. 'It was DiMatteo.' Walter said.

'What was DiMatteo?'

'He set John up. Well, I'll never know for certain I guess, but I know it was him in my gut anyway. Like you said, I've been around DiMatteo a little bit, so I know what he's like. My brother John didn't know him well . . . he didn't know how he reacts to shit like that.'

'Shit like what?'

'DiMatteo had some broads over. One of them, I don't even remember her name, can you believe that? She started flirting with John a little bit. She liked him, it was obvious. Anywhere else in the world . . . or anyone else, and that would be that. But fucking DiMatteo, you know . . .'

Vinny Bruxelles shook his head. He felt weary all of a sudden and brought his own hands up to his face and rubbed his eyes. He knew DiMatteo's type. He was an evil bastard. His mind didn't operate like a normal person's, his world consisted of himself alone, front and center, everything else happened on the periphery. He looked at Walter. The kid looked bad. Probably a week on the booze or God knows what else. His clothes dirty, in desperate need of a shave and a shower. To make it worse, he sat there now with tears streaming down his face leaving lines on his skin where they had fallen. 'Walter.' Vinny Bruxelles said 'You mean to tell me that DiMatteo killed your brother over some fucking tail?'

Walter shook his head yes. 'Apparently an ex of his, he didn't take kindly to her being all over John . . . I tried to warn him. I told John that DiMatteo don't fuck around, that he needed to walk away from that broad. Next thing I know . . . John was shitfaced see, he never did drugs or shit like that. Someone had to have slipped him something and then I come into the room and DiMatteo's being all nice to him, at least that's how it looked to John. I know DiMatteo, I know he ain't ever nice. I could see he was fucking with John. He was pressuring him to do a couple lines. John never did drugs like that before . . . maybe smoked a bone or two, but that's it. DiMatteo was being all nice to him, set him up a couple lines. He even did one first, but he must've . . . it had to be him to spike it with something you know. John took one snort, a tiny piece, wouldn't get a fucking puppy high. Then that's it . . . he was gone.'

Walter finished and dropped his face into his forearm. Vinny Bruxelles watched him convulse with tears. He stood up and put a hand on Walter's shoulder feeling something in between sympathy and disdain for the guy. He truly felt bad for what happened, but something irked him about Walter. It was mainly the fact that he just took off, did nothing to protect his own brother that night or after. Vinny Bruxelles couldn't imagine letting something like that go. The guys in the MC were his brothers, if any of them ended up like John Carson, Vinny Bruxelles thought, 'I'd have DiMatteo nailed upside down on a fucking cross in Boston Common.' He'd heard enough. He was more certain than ever that DiMatteo had the young Carson brother killed, or at least caused it. It wasn't his score to settle, but it was Billy Carson's, and he'd be the one to bring it to him. Vinny Bruxelles walked to the front door and grabbed the doorknob. He turned back towards Walter before he walked out. 'Take that money and hide out, at least a few weeks. DiMatteo knows where you are and I wouldn't be surprised if he sent some guys to spy on me. Bottom line Walter, if you show up in Dorchester or Quincy and get spotted, then my ass is on the line. If that happens, then let me assure you, our next meeting will not go so well.

Billy Carson

Billy peeked through the blinds when he heard an engine pass the house. It sounded like a motorcycle on a low gear and the sound carried past the front of the house and up the side, which meant there was someone in the driveway. He wasn't going to chance running to the side of the house to check. He barricaded the back door and window, so no one was getting in there easily. Times like these he wished he took the second or third floor apartment instead of the first. From the front window, Billy could make out McNulty's frame inside the Mustang, which he parked facing downhill across the street and a few houses up. 'Smart' Billy thought, 'Don't trust the rear view mirror. Plus if he has to run, it'll be downhill instead of up.' McNulty hadn't moved yet, but Billy assumed he saw whoever it was that pulled up. He was glad he sent Kathleen and the boys up to the lake with his father. His old man questioned the need at first, but it didn't take much convincing. 'As it turns out, it was the right move.' Billy thought. Someone was here and it had to be for him. He expected to be nervous, to have the shakes, for his heart to beat quickly and head to get light. None of that happened. He felt energy and extreme focus. 'Military training.' He said out loud to himself. 'Has to be.'

He looked out the window again. This time he couldn't see McNulty at first, until he caught his shadow behind the Mustang at the front tire where the street light had its glow. He listened intently for movement. The engine in the driveway had cut out, but he heard nothing for a few moments and cursed the unpaved path. He made his way over to the front door and stood to the side of it, at the ready. He pulled out his knife and tightened his hand around it letting the blade shine out through the bottom of his fist. The day had unraveled so quickly that he hadn't been able to get his hands on a gun. He'd had enough of guns after the army and never expected to need one again. He was wrong unfortunately. That's where he depended on McNulty and his double barrel shotgun out front. Finally he heard footsteps moving up the front porch. Then he heard the creak of the front hall door open. Someone was in the entrance hall. The sound of boots in the hall echoed loudly at first, but then all sound died out. Whoever it was had stopped to consider their next move. He heard shuffling again. A second later there was a firm knock on the door. Billy waited. He didn't move, didn't even breath. Seconds later he heard it, the door open again and the shotgun cock. He heard McNulty say 'Knees.' Then 'Billy open up.'

Billy kept the blade gripped in his fist as he turned the knob and pulled the door open. At eye level he saw McNulty with the shotgun raised. McNulty nodded. He looked down and saw a tall man kneeling down. He wore a leather vest with a TNMC badge stitched on the front over the chest. His face looked nonchalant for someone in his current predicament. Billy recognized him and smiled.

'Billy.' Vinny Bruxelles said and smiled and nodded.

'Vinny.'

'You treat all visitors like this?'

'I'm married with kids these days Vin. I don't get many midnight callers.

'Fair enough. Can you ask McNulty if I can stand up?'

'You got a piece on you?'

'Yeah. Belt.'

McNulty leaned down quickly and pulled the nine millimeter from Vinny Bruxelles' belt.

'Come in.' Billy said and opened the door. He led the way in through a large foyer and into his living room. McNulty walked behind Vinny Bruxelles the entire way and didn't lower the shotgun until they were all seated and he rested it on his knee.

'You wanna explain?' Billy asked.

Vinny Bruxelles had the napkin with Walter's address in his hand. He handed it across to Billy and let him read it. 'DiMatteo found your brother Walter.'

Billy shook his head. 'What the fuck is this guy's problem?' Billy said.

'He's got several . . . problems that is.'

'And what, he sent you out to get Walter?'

'Billy, he handed me twenty grand and told me to put a bullet in him.'

Billy felt his heart start racing. He was angry, more angry every second. He looked at McNulty. McNulty looked mad as hell.

Vinny Bruxelles continued 'I gave Walter five grand and told him to stay up north for the foreseeable future.'

After a moment Billy said, 'I appreciate that.'

'Forget about it. To be honest, I wasn't sure what you'd think, I heard you and Walter are on the outs.'

'Yeah that's true, but I don't have to like my brother to love him, you know.'

Vinny Bruxelles nodded.

'You talk to Walter . . . about what happened.'

'I did Billy, you ain't gonna like it.'

'I never expected to.'

'DiMatteo did it. Walter wasn't sure exactly how, but

he knows he did. Billy, man, it was all over a fucking girl. Someone DiMatteo used to go with apparently took a fucking liking to your brother John. DiMatteo . . . he ain't fucking right in the head. No half measures. Billy, the fat fuck has to go. He ain't gonna stop. He wanted me to hit you next. God only knows what he had in mind after that. I gotta check in with him now at his place. He's expecting me to collect dough for the job of taking you out. The man has got to go.'

'Don't touch him.' Billy said. He looked over a McNulty and saw agreement from the big man. 'I want him.'

Vinny Bruxelles nodded. 'Good.' He stood up slowly. Billy and McNulty stood up after him. McNulty handed him back his nine.

'You're going direct to his place?'

'I am. Follow behind me. Take the Buick Billy.' Vinny Bruxelles said. 'Everyone in the fucking state knows McNulty's Mustang. Give me ten minutes once I'm in to set up. I'll get DiMatteo isolated.'

'Good. How many guys he got in there?'

'My guess is at least five guys. Probably armed, maybe not. Go in hard just in case. The guys I know of are big, but they ain't fast and they ain't smart. You go in hard and don't let up until DiMatteo's in your sights, then I'd say you got a chance.'

Billy held out his hand and Vinny Bruxelles shook it. 'Thanks Vinny.' He said.

'Don't thank me yet Billy. After this, you have to disappear. My Club up in Laconia can get you cover to start. It's gotta be you though Billy. The Club can't be on the hook for this. Too many relationships at stake you get me.'

'You're doing enough.' Billy looked over at McNulty. 'Nick can get me to New Hampshire, we'll figure it out from there.'

'Good. On the other side then?'

'The other side.' Billy nodded.

'Watch his back McNulty.' Vinny Bruxelles said.

'No change there Knuckles.' McNulty said.

Billy locked the front door behind Vinny Bruxelles and he and McNulty headed out through the basement. On the way out, Billy grabbed a duffle bag he packed before with clothes, a container of gasoline and some industrial matches.

'What the fuck you doing that?' McNulty asked pointing at the gasoline.

'Diversion.' Billy said. McNulty squinted his eyes for a second, then shrugged his shoulders. They headed out to the driveway where Billy's car was parked. His Buick was midnight blue and had a quieter engine compared to the Mustang so it made sense to take it anyway.

They followed a couple lengths behind Vinny Bruxelles. Billy knew the house. It was in his neighborhood, he'd lived in that area his entire life. It seemed darker than usual. He wasn't sure if it was a cloud covered moon or just his perception that changed. He felt dread come over him. He hadn't wanted this. There was no coming back from what he was about to do. He knew better. He knew this would change the rest of his life. He could never be the person he'd hoped once this thing was done. He felt a pain in his chest as he started to think about Kathleen and his sons. They'd never look at him the same. He told himself he was protecting them here too. He was, that was a fact, but it was more than that. An urge for revenge burned deeply in his soul. It ate away at his resolve quickly. Under the mask of drugs and alcohol the last few days, he'd been able to suppress it. Today however he didn't have the luxury of drowning out his pain with chemicals. It was violence he yearned for now. DiMatteo may have been the catalyst, he may have appeared to be the aggressor, but really since the moment Billy Carson first opened that man's door and found his brother unconscious in the hallway, Seamus DiMatteo was a dead man. He just didn't know it yet. It was destined. It was written.

He pulled the Buick to a stop around the corner from DiMatteo's house. He kept the engine running, but turned the lights off. From a distance he watched Vinny Bruxelles enter through the front door. Billy checked the time on the dash. The countdown was on. The first seven minutes ticked by like decades, the last three like seconds. When ten minutes were up he turned the engine off and quietly climbed out of the car. McNulty did the same, still gripping the shotgun in both hands, looking stern and unnerved. Billy opened the trunk and took out the gasoline can. Together they made their way up the street, hugging the wall so the shadow of night cloaked their movements. Billy knelt behind a low stone wall next to the driveway. He looked around for lights on the exterior of the house, but there seemed to be none. He only had the streetlights to contend with. He told McNulty to stay put and cover and took off running down the driveway. There were three cars lined up one after the other next to the house. He undid the cap and poured gasoline over each car. Then walked back slowly using the remaining accelerant to wet a trail down the driveway to the foot of the steps leading to the front porch.

He ducked next to the stairs. He could hear voices and music inside. Through the window he could see at least three men inside nonchalantly standing around drinking. He couldn't see if they were carrying. He looked over to McNulty and counted down with his fingers from five. At five, Billy pulled out the matches and ran nearly a handful off the tarmac. They broke out in flames, which he laid down against the trail of gasoline. The gas caught the flame and singed his hand. The trail of flames took off like a comet and ran right over the cars. The cars lit up immediately. Billy could feel the heat from the fire. It was intense. He saw through the window the men took notice and ran over to the side of the house. He darted up the steps and could hear McNulty's steps right behind him. He heard commotion inside. He crouched on the porch next to the door and heard footsteps pounding through the hallway towards the front door. He gripped his open switchblade in his fist and waited. As the door opened, an explosion rang out from the first car. The blast lit up the street like daylight. The three men that ran through the door dropped to the ground for cover. Billy stood up.

One of the men recovered and jumped to his feet. Billy didn't wait for a fight. He flicked the blade around in his hand and stuck it in between the man's neck and shoulder. Blood squirt down Billy's arm when he pulled the blade out. He kicked hard at the man's kneecap and he went down reeling in pain and shock, holding his neck. Billy kicked him hard in the ribs and the man rolled down the front steps, shooting blood out of his neck. The other two men jumped up, clearly in shock. One reached for a gun at his waist. Billy's eardrum burst from McNulty's shotgun blast that shredded the man's arm. The other man held up his arms and McNulty cracked him between the eyes with the butt of the shotgun. Billy raced inside. He expected at least a few more men to jump out, but it appeared empty. He tried to move quietly and listen for steps, but his ears were ringing. McNulty moved behind him with the shotgun cocked and aimed. They moved to the back of the house. He could smell burning wood and felt intense heat. Smoke formed around the walls and ceiling closest to the driveway. The flames had run from the driveway up the side of the house. It was burning and it's wood frame wouldn't stand long. The first floor was cleared and Billy headed for the stairs. McNulty put an arm across his chest to hold him back. He took the lead with the shotgun out in front. They climbed the stairs slowly to the sound of flames licking through dry wood. They came to a landing at the second floor. Through the ringing, Billy heard a voice call out his name. He knew it was Vinny Bruxelles. He and McNulty followed the voice to a porch overlooking the backyard. They walked out through the door and onto the porch landing. From the porch he could smell the house burning and see the flames running up the side. Vinny Bruxelles stood with his arm extended and his nine millimetre held to Seamus DiMatteo's temple. Billy paused to look into DiMatteo's eyes. His fat face shook with fear and snot ran out of his long nose. Dark circles under his eyes matched the dark hair on his head that swung down to a widow's peak. Billy felt sick to his stomach. The sight of DiMatteo's scared face only enraged him further. Vinny Bruxelles slowly lowered his gun and walked over to Billy and McNulty.

Billy watched DiMatteo's face relax in relief when the gun was off his temple.

Billy smiled. DiMatteo dropped to his knees and started to plead for mercy. Billy stepped forward. He reached out quickly with his left hand and grabbed DiMatteo's tongue then swiped his blade across it. DiMatteo tried to scream, but couldn't. He grabbed at his mouth and rolled on the ground. Blood began to pour over his hands.

The flames from the house danced around the porch, trapping the heat and smoke with it. Billy turned to Vinny Bruxelles and McNulty. Both men stood staring at Billy, blackened by the smoke, wet with sweat and another man's blood. Flames grew behind him. 'Leave us.' Billy said.

McNulty looked at Vinny Bruxelles then back at Billy. 'Billy this place is going down any second.'

Billy reached into his pocket, pulled out a set of keys and tossed them at McNulty. 'Start the Buick Nicky. I won't be long.'

THE END

TOMORROW'S SUN

JIM CARSON

Jim Carson owned Beale Street Deli and every Saturday it felt like the entire city descended on the place. Jim loved this about Saturdays. His mostly teenaged, mostly hung-over staff, on the other hand were not always so thrilled.

The deli was a landmark in the city of Quincy. On the face of it however the place wasn't much to look at. It had a large blue sign out front that read "Beale Street Deli" written in very subtle block capital letters and the inside refused to buckle to the 21st century. It reeked of nostalgia and familiarity, like walking into your grandmother's house.

There were wall to wall windows with a prime corner view of Beale Street. The tables and chairs were old, but sturdy like they were built before mass-produced furniture. Even the staff, despite the grogginess accompanied with Saturday morning hangovers, added to the appeal. They were mostly local with local accents, and all had the same haircut. That was normal considering they all went to the same barber. The uniforms were antiques. They wore short-sleeved, blue-striped button down shirts that were heavy on the starch. The matching blue aprons tied around the waist wouldn't have been out of place in a 1950's diner. If you came across someone dressed like that around town, they could only be from one place. People loved it now, but the Deli wasn't always seen in a welcoming light. Before Jim took it over, it was a dated sandwich joint well beyond its prime. What Jim pulled off was nothing short of a miracle.

The success of the Deli reinvented a local business and also came to define its owner. Jim Carson became known around the neighborhood as a 'Somebody'. That didn't mean much to Jim though. Sure, he was happy that his Mom was proud of him and that she got to gloat to her friends, but his ego stayed in check.

In any other family, Jim would've been the golden boy. Then again, in any other family Jim wouldn't have his brother Danny to contend with. Danny's achievements cast a pretty big shadow. Some people would never shake that inherent jealousy. Jim Carson however, seemed to thrive in that situation. He did his own thing and that was enough to make him happy. Plus, he was newly in love, so not much could get him down.

Her name was Alex. She had dark curly hair and brown eyes and walked into the Deli at 12 o'clock on that Saturday. She locked eyes with Jim as he broke from a trance and finished making fresh pots of coffee at the far end of the counter. She smiled at him. Jim smiled back. She took her place in the line, which was moving quickly since breakfast had finished and lunch was only just beginning.

Brendan, one of the hung-over teenagers working the counter, saw her come in and said, 'You all set Alex? What can I get ya?'

'Hi Brendan, I think I want breakfast, can I get you to make me a number 1?'

Brendan stood shaking his head, 'Afraid I can't do it'

'Oh . . . why not? Even for a regular?'

'I wouldn't really call you a regular. Either way, breakfast stops at 11, so I can't do it. Jim's always on me about that.'

'Hmm,' Alex said 'So, you must turn up the heat on the grill for lunch then? And you probably just changed the fry oil?'

'Ahh . . . no we don't. We use the left of the grill for breakfast, but we keep it the same temp for lunch to keep food warm that's done and ready to go. The friolater was changed last night . . . you know, with fish & chips on Fridays, people don't really dig on haddock flavored home fries.'

'Oh, so you're out of eggs and bacon then?' She asked seeing her angle develop.

'Um . . . no' Brendan shifted and began to look irritable, 'they're just out back, but you know, breakfast's supposed to stop at 11.'

'Well . . . what could actually happen if you give in and make me breakfast right now then . . . in all honesty?'

Brendan's irritation flared up again, but he kept it in check and said, 'What'll happen is, next thing there's a line around the corner and everyone who couldn't drag their asses out of bed will be asking me to drop some home fries and do up some eggs.'

'And you know what you tell them if that happens Brendan?' Alex said. She smiled and held in a laugh, her trademark dimples formed on her cheeks.

'What do I tell 'em? Brendan asked.

'You tell them you're out of fucking eggs, but IHOP is open down the street and they do breakfast all day'

Brendan's face grew red, then he began to laugh 'Alright, alright, I'll make you breakfast then, whattya want?'

'Two eggs over easy with bacon, home fries and toast. That's all.'

'Kind of toast you want . . . white, wheat, dark rye or light rye?'

'Tough choice . . . I'll take . . . wheat. And Brendan?'

'Yeah whatsup?' he asked as he turned to tuck the breakfast slip above the grill and reach for the bacon.

'You're very cute you know that?'

'Hands off lady, you're probably my mother's age.'

Alex laughed and pretended that the comment didn't sting a little. She walked down the counter to where Jim was standing shaking his head at her. He had witnessed the encounter with utter amusement.

'Morning Jimmy' she said.

'Morning Alex, although technically its afternoon. By the way, breakfast stops at 11.'

'Anything for me though right?' She asked and winked.

Jim shook his head again, 'Guess so . . . doesn't seem to matter anyway. Poor Brendan, you turned his brain into a pretzel.'

'Oh well, wouldn't have been so easy maybe if he could've kept to a curfew last night.'

'True, true, but hungover or not, he's the best I've got,

especially on a day like today. Good help is hard to find, you know that.'

'I've heard . . . so can you join me for breakfast? Pretty please?'

'Afraid I can't. I'm catering a funeral later on up the street. I have to deliver and setup shortly.'

'Ohhh' Alex pouted and pretended to be upset. 'How about tonight . . . wait, I forgot, plans to meet your brother right? The mysterious Danny Carson, so mysterious in fact, that I've never been introduced.'

Jim smiled, 'Mysterious huh? Not sure about that.'

'So why hide him then? Ashamed of me?'

'Well . . . I didn't want to say it . . . but . . . '

'Please, like anyone would believe that. Seriously though, he's your brother and he's important to you so I'd love to meet him.'

'I know. Listen, he's here for a week I think. Maybe tomorrow or Monday night? I'll confirm once I talk to him.'

Alex smiled and reached for her coffee. 'I'm free every evening this week, so looking forward to it.'

She snuck in for a quick kiss on Jim's cheek and turned to go to the table. She glanced back and through the curly locks dangling over her eyes, Jim saw her wink at him again leaving him blushed. He watched her walk away with butterflies in his stomach and a shit-eating grin on his face.

Jim Carson

After work Jim ran home to shower and change his clothes. He rushed to turn around quickly. Less than an hour later, he went to meet his cousin Mike Riordan at a bar in Quincy Center.

As Jim waited for Mike to come back from his third visit to the men's room in two hours he watched Sportscenter highlights on the flat screen TV tucked behind the bar surrounded by the bottles of Smirnoff and Jameson.

The bar and restaurant filled up as the evening went on. It was locals mostly on Saturdays, unlike Friday evenings. Friday's were mainly the after work crowd from the corporate offices scattered around the city. 'The Sports Bar' made a name for itself with a tastefully decorated Boston Sports theme interior and menu, which also included the signature appetizer, buffalo chicken nachos. They were not from Buffalo and barely chicken, but they were damned delicious.

Jim marveled at the bartender's perfect pouring technique and motioned to him for two more Sam Adams just as Mike came back from the men's room.

Mike was chuckling to himself as he waddled over avoiding the ping-pong movements of the wait-staff and made his way back over to the stools.

'What's wrong with you?' Jim asked.

'Nothing wrong, just wishing they'd hang up more than just today's back page of the Herald. I had it read before wrapping up my second piss. At this stage I'm getting sick of staring at Zdeno Chara in action.'

Jim nodded. 'I hear ya, good defenseman and all, but

not much to look at really.'

'Exactly, so you're with me on this?'

'Oh yeah Mike I'm with you. They should really cater more for those with the acorn sized bladders.'

'Easy buddy, you know what holding it in does to ya. Plus, it's more likely the grapefruit sized prostate that's the issue, in fairness. Anyway, you order two more?'

'Yeah, Fast Dunny's working on it now'

'Who the fuck is Fast Dunny?'

'The dude in the short sleeve button-up behind the sticks.'

'That fat bastard? Doesn't look that quick to me. Why they call him that?'

'Don't know man, ask him.'

Mike raised his voice so the bartender could hear him, 'Excuse me, bar man, why do they call you Fast Dunny?'

The bartender gave him a look like he complimented him on a nice watch while shoulder to shoulder in the men's room. 'Hey, go fuck yourself champ, I guess you don't want this beer after all.'

Mike was taken aback by the bartender's fervor and apologized, 'Woah, hey sorry buddy, I . . . ah didn't mean to offend . . . how much for the round?'

The bartender regained his composure and rang up the beers at the register. '11.60' he said.

Mike handed him $15, 'Keep it man, no hard feelings.'

Jim proceeded to laugh his ass off at Mike's altercation. 'So you wanna know?'

'Wanna know what?' Mike asked, feeling irritated at the bartender's outburst.

'Why they call him Fast Dunny'

'Yeah, sure then, what the fuck, why?'

'He's got a wooden leg man . . . it's one of those ironic nicknames . . . he's not that fond of it either. You probably gathered as much.'

'Hmm' Mike said and tapped his index finger over his lips, 'Figures'

Jim scrunched together his eyebrows 'What figures?'

'Well, when he said 12 bucks for the two beers, I thought to myself, "What a fucking pirate" . . . so . . . it figures that he's just an eye patch and a sword away.'

Jim shook his head, 'You're fucked man'

Mike grinned 'Hey you brought it up asshole'

'Yeah, yeah, I know. Hey you want to know the funny thing?'

'What else man, come on?'

'His name's not even Dunny. I think it's Sheehan or something.'

Mike laughed again, harder this time, 'Why the fuck do they call him Dunny?'

'Pfff' Jim puffed his cheeks and blew air out, 'No frigin idea man.'

Jim loved this about Mike Riordan. They could just spend hours together with brains shut off just shooting the breeze about anything and nothing all at once. He found it to be the perfect escape. Not that he was escaping anything really, but with the business and pressures of everyday life, everyone needs an outlet. Otherwise they'd go crazy. Jim knew this, and catching up with Mike was one of his favorite past-times. It had been for as long as he could remember. They're cousins, but not in that "See you on Christmas way". It was more like they were friends, same age, same town, same schools. They were close. They were pretty much like brothers minus all the animosity that comes with sharing a bedroom growing up.

Mike acted funny and sometimes not all there mentally, but in reality he was plenty there. He had a job that he went to each day. He had a family, a wife and two young daughters. He had his priorities straight that was certain. His girls came first and foremost. Everything else was at least a mile away. Even meeting Jim on Saturday night was really only a favor. It was just to keep him company until his brother Danny showed up.

'So when's Danny flying in anyhow Jimmy?'

'Actually, he flew in yesterday as far as I know.'

'Oh . . . really'

'Yeah, he had a business meeting or something yesterday evening. Then he went straight to Mom's this morning.'

'Ahh well, gotta prioritize man.' Mike took a sip from his beer, then put it back on the wet coaster and began tapping the glass with his wedding ring finger. 'Business meeting huh? So Danny's still a big shot then? Even back in Boston?'

Jim shrugged, 'Don't think big shot is the right phrase. He's a smart dude with some drive to him that's all. I doubt he'd sell his soul enough to be considered big-time in the corporate world.'

'Fuck that man, people like those hard-nose, straight talking types.'

'On paper sure maybe they do' Jim said 'but not in the real corporate world. It's all perception. People say they want someone to stand up and speak his mind. But that's all bullshit as soon as what you say and what the bosses want to hear don't quite reconcile.'

'Spoken like a jaded man Jimbo. Guess that's why

you're back flipping burgers.'

Jim laughed, 'You got me pegged Mike, that's me alright, best burger flipper in Quincy.'

Danny Carson

Danny Carson took his Father's antics personally. Growing up, anytime his Father fell off the wagon or disappeared for periods of time without notice became permanent scars on his memory. Every time Danny lay awake at night listening to the old man yelling violently at his mother it pushed him closer to his boiling point. Even today he knew his impatience and his quick temper with people could be traced back to those experiences. It was like inside he was permanently waiting for his father to come home from the corner store. As a kid Danny never understood why it took so long, the corner store was less than 5 minutes away on foot. There were also those times they'd be locked in the car outside some run down house in Roxbury. Danny had to struggle to keep Jim from freaking out and running out of the car. The nerves had stuck with him. He bit his fingernails down to the cuticle still to this day.

Danny never used those experiences as an excuse however. Too many people get into some bad times and blame it all on their childhood. To blame his father for his own shortcomings, he thought, 'No way, because that's exactly what the old man would do.'

Danny did however use that fire inside him to drive himself forward. He was the prototype for what shrinks call 'overachiever'. It didn't matter in what, school, sports, social activities, anything. Danny always went hard after it.

He was never really the best at any one thing, but he was never bad at anything either. Plus he was always out-hustling everyone. In sports, he played hockey and baseball. He wasn't great, but he always tried harder than everyone.

Sports were fun for Danny, but they weren't what he was working for. It was academics where he really thrived. Whether it was words or numbers, he always just seemed to get it. He loved the fact that he got it. He wanted to be the smartest guy in the room, always. That was his strength, but also his weakness.

To some people, Danny was cocky, even arrogant. This probably led to most of his coming of age fist fights. His stubbornness didn't help either.

He had a softer side also, it just didn't show up as often and it didn't show to everyone. His teachers loved him, his mother did, Jim, his friends and of course his wife. He probably figured that was enough and everyone else could just pound sand.

He was pretty smooth though despite this. He always had some angle. Things weren't always as they appeared with Danny. It was just his mind, always in overdrive, rounding third when you thought he'd slide into second.

That sharpness is also what made him successful. He got into the corporate world and fought tooth and nail for everything he got. He wound up in Ireland working in a company's European headquarters. No one from home knew exactly what he did, so he mainly just told people that he's in finance, which is about as vague as he can get. He preferred not to talk about work at home anyway. He preferred to come home and hear how everyone else was doing. That was just one reason of many that his first stop was always a visit to his Mother. She usually kept him well briefed on the comings and goings of the neighborhood, or as he called it, 'Who's doing who and who's getting fat.' The problem was, once he was there, she'd never let him leave.

So instead of the agreed 8 o'clock, it was closer to 9:30 when Danny finally walked into The Sports Bar and found Jim laughing at Mike, who was making an exaggerated gesture of a cook flipping burgers with a spatula.

He pushed his way through a group of sun-stroked men with beer belly's sticking out through their polo shirts. As he approached he caught Jim's eye and gave him a wide grin, 'I know I'm late, but it's a bit early for charades don't you think Mike? Let me guess though, it's your wife trying to cook?'

Mike turned and smiled when he saw Danny and laughed, 'Fuck that' he put his hand to his head like he was making a phone call, 'this is my wife trying to cook'.

Danny and Mike gave each other the guy half-hug half-handshake. He did the same for Jim only followed by a quick slap on the back of the head. 'Good to see you boys, how far ahead are you?'

'About 3 and a half' Jim answered, 'what're ya having?'

'Sam Adams . . . draught and the real one, not that nasty summer ale'

Jim nodded to the bartender and tapped his glass and gave him a three sign.

'So, Sam Adams?' Mike asked, 'I would've thought you'd be hooked on the Guinness now living over there.'

'When in Rome Mike . . . Plus, it tastes much better there. Ask any older Irish guy and he'll tell you Guinness doesn't travel well.'

'What the hell's that mean?'

'No idea, just something they all seem to agree on. How about this, 'What's for you won't pass you. That's a saying all the mother's seem to agree on.' Danny turned and accepted the beer from the bartender's hand and nodded in thanks.

Jim laughed, 'Sounds too optimistic to be Irish, they must've stolen that from the Chinese or something.' He took his beer from the bartender also and handed him an empty glass. 'So Dan, what's Ma up to?'

'Nothing much I guess. She was just telling me about her new job and everything. She said she's back in a clinic so she's happier.'

'Yeah, she told me that, she likes it better, at least the doctors don't treat the nurses like shit in the clinics.'

'She said that too. I have half a mind to have a word with one or two of those jerk-off doctors. Some of them with a God complex need to come down a notch.' Danny said.

Mike laughed, 'God complex huh? Man all you educated types have ego's bigger than your dicks. I bet you both spend most of your day bossing us regular folk around.'

Jim turned to Mike with a raised eyebrow, 'Ah, regular folk, huh Mike? Last I heard you've been throwing your weight around too champ. Aren't you the foreman on that Neponset bridge project?' Jim asked.

'Hey, if I'm wearing a tool belt, I'm still regular folk.' Mike considered his own logic for a second and took a sip from his beer. 'Who am I kidding, I don't wear a fucking tool belt anymore, I just walk around with a clip board and a tape measure . . . oh well, looks like we're all assholes then, must be genetic. Fuck them if they can't take a joke.'

Danny laughed and shook his head, 'Hey, you know something? Every time I come home I spend so much time around this neighborhood catching up and I never make it into the city. Can I interest you fellas in hitting the town for a few? Nothing crazy, I just feel like something different.' Mike and Jim looked at each first and shrugged. Both then nodded to Danny in agreement.

'Plus' Danny added, 'I think the bartender keeps shooting dirty looks over at me.'

Jim and Mike looked at each and laughed.

'Yeah Danny, what'd you say to him anyway?' Mike asked.

'Hell if I know' Danny answered, 'but I think it has to do with his limp.'

Jim Carson

Jim had the bartender close the tab and call them a taxi. He insisted on picking up the bill for the last few rounds. The taxi picked them up twenty minutes later outside the bar in Quincy Center. Danny asked the taxi driver to take Quincy Shore Drive so he could cruise down Wollaston Beach. It was a warm spring night so along the beach front was still busy. There were couples out walking dogs and small gatherings of high school kids across from Tony's Clam shop holding onto fast-melting ice cream cones. They drove past the bar that had the doors open with people smoking on the patio out front. All along the street you could hear music from the bar playing. It was a local band, The Junkyard Dogs blasting out a blues rock.

They hit a string of green lights starting with the Squantum intersection and all the way over the Neponset River Bridge. That meant they were on 93 North in about 2 minutes. When they hit the highway, an old U2 song came on the radio. Mike motioned for the cab driver to turn it up. Jim rolled the window all the way down and let the warm breeze hit him in the face. 'What a night' he thought, as he sucked in the familiar Boston Harbor air. The sun had gone down an hour ago and the city up ahead was lit up. Jim looked over at the two guys and each were smiling. Jim knew they were all thinking the same thing, nostalgic all of a sudden for simpler times. Laughing with friends, heading into the city without a care in the world 'At least that's how it seemed in retrospect'. It was safe to say they all missed those days sometimes. Although each knew those care-free times were well and truly behind them.

The view and the smell of the sea brought Jim back to his early twenties, leaving a bar on Dorchester Avenue before going to close out the night at JJ Foley's in town. 'Yeah' Jim thought, 'We all missed those nights'. However, he knew memories like that often came shaded through rose-tinted glasses. He knew it was a passing feeling, but it was nice while it lasted.

The taxi dropped them close to Boston's North End. They walked over to the bars on the waterfront. The city had a good buzz, especially considering it was not quite summer. They grabbed a table on the patio of one of the bars overlooking the harbor. The atmosphere was perfect. It was steady, but not so packed and loud that they would get bored staring at each other or struggle to get served. An attractive young waitress took their order and within a minute there were three Jameson's on the table. The whiskey was Danny's idea, but he regretted it immediately when Mike took his down in one shot and said, 'Should of ordered a few beers to go with that Danny boy.' Jim just snickered because he knew Danny was not impressed. He signaled for three beers from the waitress.

Danny turned to Mike and said, 'I would've Mike, if we got Jagerbombs or Sambuca you asshole. That's good whiskey, you're supposed to enjoy the taste not suck it up like a wet-dry vac.'

'My bad Danny, I didn't realize booze came with instructions.'

'Alright, alright' Jim said, 'Enough bitching already, beers are on the way.' He turned to Danny and said, 'Hey Dan tell me about that trip to Israel for work. What's it like there?'

Danny stopped his lingering glare towards Mike and shifted towards Jim, happy to have a change in subject. 'It was strange actually. Tel Aviv's a really nice city I thought, great weather, a lot of young people, good bars, nice restaurants. I even went to a pretty sweet brew house. They have this Israeli ale called Dancing Camel, if you ever come across it, give it a whack . . . delicious. The only problem was that the whole time I always had in the back of my head where I was . . . I mean geographically. So that made it kind of tough to relax. I guess if you're born there, you're just used to that.'

'Weather was good huh . . . fucking wicked hot there I bet?' Mike asked

'Not really actually, probably 70's, really nice, it wasn't summertime though, so not sure how it gets around then. It was pretty sweet though, the hotel was along this promenade on the beach, so I jogged along the Mediterranean every evening. It was beautiful. Only one problem . . . the cats man. There were stray cats all along the promenade, and these fuckers looked way too big and well fed for stray cats, so you know they were dangerous.'

Mike gave Danny a confused look, 'What the hell are you talking about cats for?'

Jim started to laugh and turned to Mike 'Did you forget Mike, Dan here has somewhat of a feline phobia. He's had it forever.'

'Not forever' Danny corrected, 'Only since that crazy asshole down the street opened the door for us trick-or-treaters with a mutant cat in his kitchen. It had a cat face and was about the size of a St. Bernard.'

'Yeah boys, sorry, but I'm fucking lost' Mike said while

scratching his head.

'Let's just say Danny hasn't been the same since' Jim added.

Danny winced, 'I actually don't even want to talk about it anymore.'

Mike said. 'Okay I get it, kind of like Batman and bats, only without all the cool shit, like crime fighting and the Bat Mobile. Anyway, you make it to Jerusalem?'

Danny's eyes twitched suddenly with excitement, 'Oh, yeah, what an incredible place. I've never seen anything like it. You can't help but get caught up in the history, everything's so ancient. To actually stand on the ground where Jesus Christ himself stood, it's a pretty special feeling. I don't know man, just to look at the city and consider how much blood's been spilt in the last two thousand years over pretty much a claim to this place. It was wild.'

'Yeah, and the kicker is' Mike said, 'You got three religions battling over it and they're all probably talking about the same frigin God.'

Jim looked surprised and asked 'When the hell did you get so political Mike?'

'Was laid off during the winter Jim, I was hooked on the History Channel and Discovery HD. That's some compelling shit.'

'What is?'

'Fucking history man'

'Pretty ambiguous there Mike, but I get your point.' Jim turned back to Danny, 'I heard you brought Ma back some cross Dan.'

'Yeah, a Jerusalem cross. It's one big cross in the center and four smaller crosses surrounding it.'

'What's it mean?'

'I'm not 100% positive, but I do know it's supposed to represent Christianity as a whole, meaning all sects, not limited to just Catholic or Orthodox or whatever. I think it's based on some of the Crusaders' crosses, maybe the knights from Malta, but I'm not sure.'

'Sounds like something right up her alley anyway, I bet she loved it'

'Hope so . . . hey, I almost forgot.' Danny dug into his pocket and pulled out a tiny wooden case and handed it to Jim, 'I got you something too Jimmy. Happy early 30th, I figured I might not be able to come home for it, so I picked this up in Jerusalem too.'

'Thanks Dan, you didn't have to do that.' Jim rubbed his hand over the smooth wooden case and noticed the almost silky feel to it. He held it up to the lantern to look at it in light and noticed the slight grains and color changes throughout.

'Hang onto that case too actually, it's hand-carved olive wood, but go ahead open it up.'

Jim put the case back on the table and opened it. Inside there were two shining cufflinks that look like ancient coins, rimmed with gold and gold fasteners.

'They're ancient Roman Empire coins. I remember you used to be big into Julius Caesar and the Romans. They're authentic, at least they better be, that's what the guy who sold them to me said. Anyway, I thought you might like them.'

'Are you kidding me, I love them Danny, thanks bro' Jim got up and gave Danny a bear hug.

The waitress came back balancing a tray with three beers on it, 'Sorry for the wait fellas, I would've put a rush on it if I knew you'd get so emotional over it.'

Mike called the waitress around to his side of the table to pay. He winced as reached into his pocket. His hands, like a lot of builders, were tough and callused, but also dry and riddled with tiny cuts from vigorous hand-washing. He pulled out a worn leather wallet that was speckled with paint and stucco. He found a twenty inside, pulled it out and handed it to the waitress. 'It's just a brotherly love moment, that's all. Feel free to stick around and talk to me, I'm feeling left out.'

'Love to, but I've got other tables' she went to hand Mike the change, but Mike waved it away.

They finished another round of drinks before the breeze picked up off the harbor and it grew too cold to sit outside on the patio. They decided that was their cue to leave and got the waitress to call a taxi.

The taxi dropped Jim and Danny off at Jim's apartment across from the Cedar Grove cemetery. They split the taxi fare and prepaid for Mike to get back to Braintree. It was the least they could do considering they made him abandon his truck in Quincy.

It was quiet which made sense since Jim's neighbors for the most part were one leafy park, a little league baseball diamond and a few thousand corpses resting across the street.

Jim moved to this two-family house in the last couple of months. Since he moved in, the place had really grown on him. He liked it much better than his old bachelor pad over at the renovated chocolate factory. This place had three bedrooms, a kitchen, dining room, big living room and even a spacious entrance hall. It also had a front porch overlooking the cemetery grounds.

Jim showed Danny the spare bedroom and gave him the tour of the rest of the apartment. He lent him an old Suffolk University hoodie to throw on and they sat out on the front porch for a nightcap.

'Big place you got here Jimmy. How about you tell me now why you got three bedrooms? You holding something back?'

'You're always observant Dan, I'll give you that. Don't read too much into it though' Jim said. Jim was glad it was dark, as he knew his cheeks started to blush at the question.

'Good, I hope I would've heard something about it at least. Seriously though, Ma mentioned your girlfriend. Alex right? Getting pretty serious I gather?'

'You could say that. Still can't believe you've never met her though. She's moving in man, end of the month as soon as her lease is up on her current place. Half the shit here is actually hers.'

'Haha' Danny laughed, 'I was gonna ask about the throw pillows alright. I thought that was a bit strange for a grown man living on his own.'

'Nah, that's her. I stick to pillows people actually use.'

Jim reached down and popped the top off two bottles of beer at his feet and handed one to Danny.

'There's more too Danny . . . I bought her a ring. I haven't given it to her yet or anything though. Her father's kind of old fashioned so I want to go and ask him first.'

'Jesus man, that's great news' Danny threw his hand on Jim's shoulder and gave it a squeeze 'Congrats Jim.'

'Don't congratulate me yet bro, wait until she says yes first.'

They talked for a while more after that. Jim told Danny more about Alex. He talked about how they met at the deli when Jim first worked there years ago when her uncle owned it. And how her family had moved to the U.S. from Romania when she was about 8, but she has no trace of an accent. He told him how she had gone to private schools and never really hung around the neighborhood but was still very street savvy and down to earth.

Back when he was just a part-timer at the Deli, he had always timed it so he could wait on her whenever she came in to eat. After a while he began timing it so he could take a break and eat with her. All through college they kept in touch, but really only as friends. When Jim took over the Deli as owner she still kept coming in. By that time, she was just coming in to see him.

Danny sat and listened to every word his brother said. The more he heard him gush about this girl, the more he knew he liked her already. He liked her because she made Jim happy and even though he had a pang of jealously over it, he knew Jim deserved to be happy. Jim was always the kind of guy Danny wished he had been. Not that Danny was a bad guy, but he could never just be happy. He was never content with anything. It was part of what made him successful, but it also drove him crazy. Sitting there with Jim just hanging out, relaxing and talking, made Danny wish (and not for the first time) that he could be there more often. He wished he was there more for Jim, for his Mom, everything. Part of him knew that it was a futile feeling however, plus it was probably too late anyway, each had their own lives now.

After finishing off the beers that were in the fridge, the two brothers said their goodnights. Jim had to open the

Deli in the morning and was already sacrificing a good portion of his sleep, not that he minded one bit. Danny agreed to meet Jim and Alex the next night for dinner in Quincy Center around 8:30. Danny promised to be punctual this time and even offered to pay for it if he was late, something he probably planned to do anyway.

Brendan Maguire

Brendan Maguire was a bright kid. He made good grades in high school without over-exerting himself. He also worked up to 25 hours a week at the Beale Street Deli. He worked there since sophomore year and also picked up more shifts during the summers.

By senior year in high school, his parents knew he and his friends were into drinking. They figured most kids were at that age. They also figured he was smart enough to be responsible. They were probably not the first parents to make that mistake. Most weekends, Brendan left his car home and headed out on foot with his friends. Usually they'd head down to Merrymount Park, which had basketball and tennis courts out front and dense woods in the back. The woods were where they usually stashed the coolers of beer. They'd hang out on the courts until 10, when the basketball court lights went off. After that they'd head deep into the woods and continue drinking. If it was a really good weekend, someone's parents would be out or away and word would get around of a party.

It was that kind of night when Brendan and his friends headed to Dora McBride's house on a side street off of the beach. Her father was a Boston cop and more often than not he'd either be working or blowing off some steam at one of the bars in North Quincy on weekend nights. Brendan had heard that Dora's mother took off years ago and was barely heard from anymore. Reports of why she left were mostly speculation, but he heard that she left because she couldn't handle the pressure of being married to an alcoholic cop. Maybe it was the combination of the two that turned her stomach. Either way, she left one day and that was that. Dora for her part seemed older than her 18 years. She was kind of a bad-ass in Brendan's eyes and more than a little intimidating. She took a liking to Brendan though and they hit it off pretty well. They had begun some form of a relationship, but he wouldn't call her his girlfriend. She always seemed to have the upper hand however and this left Brendan always trying to impress her. For a pretty smart kid, he made some bad decisions. He started dabbling in soft drugs first like smoking weed and occasionally eating mushrooms. He balked at anything harder than that like cocaine, pills or heroin, which had a strangle-hold on much of his generation. He wouldn't take any of that himself, but eventually he did try to gain her favor by creating a supply line between the source, Dora's 25 year old brother named Flynn and the end users, Brendan's buddies and classmates.

Flynn was like many misguided, under-educated young men in Boston. He had a quick temper and faster hands. He made a name for himself as a teenager in the Golden Gloves boxing tournament. The local trainer was connected with big-time drug dealers from South Boston. He lived to recruit the city's impressionable young tough guys into his ranks. He trained fighters and often times he turned fighters into enforcers. He gave them some small cash, which they had never seen before, and promised more if they could deliver results.

Flynn turned out to be the cream of this crop. Also, Flynn's old man was a cop, so he availed of some additional protection, at least while he was a minor. No cop wanted to be responsible for putting another's kid into juvenile hall.

Flynn played this card as often as he needed. He felt he deserved any leniency thrown his way. Therefore, he had pretty much run amuck and did whatever he pleased from about the age of 15.

When he met Brendan, he didn't mind one bit that he was doing whatever with his sister. He felt so unthreatened by him he almost pitied him because of how out of his depth he was in dealing with Dora. He wasn't one to leave the exploitation of individuals to amateurs however, so when he saw the grip that Dora had on this kid, he saw opportunity knocking.

Of course Brendan and his boys wanted to get in tight with Flynn McBride. That was like instant street-credit to middle class white boys. So Brendan started introducing people he knew that were looking to score to Flynn. After a while, Flynn no longer wanted to deal face to face with these newbies, so Brendan started working as an intermediary. He'd bring cash to Flynn for whatever was available. For Brendan's friends and acquaintances it was mainly pills, downers like OC's and Percs that they wanted.

Somehow that stuff started out as less offensive and taboo than cocaine. Unfortunately for many, it was also the first step towards sticking a spike in your arm.

As Brendan became known more and more among his peers as someone who could supply anything, his confidence started to increase. It grew to the point that eventually he had the balls to ask Flynn to front him some product. Flynn agreed. All he could see was dollar signs those days. Most of those dollars were finding their way immediately up his nose, so his decision-making ability was more impaired than usual.

He should have known that Brendan didn't have the muscle to keep an eye on his merchandise or even make an attempt to protect it.

Brendan listened to him from outside Dora's house days before. 'He basically served it on a platter to those Mattapan brothers and they even felt bad for him and barely even roughed him up for it. What the fuck was that retard doing on the Milton Street trolley anyway? He's from fucking Wollaston Hill?' Flynn had screamed at Dora when she gave him the news. 'How much is he fucking down?'

'Twenty-five hundred he said' Dora replied.

'Well tell that fucking chicken-shit he owes me five grand. There's a mark-up for making me look fucking weak.'

Brendan knew he had to go to Dora's party on that Saturday night. He also knew he had to have some kind of plan for getting Flynn's money back. So when the Deli closed up shop in the evening, he said goodbye to Jim, but not before he pilfered the spare set of keys to the Deli's office. Brendan knew that if it was busy and they closed late, that Jim wouldn't have time to make it into the bank to deposit the day's take. When that happened, Jim had to either take the cash home with him or drop it into the safe downstairs.

Brendan figured there'd be at least five grand in there from a Saturday, especially one that was so busy. All he had to do was give Flynn the keys and explain the operation. Go in, middle of the night, pop the lock on the safe, grab the cash and head out. It was such an old building, that there were no cameras inside. Jim was waiting until after spring to get them installed. As far as the alarm was concerned, Brendan knew the code. He had watched Jim punch it in about a hundred times.

Brendan and a few friends got to Dora's house just after 11 on Saturday night. They hung out drinking beers in a friend's mother's basement and playing cards for most of the evening. Brendan wasn't very vocal about his current predicament, but his friends knew something was troubling him. They played a few hands of poker early, but Brendan just kept folding before the flop.

He didn't even argue when someone put the TV show Cops on, which was the first time in his life that Brendan didn't complain about having to sit through that garbage. The boys were pretty clued into the type of business that Brendan was involved. It was one of his buddies that he went to meet in Dorchester that day. His buddy worked at a pizza shop in Dorchester and had an aunt living in Mattapan. It was her house he and Brendan were headed to so they could try and get a ride home when they got jumped. Since then, word had spread that Brendan was in a jam with Flynn McBride. However, Brendan would never tell them what his plan was. Half those guys had worked for Jim before and the other half were regular customers.

The door was unlocked as usual at Dora's, so Brendan knocked, trying to keep his hand from trembling. 'Hello . . . Dora?' He said and walked in. The kitchen was on the left, it was run down with old wooden cabinets and worn wallpaper.

Brendan saw empty Bud Light cans upside down in the sink and a pizza box on top of the stove. He heard music coming from the back porch and could smell the familiar mix of cigarette smoke and marijuana drifting from the open windows.

Dora called up from the basement, which was set up as a lounge with a makeshift bar, a couple of couches and an out of place pool table. Brendan looked back at his friend and motioned for him to bring everyone downstairs to Dora. He said he'd be a minute and continued through the hallway to the back. He knocked and opened the screen door to the porch.

Flynn and his side-kick named Mike Faye both stopped talking and looked up when they heard the screen door squeak open and saw Brendan walk through it. They were both sitting in what looked like old, rotted Adirondack chairs. Flynn was holding a half smoked joint and his eyes were glazed over. His hair was buzzed down to a 3-blade and he was sporting a chin strap beard, roughly about the same length as his hair. He had on baggy jeans with flip flops and a ratty t-shirt. He looked like he was on the final stages of a bender. 'It's strange' Brendan thought 'I've never seen him so mellow looking.' That changed as soon as Flynn spoke.

'What the fuck are you looking at, you fucking coward? You have my fucking money or should I let Dozen here chew your fucking fingers off?'

Dozen was Mike Faye's nickname. Although only very few people called him that. Rumor was, he was a fat bastard of a kid growing up and could always be found in Dunkin Donuts ankle deep in Boston cream donuts. So naturally, Dunkin Donuts became Donut, which became Donuts, plural, which became Dozen. After his heroin problem really got off the ground though he got so skinny it became more like one of those ironic nicknames. Either way, Brendan called him Mike, for fear of getting cut up, or worse.

'I was hoping I could talk to you a minute Flynn, about what I owe you?'

'So . . . talk mothafucka, I'm already losing interest and think I might let the big dog loose on ya' he said and pointed over at Dozen with the joint between his index and middle fingers.

'I was hoping I could talk to you in private. I have an idea on how to get your cash back.'

Flynn leaned forward and put his elbows to his knees. He took a drag from his joint and holding the smoke in his lungs he said, 'You got something to say to me, say it now. No secrets between me and Dozen.' Dozen nodded in agreement.

Brendan shrugged. He figured he had no choice but to let Dozen in on the plan too. 'I work at a Deli, you know that right?'

'You gonna pay him back in fucking pastrami, dip shit?' Dozen asked.

'I took the keys tonight, and . . . I think there's at least a few grand in the office safe.'

Flynn leaned back again in his chair, 'So why the fuck are you standing here! Go get it and fucking bring it to me.'

Brendan shifted his feet at the sound of Flynn's raised voice again. He dug his hands in his pockets and continued. 'It's not that simple if I don't want to get caught. If I use the keys to get in and clean the place out he'll definitely know it's me or at least someone who works there.' Plus, Brendan thought to himself, 'Jim probably wouldn't be insured for that.'

'Why would you getting caught be my problem?' Flynn asked.

'It's not Flynn, I know that, but if you think about it, I did funnel a good chunk of business your way. If people that know me see me go to jail or something, they might be scared off going to you for anything.' Brendan answered.

'Well, I'll tell you what I think . . . I think that's a weak-ass excuse because the bottom line is, I don't need fucking shit from you. You think one of your fucking bed buddies wouldn't just take your place? What the fuck would I need with someone who just ups and loses my shit without a fight? Actually, now that I think of it, get your fucking faggot ass out of my house!' Flynn sprung to his feet and fired a half-full beer can towards Brendan that hit him square on the chin.

Brendan flinched to brace himself but was too slow and stumbled back into the screen door and made it rattle, nearly knocking it off the hinges.

Brendan, while holding the newly formed cut on his chin, turned and struggled to open the door and step over the threshold. Flynn took two quick steps forward, pulled him back and slammed the door shut. 'Where the fuck do you think you're going?'

'I was leaving Flynn . . . I thought you said . . .'

'I'm up now asshole, sit down and tell me about this place, we're going tonight.'

Jim Carson

Jim's alarm started screaming at 4:30 in the morning. He reached over to the side table to grab his cellphone and turn off the alarm. He knocked over a couple of books and half a glass of water in the process.

He flicked the lamp on and sat over the side of his bed. He wasn't really hung-over, but definitely more tired than usual and could feel those few drinks from the night before. Jim was not a snooze button person when it came to alarms. He knew that was a slippery slope, especially when he had staff waiting out in the cold for him. He played through the pain of getting up right away and jumping into the shower. At least it was warm, which made it easier to roll out of bed.

Typically Jim would not do any drinking the night before an early start, but having Danny home was an occasion to celebrate. Also, working on Sundays was such a rare occurrence, he felt he could endure this one time. Generally he'd never open Sunday mornings unless some sort of event required it. That Sunday, he felt he had to open as most of his geriatric clientele were headed to an anniversary mass for one of the volunteer workers at the senior center. With the early Mass on at about 6am, he promised the center's coordinators that he'd be open for breakfast afterwards.

Therefore, there he was digging around under the bed for his other shoe. He was trying his best to keep the noise down since Danny was still sleeping in the next room, but he'd forgotten to lay out his stuff the night before. He went right from the porch with Danny to talking on the phone with Alex before he fell asleep. He gave her the good news, that they were meeting Danny later for dinner, so she'd have her chance to meet him at last. Alex was thrilled and she promised to drop by for breakfast early at the Deli before she went out to buy something to wear.

Jim left the house mostly awake. At least he had showered, shaved and dressed by 5am, just a few minutes behind schedule.

At that hour anyway, the drive to Quincy was quick with no business traffic on a Sunday. The clock read 7 minutes past 5 when he put the car into park in the deli parking lot. He got out and walked around to the front. He reached the door and fumbled for a second with the keys to open the lock. He walked in and headed over to punch the code into the alarm system, but noticed it was unarmed. 'That's odd' he thought, 'I guess I did leave in a rush to go meet Mike and Danny.' He couldn't actually remember setting it. 'Oh well', he figured 'must've just forgotten'. He let it go and walked behind the counter. He turned the coffee machines on first and set a pot for brewing. It was still early enough that he could setup and enjoy a coffee at the same time. He continued over to the grill area and crouched down to turn the dials on, left side on low, right side on high. He stood up and held his hand over the back to make sure the flame had lit. 'It wouldn't be the first time the old grill's pilot went out.' When he felt the heat start to rise he nodded to himself happy to avoid a morning of repairs.

He switched on the friolater next and then checked the small refrigerator and was happy to find someone chopped up the potatoes and onions the night before. 'That would do for the first round of home fries.' Happy that all that needed turning on was on, Jim went over to the front door again and put the keys in and locked the door. He did that every morning when setting up alone and heading to the back or downstairs to the office.

Jim poured coffee into a mug and dropped in some milk and turned to walk out back to grab the cash till from the office. He hit the light switch on his way around the kitchen and was about to take his first step downstairs when he saw something strange in his periphery.

The back door dead bolt had been pulled open and the door was just slightly ajar. He tried to remember whether he had noticed it when walking around the front, but was drawing a blank. He took two steps back from the stairway and the realization hit him. He felt a burning feeling in the pit of his stomach. His saliva dried up and he couldn't swallow. His blood rushed to his head and caused an onset of dizziness. Then he heard something, a rustling noise from downstairs. It could only be someone looking for something in the office.

He heard a noise to the left of him. It came from the walk-in fridge across from the back door. His body jolted left quickly and he was a meter away from a pale, thin man carrying a case of bottled cream soda. The man froze at once, his gaunt face showing surprise.

Jim recognized the man from around the neighborhood, a known drug addict and all around scumbag.

'Oh fuck' Dozen swore and dropped the bottles crashing on the floor. He made a move for Jim, but Jim shot up with his right hand, throwing his hot coffee in Dozen's face. Dozen took a step back and yelped, going down to a knee in the process. Jim turned to run towards the front but lost his footing in the spilled soda that gathered around his shoes. He scrambled quickly to his feet and turned back around just in time to see Dozen leap again towards him. This time he had a knife. Dozen swung the knife with his right hand, stomach-height but Jim jumped back in enough time and rifled the empty coffee mug towards Dozen's head. He missed. Dozen recovered and thrust the knife straight towards Jim's stomach. Jim shifted his feet back quickly to avoid the cut and this time reached forward and managed to grab Dozen's forearm. The knife caught Jim in the stomach, but didn't hit deep. In one motion, Jim slid his hands down to Dozen's wrist and twisted it so the knife turned upwards. Dozen's wrist made a popping noise and his head and chest lurched forward. Still putting pressure on the wrist Jim let loose with a kick that hit Dozen square on the bridge of his nose. The crack echoed in the kitchen and Dozen's broken nose exploded in red immediately. Jim followed up right away with an elbow to the back of his neck and then hooked him to the ground still holding on to the knife hand. Despite the blood, Dozen still fought and Jim was on top of him trying to knock the knife free. That's when Jim felt a blow from behind. Something hard and heavy thumped him on the top of the spine and he immediately fell to the side and rolled onto his back. He could see clearly. He didn't feel pain, but a sting and then he was numb. He knew then he was done for. As he was pounded on, he shut his eyes to avoid watching the repeated blows. His mind began to flicker, flashes of Danny and Mike laughing, his Mom smiling, even his father, and then finally Alex, her face, those dark eyes, those curls, her dimples, and then it all faded and he saw nothing but black before he drifted from consciousness.

Brendan Maguire

It dawned on Brendan what he had done the moment he watched Jim Carson turn the corner and let himself into the front door of the deli. He sat there frozen with fear in Flynn McBride's truck. Maybe he realized his mistake before that too. As the night turned to early morning, he watched Flynn fill himself with whiskey and red bull. Then he watched him snort lines of cocaine off the patio table. He knew all along the type of person Flynn was, but he still served this up to him on a platter.

'Who am I kidding', Brendan thought. About a year ago, he watched Flynn jump an old homeless guy and repeatedly kick him in the face. The whole time Flynn was laughing hysterically. He knew he shouldn't have gotten into bed with this animal. Now this happened. He knew he was wrong, he just wish he'd realized sooner. He tried to back out that night. When he did, Flynn put lit cigarettes out on his arm until he handed over the keys. Then he was dragged at Dozen's knife point to the front door until he disarmed the alarm system. As soon as he saw Jim, he remembered bitching to him about having to chop potatoes and onions before he could go home. That was at work the night before. How could he forget, the memorial Mass was this morning. Of course Jim was opening the Deli for that.

Brendan's brain was too occupied with dread when he saw Jim walk in. It couldn't send signals to his legs to move. He needed to do something fast, take some action, but nothing came to him. Or maybe too many things came to him. Finally, he knew he was fucked and he had to try and intervene. He had resigned to whatever fate lay ahead when he jumped from the truck and bolted to the front door. He nearly knocked himself out running into the door, which didn't budge. He grabbed the handle and pulled at it frantically until he saw the keys dangling from the other side. Jim had locked himself in. Brendan grabbed his phone and dialed 911 as he sprinted around the back. The call connected as he reached the back door but he dropped the phone when Flynn flung the door open and ran towards the car. 'Hurry the fuck up he yelled' as Dozen followed behind him holding his nose, with blood all over his face and shirt.

Brendan stumbled to his feet and grabbed his phone. He heard the operator and spoke quickly 'Robbery in progress right fucking now! It's at The Beale Street Deli in Quincy!' He ran through the kitchen and stopped short then. His hand dropped to his side with the operator still asking questions. He could already hear sirens getting closer and realized one of the neighbors must've already called the police. Brendan couldn't think. He thought he might be in shock, he lifted the phone again and said, 'Please, you need to send an ambulance now . . . my name's Brendan . . . Brendan Maguire.' He let the phone drop slowly from his hand. He walked forward into the kitchen and knelt beside Jim, who was laid out motionless on the floor. He knew absolutely nothing about first aid. He could plainly see that Jim was unconscious and he couldn't see his chest moving. Brendan was suddenly light headed. The dizziness made him sit back and lean against the oven that was behind him. His own breathing became difficult. He started to panic when he realized he couldn't take in a deep breath. He felt like someone was sitting on his chest. He leaned on his elbow so he was parallel with

Jim, but he couldn't stomach the sight of Jim sprawled-out and lifeless. He laid down on his back and shut his eyes. Within seconds he too was lying unconscious on the ground. The only difference was that Brendan's chest was moving up and down as he was still breathing. Jim Carson was not.

Danny Carson

There was a car's horn blaring in the final minutes of Danny's dream. He heard it, but didn't wake from it. A vicious pounding on the door downstairs and frantic calling of his name did wake him up however. He jumped from the bed at the sound. It took him a moment to remember where he was. It was his first time staying at Jim's new apartment and he was suffering from jet lag and a mild hangover. He pulled his jeans on quickly then ran out into the hall and down the stairs, putting his t-shirt on in the descent. Through the door, still knocking loudly was his cousin Mike.

Danny felt confused at the disturbance and dread began to set in. He undid the lock and opened the door to let Mike in. 'What the fuck Mike?' he asked with concern his is voice.

Mike was out of breath and hoarse from screaming outside. 'Get your shit Danny. Something's happened to Jim, we need to go to the hospital now.'

Danny's heart began to race and his hands were shaking. He ran to the top of the stairs and grabbed a pair of sneakers and quickly pulled the apartment door shut. He ran back down to the bottom and followed Mike out who had already gone to the truck and was starting the engine. Danny jumped in the passenger side and Mike hit the gas aggressively before Danny even had the door shut. Danny held on tightly to the side handle to keep from falling into Mike's lap.

'Jesus fucking Christ Mike, what happened? Tell me something for Christsakes.' Danny said.

'I don't know much so far, but I'm waiting for a call for

more information. There was some kind of break in at the Deli or something man. Some guys ransacked the place and Jim got beaten . . . badly.' Mike answered.

'Fuck. Is he okay Mike?'

Mike didn't answer and didn't look over at Danny either. He just continued weaving in and out of lanes to avoid hitting cars from both lanes of traffic.

'Answer me damn it!' Danny yelled at Mike and smashed his fist hard against the dashboard.

Mike finally looked over at Danny briefly. 'It doesn't look good Danny' he said, showing clear signs of shock, 'He may not make it.'

At Mike's words, Danny leaned back against the passenger seat and ran his hand through his hair. 'Fuck' he said.

Mike continued driving, whipping precariously through morning traffic and within 10 minutes he pulled the truck up to the emergency room entrance in Quincy Medical Center.

'Go!' he yelled to Danny.

Mike didn't have to say it twice as Danny pushed the door open before the truck had stopped and jumped down to the sidewalk. He went down to one knee when he landed before hopping back to his feet and running through the automatic doors. 'Jim Carson!' he asked reception and they gave him directions to the surgery waiting room.

He ran over and hit the elevator button several times until the doors chimed open. The elevator was empty and he pushed the 3rd floor button for surgery. He hopped up and down waiting for the elevator to open up.

When the doors opened he ran outside into the hall. A

sign on the wall pointed right towards surgery and he ran flat out until he entered a large waiting area. He slid to a stop when he saw his mother sitting down staring blankly before him. There was young women sitting next to her with tears slowly streaming down her face. Her hands were gripping the sides of her forehead and strands of dark curly hair rested over her fingers. Danny walked over slowly towards them and said 'Mom' to get his mother's attention, but her focus on the floor didn't waver. He knelt down slowly in front of the young women and looked into her eyes. She looked at him momentarily startled. Danny thought he saw recognition in her eyes. 'Danny?' she asked.

He nodded 'Yes, it's Danny. You're Alex?' he asked

'Yes' she answered.

'What have you heard? Where's Jim? Is he gonna be okay?' Danny asked.

She continued looking in his eyes and Danny saw her struggling to fight back tears. 'He's gone Danny. The Doctor said . . . he's gone.' she answered.

Danny dropped down to both knees. He felt sick and could feel bile building in the back of his throat. Suddenly and uncontrollably, he began to sob. Through the tears and shaking, he felt Alex's hand touch his face and then rub the back of his head. He felt on the verge of collapse until she pulled his head to her chest. Danny felt his tears soaking her shirt through to the skin, but he couldn't move.

Minutes later, he heard a set of footsteps approach behind him. He slowly pulled himself away from Alex, looking into her sad eyes as he stood slowly. He turned around to see Mike standing with his cell phone still in his hand. Mike's face was ghostly white at the realization that Jim was gone. He asked Danny 'Is he . . . ?'

Danny nodded slowly and used the back of his sleeve to wipe his eyes dry. 'What did you find out?' He asked as he walked closer to Mike.

'I know who did it and I know where he lives. His name's Flynn McBride, lives off Wollaston beach.'

'Let's go.' Danny said with finality.

Mike nodded with agreement and they both started into a jog towards the elevator. When they hit the ground floor at reception, both men picked up the pace and ran outside. Mike led Danny to the truck. Once inside, Mike reversed out slowly from the parking spot then slowly turned onto the main street. As they left the hospital grounds, Mike stepped on the gas and sped down the hill and took a left at the bottom of the street, then a right onto Furnace Brook Parkway.

Danny could feel his hands begin shaking again uncontrollably. The sick feeling in his stomach stayed with him, but he no longer had the urge to vomit, it was now more of a burning feeling. Within minutes they approached Wollaston Beach and Mike quickly swung the truck onto Quincy Shore Drive, then almost immediately off again up a side street. He pointed at the house a hundred yards ahead.

Danny felt his blood run cold looking at the quaint front lawn that housed his brother's killer. He felt nerves build up and the shaking increased. He noticed three cruisers had already circled the house. As Mike pulled the truck to a stop, Danny watched the front door open. A young man was being escorted out of the front door by a police officer.

'That's him' Mike said.

Danny held his breath for a moment. Then he jumped out of the truck. He started walking towards the men quickly and broke into a sprint when he reached the side walk. He ran right for Flynn McBride. He had tunnel vision and could see nothing but McBride in front of him. He could sense blurry blue uniforms running towards him from multiple angles. He didn't yell anything or make any noise at all. 10 yards away from McBride he tightened his fist in preparation for the fight. He raised his arm, but as he did, he felt a stiff impact hit into his left side and immediately he fell to ground. He wrestled on the ground momentarily with the officer that tackled him until he felt many more hands pulling at his limbs. He stopped fighting and felt a number of punches from outstretched arms. He wheezed and tried furiously to take in a breath. Either the tackle or the fall had punched the wind out of his lungs. He could hear Mike in the background yelling for mercy and he felt hot tears heavy in his eyes once again as he watched the officer put McBride gently into the back of the squad car and slam the door shut.

A Funeral

The funeral for Jim Carson was held in Saint Gregory's Church in Dorchester. It was the largest Catholic Church around, which was needed since so many people had gathered. Also, it made sense to hold it there, since it was seconds from Cedar Grove cemetery. Jim enjoyed sitting out on his front porch so much, looking into the landscaped grounds of Cedar Grove cemetery. No one could have known that he'd be a permanent resident so soon. Danny was sure that Jim would've found humor in that somehow. No one else found humor in what had happened however, the circumstances that brought them together were terrible.

Instead of meeting over laughs and dinner, Danny had met Alex in the hospital waiting room. Instead of sharing stories about Jim's idiosyncrasies and how he was so laid back he was nearly falling over. Alex had comforted Danny, actually holding his head to her shoulder while a grown man sobbed. She was strong for him and for Kathleen showing the gritty exterior that comes with being a first generation daughter of immigrants well used to pain and suffering. On the inside however, she was bursting with flames. At home later that day she broke down in the shower, as if the water flow from the pipes was a signal to her body that it could release those tears she had held in restraint.

Mike Riordan gave the eulogy at the funeral at Danny's request. Mike barely held his composure throughout and every so often his voice cracked, especially when he made eye contact with his wife and saw her between his two girls, holding the youngest child's head on her lap. All three had red teary eyes. Even the priest had a difficult time with the service, recalling Jim as an altar boy dropping the cross at one Sunday service and his awful timing with the bells during communion.

Danny was glad Mike could give the eulogy and he was proud of him. Mike had been much closer to Jim growing up whereas Danny felt at best, he was neglectful and at worse a bully. That was now his biggest regret. Mike managed to make people smile during the service with his witty tales of youth. He even told the story of when he and Jim were about 13, and Mike had actually managed to finally push Jim so far to the edge, that he punched Mike in the face. The people laughed especially those that knew them best, including how resilient Jim was, but how irritating Mike could be.

Danny laughed and cried simultaneously. He looked back to gauge the crowd's reaction and stiffened with cold when he noticed his Father standing in the back of the church. He had snuck in late and didn't seem to be alone, a tall dark-looking man in a suit and tie right next to him. It was most likely his guard or some policeman. He saw the aging face of a man so familiar, hair longer than normal, slicked back, thinner than he remembered and with a goatee speckled with gray. Danny peered at him in astonishment and noticed he was not just standing with his hands neatly behind his back. He was actually cuffed. Billy Carson made eye contact with Danny and nodded his head slightly. Danny turned abruptly back around. It'd been about years since he'd seen him, 'He has the audacity to show up now?' Danny thought. He had disappeared by the end of the service. Danny stood on the steps of the church afterwards, looking across Dorchester

Avenue. He was looking left towards the Carney hospital and right towards Bakers' Chocolate factory, but the old man had vanished like the ghost that he was. As the people filed out of the church, they engulfed him and his mother with hugs, apologies and condolences. Danny let the memory of the ghost subside. His anger at those who had done this to Jim had now dulled any feelings of animosity towards a man that had become merely a figment of his imagination.

Brendan Maguire

Brendan never thought twice about whether he'd cooperate with the police. He felt his actions had led to this terrible event and he was willing to own up to his part. Brendan's parents got him an attorney. He didn't want one. At that point in time he didn't care about the outcome. Thankfully for him, even the first officer on scene and the detective assigned the case could see his fractured state of mind and reiterated time and again it was his right to ask for an attorney.

Ultimately Brendan and his attorney asked for very little. He volunteered to serve as a witness for the prosecution in the trials of Mike Faye and Flynn McBride. In return, Brendan was granted some leniency on his sentence and also was placed in a separate prison from McBride and Faye. It was a lower scale facility, with prisoners guilty of less severe crimes.

The State of Massachusetts got Mike Faye hooked on several charges, including unlawful entry, armed robbery, assault and battery, and eventually on murder in the second degree. He could've copped to manslaughter and had a few years lumped off his sentence, but he refused to roll over on Flynn McBride. For this, Dozen was given absolutely no leniency from the Judge. He saw 5-10 years tacked onto his 15 for murder. So, pretty much, the judge told him to get comfortable in Walpole, because he was in there for a least 20.

Flynn McBride didn't skate on all charges, just the most serious. Testimony from Brendan Maguire as eyewitness and concrete fingerprint evidence put him inside the Deli, so they got him for attempted larceny. Also, when Quincy police picked him up he was holding a small quantity of cocaine, so he was hit with a minor possession charge as well.

In the end though, no physical evidence could link him to the attack on Jim Carson. Whatever he had used, which was a meter long piece of wood used for stirring soup, had left the deli with him. It probably ended up in a fire place. The police and investigators did what they could to make an example of Flynn, but it was fruitless. Everyone knew it was him who beat Jim Carson to death. But no evidence or testimony from Brendan could actually directly link him to the attack, at least not beyond a reasonable doubt. All it would've taken was even the slightest cooperation from Mike Faye, however Faye took all of it on himself.

He took total responsibility for the attack and subsequent killing of Jim Carson. And so, for the death of Jim Carson, the main person responsible had walked pretty much scot-free, less than 2 years in jail. He was thrown in, a murderer, with the car boosters and petty thieves, still cocky, still bragging, and out in less than 24 months.

Brendan looked up from the letter he was writing and stretched his neck out of the bunk to look up at João, 'Hey J, how are you coming along with the Lonesome Dove? Great isn't it?'

João, kept his left thumb on his page and leaned on his elbow to look at Brendan's outstretched neck, 'Damn Brendan, this book's about a thousand pages long. You know I only got another 6 months inside . . . I'll never

finish that. Plus man, you know me ingles no is good.'
Joáo joked with a put-on accent.

'Yeah yeah, whatever bitch' Brendan replied picking up
the letter from his chest and started going over the
wording again. 'Everyone knows you went to private
school down in Fall River. Just cause your parents gave
you a name no one can pronounce, doesn't make you a
Brazilian national. Also, I've seen you play soccer and
you're a disgrace to your ancestors.'

'I'm Portuguese, not Brazilian man, suppose we all look
alike to you?'

'Who's we then? If you're Portuguese, that's European
asshole. I would've pegged you as Puerto Rican if
anything.'

'Whatever you say muchacho, I am pretty damn good
at baseball too. Maybe I am fucking Puerto Rican. You
think my folks lied to me? Maybe I'll start calling myself
Juan.'

'At least people can say that name, maybe turn Pires to
Perez too while you're at it.'

'Of course bro, I'd say my father would love that.'

'You are in a cell man?' Brendan said jokingly, but
regretted right after

'Hmm, good point man, guess that ship has sailed
already.'

'Ahh, you know I'm playing J, your folks still love you.'

Yeah I know man, can't say I done them proud though
brother.'

'You will man, just keep your nose clean after this
round . . . still early, you got time to turn it around.'

'Thanks preacher boy, think you're throwing stones
from the porch of your glass house there cousin.'

'Guess you're right man . . . Obrigado'

'Haha, fuck you asshole' João said as he lay back against the pillow and resumed from his spot in his book.

Brendan was put in a cell from the start with João Pires. You could call him lucky to a degree. João was about the same age, maybe a little older, but he was in tight with most minority groups. The place wasn't Shawshank or anything, but still tough enough that a clean cut boy from the suburbs wouldn't last long alone out on a limb. João and Brendan hit it off pretty quickly despite not having a great deal obviously in common. The troubled son of a Portuguese immigrant from Fall River and a middle-class college bound Irish-American from a quaint Cape Cod style bungalow didn't seem like a good match.

Their circumstances weren't that dissimilar however. Both, deep down, were good people whose moral compass hit a temporary dead zone. Both were from hard working, values-driven families. Where Brendan mixed himself up with the drug scene, João's poison became taking things that didn't belong to him, mainly sports cars. Regardless, they both ended up in a correctional facility for relatively short stints in jump suits. João had about 3 months in when Brendan joined him, but he knew people inside already. He wasn't tied in with gangs or anything, but when you grow up in tough neighborhoods you get to know tough people. So, João had a leg up on learning the ropes of the place and learning how to cope with life on the inside.

By the time Brendan showed up João had somewhat of a routine down. They were locked up for almost 17 of 24 hours, minus maybe 8 for sleep during the night, so you're looking at 9 hours give or take of pretty much nothing.

João showed Brendan the prison workout routine, which consisted mainly of push-ups, lunges, squats, sit-ups and the plank. Brendan got João hooked on stories. The prison had a three-at-a-time book limit per person per cell, so Brendan would have his mother order them online and ship them in intervals. It was prohibited to give the prisoners books or anything else during a visit, so that was the easiest way. If he started getting through them too quickly, he'd have his mother address the books to João. He figured they're all going to the same place.

The rest of the time they were loose in general population, which consisted of rec time in the yard, jobs and eating. Brendan was surprised at first how well they were fed. It wasn't gourmet by any stretch of the imagination, but it was okay and you could get three square meals a day.

He guessed it was probably the path of least resistance for the prison and it went a long way in keeping the atmosphere cool.

It was during the general population time where Brendan's friendship with João, and João's network became so obviously important. Word was out that Brendan had given up information on McBride, so there was always a chance of someone trying to make an example of him.

During rec time, it was outside when you could see the cliques and class system develop. Many of the inmates were short to medium timers, but there were still some tough dudes walking around that would rough you up for next to nothing. 'At least there were no serial killing psycho's floating around.' Brendan thought. Still, he never quite found comfort in that thought alone.

Brendan and João walked outside together. It was a decent day weather-wise, a few clouds floating around, but they were puffy white ones with no threat of rain. There was a good portion of sun getting past the clouds as well, and best of all no humidity. 'Nothing worse than very hot and very humid, especially trapped with hundreds of caged convicts,' Brendan thought. 'Humidity always seems to bring out the worse in people, making even the most docile riddle with agitation.' Had he not been where he was, he'd have nearly called it pleasant.

The two boys walked through the yard past a couple of weight lifting areas. Brendan liked to work out, but he felt those dudes pumping the weights were not an approachable bunch. He figured he could stick with the Count of Monte Cristo workout at least until his time was up. He was safer that way.

He and João did play basketball however. Brendan was more of a hockey fan growing up, but everyone growing up where he did played at least some hoop. It was a convenience thing. There were courts everywhere and all you needed was a ball.

Brendan followed João over to behind one of the hoops. João fist bumped with a few guys stretching out under the net and asked if they could get in. The two of them made 10 in total looking to play, so they decided to run full court. They lined up at the foul line to shoot for teams, first five to hit a free throw. João and Brendan ended up on the same team with two Brazilian guys and an Asian guy named Nguyen. Brendan was a head taller than everyone else on the team so he won the job of center. The other team was better for size. There were two white guys, one tall and stick thin called Jason and another older guy they called McNally, who had graying, balding hair but was built like a cathedral. There was also a shorter black kid named Ray, who they all knew because he was the best on the court almost every day. The Chang twins rounded off the side. Brendan didn't really know them, but apparently they ran with some of the Chinese Mafia near Kingston Street in town and both got done for breaking and entering. Brendan didn't think they were really twins, since besides both being Chinese, they shared no resemblance. He wasn't sure whether they were even both named Chang or if it was a nickname.

There were no jump balls on the court. Instead of a tip off, the first to hit a 3-pointer started with the ball. Nguyen hit a 3 after Ray missed his attempt, so Brendan kicked the ball in from under the net to João to start it up.

João took the ball up in a slow jog, letting his team set up. Ray was guarding and gave him plenty of space to start off. João took it over half court and caught a look from Nguyen. João dribbled hard right like he was driving, at the perimeter he stepped back and crossed over to his left to change direction. Ray back-pedaled and corrected, but as João went left Nguyen set a solid pick on Ray. Ray yelled 'switch' and McNally stepped over to guard João. João caught Brendan's move from the right side to cut in past Jason to the hoop. João hit Brendan with a perfect pass rifled from his left to Brendan's chest and Brendan lofted in the easy lay-up.

João started back pedaling on defense and fist-bumped Brendan on his way past. McNally let off a tirade of f-bombs in Jason's direction for getting beat to the inside.

McNally checked the ball in to Ray who decided to take it back hard. Ray was quick past half court and stutter-stepped Nguyen to the right, only to spin off him to the left when Nguyen went for the reach. Brendan and João stepped up to double on Ray, but Ray was too quick. He faked right again and Brendan bit, then he dribbled through his left leg to go left only to go behind his back, again to his right. He beat João with that move then hit the empty lane to the basket. Ray laid it in and ran back on defense only after some good-natured ribbing in João's face.

The game went back and forth at a fast pace until it was tied up at 17. With the game close and both teams wearing down, that's when each started launching 3's. Ray dribbled up the right wing, then held up for McNally to shake loose one of the Brazilian contingent on the perimeter. Ray fed him and McNally launched a 3 that fell in off the glass. Ray yelled something to McNally about being old school, but McNally was too into the game to joke at this stage.

João ran the ball up past half court then slowed the tempo. He was looking for Nguyen, who was scrambling, trying to get loose for a 3-pointer.

Meanwhile, Brendan tried to gain position down low on Jason for the rebound. The two had been grappling with one another all game. Jason had snuck in several elbows to the ribs and knees to the thighs on Brendan, all the while giving him verbal jabs under his breath.

Jason kept on him. He was calling Brendan Sinatra, saying how he'd heard Brendan loved singing to the cops. Brendan tried to keep his head about him. During the game Brendan realized, Jason was obviously one of McBride's boys or at least an acquaintance. He was wishing João hadn't talked him into playing basketball at all. He knew Jason was trying to goad him into something. The guy was thin, but he was lean and wiry and looked well able to scrap. Brendan thought he must be local, an older dude from Quincy maybe, but he wasn't immediately familiar.

Brendan stood his ground for the time being, and Nguyen got loose at the top of the circle. João fed him a bounce pass, which he fielded and fired to the basket with a quick release. The shot was just wide and clanked off the rim and back board towards the right. Brendan crouched, and then leapt for the rebound. Jason saw Brendan poise for the jump. He planted his left foot on Brendan's toes, then with a quick pivot, turned and caught Brendan's nose with his right forearm just as Brendan went for the leap. He connected cleanly and everyone on the court heard a crunch.

The crowd that had surrounded to watch the game's end now started roaring. Brendan clutched his face and went down immediately. He felt a shooting pain through the center of his brain. He tasted the bitterness of blood almost instantly and could see only blurred colors through the tears that sprung to his eyes. He heard shouts from the court and from the crowd. Some were roars of outrage, others of encouragement. Then he felt a thumping pain in his ribs and knew he was being kicked. He pulled his legs into a fetal position to try and block it, more concerned with keeping his arms over his head.

João had cut towards outside the key to follow his shot. He hadn't seen the initial forearm to Brendan's nose, he did hear a thump and a crack however. When he turned, he saw Brendan fall to the ground. He stopped his run to slow it down and check on Brendan. It wasn't until he saw

Jason begin kicking Brendan that he realized what was going on. A crowd seemed to gather immediately and Jason kept beating on Brendan, aiming punches and kicks at areas not covered up.

João was quick to act. He shoved his way through the dense crowd of rowdy onlookers that had developed. He saw an older white guy grab hold of Jason and tuck something into his hand. João saw a flash of light from the object and it was clear right away it was a blade or at least something sharp. He managed to pick up the basketball which appeared near his feet and rifle it at Jason right as he took a swipe at Brendan's side with the blade. The ball struck Jason hard off the face in mid-swing, disrupting his attempt, although he had managed to slash Brendan's outer arm around the triceps. Jason was momentarily stunned by the hit and faltered slightly, taking a step back. A lane opened up for João and he ran right at Jason and tackled him to the ground.

By this time the shouts of the guards could be heard loud and clear and the crowd that had gathered to see blood was dispersing to avoid the guards' wrath. Jason was more than a head taller than João and had much longer legs and arms. However, João was pretty well built for his height, put together like a wrestler so he was showing a slight edge. He wrestled Jason to the ground trying to grab at his arm that held onto the blade. His hands were getting cut, but it appeared to only enrage him further.

João managed to land a couple of rights and one or two head butts, but Jason kept scrapping.

The guards finally made it through the crowd and one guard swung his baton at João's back and neck. He refused to stop fighting though and so did Jason. João jumped up and grabbed at his eyes after another guard tried to pepper spray Jason to get him to stop fighting. Joáo's arms were finally yanked free by the two guards and they pulled him off of Jason. Joáo grabbed at his side as the guards pulled him away and grimaced in pain. He stopped fighting then as the two guards that held him led him away.

From the ground, Brendan looked over and noticed Joáo's hands, which were covered in blood and sliced, like he had punched through a few windows. He saw the red patch growing under Joáo's shirt near his abdomen.

Within just a few steps he watched as Joáo's legs gave way as he stumbled forward and he passed out.

Brendan woke hours later to a nurse changing his bandage that was wrapped around his left arm. He tried to smile at her but the nurse offered nothing in return. He tried to talk but found it too difficult to speak. His throat felt raw. He rubbed his neck with his right hand and the nurse understood his gesture.

'Throat's going to hurt for a while. Your nose is all taped up so there's no air getting through so you're breathing only through your mouth. I'll have them bring you a drink.' She finished the wrapping and taped up the gauze. She nodded to his arm and said, '25 stitches in all, clean slice luckily, but you'll probably have a scar anyway. Whatever got you was very sharp.' She finished up and turned to walk away. Before she left she said, 'There's two policemen outside the door. There's a buzzer on the table to your right. Press that if you need anything urgent. I'll see to it someone brings you something to drink.'

She left then and Brendan felt more alone than ever

before. 'They must have given me a sedative to knock me out' he thought, 'probably to reset the nose bone.' He could feel the pain all the way through to the back of his head. He couldn't see himself but he imagined he looked rough, probably two black eyes to go with this gauzed up nose. He felt rough anyway. He felt furious too, with himself that is. He should have been more careful. He never should've jumped into a basketball game. It made him an easy target. 'Someone would have come at me regardless' he figured, 'so no point in dwelling on this.' If anything, having it happen so publicly was probably a blessing. At least João was there and had his back. He'd most likely be dead otherwise.

Once he thought that, he remembered João. He had no idea what happened to him. He didn't know if he was okay. He thought, 'Was he in trouble with the warden? Was he dead?' A whole new feeling of dread swept over Brendan. 'Have I sent another person to his death?' He wondered. He was sure he could not carry on any longer if so. And with this thought he clenched his eyes shut and forced all the pain towards the front of his head and let the slow tears trickle down his cheek until he dried out and there was nothing left to pour out of him.

Brendan Maguire

The State of Massachusetts let Brendan recover for about a week and a half in the hospital. He was still bruised and cut when he was led back into his cell by one of the guards, but he looked better than he had a week ago.

The bandage around his nose had been reduced to a strap and he had to see the prison nurse daily so she could change the bandages on his arm.

The doctors warned him off any sports for the next month at least. This meant very little to Brendan considering he didn't have the slightest intention of joining anymore pickup games. He was dead set against even going into the prison yard for rec time. He figured he'd just wait out those hours in his cell.

During his stay in the hospital, he learned that Joáo had a real close call with a stab wound to his abdomen. The surgeons had worked on him immediately, which was lucky for him because there wasn't enough time to bleed out. After surgery, the doctors had kept him sedated most of the time. There was some worry of infection Brendan heard, but Joáo made it through.

Brendan also learned that Joáo would serve out the next few months in a rehab facility, which meant Brendan would be out free before Joáo made it back to finish the remainder of his sentence. Apparently there was no disciplinary action taken against Joáo as several guards testified to his involvement as self-defense. The whole thing was a relief to Brendan. He never meant to drag Joáo into his troubles, he was sure Joáo had his own shit to

115

deal with. But knowing now that he was okay, Brendan couldn't help but feel happy that João was there to jump in.

He still wasn't comfortable that everything had blown over. He hadn't heard anything about that guy Jason, and God knows who else was floating around those jail cells on Flynn's behalf. So when the cells were open the first time for chow, Brendan entered the walked out filled with trepidation.

When he grabbed his tray he noticed his hands were visibly shaking. He slowly joined the line and took his turn reaching for food. Each stretch drew pain from his wounds. His eyes darted back and forth in an attempt to keep watch of his periphery in case of any sudden attacks. He decided if approached, he would first swing his tray, then try for a kick in the nuts, then run. Thankfully no such attack ever came. Once he was served he scanned the room for an area that was quiet. He headed towards the back corner of the canteen close to the exit doors and found a seat at an empty bench. He realized he was starving and couldn't remember the last thing he'd eaten. He began tucking into his plate and forgot all his worries for the moment.

As he was shoveling the last of his instant mash potatoes into his mouth, he heard the clank of a tray being put down in front of him. Brendan flinched and slid back sharply in his seat.

'Relax kid' the stranger said, 'if I was gonna go at ya, you wouldn't have heard me coming.'

'That's reassuring' Brendan thought, but just said 'Oh'.

It took a few seconds, but a look of recognition must've come across Brendan's face. The man noticed the look and asked, 'So you know me huh?'

Brendan tried not to nod, he didn't want to over step his boundaries. He just said, 'from the basketball game right?' I think the guys were calling you McNally.'

'That's me' the man said, 'except it's not McNally, its McNulty.'

Brendan said 'Oh, sorry, I thought I heard McNally.'

'You did' McNulty said, 'You think I tell every fucking asshole in here what my real name is?'

'No sir' Brendan answered

'That was rhetorical champ, and keep that sir shit for your grandfather.'

'Uh okay' Brendan said safely, not knowing where this was headed.

McNulty started into his food and chewed the burger beef for about thirty seconds before taking a sip of his drink and cleaning his mouth with his sleeve. 'So . . . believe it or not handsome, I'm not here to chew the fucking fat and make nice nice.'

'I figured as much' Brendan said.

'You would' McNulty said raising an eyebrow, 'I heard you weren't such a dumb shit. Although truth be told, ending up in here across from me isn't what I'd call intelligent. Anyways . . . the point. I know something you might like to hear.'

'Oh' Brendan said 'Thanks.'

'Don't thank me, remember I did sit and watch you get your balls handed to you by the white Snoop Doggy Dog, figured I owe ya. To be honest, I had heard about you before. I heard that you got Jim Carson setup and left for dead . . . figured you were as good as gone. If you knew the Carson's as well as I do, Flynn McBride's recourse on your actions never would've even crossed your peanut sized mind. That fucking faggot's baby carrots compared to Carson's crew . . . especially behind fucking bars.'

Brendan visibly shrunk in his seat. 'I wouldn't have blamed them if they did . . . I never meant to . . .'

'Save it junior. I'm not your fucking priest and I'm sure as shit not your lawyer. Anyway, my story . . . I was waiting for word to come down the line to take you out. I assumed if I wasn't asked myself, I'd at least have heard through my channels. When said information never showed, naturally I became less and less interested, and before long it found its way into the 'who gives a fuck' part of my brain. It wasn't until I saw you get your roof beat in by that skinny douche bag that my interest was once again piqued.'

'Well, I'm glad my getting my ass kicked interests you.' Brendan said and immediately regretted his tone.

McNulty shot him a quick look of irritation, paused briefly, then continued. 'So, I made some inquiries into your situation. What I found out was 'A' what you already know, McBride wanted a message sent, which was obvious. And 'B', the curveball, word was out from Carson to let you go on about your business. He wanted you left alone . . . if you can believe that.'

Brendan leaned forward on his good arm showing his interest. 'Why I wonder?' He asked.

McNulty smiled, 'Same fucking thing I said. I couldn't figure it out. So I put a few calls in. It turns out, some broad had nearly begged Carson to leave you alone.'

'Some broad?' Brendan asked. 'What girl could that be?' he thought, 'doesn't sound like Dora.'

'Some foreign broad I think.' McNulty said, 'Alex

something or other. Some Greek name maybe.'

'Alexandra' Brendan said. 'Alexandra Dumitru. It's Romanian actually.'

'What the fuck's the difference' McNulty said, 'Whatever the fuck, she saved your ass somehow. I heard she went out with the Carson kid who got killed.'

'Wow' Brendan thought, then he said, 'I can't believe that. I guess I'm lucky it was her. Jim always said she was special . . . always said she was different than other girls around here.'

'Well don't go getting emotional on me anyway.' McNulty slid back in his seat and made like he was getting up. 'You are fucking lucky ya know. Fucking horseshoe up the ass lucky, anyway kid, keep your head down and finish out your bid.' McNulty started walking away, but stopped and turned on a dime. 'Oh, and don't worry about that string bean Jason kid. Turns out he went at you because he owed McBride. He's a junky. Hit you to clear up a debt. Stupid bastard popped your Brazilian buddy though and is now going up for attempted murder. Heard a good few years are being tacked on to his sentence, so bottom line, he's no longer staying at this country club. Good news huh?' Brendan just nodded in agreement and watched McNulty turn and walk away.

After Brendan's little talk with McNulty, he felt a strange sense of relief. Over the next few days his routine, mundane as it may have been, got back in full swing and for the most part his anxieties seemed to melt away. This wasn't solely down to the information he received, although that did change him. It was more that he felt he had gotten over one big hurtle. He could now see a light at the end of the tunnel, the light being his freedom, the tunnel being the next few months.

Brendan welcomed the thought of leaving that place, but he also experienced a sickness in his gut whenever he tried to figure out what to do when he got out. Not so long ago, he thought, 'I was an aspiring college student. Maybe not headed for big things or greatness, but headed in an upward trajectory nonetheless. Now what' he pondered, 'now what is there for me?' He knew however that no one was to blame for his path and where it took him but himself. His parents hadn't raised him that way. They were great role models. They were honest, hard-working people. They were always supportive, never smothering and he had shamed them. That was his thank you to them after 18 years of love and support. He had made them outcasts in their own town for actions he had taken alone, not them. They tried to keep their heads high and go about their lives as normal, but Brendan could see the circles under his parents' eyes on the occasions they'd visit. He saw the weight of the last year or so dragging them down, faces worn, ostracized by friends and neighbors. They had withdrawn from the community. His father, once a proud and vibrant man, now looked torn and dark to Brendan. He even struggled to make eye contact with his son when they spoke.

Brendan was sure he wasn't strong enough to go through what they had or bold enough to join them in misery, so he knew once he was out, he was gone. He didn't need to go far, but he needed to go.

With João still in recovery, it ended up that Brendan would serve the remainder of his sentence in his cell alone. At first this lonesome period drove him crazy with unwanted introspection. After a while however, Brendan began to cherish this time alone with his thoughts and imagination. It was during this period that he began to write. For hours each day he would lay on his bunk, face first with a pillow under his chest and a notebook and pen at the ready. It started with letters. He wrote letters to everyone, not so much letters to say hello, but letters of apology. He wrote to his mother and father often. He thanked them, tried consistently to cheer them up. He wrote to the parish priest. He didn't know why really, he wasn't really religious, but he felt like at least he would likely read them. His hand broke into cramps often when he started writing initially. He hadn't hand-written anything in years. His penmanship was atrocious and he often needed to rewrite letters slowly in better hand.

Brendan felt bold in doing so, but eventually he began writing to Alexandra. He even once wrote to Mrs. Carson. He wasn't sure if they'd even read it. He thought they'd probably toss it into the fireplace.

He wasn't sure why he did it. It wasn't forgiveness he sought, he wasn't that naïve. It was more he wanted them to know that he realized what he'd done was wrong and could never be put right. He did apologize, but he never once asked to be forgiven, nor did he ask for a letter in return. He never received one either. He even once wrote a letter to Danny Carson. Afterwards he thought better of sending it and ended up tearing it into a thousand pieces and flushing it down the toilet.

Eventually, he ran out of things to say in letters. It was then that he let his imagination run wild and began writing fiction. Living inside his made-up world became like a drug. Day and night it's where he was, stopping only to eat and go the bathroom and sleep occasionally. And before he knew it, Brendan was escorted from the prison with his notebooks in a plastic stop & shop bag, wearing the same clothes he did when he entered.   He left the gates and walked into his mother's arms, but by this time, it had all changed and he was no longer her boy.

Mike Faye "Dozen"

When Mike Faye took the wrap for Flynn McBride he thought he was the hard guy. Only a rat would roll on a buddy and Flynn was his friend. He truly believed he'd do his time and probably get paroled after 10 years. He wasn't looking forward to it or anything, but in his head it wasn't just the best option, it was his only one. Plus, he figured he would've killed that guy Carson on his own, 'Only the bastard knew how to fight. Fuck him anyway' he thought, 'only a few lucky shots'.

When he first arrived in Walpole he thought he'd fit in great. Actually at first he kind of did. The first while he met a few inmates just like him. Guys that were in there because they were too tough to give in. 'Fuck 'em, give me whatever time you want Judge, I'll do that shit on a headstand.' There were plenty of young puffed out chests walking around telling each other about their escapades, telling people why they're in, how they got caught and basically running off at the mouth. Mike liked these guys. They were just like him. They were his kind of people. Gradually however Mike began to notice a lot of other types around, quieter types, dangerous looking types. He began to notice the looks from these men.

Eventually he got the feeling that maybe these were the men, and he was merely a boy amongst them. Once the initial period of settling in was over, he began to realize that maybe his pack, the guys like him, were not the right ones to emulate. He saw how these hard, stone-faced inmates looked at guys like him. They weren't respected. They weren't feared. They were a joke. That meant . . .

he was a joke.

He wished he had never walked around telling people to call him Dozen. Like anyone really gave a fuck about his nickname. But it was too late, soon as his nickname went around, on came the jokes, with all types of sexual innuendo. He knew this was not the place to be associated with sexually ambiguous nick-names.

Dozen was never attacked in the shower or anything, but he couldn't help but think his time would come. He'd seen plenty of movies. He knew what happened in prison. 'That shit ain't worth taking for anybody, for Flynn or anyone else' he thought. Fortunately, but unfortunately for Dozen, no hard-man had taken a shine to him. Maybe if one had he'd have been able to protect him.

Dozen's cell was on the second floor, and as the doors opened for dinner one evening he walked out of the cell and took a left to head for the stairs. Maybe if he'd noticed the lack of people in the halls or a lack of guard presence he would have turned back and skipped dinner that day . . . but he didn't. He didn't notice anything different, so he didn't turn around. He continued walking, rolling his shoulders forward in a hunch which he had developed only recently. The more confidence he lost, the further forward his head lurched when he walked.

He experienced an eerie feeling as he walked past an older man; a man with straggly looking salt & pepper hair and a matching goatee. The man was staring at him intensely, that's what Dozen noticed. Dozen dropped his eyes to avoid the gaze. He couldn't bear the man's fervent eye contact. He focused his own eyes on his feet and thought to himself, 'keep walking, don't say shit.' He even didn't react when the man brushed a shoulder against him as he walked past. Dozen tensed at the contact, but kept the same pace moving forward. He could smell the man's deodorant and feel the heat of his body temperature as they grazed shoulders. He couldn't fight the urge and after a few steps he turned to glance back at the man that had put such fear into him.

As he did this, he saw the flash of a movement close to his face and felt something like cloth around his neck. As he gasped for breath, he then felt a shove at the top of his body and something trip his feet.

As he flipped over the bars on the balcony, he saw a blur of colors which he imagined were faces. The rope wasn't long though, so his descent was brief. He felt a tug and then nothing at all.

A guard on the ground floor of the prison had entered the area just in time to hear a popping noise. He thought at first it was the sound of a light bulb bursting. But, when he looked up to check which bulb had popped, he saw a man hanging lifeless from a make shift noose crafted from a pair of prison trousers tied to the railings and what looked like a rolled up pillow case hooked around his neck. Mike Faye died on impact from a broken neck.

Alex Dumitru

Alexandra still managed to smile whenever she thought about that day with Jim when they found out Theresa was on the way, although they hadn't known whether it was a boy or girl or even cared at that stage.

She remembered Jim's confused look on the couch trying to enjoy his Sunday ritual of reading the newspaper and drinking coffee all day. She had told him gently what she was feeling and tried to get him to deduce the meaning. This was all in vain of course and so 'enough with the subtleties' she thought, and blurted out, 'Jim, I'm over a month late for my period. I think I might be pregnant.' He had sat there for a few seconds looking up from his paper, looking all of 12 years old with his raggy old plaid bathrobe on and huge race car slippers on his feet that he got in the Deli Christmas grab the year before.

He appeared to be thinking deeply about what to say, although it just as easily could have been his peeing in his pants look, with his brow furrowed, lips pursed and his hair still in the bedhead style he woke up with. 'Well?' Alex finally had to say to break his concentration. That's when his face finally relaxed and a broad smile gradually made its way to the surface. 'Well, if it's true.' he said, 'then I couldn't be happier.' Alex saw him toss the paper aside and jump up to hug her. Her anxiety about telling him melted away in that instance.

She made him, actually, forced him to change into clothes and brush his teeth and hair before they could run to CVS to buy a test. Jim drove and he had a new found cautiousness to his driving, Alex recalled. They smiled to each other without speaking during the short drive up to Dorchester Ave. She saw his face blush briefly when they were in the family planning section and the after-church crowd paraded into the shop. That's the Catholic upbringing she thought. He never wavered though. They had stood shoulder to shoulder in the line to pay. She could still feel the heat from his hand when he squeezed it tightly to let her know he was still excited. They paid at the counter and withstood the glances of curiosity from some people and of disapproval from others, mainly the older women in pink outfits with crosses around their necks, and reddish freckled faces from the early spring heat wave.

The drive home again was riddled with anticipation. Not so much however as the three minute wait after peeing on the stick. Jim had insisted on pacing back and forth for the full 180 seconds, stopping only once to say, 'you washed your hands after, right?' He winked then and kept pacing.

The oven timer buzzed after what seemed like eternity. They gave each other one last encouraging look before they feasted their eyes on the results, 'Plus sign means positive, means yes we're having a baby' Alex thought to herself as Jim lifted her and kissed her.

That was two months or so before Jim was killed. She had begged him to hold off telling people until after the first few months. He had been aching to tell Danny, and they had agreed to tell him together that night for dinner. Of course that day never came and so Alex never could quite find the right time. She hated herself for asking him to keep it from his brother, but after not telling Danny at first, she couldn't bring herself to do it. Of course eventually word got out. Her parents obviously had to know as she had moved back in with them temporarily. A thousand times after Danny left to go back to Ireland she tried writing, tried to get the strength to call, but she always failed. When Theresa was born she told them all, but by that time Danny had begun his downward spiral and was barely coherent and really just lost in himself.

His apparent indifference pained her, but deep down Alex felt she was to blame. Where she found empathy was even stranger. It had begun with a letter to Mr. Carson, Jim's father. His response was kind and empathetic, not at all what she had expected from the man Jim had described. She had even paid him a visit in prison. She didn't ever ask why he was there or what he'd done, or even when he'd be out. It was good enough for her to have some connection with Jim's family. It was good enough for him to have someone to talk about Jim with. She knew the main thing they had in common was that they both thought they'd always have more time.

Danny Carson

Danny saw the email from his boss had come through at about 7:30am. He heard his phone vibrating on the table next his bed. He struggled to scrape the sleep from his eyes as he punched the pin code into the phone's touch screen. He always botched the first pin attempt in the mornings these days. He chalked it up to waning eyesight, fat thumbs and an over sensitive key pad. He noticed the time on the phone read 9:52am. The buzzing must have been a message reminder. He either slept through his alarm or heard it, turned it off and fallen back asleep all without realizing.

Danny shook his head awake and rubbed his eyes with his fingers. He slid back in his bed and propped himself against the headboard. The covers slid off him as he sat up and he felt the cold air sting his bare shoulders. Danny looked to his left out of habit, expecting to see his wife Michelle sleeping soundlessly next to him. 'Must've been dreaming again' he thought. It registered that he'd been living alone in a one-bed apartment in Harold's Cross for a while now.

The realization dampened his mood and once again he could barely stomach the thought of walking into that soulless glass building for work in the morning. He would have to pull himself together to give the impression he gave a damn. Although that'd be tough to pull off when walking in about two hours late.

He jumped out of bed and hustled to the closet to grab a towel. He rushed to get the shower going with hot water to melt away the coldness from the apartment. It was an old building that was not well-insulated. Plus the only heating in the place came from two space heaters, including one in the bedroom that didn't work.

After the quick shower, Danny brushed his teeth and rushed through a shave. He threw on his cleanest suit and the least-wrinkled shirt from his closet. He grabbed his three-quarter length pea coat off the hook by the door and tossed a scarf across the back of his neck as he walked through his dark hallway to the front door. He heard the heavy door slam behind him as he left and hustled down the front steps. He pulled his coat on and flicked his collar up to try and block some of the cold wind from getting to his ears. It was gray out and cold, 'but at least the rain had held off' he thought.

As he turned on to the Grand Canal towards Ranelagh he picked up his pace. He sped up to increase his body temperature not from any sense of urgency.

Danny reached Harcourt Street about 15 minutes later. He was sweating a little from the walk and he stripped off his coat after walking into the building. The receptionist gave him a knowing nod, which to Danny smacked of judgment. Danny returned only a slight eyebrow raise as he turned the corner and hit the elevator button.

He took the elevator to the sixth floor and fumbled in his pockets for his badge to get through the hall door. He found the badge in his inside coat pocket and swiped himself through to the floor. He crossed the small kitchen area and headed down the hall to his office. He hung his coat on the hanger in the corner and switched on his laptop.

Danny decided there was no point in putting off the inevitable, once the PC was starting up, he headed the few doors down to speak to his manager.

When he reached the office, the door was open and Danny leaned his head in while he knocked on the glass. 'You wanted to see me Kevin?' he asked.

Kevin looked up from his monitor and answered, 'Yes Dan, come on in and shut the door behind you.'

Danny stepped in and shut the door.

'Grab a chair' Kevin said and pointed with his palm open towards the chair across from his desk. Danny walked over, sat himself down slowly and folded his hands on his lap.

Kevin used the mouse to close a couple of windows on his PC then turned to face Danny at last. He took a deep breath before he started talking. 'This isn't an easy conversation to have Danny.'

Danny remained still and just waited for the punchline. He did scrunch his forehead slightly to show Kevin's words had registered. Kevin opened the drawer on the right-hand side of his desk and pulled out an envelope. It wasn't sealed, so Kevin opened it and pulled out a letter and slid it across the desk to Danny.

Danny perched himself forward and started to read through the letter without touching it.

Kevin pre-empted his response and said, 'it's not a dismissal letter Dan, but it is your final, written warning.'

Danny quickly scanned through it and looked back up at Kevin when he finished. Kevin nodded at him and said, 'It's signed by me and our Human Resources Business Manager. Technically, she's supposed to be in this meeting, but after you didn't show up at 9 this morning, she couldn't keep cancelling her other appointments all day until you decided to waltz in.

Danny gave a slight nod to indicate he understood the criticism. He said, 'The letter says there have been several complaints about me. Why is it that people can complain about me, but not to me? Where I'm from if you have an issue with someone, you bring it up to him first.'

Kevin gave a shrug and looked around his office. 'Look around you Dan. We're not on a building site in Downtown Boston here. Not everyone is comfortable with bringing their issues to your face. Besides, you haven't exactly been the most approachable person around the office here have you? People think you're liable to snap any minute.'

'Well Kevin, who are these people anyway? Who's them and they? Is it some big secret? And what are their complaints?'

'Danny!' Kevin said then slapped his hand down hard on the desk. The months of leniency and aggravation started to burst through to the expression on his face. 'Forget them and they. Consider my opinion and my complaints. Consistent tardiness, numerous missed deadlines, and never mind your negative attitude and constant insubordination . . . I mean, you come in here reeking of booze 3 out of 5 days . . . its fucking enough!' He hit the desk again, this time with a closed fist. 'It's been over 2 years since your brother died for Christsakes. You need to move on now!' Kevin leaned back in his chair and puffed his cheeks out. He let out a long, slow breath. Right away, right after he said it, he wished he hadn't, not like that anyway, but his emotions got the best of him.

Danny sat silently; his stare began to pierce through Kevin's chest. His jaw hardened as he clenched his teeth so hard that he thought they might crack. Danny felt the blood rush to his head and the dizziness that comes with adrenaline releasing suddenly and intensely. He fought hard against it in order to swallow his rage back down. He began to see red and flickering stars. His mouth had been stripped of any saliva. Finally, after a few aching seconds, he felt his lungs give way and he took in a deep breath. When he let it out, he felt the fury begin to dissipate. He raised his eyes finally to meet Kevin's. Kevin's own face showed signs of a struggle to remain firm. Danny could tell it was also masking some fear and he thought perhaps some sorrow as well.

Danny stood up and picked up the letter from the desk. He folded it and put it back into the envelope. He turned and began to walk out, but took two steps towards the door then turned back to face Kevin again. He said, 'Killed'.

Kevin looked up at Danny and asked 'What's that Dan?'

'My brother didn't die Kevin. . . He was killed.'

Kevin's face hardened and his eyes glanced down to the floor, then back to Danny's. He shook his head slowly in acknowledgment, 'Ya, I know Dan . . . I know'.

Danny raised the letter to his forehead in a mock salute and left Kevin's office then. He walked into his own office and grabbed his coat off the hook. He walked out and stepped into the open elevator and stuffed the letter into his pocket. He took the elevator down to the ground floor and walked back through reception towards the exit. The same receptionist gave him another funny look. Danny held up his middle finger at her as he walked past and said, 'mind your fucking business' before leaving through the rotating doors.

Danny crossed the tram tracks on Harcourt Street to head for the bar across the street. He paused when he reached the stairs and thought better of going in, 'too likely I'd run into someone from work' he thought. He decided to walk for a little while to see if he could calm himself down. He started up Harcourt Street towards Stephen's Green. He tried to lose himself in the walk by focusing on the lines of brick buildings on both sides of the street. He remembered how quaint he thought they were when he first moved over. Much of Dublin, at least the parts that looked like this, reminded him of Beacon Hill in Boston. 'All built by the Brits most likely' he thought 'It's too bad much of the old offices that inhabited these areas fell victim to the fizzled out economy'.

When he reached the first gate to Stephen's Green, he entered the park and slowed his pace. Despite the cold, there were plenty of people wandering within, most likely out of the office to stretch the legs and grab coffee to hold them over until lunch.

Danny walked on through the center of the park past the fountain and found an empty seat on the bench that looked across a landscaped green. He dug into his inside pocket and pulled out his phone, 'No missed calls, no messages . . . Christ, not even an email.' He wondered if he had already successfully alienated everyone he knew. Michelle wouldn't talk to him, his mother only depressed him more, his father . . . well, no chance there. Maybe Jim was his only link back to his old life . . . his real life. 'Maybe after all, my brother was the only one that cared' he thought. He wished silently that he would have been a better brother, but it was too late now. There was no chance at redemption as far as he could see. Revenge still stirred in his stomach however. As soon as he thought this, he was interrupted by a sudden clang on the other side of the bench. He looked over to his right and saw that it was a plastic bag with a couple of loose tall beer cans that made the noise. The man carrying it could barely hold himself up long enough to turn around and plop his backside on the bench. Danny crinkled his nose at the waft of odor that floated his way. It was a mix of slime and stale booze that only a homeless heroin addict could perfect. Danny looked at the man. He had a hood up over a wind-blown red face and dirty reddish hair and eyebrows. He might've weighed max 120lbs with all his clothes on.

Danny took his new neighbor's presence as a cue to leave and gathered himself before standing up. The man grunted something that Danny couldn't make out, nor did he care to. He just kept walking, this time out of the park and down to Grafton Street.

He turned right after a block or two down Grafton Street and headed straight to a pub, one that had grown quite familiar to him over the last year. When he sat at the bar and ordered a Guinness, it dawned on him that really his stroll in the park was nothing more than a distraction. It was just something to do until the clock struck noon, nothing more, nothing less. For a second this thought left him with a guilty feeling. Within seconds, it had drifted away.

Mike Riordan

'Daddy! Daddy!' Rebecca yelled to her father while kicking the heels of her feet against her plastic car seat in the back of Mike's 4-door pickup truck. 'Are we going to the plaza?' she asked.

'You know what she's gonna ask' Mike's wife Elaine said. She was smiling and rolled her eyes. 'You'll notice she never dares to ask me. She's too used to me saying no.'

Mike finished leveling out the truck in his parking spot and put the transmission into park. He winked at Elaine as he turned around to face his daughters Rebecca and Ashley. 'Yes, we're here at the plaza Becky, just like we said, so Mommy can go shopping.'

'She wants ice cream Dad!' Mike's older daughter Ashley said with a look that said she couldn't be bothered with such childish requests. 'She always does!'

'Not always!' Becky shouted, 'just Brigham's'.

Elaine turned around then and gave the girls a look that said 'No Anything if the yelling keeps up'. It was a look they both knew well.

'Okay, Okay girls, maybe if you stick by us the whole time while Mom does her shopping, you'll be rewarded with some Brigham's Mike said as he climbed out of the driver's seat and opened the back door to get Becky out of her chair.

'Thanks Daddy, we won't run away' Becky assured him as he helped her out of the chair. He took her hand then in his and locked the doors as they walked towards the entrance.

They walked into the plaza through the main entrance at the front of the parking lot. Mike was glad to see the mall wasn't too busy, at least not busy for a Thursday, which could generally be hectic. Living close by and living with just his wife and his girls, a one-man show, meant Mike spent more time at the plaza than he cared to admit.

Elaine had insisted that he came along this time. Since he'd been picking up side work to balance off the Union layoffs, they hadn't had much time to do things as a family. It wasn't an ideal day out for either of them, but they had a wedding to go to the following week. Therefore she needed a new dress to wear. 'Need is a strong word.' Mike thought. 'At least the girls could run around and enjoy themselves, even if I'm miserable.'

Elaine led them through a few shops, then decided after an hour of disappointments that she'd be much faster on her own. She went off to the Nordstrom woman's section, while Mike agreed to head to down to Brigham's and feed the girls while they waited for her to pick out a dress.

Mike made his way towards the escalator with his two girls in tow. He stood in front of the escalator and made each child get a grip of the railing. At the bottom of the ramp they made a 180 degree turn towards Brigham's Ice cream parlor. When Becky saw the sign, she started to pick up her pace and Mike felt his hand jerk forward slightly as she tried to run. 'Relax baby, we'll get there soon enough' Mike said. They passed a shoe store and Mike peered into the window as he continued to walk trying to see the price tag on a pair of work boots in the front window.

He stopped quickly as two teenage girls nearly knocked him over, walking passed quickly, both staring at their respective cell phones.

Mike found himself standing in front of a book store entrance as he recovered his footing. He looked into the store at the group of people lining up, he couldn't help feeling a sense of familiarity. The guy signing books, presumably the writer looked really familiar to Mike, but he couldn't place him.

Mike stood still for a minute, and finally it struck him who he was looking at. He noticed the billboard in the window, 'Meet Boston's own Brendan Maguire.'

It was a name that Mike knew intimately. That name had crossed his mind through day dreams and nightmares alike. Mike froze when it all came together for him. He didn't know what to do. Finally, he had to succumb to his daughters' impatience as they both frantically pleaded with him to keep walking. He moved slowly, more deliberately towards Brigham's and walked in and slid into a booth and just stared blankly.

Elaine paid for her new dress by credit card. She lugged her bags onto the escalator and breathed a deep sigh of relief that her shopping was done. She found a nice dress that fit well, without breaking the bank. This was nearly a cause for celebration.

When she walked into the restaurant the hostess with the funny pointed hat directed her to the booth where her family was sitting. She walked through the seating area and found the girls with Mike sitting in the second-to-last booth. There were chicken finger plates with french fries in front of each of her daughters, which seemed normal. She saw nothing in front of Mike which seemed strange. Also, his complexion was pale and there was a distant look on his face. Elaine slid herself next to Ashley on the booth and across from Mike. 'Are you feeling okay hon, you aren't looking too well?' She asked.

'Huh?' Mike said, looking up at her as if he just realized she was there. 'Oh, yeah. Sorry, was just thinking about something.'

'You're not eating? That's not like you.'

'Not hungry babe, I'll get something later maybe.' Mike raised his hand and got the waiter's attention to give a signal for the bill.

'We're leaving? I haven't eaten yet.' Elaine said confused.

'Sorry' Mike said, 'I forgot, I gotta call from a guy I was doing some work with. I have to go price a roofing job.'

'First I heard of it, I thought this was a family day today?' Elaine asked.

'I know honey, I'm sorry, like I said, I forgot about it. I'll leave you money to order something.'

'It's not about the money, forget it Mike . . . whatever.'

Mike paid the bill and got a quart of ice cream and some hot fudge to go so his daughters were kept happy. He still wasn't quite sure what he was going to do, but he knew he had to get his family home and had to be alone to think for a minute.

It only took about 10 minutes to get to their house, including the time it took to carry Becky into the house and put her on the couch for her nap. He tried to appear normal but it was difficult to do this with so many thoughts racing through his head. After getting the girls inside he grabbed his work folder and tape measure to keep up the charade and hustled to get out of the house.

Mike drove directly back to the plaza and parked right outside the front entrance. The parking lot had already started to clear out as the families shopping for the day loaded up their cars and left. He sat in his truck for what seemed like an hour, but was more like 10 minutes, just trying to figure out what to do.

Mike decided to pull into a parking space and walk back inside. He entered the plaza again through the front doors still unsure what he was planning. He just knew that he should at least get one more look at the kid to be sure it was him.

When he got back to the book store however, he found the grates lowered and the shop all but empty. It had closed in his absence. He felt a rush of anger for a brief moment, but it flamed out quickly and gave way to a strange feeling of relief. 'Maybe it was better this way' he thought.

He realized he was loitering and probably drawing attention to himself, so he headed back towards the way he came in. As he walked towards the exit, he glanced into the restaurant that was attached to the mall. It was definitely still open, there were a few people in having an early dinner. He stopped walking when once again he had a feeling of familiarity sweep over him. He put his face all the way up against the glass this time to be sure. He stared right into the eyes of Brendan Maguire, sitting alone at a tall table with a coffee in front of him. Brendan saw Mike, but made no movement to leave. In fact he kept eye contact as best he could. Mike was hit with lightheadedness, but he blinked it away as he entered the restaurant. He walked past the smiling hostess and ignored her greeting. He crossed the bar area and stopped when he reached Brendan's table.

Brendan was in a tall chair, so even with Mike standing,

they were still roughly eye level. They remained in their places for about 15 seconds before Mike finally let out a deep breath. His shoulders drooped noticeably as he did, his posture going from hunter to victim in one motion. Brendan held out his palm towards a chair in a gesture for Mike to sit down. Mike glanced sideways back at him, but still pulled the chair over and took a seat.

'Do you want a drink or anything?' Brendan asked.

Mike said nothing but shook his head 'No'.

'What's that you're drinking?' Mike asked.

'Just coffee' Brendan answered. 'I don't drink much really.'

Mike nodded like he was agreeing with something Brendan said. 'I often thought about what I'd do if I ever ran into you.'

Brendan just kept looking at Mike, letting him go on in his own time. 'I always told myself I'd kill you ya know . . . Never thought about how or when . . . just thought that I'd do it. Even bought a gun . . . sits there in my closet just haunting me.'

Brendan's expression didn't change, but he paused for about 30 seconds, 'can't say I'd blame you if you did.'

'Yeah, well. I'm not gonna kill you . . . I think we both know that.'

Brendan nodded his head slightly reassured.

'Why did it take until now to run into you? I heard you got out a while ago?' Mike asked.

'I couldn't take moving back here.' Brendan answered and then reached for his coffee. He took a sip and continued. 'My publisher had to beg me to make an appearance. This is actually the first time back home since I was out.'

'I see . . . staying long?' Mike asked.

Brendan shook his head 'No', 'I fly out before the weekend's over.'

Mike raised his eyebrows, 'short trip then I guess. Where you flying too? Or are you keeping it close to your chest?'

'No, it's no secret. I'm not hiding Mike, I've accepted that I may reap what I sow at some point. I'm living just outside Philly.'

'Many writers out that way?' Mike asked.

'Writers? . . . Not that I know. I wrote once, that's all. Might write again, but I'm not rushing into it. I work out there though . . . well volunteering any way.'

Mike nodded, 'Soup kitchen or something?'

'Nah. No soup kitchen. I work with teenagers just out of juvy. Started off as part of my parole, but I've kept it on since. It's not much, but I guess it makes me feel like I'm giving back something. Probably not what you want to hear I know.'

Mike lightened his mood. 'Sounds like a tough gig man. Dealing with groups of thugged-out teenagers, I'm sure it ain't easy.'

Brendan shook his head slightly. 'Wasn't easy at first definitely, but it's gotten easier. I've gotten better at it. It's funny actually, it was something Jim taught me that got me through the first while. I asked Jim once how he kept his staff in line without being a prick . . . a good few hard-necks put in time at the deli. He told me about an experience he had back when he was a teenager working with kids in the Quincy rec gyms . . . Sterling middle school I think. He said he showed up the first day and got pushed, spat at and everything else by a few of the wise-ass kids in the gym. He was almost afraid at first, he wasn't much older than those kids ya know . . . and he was extremely outnumbered. He didn't know what to do with them. He went home after the evening rec time and thought about how to approach the next time he dealt with them. He thought about the group and began to think about a few of the kids that stood out . . . there were maybe two or three who . . . didn't look like the ring leaders or anything, but when they spoke the others listened. He remembered that the other guys, those trying to cause trouble, would do something wise and then look to them for some kind of approval. So Jim said he made it his goal the next few gym sessions to try and get to know these few . . . talk to them, see what made them tick. He said he just knew if he could get those few guys on side he might have a chance with the rest. So that's what he did. He won over those few kids. He got them on his side, and immediately he noticed the change in the group. By the end, that group of young kids grew to love Jim . . . grew to respect him . . . and he always talked about that being one of his favorite experiences. So . . . I basically tried the same approach. It works . . . not always, but mostly, it works. I guess that's kind of like my homage to Jim. . . Sorry Mike . . . I carry on a bit . . . and I . . . I know you don't need to hear this.'

Mike pushed back in his seat and winced as he made to get up from his painful joints. His eyes were glistening. At some point while Brendan spoke, tears formed in Mike's eyes that he fought back. 'Actually Brendan . . . I think maybe I needed to hear something like that.' He rubbed his eyes with his fingers, 'My family's waiting for me. I should get home.' Mike tucked in his chair and started to walk away.

Brendan called, 'Mike.'

Mike turned and looked at him again.

'I am sorry.'

Mike pursed his lips for a second and swallowed. 'I know you are kid.' Mike left the bar then and walked back to his truck. As he started it up, he smiled at the thought of his family and felt a wave of loss as his cousin Jim crossed his mind again.

Danny Carson

Danny didn't leave the pub for the rest of the day. Even when the daytime crowd left and the after work patrons gathered in he didn't wrap it up. He wasn't drinking quickly, but he was drinking steadily. After a few hours of pouring pints of Guinness down his throat, the cotton-mouth finally got to him. He ordered a pint glass of water and took it down in two gulps. The coldness gave him a frozen headache and he winced with pain. He switched to Captain and Cokes to fend of his tiredness. The Captain was sweeter and easier to swallow and the Coke gave him the caffeine boost to keep him upright. He had been there for hours. Luckily for him the bartenders had changed shifts a couple times, so it wasn't as obvious to them that he hadn't moved from his seat.

Pretty soon, the lights were dimmed and the music came on in the background, which caused the chatter volume to increase as well. The caffeine's kick only lasted a little while, so Danny eventually grew tired again. Throughout the afternoon he had been checking his phone constantly, holding out hope that Michelle would call or text. As the afternoon faded into evening his patience with waiting dimmed at the same rate. He dialed Michelle's number a few times, but it went straight to voicemail. He followed the calls up with texts, but there was never any response. As his head began to increase in weight and nod forward, he decided he'd had enough. He stuffed his phone back into his pocket and closed out his tab.

He slid his chair back and stood up and felt a sudden

onslaught of dizziness. He stumbled forward and fell into a group of guys standing in a semi-circle around a ledge against the wall. 'Sorry' Danny slurred as he tried to right himself. One of the guys, a stocky man with strawberry blond hair and a scarf around his neck took exception to Danny bumping into him and spilling his drink.

He turned and shoved Danny making him sway backwards and fall into another table. Danny climbed back up apologizing to the table of girls he landed on. When he was on his feet again, he walked by the group of guys again, who were now looking at him in amusement.

'Fucking take it easy asshole, it was an accident.' Danny said to the guy with the scarf.

'Oh! He's a focking yank!' the guy in the scarf shouted in his South Dublin accent, looking to his friends for approval.

Danny stood still for a second. Feeling slowly crawled back to his limbs as the adrenaline seemed to counteract his drunkenness. He smiled at the table and pretended to join in the laughter. 'Yank huh? That's funny.' Danny made like he was going to walk past, but then spun his left foot in a pivot and threw a left hook that hit the scarf guy square in the mouth. The punch knocked the guy into his friends crying and bleeding all over his scarf. One of the other friends threw a punch at Danny, but he pulled his left arm back to cover his face immediately like a boxer. The blow hit him in the bicep and he countered with a quick right cross to the man's face that drew blood from the nose.

The fight caused the people in the pub to scatter, leaving an opening for two bouncers to grab Danny by the arms from behind. Other guys from the table tried to get in to punch Danny but he fended them off with kicks to the groin and face before they could get in close.

The bouncers dragged Danny out front, going hard through the double doors, almost knocking over a couple of patrons on their way into the bar. A third bouncer, presumably the doorman, ran out to Dawson Street and flagged down a taxi, which is where the two others deposited Danny. Danny ceased his tirade once they got him outside. He went quietly into the back of the taxi and just told the driver, 'Harold's Cross.'

The next morning came quickly for Danny. When he woke up, his mouth was sealed shut with dryness and his head had a freight train running through it. He got up to go the bathroom. While washing his hands, he noticed how swollen his left hand had gotten. Flashes of the altercation the night before ran through his head. He found an ice pack in his freezer and popped it over his hand and tied it down with a dish towel. He didn't bother looking at his phone. He knew there'd be no messages from Michelle.

He poured a glass of club orange and took it over to his table. 'It's time' he thought to himself 'I've waited long enough.' He opened up his laptop and turned the machine on. When it started up, he cringed at the wallpaper on the screen's background. It was a picture of him and Michelle on Rossnowlagh beach in Donegal. 'Feels like a different life' he thought.

He opened up the internet explorer and typed in the web address for Aer Lingus's website. He booked a ticket to leave for Boston the next day.

Once it was booked, he went and found his pants on the floor next to his bed. He found his phone in the pocket and typed in, 'I fly in tomorrow. 3pm. Danny' and sent the text to Mike and his mother.

Flynn McBride

Flynn stopped on the makeshift wooden steps to readjust his grip and wipe the sweat from his forehead with the back of his forearm. He couldn't remember being in such bad shape. The back and forth carrying of tools up to the landing had his leg muscles aching and his lungs nearly wheezing.

He put the nail gun set down from his right hand so he could readjust the table under his left arm. If the foreman saw him, he'd definitely get an earful for carrying too much up at once. Then again, if the carpenter's steward saw him, his foreman would probably hear it from him since the laborers were supposed to have everything setup before the carpenters even clocked in.

Not that it mattered, but it wasn't his fault that there was an accident that morning heading into the city. With that, plus the random road works, traffic was worse than normal.

Once he got his grip back and his breath, he bent down and reached for the nail gun to start up the steps again. He could hear some noise coming from up top and heard one of the carpenters yelling for his gear, 'Probably that loud mouth Lentini' Flynn thought, 'he never shuts his fucking trap.'

'Two seconds!' Flynn shouted back and double timed it up the last few steps to the landing. When he got to the top, he saw Lentini standing back looking impatient. His belt was on, but his hard hat was turned backwards and he was lighting a cigarette, which indicated he was taking a break. A much younger man, who looked to be an apprentice stood next to Lentini and looked like he was trying to do his best imitation.

'Bout fucking time you showed up McBride, its nearly fucking coffee.' Lentini cackled to himself and his sidekick did the same, exaggerating the joke's actual effect to please his mentor.

Flynn placed the nail gun case down and struggled with the table saw for a moment. 'You don't look too fucking pushed Lentini . . . I thought you couldn't smoke on the premises?'

Lentini shrugged his shoulders with indifference, 'Who's fucking smoking?' He looked to his apprentice, 'you smell smoke kid?'

Laughing too loudly again, the kid shook his head no. 'See McBride, no one's smoking, what are you gonna rat me out? That'd get you shanked in prison . . . but I guess I don't gotta tell you that.' Lentini said.

'Fuck you' Flynn answered and then looked around for somewhere to put down the table saw. He looked over at Lentini, 'Where's the best place to put this?' he said holding up the saw.

'Usually on the table setup on the saw horses, but my fucking laborer never set them up this morning.'

Flynn sighed heavily 'Right' he said and placed the saw on the ground next to the nail gun. 'I'll be right up with them.' Flynn turned to head back down the stairs again. 'Take your fucking time McBride. We're paid by the hour here anyway.' The apprentice laughed out loud this time. At least this time his amusement was genuine.

Flynn headed down the stairs, faster this time and fumed more and more with each step down. The laughter seemed to decrease in volume and he eventually put it out of his mind.

Flynn got pretty much straight into demo work after that. On another section of the job site he and a few other laborers were called over and handed sledge hammers, crowbars and little white dust masks. They were tasked with clearing out and taking down an old decrepit bungalow, or at least that's what it was as far as they could tell. One of the guys said it was most likely an old rectory for a parish that no longer existed. Holy or not, it wasn't owned by the Church anymore and either way, it was coming down.

Most of the laborers were not happy with demo duty, especially when it involved old dusty buildings, but Flynn relished the opportunity to release some of his aggression. He went straight for it, swinging his hammer at full tilt and digging the dagger end through some old wood paneling, nearly tearing the wall off in one fevered tug. Next, he bust through as much wood framing as he could with the hammer, then pried off the remainder with a heavy crowbar.

Others took short breaks, either to smoke or chat. Flynn kept at it however and many of the guys showed flashes of intimidation at his violent spectacle. Flynn had moved on to the sledge hammer to take out the concrete base when he finally stopped for a breath. At that time he noticed that many of the others had dropped their tools and those with belts dropped them in place. Flynn realized it was time for lunch. He reluctantly leaned the sledge hammer against what remained of the wall. He reached to his face and pulled the mask down from his mouth and let it hang around his neck. The lingering dust started to creep into his lungs immediately, so he cupped his hand over his nose and mouth and headed toward the opening to follow the others out.

When he reached the outside, everyone had already dispersed. He hadn't expected that anyone would wait for him or anything, the Union could be as bad as high school as far as cliques were concerned. Flynn had eaten alone almost every day since he started the job, 'why should today be any different?' He thought. He headed off the site to cross Huntington Ave over to the small parking area outside a bar called the Squealing Pig. He unlocked his truck and reached behind his seat for the mini cooler that held his lunch. He walked around back and dropped the tailgate to his beaten down pickup truck.

He propped himself up on the bench and took a deep breath once he had settled. As he opened the cooler and began tucking into his lunch, he heard the chatter of voices and saw a group of carpenters and a few laborers sneaking into the Squealing Pig. 'Another liquid lunch' he thought 'at least I don't need to rush back. God knows those fuckers won't.' Flynn couldn't help from seething with jealousy when he thought of that group of guys drinking some beers over lunch. He hadn't had so much as a drink since he was released. His sobriety was a parole requirement and he was in West Quincy twice a week pissing into a cup for drug testing. He'd been clean for a couple months at least, but the lure to stray was constant. This only added to his aggression, which was fierce to begin with.

Flynn hated bending to anyone's rules, but his old man had called in several favors to get him sprung as soon as he did. He also set him up with the Union for his job. Out of work cocaine dealers were not exactly marketable . . .

not in any field.

Flynn took about twenty minutes for lunch. He lit a smoke while packing up the truck and walked slowly back to the site to give himself enough time to enjoy it. When he got back to work there were noticeably fewer people around and those that had stuck it had tailed off and worked at a slower pace. 'Start nothing new after 2' he had often heard some of the guys say with a touch of pride. Flynn didn't find those quips funny, but he couldn't argue with the motto. When it came down to it, he hated working. He only hustled through his work because it made the time go by faster so he could leave.

After a slow couple of hours, the clock hit 3:30 and the laborers stopped for the day. Flynn had started wrapping up his tools for the day when he heard a commotion outside. He peaked out to see a couple of men yelling at each other and being held back by a few guys from attacking the one another. Apparently one of the carpenters thought he'd speed the day along by lifting and stacking some of the two-by-four's to store for the night. The labor steward took exception and laid into him, something about letting the laborers stick to the laboring and carpenters stick to hammering shit. 'Fucking politics' Flynn thought, 'just like fucking prison' everyone at each other's throats, carpenters and laborers arguing with each other, stopping only to make fun of the plumbers and electricians, who were apparently 'primadonnas' mainly because they wanted a clean workspace. 'Fuck it' Flynn thought, 'Let 'em beat each other's' heads in, free entertainment anyway.'

Flynn walked around the mayhem and dropped his demo-tools off over at the cages. He flicked off his hard hat once he left the gates of the job site and headed across the avenue back to his truck. He found the keys dug into one of his deep Carhatt pockets and opened up the truck. He lifted the seat back and popped his hard hat and work jacket in the fold behind the driver's seat. He lit a cigarette just as he sat in and shut the door. He struggled to roll the manual window down quickly as the smoke began to sting his eyes. He took a heavy drag from the butt when the window was open and sighed loudly as he exhaled. Getting home in the evening was almost always the toughest part of his day. Traffic going south on 93 was brutal every day. It was the only time he ever considered making friends at work, to use the carpool lane. He'd have chanced it alone if he wasn't already on thin ice with law enforcement. 'The Staties are always setup to catch the chancers anyway.' He thought.

He found a classic rock station that was more music than talk and headed off on his journey. As expected the highway traffic was crawling from South Station to Dorchester. It didn't open up until a little while after the JFK exit.

He jumped off the highway two exits later onto Adams Street. During his hour in the truck he had talked to Dora and told her he'd come by her place with a pizza for dinner. By the time he picked the pizza up in Lower Mills, it was nearly cold. He paid for it and headed around the corner to Dora's apartment. He decided to leave the truck in the spot he took in the CVS parking lot and walk to Dora's since on street parking was tough to find in front of her place.

He glanced over at his truck as he tried to remember if he'd locked it. He was hit with a feeling of déjà vu when he saw an 80's model Buick parked next to his truck. It was familiar for some reason, but he couldn't place it.

He decided it stood out simply because of its newness. For an old car, it looked like it was just driven from the manufacturer. That was odd to him. 'Fuck it' he thought, 'pizza's already cold, better get to Dora's'. Then he took off down the street.

Flynn walked up the front steps to Dora's place a couple minutes later. He balanced the pizza on top of his left hand and reached to open the screen door with his right. He flung the door open and shoved his hip against it to keep it from springing back. The main door was ajar so he leaned his elbow against it to prop it open more. 'Dora!' he yelled, 'you home? I'm coming in.'

Flynn walked into the apartment which opened into a spacious living room. Dora peaked her head out of the bedroom door, with a cordless phone held to her ear. She gave Flynn the 'one minute' signal and pointed to the kitchen.

Flynn walked through the living room and over to the kitchen. It was more like a kitchenette since it was open and pretty much the same room as the living room except for the open doorway. He placed the pizza box on the table and opened it up to take a slice. He found some paper plates on the counter and took out a couple slices and dropped them onto a plate for Dora. He took his first bite while standing over the sink when Dora came back into the room. The pizza was kind of cold, but still tasted excellent.

'Standing over the sink doesn't mean you don't need a plate. I'll have mice if you keep that up.' Dora said.

Flynn replied with pizza still being chewed in his

mouth, 'hate to break it to you, but you probably already do. All these old houses have 'em.'

'Yeah but you don't need to leave a trail of crumbs directly to my kitchen for them. Give them a challenge at least.' Dora said. She took her plate and a Pepsi from the refrigerator. She jumped up then onto a stool at the kitchen counter. 'Ugh' she said when she looked at the pizza, plain cheese . . . you mean to tell me of all the toppings around, you just stuck with plain cheese? How adventurous of you.'

Flynn shrugged, 'I'm a minimalist when it comes to pizza . . . Base, sauce and cheese. That's all.'

Dora sighed loudly, 'Yeah, I've heard your 'less is more' talk in relation to pizza a million fucking times at this point, I got it. Still, you could've gotten half and half.'

'Maybe next time' Flynn added.

Dora took a bite from her slice, 'Ahh, its fucking cold too! You're on fire today.'

'Traffic sucked, you know how it gets in the afternoons. Hey, what's up with you swearing so much? Makes you sound . . . I don't know . . . trashy or something. You should quit that.'

'Well if it isn't the pot calling the kettle black . . . anyway, when you're brother's a jail bird, it comes with the territory. I could talk like Jackie Kennedy and people'd still call me trash.'

'Hey, fucking watch it alright. I don't need to hear that shit from you.'

'Language Flynn? Hypocrisy doesn't suit you.'

'Fine forget I said shit then.' Flynn stopped talking and turned to open the refrigerator door. He stood with the door open, leaning on it trying to make a decision.

'Is there a reason you're wasting my electricity?' Dora asked 'Can I help you with something?'

'Yeah . . . any rootbeer?' Flynn asked as he crouched down for a closer look.

'Strangely enough, yeah I think I do have some. Check the bottom drawer, there should be some cans there. They must be yours, who the hell else drinks that crap.'

Flynn found the cans and grabbed one. He stood back up and closed the door, 'not my brand, but it'll do the trick.' He cracked open the can and took a long sip followed by an 'Ahhhh'.

'Whatever, weirdo' Dora said and went back to her pizza.

Flynn put another two slices on his plate and took those, along with his root beer, into the living room. He found a spot on the couch and pulled the coffee table closer towards him. 'So, who was that you were talking to when I walked in?'

Dora looked suddenly uncomfortable 'No one, a friend.'

Flynn crinkled his forehead in a confused face. 'What? What's that supposed to mean? I don't give a shit about any boyfriends, who was it, I'm just making conversation.'

'No one, I said' Dora said again.

'Stop being so fucking shady, now I'm curious, it was obviously someone that I shouldn't know about, so fucking what.'

'It's none of your business Flynn, I don't wanna hear it from you that's all.'

'What. Quit being a bitch, I was just asking. Now you can bet your ass you're gonna tell me. Who could you possibly be talking to that could piss me off? Unless it was our bitch of a mother or something.'

Dora's face reddened at the mention of her mother. Flynn picked up on it immediately and gasped. 'Don't even fucking tell me you've been talking to her? Please don't say it.' Flynn got up suddenly from his seat and folded his hands at the top of his head.

Dora seemed to shrink into her seat as he walked towards the kitchen. 'That was fucking Ma wasn't it' He yelled at Dora, 'don't tell me she's fucking back around here.'

'It was her' Dora answered 'and stop talking about her like that. She's my mother too. I have a right to talk to her.'

'Does Dad know you're in contact with her?'

'No, Dad doesn't know anything. It's none of his business either who I talk to. She's back now and she's different. She apologized . . . '

'Bull Fucking Shit Dora and you know it' Flynn cut her off. 'How much money did you give her so far huh?'

'I didn't give her any money!' Dora screamed. 'I told you it's not like the other times. It's different now . . . she's different now.' Dora pleaded as her voice cracked with the onslaught of tears.

Flynn just shook his head in disbelief, 'Ya know something kid . . . you're fucking delusional. That bitch'll keep coming around you until she spots her chance to rob you blind. Take my word for it.' Flynn turned then and started walking to the door. 'I can't deal with this bullshit right now, good fucking luck to ya, you'll see.'

As he walked out the door, he slammed the heavy door behind him firmly and let the screen door slam shut too for good measure. His head was still shaking in disgust as he pounded his way up the street to his truck while Dora peered through the living room window after him, cursing him for even showing up in the first place.

Danny Carson

The airplane shifted direction slowly. As it turned, a gleam of sun shone through the open cabin window. Danny felt the heat from the glare and saw deep red as the light hit his closed eyelids. He turned his head away from the glare. He rubbed his eyes to wake himself up. He had drifted in and out of consciousness throughout the flight. Despite downing a number of over-the-counter sleeping tablets, he couldn't string together a consistent 6 hours of sleep. He woke several times from a multitude of nightmarish ramblings in his head that only slightly diminished in comparison to his real life anguish. Each time he woke up it was with a sudden jerk. The girl next to him no doubt wished the flight a hasty landing. She had relinquished the shared armrest without debate and had clung to the other neighbor's side. Whether or not they were travelling together didn't seem to factor into her decision.

Danny empathized with the girl, but it could've been worse, he thought, 'at least there's no stench of booze coming off me'. Although, he pondered whether the lack of booze in his system could have factored into his nightmares . . . brought on by the toxins leaving his bloodstream at last. He shut his eyes again, deciding to sleep again while he had the chance. As soon as he did, however, he felt a soft brush against his forearm. He opened his eyes again, this time to a woman in the turquoise green outfit of the airline staff. 'Excuse me sir' she said, 'we're now making our descent into Boston, could you please pull the seat back forward for landing and open the blind fully.'

Danny shook himself awake again, amused by the computer element to the woman's request. 'ah yes, thanks' he replied as he adjusted his seat forward. 'Excuse me, miss?' he asked the stewardess. 'Could you please tell me the local time?'

'Sure, it's 10 to 2 and we should be on the ground by 5 past.' She replied.

Danny nodded in thanks and took his watch from his wrist. He wound the hands back to set the watch to local time. He smiled to himself and said, 'it's like going back in time.' The young girl next to him hesitantly turned to him and asked 'Pardon? Did you ask me something?'

Danny looked at her slightly surprised at the interaction as he thought he'd said that only in his head. He answered, 'Sorry, was just saying to myself it's like going back in time . . . ya know . . . left at 2pm, land at 2pm, like the last few hours didn't happen.'

The girl scrunched her eyebrows and fought the urge to roll her eyes. Danny picked up on the disinterest and in an attempt to save face continued, 'Sorry, I must sound like a freak. I didn't realize I had said that out loud.' His face reddened as his blood rose to his cheeks in embarrassment. He smiled apologetically and turned back to look out the window.

'Okay' she said and immediately dug into the inflight magazine. Danny sat back in his chair and now embarrassed, shared her wish for a fast landing. 'She must think I'm a psycho' he thought. He popped a few pieces of chewing gum into his mouth and chewed. He swallowed his saliva every few seconds in hopes that his ears would pop and bring relief to his congested head, which felt ready to explode.

Once the plane touched down at Logan airport, Danny's thoughts about why he was here and what he was intending to do began to overwhelm him. He tried hard to push them away. He tried thinking of mundane things, like whether his bag would show up and how much a taxi would cost. The seriousness of his intentions could not be brushed aside however, and his conscience constantly nibbled away at his composure like a finicky child's approach to eating lunch. There were moments where he swore he could feel his soul disintegrating, pulled and dragged and melting away in the sun. He couldn't help but think of those Salvador Dalí paintings. 'Maybe that's what he meant when he stretched those clocks across the canvas' he thought to himself. He longed for blind rage at times like these. 'At least rage would push me forward'.

As he approached the counter, the close-cropped man at passport control welcomed him home in what Danny felt was a sardonic demeanor. He shrugged off the non-insult and proceeded to baggage claim to collect his luggage. International baggage claim in Logan airport never seemed to change. It was always the same lonely, sterile room, crawling with customs officers with 1990's hairstyles and sniffer dogs making the rounds. Danny allowed a chuckle to himself when he thought about the customs agents, had they all become a parody of themselves . . . transformed into walking cartoon characters.

He picked up his bag and walked over to the desk and handed the customs card to an officer. The man was no older than 30, but he had what looked like his father's moustache. The man looked Danny up and down for a moment, and then waved him through.

As he walked out to the arrivals hall, he saw throngs of friends and families eagerly awaiting the arrival of some loved one. Nostalgia gripped him as he remembered those times when Jim and his Mother had met him in that very hall. 'It had meant so little to me at the time' he thought 'funny how perspective changes you'. He headed through the crowd and found the exit to the taxi rank. The bite of the cold stung him as he walked outside. How easily he had forgotten the Boston winters. They are a different level of cold altogether. He greedily jumped into the first taxi available and rubbed his hands together to hurry up the warmth. 'Where to buddy?' the driver asked in that familiar twang that was like music to Danny's ears. 'Quincy Shore Drive' Danny answered, 'I don't know the exact address, but I know which house it is, so I can tell when we're near it.'

'Just yell "when" champ, I'll slow this jet down and you can barrel-roll outta here.' Danny laughed in response, happy to engage in some small talk to take his mind away from more damning thoughts. 'Thanks man' he answered, 'Glad I wore my hockey equipment now'.

Danny paid the taxi driver with a fifty dollar bill and told him to keep it. 'Big tip buddy, you sure?'

'Hey, you stopped the car long enough for me to walk out, it's the least I could do.' Danny replied.

The man nodded his approval and continued, well I'm much obliged then stranger, thanks a lot. May God watch over you.'

'Only when I'm sleeping, I hope.' Danny answered, 'Take it easy.' Then he jumped out and shut the door firmly behind him. The driver went to open the door to come around and get the bag from the trunk, but Danny waved him off, 'I got it man, watch your mirrors. Cars fly by on this street.' He pulled his bag out, a small dark duffel bag . . . just enough for a short trip. He flung it over his left shoulder and slammed the trunk to the old Ford shut with his right hand, tapping twice on the back to say goodbye like he was shooing a horse.

He crossed through the small parking lot, squeezing through a couple of tightly parked cars in the process, careful not to take a mirror or two with him. He paused at a set of twin doorways, hesitating to remember which apartment belonged to his mother. 'Has it been that long?' he asked himself.

He decided the porch with the wind-chimes could only belong to his mother, so he took the small steps to the door and rang the doorbell. He turned to look out at the street and thought 'cold and icy all day and the cars still whiz by both ways, one way speeding up to hit the bridge, the other way still lead-footed from the highway.'

He was making 'o's with his mouth and blowing out frost for about 30 seconds until he heard a lock switch open and chain being removed from the door. He peaked in to see a shadow through the door's glass-framed center. With one final sound of a bolt-lock being freed, the door opened slowly to reveal a familiar yet different face. It was a face that Danny knew so well, but one that also aged so much.

His mother's face had thinned greatly in such a short time. Danny thought, 'It had to have added 10 years to her appearance.' Also, her hair, once thick and auburn, was now shorter, still thick, but unmanaged and much grayer than he recalled. She smiled when she realized who had come to visit, and that smile at least had remained timeless, a permanent imprint on Danny's psyche.

'My son returns at last I see . . . and appears . . . what's the word? Stunned into submission and silence. Have I changed so much Danny that you've forgotten me? Or have you been struck dumb and mute by a greater power?'

Danny smiled realizing her wit had not failed her either. 'Hi Mom, it's just that . . . your hair . . . um . . . your hair looks different. I don't remember it ever being so gray.'

'Well' she replied, 'it's been gray since you were 15 years old, I just lost interest in dying it. Maybe next time you visit, you'll give me more than a 24 hour notice and I'll have time to prepare myself to your standards. Now, get in the house before those ears catch frostbite, you were never a good listener at the best of times.' She said as she shoved open the door and turned to walk into the living room.

'Sorry Mom' Danny muttered. 'That was rude, you look great.'

She turned around to face him with flared nostrils and raised eyebrows. She put her arms around Danny and squeezed him tightly. 'Thanks Danny' she said, 'but lying won't get you far.'

Danny hugged her back and felt a feeling of guilt wash over him. He felt guilty for leaving . . . guilty for coming home. Pretty much, he felt guilty for everything.

After a time they both slowly backed away from their embrace. His mother turned around and headed through the hallway. Danny followed her into the apartment hall for a few steps until he branched off left into the living room, while she continued towards the kitchen. Danny slowed as he turned into the living room, his mother's voice sounding distant asked if he wanted something to eat. 'Yeah sure, anything thanks.' He answered.

Stepping into the room he noticed that although it was a different building, it was dressed up like a familiar family room he'd know through all his years growing up. The same charcoal gray, fabric couch with a hand knit afghan draped over the high back, the same pine-wood stained rocking chair placed neatly under a tall reading lamp and angled to face the doorway and not the TV. Memories of Sunday mornings and snow days home from school swept over him as he entered the time capsule that was his Mother's living room.

He shut his eyes for a moment and could hear his mother clanging pots and dishes in the kitchen. 'She never could let anyone sleep once she was up.' He thought. He smiled to himself as he walked over to the fire place, catching a glimpse of himself in the mirror behind the mantelpiece.

The smile looked lost on his face or maybe it was more just unaccustomed to the motion, his facial muscles obviously out of practice.

In the mirror he looked much like he felt, tired and aged. His hairline hadn't yielded to time and the color hadn't gone gray, but his eyes looked worn. There were dark circles under them and lines at the corners. Both looked of the permanent nature to him. Also, his formerly athletic neck and shoulders seemed to have softened under a layer of cushion that had gone surprisingly unnoticed until that point. His smile faded at the extent of changes in himself and he averted his eyes from that dark stranger's reflection. His eyes moved to scan the framed photographs around the mantel, which for the most part chronicled his very existence. He focused in on a photo of he and Jim. It was one from Veteran's Stadium in Quincy from Jim's high school graduation. He remembered with painful clarity how he had rushed through the family's celebration afterwards. It was all so he could head off with some friends down to Cape Cod to celebrate finishing out the spring semester. 'Always so goddamn busy' he thought 'and for what? To suck down a 30-pack and watch fucking baseball with a bunch of guys I haven't seen or heard from in over 10 years.'

With his mind meandering, he hadn't noticed that his Mother had stopped slamming dishes in the kitchen and stood behind him quietly in the doorway. She stood calmly watching him and finally she cleared her throat gently and spoke. 'Jim was glad you made it that day.' She said. 'It meant a lot to him.' Danny, slightly startled by her voice, noticed her behind him in the mirror only after she spoke. He looked away from the photo and turned to face her before sinking into the rocking chair and pushing off on his toes.

'Yeah, some brother I was. What did I stick around for . . . like 20 minutes?' He drew his hand up to his chin as a wrinkle of irritation ran across his brow.

His Mother stepped further into the room crouching down to meet his slouched posture at eye level while he slowed down his rhythm in the rocking chair. 'You were 20 years old Danny. That's what people do when they're 20 years old. They live in their own world. They have their own friends and their own lives. Don't think for a second that Jim didn't understand that, because he definitely did.'

'Oh, I'm sure he did.' Danny said with more venom than intended. 'Leave it to Jim to not hold a grudge for me being a lousy brother. Water off a duck's fucking back with him . . . always.'

His Mother left her crouched position and stood back up. She drew her hands to her hips and her face turned disapproving. 'You still don't get it do you Danny? You still don't understand. For a smart boy, you don't pick up an awful lot. You're always in a competition . . . Always!' She yelled. 'But, you're missing the point when it comes to Jim. He never held a grudge simply because you were his brother and he loved you . . . he got you. That's something you couldn't and I guess, still can't see for yourself.'

'Oh come off it Ma. What's there to get? What do I not get?' Danny asked.

'Mainly . . . my son . . . it's that you are and only ever were in competition with yourself. You . . . no one else. You're in some kind of race Danny and your moving fast. The only problem is, you don't realize that there's no one else around you. Not in front of you, not behind you. No one . . . nowhere. You're an island. I mean . . . just God help you sometimes Danny.' She finished and turned away and pushed her palms to both temples in frustration.

'God huh?' Danny asked. 'I don't think you should "God" me anymore Ma. I've heard just about enough of God.'

His Mother turned back to face him again and ran her hands through her tangled hair. 'Enough of God, Danny? Really? What, you don't think he exists now?' She asked with a look of concern emerging on her face.

'I don't fucking know Ma. Maybe he does, maybe he doesn't. But if he does, he's asleep at the wheel half the time.'

'I don't like that kind of talk Danny. That's not how I raised you.' She said. 'What happened to having faith? I always thought there was strong faith inside you.'

Danny's shoulders softened as he leaned forward in the rocking chair with his head in his hands and his elbow's heavily on his knees. 'I'm sorry Ma. I guess all I'm saying is that sometimes . . . I feel like he's doing nothing . . . except sitting up there, wherever he is . . . Shooting arrows with his fucking eyes shut.'

His mother's face buckled in a frown. She looked to be on the brink of tears only unable to produce anymore. She turned to leave the room, but turned back abruptly and asked Danny. 'Why did you come here Danny? Why did you come home?'

Danny's gaze stayed towards the floor as he pondered the answer to her simple question. A simple question with a not so simple answer, not one at least that he would give her. She shook her head disapprovingly, 'Nothing Danny? Well, at least tell me why you're here in my apartment then. There's plenty other places to go. Why are you here?'

Danny slowly raised his eyes to meet hers, suddenly looking quite young and quite old all at once. 'To sleep Mom. Really, I just wanted to sleep for a little while. Is that okay?'

'The couch is yours Danny.' She said leaving the living room. ''Stay as long as you want'.

Brendan Maguire

Brendan sprawled out on his hotel bed at the Marriott in Quincy Center. He laid there with his hands clasped across his chest still fully dressed except for his feet. He had ditched the shoes in the middle of the floor at his feet, next to his packed suitcase, and found his way into the hotel's standard-issue room slippers.

The TV was on, but he had turned the volume down to zero. He preferred the sound of cars from the highway speeding in the distance and the hum of the central heating system to the repeated Cialis and Viagra commercials that ran on an endless loop on the History channel.

His face held a whisper of dark stubble since he hadn't bothered to shave in the last 36 hours or so. 'At least I showered and changed my clothes' he thought. 'That was progress for someone cooped up nonstop in this asylum for what feels like eternity. It's like prison all over again, except for the maids of course who do nothing but look at me like I'm an eccentric, a modern day Thoreau or a fugitive hiding out . . . or some combination of both.' His patience had begun to fray after 24 hours of waiting for the phone call that may or may not arrive. His instructions were to do his one appearance, and then haul ass back to the hotel and stay put until his services were needed. No cellphones were the rule apparently, so he'd been forced to stay locked in the room under a bogus name waiting for a phone call that may or may not come.

He couldn't help but chew on his fingernails while anticipating the details of the 'favor' that had been asked of him. He got to a point where there were no fingernails left and resorted to biting and picking at the skin on his fingertips, a terrible habit he'd developed at some stage recently.

The phone rang loudly all of a sudden and Brendan jumped at the sound of it. He'd expected the noise to come for so long, but he never wished that it would. The ringing caught him off guard so much that when he leapt up, he tripped over his scattered shoes in a panic to answer the phone.

He managed to answer finally by the fourth ring with a heavier breath than he expected. He breathed into the receiver, 'Hello?'

A familiar voice responded, 'Hey smart-guy, what disgusting habit has you so out of breath?'

'Ah . . . it's nothing.' He answered, 'I just tripped that's all, the phone ringing caught me by surprise.'

'Yeah? Well, glad I called. I feel like I would've had to do CPR on you if I'd decided to knock and you're really not my type. Listen junior, you know my voice right?'

'Um, yeah, it sounds familiar. It's Mc . . .' Brendan started.

'Don't. Fucking say my name guy are you shitting me?'

'Sorry, yeah of course.' Brendan had forgotten how charming and frightening his old prison pal McNulty could be.

'Now, Junior, what I want you to do is very simple.' McNulty continued, 'It's nothing dangerous and it's nothing illegal.'

'Good, okay, sounds good, I was worried for a while. What is it?' Brendan asked.

'I can't spell it out over the fucking phone guy. Put your

fucking dress and high heels on and go check out at reception. There's a letter waiting for you behind the front desk. That'll lay out everything I need you to do.'

'What if there's questions or anything?' Brendan asked 'Can I contact you?'

'Don't worry there won't be and you most certainly cannot contact me.' McNulty answered. 'Listen . . . a retarded chimpanzee could do this thing for me, so I trust you can manage it also. Now . . . get your ass down there, pretty fucking please.'

Brendan heard the phone click as McNulty hung up. His mind filled with a crippling doubt at that moment. 'Redemption' he thought 'It's my one real chance at redemption.' With that thought he bent to put his shoes on and grabbed his case to move out. He caught a glimpse of his reflection in the mirror on his way out. He paused briefly, just enough time to shrug to his own reflection. He headed out the door and pulled the key card from the light slot and let the heavy door slam shut behind him.

He waited until he was sitting in the back of a taxi out front of the hotel before he opened the envelope. When he did, he found a card inside with an address neatly printed on it along with a small torn piece of paper with the following note scribbled on it in messy handwriting:

"Junior - Let Dora know your plans for tonight. You're meeting friends at Mackin's Saloon in Quincy Center. Make sure she relays your plans to her brother. Then get your ass on a fucking train back to Philly."

Brendan stuck the address card in his pocket. He crumbled the note in his hand, then popped it in his mouth and chewed quickly. Still chewing, he caught the taxi driver's eyes in the rearview mirror. He gave him a confident nod and said, 'head towards Dorchester, I'll show you where to drop me.

Danny Carson

Danny listened to the familiar sound of metal grating the pavement. He knew right away it must have snowed while he slept. 'Enough to have someone's pick-up truck scraping a snow plow on the ground' he thought.

He had expected to dream. He always dreamt. Even long days at work made him dream. So when he shut his eyes only to blink them open what seemed like a second later, he didn't feel refreshed. He didn't feel like he'd slept at all. He wasn't alert or rested or any different at all from when he'd first laid down. 'Maybe slightly less of a headache' he thought, 'but just barely.' Time must have past however since it was pitch dark out and not a sound could be heard in the house. He searched for words to describe how he felt as he laid there staring at fringes of light from beyond the cracks in the window shades. It wasn't day light that split through, 'too late for that this time of year. It must be a street light just outside the apartment. That must be hell, sleeping with that burning flame in your periphery each evening.' He tried to think of the right adjective to describe his mental state, but he couldn't put his finger on it. His mind grasped at his rusty vocabulary, 'trapped, stuck, down in a hole, stuck in the middle, boxed in, boxed out, boxed off, punched out, cornered, back against the wall, just fucking lost.'

He sat up quickly and inadvertently kicked the blanket to the ground as he swung his legs around to plant his feet on the carpet. As he stood up he heard the floor boards underneath him creek, 'better the floor than my knees' he thought. He walked slowly across the dark living room into the darker hallway. It felt much later than it was and he felt childish all of a sudden and just plain dumb when he realized he had been tip-toeing like it was Christmas morning. There was no one there to wake up. When he flicked on the kitchen light, the note on the refrigerator confirmed his suspicions that his Mother had gone out.

The note was brief and written in a familiar scribble. It read, 'Had to run some errands, help yourself to any food. Sorry, but needed my car. Love Mom.'

Danny opened the fridge to find a plate of dinner made for him and covered in plastic wrap. He thought better of eating it, 'stomach might react badly to a healthy meal'. Plus he needed to get moving. He kicked himself about the car. He thought he'd have no problem borrowing it and had assumed it to be his main mode of transport. Instead he rifled through a pen jar for train fare. He grabbed his toothbrush from the duffle bag and brushed his teeth in the bathroom. He winced at the strong cinnamon flavored toothpaste, which was the same shiny red tube he hated as a kid. He found some blue Listerine under the sink which he gargled with for a minute to wash the remnants of the red poison from his mouth.

He changed into a dark sweater and warmer shoes, then grabbed a black winter hat and his leather gloves from his bag. On his way out he found the spare key hanging on a hook near the door and stuffed it into his pocket just before he pulled the door closed tightly behind him.

The streets were cleared but there was a dusting of fresh powder on the sidewalks, about 2-3 inches thick. The snow was light however and easily kicked away, 'too cold to snow heavily' he thought and peered into the glare of the streetlight to judge how hard the snow was falling. It was the same method he and Jim used as kids. They would always take shifts watching around the glow of the streetlights, elbows on the window sill, hoping to see fast-falling, heavy white crystals that meant a likely day off from school. This time however, he saw barely anything as the snow that started earlier tapered off to an occasional flurry. The childhood memory rekindled a practiced pain in his chest. 'Not so much a pain' he thought, 'as a dead weight'. Sorrow and guilt gripped him each time he remembered moments with his younger brother, which was often. The ghost of Jim Carson walked next to him on most nights and this one was no different. He half expected to see parallel footsteps matching closely to his own in the fresh powder. He stopped at the edge of the curb and peered down at his feet. He looked quickly behind him to his left, then to his right focusing on the untouched snow lying motionless on the sidewalk. Reassured of his sanity, he shivered as he tried to chase the thoughts away from his mind. He continued on and stepped into the street. He crossed carefully as several stalled construction works made it more precarious than necessary. He leapt over a large pot hole to avoid the splatter of its contents that included dirt encrusted ice water. He high-stepped over the tall temporary curb. Safely across the street, he started over the hill past a couple of low budget chain restaurants and past the old high school on his left. At the school crosswalk, he sped up to a jog towards a drive-through parking lot with a side passage to the train station. He heard a prolonged horn sound behind him and turned back to see a dark hooded figure make a hand motion to the beeping driver and continue at pace in the same direction as himself. Although dressed in black on a dark night, Danny could still make out a sizable frame underneath the man's clothing. Under the street light the figure cast an eclipsing shadow and it moved with an easy agility that defied its size.

Danny pulled his gloves tighter onto his hands out of habit and flexed his fists to stretch the leather to form. He tugged his hat down lower to cover the bottom of his ears which had become exposed during his trot across the street. He cut through the side passage way that led into the train station's commuter parking lot. He quickened his pace towards the back steps and took the stairs with speed two at a time. Pushing his way through the cold and huddled crowd that was waiting on buses in droves, he slipped through the swinging doors into the train station. He pulled his right glove off to dig out his coins and popped the change into the ticket machine. He waited for the Charlie card to spit out and grabbed it quickly as it did. He shot through the barrier as he heard the sound of a train approaching the platform. The doors opened just as he reached the bottom step and he walked onto the first car. The empty train brought relief as he didn't have to hustle for a chair. He felt weak and had hoped for a seat and some personal space.

He walked to the end of the car and grabbed an empty two-seater for himself, spreading out to deter any potential neighbors. When he heard the beeping sound that precedes the doors closing, he shut his eyes in quiet relief and exhaled slowly a breath he only just realized he'd been holding. The doors started to close, but a loud thump of the brakes indicated that someone made the jump just in time. The doors opened again slowly, then slammed shut within seconds. Danny sensed the heat of human presence and opened his eyes to see a beastly sized man dressed in all black take the empty seat directly across from him. Danny's eyes followed the figure from his wet work boots, past his tight peacoat and up to his face.

His mind cleared as he saw a familiar face and he laughed gently to himself in mild disbelief. Danny felt a flood of forgotten memories from long ago as he continued to stare directly into McNulty's eyes.

McNulty was first to break the silence and asked quietly 'You believe in coincidences Dan?'

Danny's slight smile faded with his answer, as he felt a rush of rage building, 'Fucking Bullshit. Let me guess, of all the gin joints in all the world, right McNulty?'

McNulty shrugged his shoulders, 'I see you still have trust issues Danny. I'd hoped you grow out of that.'

Danny coughed a laugh with disgust, 'Oh . . . don't get me wrong, I trust plenty of people McNulty, just not you or anyone else even loosely affiliated with my old man. You should know that.'

McNulty shook his head disapprovingly, 'You shouldn't harbor ill will Danny, it'll eat you alive from the inside out. You may not like me or trust me, but I'm old enough and bad enough to be damn certain of that.'

Danny coughed into his hand and rubbed the day-old stubble on his chin. He pulled the tight wool hat from his head leaving his hair in disarray. 'Alright McNulty' he said and leaned his elbows to his knees to draw him closer into the conversation. 'I didn't wake up this morning to bicker with some of my father's old homeboys . . . so I'm sorry okay, my bad.'

'Likewise Dan' McNulty answered and leaned back into his seat. 'I meant no disrespect either, I'm sure I caught you by surprise.'

'Yeah I guess you did' Danny answered 'So maybe now you'll tell me then huh?'

'What's that?' McNulty asked.

'Listen man, we both know this was no chance encounter. I'm not that unlucky. Sift through the bullshit man and tell me. It was you following me and doing a pretty bad job of it. I'll admit you move well for a man of your . . . girth, but not the most subtle approach now is it?'

McNulty chuckled in what seemed like agreement. 'Following you . . . maybe, but not in the way you think Danny. I heard you were back, so I came by to say hello. I saw you in the distance.' You have the same angry strut as your old man, so I knew it was you. So I tried to run and catch up to you.'

Danny was skeptical by nature and already decided whatever McNulty said was going to be a fairy tale, but he decided not to push it too much. 'You heard I was back huh? Sure you did, news must have travelled fast then.'

'We're in a new world kid' McNulty replied. 'News is instant and endless if you ask me.'

'Whatever' Danny said, 'anyway you're here now, what is it you wanted to say to me?'

'Just one question really . . . and one simple request, that's all.'

'Okay then' Danny answered, relieved with what he hoped would turn into directness. 'Ask your question, then we'll see about that request.'

'Simple Dan. Why are you here?' McNulty asked.

Danny's face scrunched into confusion. 'What . . . I can't visit my home now?'

'Visits are planned and vacations typically last longer than 3 days Danny. 72 hours is just enough time to get into some serious trouble.'

'You're certainly well researched, I'll give you that McNulty. Now how you got my itinerary I'm not even going to ask because I don't think I want to know the answer. Regardless, I wouldn't worry your head about me and trouble. I'm not here for trouble.'

'Well now it's me not trusting you Danny boy. Funny isn't it?' McNulty said as he stood up slowly, holding onto the pole for support. The train began to slow as it approached Quincy Center station. Anyway, Danny, good seeing you, but I gotta date to meet an old friend so this is my stop.' He walked over and with a head nod turned to look out the door.

Danny sat still, confused with the whole conversation. He asked, 'Hey McNulty. I never heard your request. Let's have it.'

McNulty turned back as the doors opened 'Oh right' he said 'I forgot. It's an easy one Danny. There's nothing but badness here for you now boy. My request . . . is that you go home. And do it soon.'

'I am home' Danny said 'Did you forget that?'

McNulty stepped out off the train, but turned back to Danny from the edge of the platform. 'Not no more kid. Your home's 3,000 miles east on a moss-covered rock in the Atlantic. Take it from me, go there and try to get your life back.'

The doors closed then and as the train slowly chugged away from the platform Danny watched McNulty. He watched him stand there very still with a waved hand in the air until he finally faded from sight. Danny sat back into the chair and put his hat back on tightly. He breathed in and out deeply and drifted into a dreamlike trance pondering just what meeting McNulty meant. He shut his eyes and rested in the comfort that even if he fell asleep, Braintree was the last stop on the Redline.

Brendan Maguire

Brendan walked around in Dorchester Park for the better part of an hour. He was trying to muster up the courage to face Dora, someone he once felt so strongly for . . . and possibly he'd even face Flynn, someone who routinely crippled him with fear. There was always the chance that Flynn could be just around the corner, waiting to pounce on him.

In the large, woodsy park in the middle of Dorchester, he had started out by sitting on a bench near the kids' playground, but when people started to realize he was alone and not with any of the children playing, he sensed their apprehension and felt it was time to move on. He strolled aimlessly for a time through the tarmacked trails and stood for a while at the top of a hill overlooking the baseball diamond.

As it grew dark and began to flurry, the silent woods began to haunt him and he headed out of the park down a side pathway towards the dim streetlights on Richmond Street. At the bottom of the lane way, he took a right and walked the 50 yards or so to the address he'd been given from McNulty. He thought about how if things had turned out differently, much differently, he could have been quite familiar with this address.

He thought longingly about Dora as he loitered across the street from her apartment, trying to be as nonchalant as possible. The shades were drawn but there were lights on and he was certain that the flickering he saw belonged to the television. He gathered himself after a minute of mental preparation and headed across the street. Ascending her steps he knew this was not going to run as smoothly as he'd hoped. He could just feel it. Before he even reached the landing he heard movement from the inside and a porch light came on followed immediately by a door opening.

Brendan froze, and for a second he nearly toppled over in surprise, completely caught on the back foot. He hadn't expected even an answer to his knock at the door, never mind a pre-emptive strike. As his eyes adjusted to the light, he saw her silhouette emerge from the doorway.

'Can I help you with something? Dora asked, trying to hide that she was clearly startled herself by a stranger lingering outside of her apartment. 'I saw you across the street, what are you some kind of pervert?' She held up her phone and said, 'All I need to do is hit 'talk' and the cops will be on the way.'

'You don't need to do that Dora.' Brendan said, after regaining his footing.

The use of her name seemed to startle Dora again, but this time only momentarily because of its familiarity. 'I know that voice' she said as she edged slowly onto the porch from the door threshold to peer closer.

Brendan finally took another step forward, entering the landing of the porch. When he did, the light shone bright on his face, unmasking him to Dora's eyes.

He shielded the blast of light from his own eyes and noticed Dora take a step back into the doorway to steady herself. Brendan paused, momentarily at a loss for how to proceed. He half raised his hand in a wave, but thought it awkward and inappropriate as he cut himself off in mid motion.

Dora grabbed the door quickly and Brendan panicked as his opportunity to speak drew dangerously to a close.

'Wait! Please.' He said more forcefully than he'd intended.

Dora stopped from closing the door, but stayed huddled next to it, still poised to shut it fast if necessary. 'I'm just here to talk Dora' Brendan pleaded 'that's all. Please.'

'Well I've got nothing to say to you, and I'm even less interested in hearing you out.' Dora replied.

'But, that's why I'm here' Brendan answered then paused, frantically thinking of what to say next as the speech he semi-prepared for this encounter fell from his memory. 'I came here to clear the air with you . . . and your brother.'

Dora laughed suddenly, a mean laugh, 'You think Flynn's ever gonna forget about you?' she asked. 'Jesus Brendan, you've got no clue. I . . . I think . . . you should just go.' She said, then she moved to shut the door for definite this time.

Brendan reacted instantly and stuck his foot in the doorway just in time to prevent the door from slamming to a close. The door popped aggressively off the rubber from his sneaker and caught Dora by surprise. She stumbled backwards into her living room.

Brendan lurched forward and grabbed her before she could fall over. He had reacted from instinct so quickly that before he knew what he was doing he found himself standing close to her, holding firmly onto her arms, their faces barely inches apart.

They stood silently for a moment that felt much longer than it was. Her eyes, which at first showed fear, relaxed and he watched her pupils dilate, eyes shining bright blue before his own. He had forgotten how attractive her eyes could be when they smiled and how beautiful she was when her shiny red strands of hair draped the edges of her cheeks. He inched closer to her face with his own and pulled her arms closer to him. As he did, he felt her arms tense at first, but then relax slightly as she slid her wrists and forearms around his waist and she moved her lips the final inch to press against his own.

Afterwards Brendan didn't dare drift off to sleep. He laid on his side and gently rubbed her bare shoulder as he watched her eyes struggle to remain open, eventually giving in to the urge to close completely.

Brendan wrestled with his thoughts as he tried to figure out his next move. His stomach ached with butterflies and he felt at any second he could vomit. Things had not gone as planned, not even slightly. This had just happened. He couldn't articulate how he felt. He obviously still loved her and he guessed she still felt something for him. He hoped she did at least. However, it was difficult to fight back logic, no matter how hard he tried. 'Anyway that this shakes out' he thought, 'it does not end up with a future for us.'

He reached down to the floor and into the pocket of his crumbled jeans and pulled out his watch, startled to see nearly 2 hours had past already. Decision time was upon him and he knew it. He slowly lifted the covers off himself and slid his legs out from the bed. As he pulled his jeans on, he heard Dora move and turned towards her as she asked, 'Where are you heading so soon?'

Brendan knelt back on the bed and leaned over to kiss her. 'Just to the kitchen' He answered 'Need a drink, don't worry. Stay there. I'll bring you some water.'

'Okay' she answered and shifted to her other side in the bed. The blankets slipped down her shoulder and Brendan felt physical pain at seeing how beautiful her white porcelain skin looked next to the shine of her hair. He knew he had to leave now or he would never again have the strength to do so. 'It's like pulling off a Band-Aid.' he thought.

He silently lifted his shirt and sneakers from the floor as he left the room. He put his clothes back on in the living room quickly and quietly. He went to the kitchen sink and ran the faucet. Meanwhile he found a pen and pad of paper in the utensil draw. He began to scribble down his note to Dora, knowing full well that any attempt at an apology would sound merely empty or worse, callous.

He kept the note brief, ending with a reassurance that he meant to make amends with her and Flynn and carefully noted his plans to meet some people that night at Mackin's pub in Quincy Center. Feeling as empty as his written words, Brendan slipped out the front door and started off briskly down Richmond Street towards Adams Street. He began in a walk that quickly went into a jog, then a flat out run, stopping only about a mile later at the old chocolate factory where he took the steps down to the trolley station at the Milton Stop to wait for his train. 'Running again' he thought as he tried in vain to catch his breath, 'always running'.

Flynn McBride

The prison psychiatrist once told Flynn of a theory that basically, in his understanding, amounted to drug and alcohol abuse during early adolescence can stunt your emotional growth. She said that in one breath and in the next told him that it didn't mean he could use that to rationalize his actions. She had said it so that he could recognize a shortcoming in himself and start to use that knowledge to try and control his urges.

Logically he understood it because it made sense. Obviously filling your body full of chemicals and killing off brain cells from an early age had a negative effect on you. Later when he thought more about it, he decided he definitely believed it. There were many things he had done in his life that he now wished he'd done differently. Not just the obvious big things, but also the small things he had done, to people he loved that he never before thought twice about. How many times had he blown up at Dora for little to no reason, leaving her a nervous wreck half of the time. When he thought about it, she was really the only family to him that mattered, probably the only person he had any significant connection to in his life. He thought about how often she had covered for him, taken care of him, protected him in a way. He had never said thank you, and never even showed the slightest hint of appreciation. He just continued on doing what he does, stirring up trouble and leaving her to deal with the consequences. 'I was gone for 2 years, who else did she have?' he thought, 'no wonder she had tried reconnecting to our mother, with me as a brother and a drunk and distant father. How could I blame her?'

He had been pondering all this and more while sitting on the tailgate of his truck, chain-smoking and watching airplanes fly overhead at Castle Island. Even if it was in the middle of Southie and was always packed with people, there was something relaxing about the old fort.

After the argument with Dora, he drove his old truck around aimlessly for a while until economic realities set in and he needed to stop burning through his gas since it was needed for the work week. The rage he felt leaving Dora's apartment subsided with time. As was the usual case, immense guilt set in shortly thereafter. Guilt was how he operated. Usually, he turned guilt away from himself into anger at those who he felt guilty about. Strangely this time however, he felt he couldn't do that. Not to Dora, not anymore. When it became too dark to see the planes land anymore, he grabbed a couple of hotdogs from Sully's, the burger and ice cream institution on Castle Island and had them both ingested before he reached Dorchester. He stopped at the florist across from Cedar Grove cemetery and was able to pick up a bouquet of flowers just before they closed for the night.

He drove around the corner and parked, blocking the driveway to Dora's apartment minutes later. He felt like she had to be home, but there seem to be no lights on that he could see. There was an eerie darkness to the street that night as it seemed all the street lights were enveloped by red, yellow and brown leaves. Flynn shivered when he opened the door, realizing the temperature dropped significantly with the transition to darkness.

He walked tenderly up the porch stairs, sliding the light covering of snow off the edges of the steps with his boot. He rang the doorbell and waited patiently for a response.

After a minute, he rang the bell again. He thought maybe she had actually gone out, but part of him just knew she was there. He opened the screen door and tried the knob to the main door and found it opened. He walked in slowly, knocking on the door again as he did so and gently called Dora's name. The lights were off in the living room and kitchen. He saw an old glass vase on top of the refrigerator and got it down. He ran the kitchen sink and rinsed out the vase. As he did, he noticed a note scribbled on a loose piece of paper on the counter. He read the note carefully. Any other day of his life, he knew it would've driven him to rage. Today for some reason, he felt only sorrow. It could've been the smudged ink from what looked like painful tears touching the parchment. He put the note down carefully where it had been before and filled the vase up with lukewarm water. He cut the flower stems at an angle with a pair of scissors from the fork draw and put them into the water.

He noticed as he turned, a dim light came on in Dora's bedroom. He walked back through the living room and knocked lightly on the bedroom door. The door opened slightly with the weight of his fist. 'Dora?' he called again and pushed through the door slowly. 'You okay?'

He felt his own eyes well up with tears when he saw Dora. She sat on the edge of the bed next to the lamp on the bedside table. Her red hair covered her hands, which in turn covered her eyes. He walked slowly towards her and knelt down slowly in front of her, bending his head low to try and get a look through her hands to her face.

She removed her hands finally and dragged her hair back behind her ears. Flynn noticed the edges of her red hair were darker than the rest, wet with tears. Her eye's, though bright blue were rubbed red around the edges and they matched the red from her nose that also gave away that she'd been crying. She didn't speak at all. Flynn had rarely seen her in such a state, if ever. He always thought of her as the toughest girl he knew, and she was, which made it all the more painful to watch her now. 'I'm sorry' he said. 'For everything I mean, not just today. I love you, I've never actually told you that . . . and you're all the family I've got. I promise, from now on, things'll be different. I mean it. You may not believe me right now, but they will.'

Dora just nodded in agreement. After a period of silence she answered, 'I love him Flynn. You need to fix this.'

Flynn felt his eyes grow heavy with water again. 'I know' he responded 'I will fix it. I read the letter. I'm going now.' He squeezed her knee, and she put a hand over his, as he got up from the carpet. Neither of them said anything else. Flynn walked slowly from her room and through the living room to the front door. He closed the door behind him when he left, making sure the lock caught this time. He started his truck and wiped his eyes dry with his sleeves. Driving away, he thought about how for the first time really in his life, he was going to do something for someone other than himself and he felt good about it. It was like a small weight from a big pile had just been removed from his chest.

Flynn pulled up the hill and swung the old truck into the bumpy dirt parking lot behind Mackin's Saloon. He knew what he had to do and he knew why, but the thought of entering a barroom made him nervous. Since his parole, he'd managed to stay clean, but not without significant mental effort on his part. One way to stay off booze and drugs was to stay out of the places where they existed. He kept out of bars and he'd kept as far away as possible from anyone from his past drug exploits. He got out of the truck and shut the door hard to make sure it would stay closed. He felt like gravity was heavier than normal. His legs moved sluggishly with the strain of his long emotional day.

The parking lot was emptier than he'd expected, 'Especially for a place that was supposed to be hosting a party.' he thought. 'Maybe I'm early.' He swallowed a gulp of saliva and took a deep breath outside the front door. He hoped he wouldn't see too many people from his past sitting inside the local barroom. After a final moment of deliberation, he turned, put his head down and walked through the heavy wooden door.

Inside was slightly brighter than the dark street outside. The bar looked the same as he remembered. It was still one of the few popular bars in Quincy that looked like a local boozer instead of one refurbished to look like a night club. He recognized the female bartender, but couldn't remember her name. He didn't recognize the man sitting on a stool next to the front door, presumably checking ID's. No one asked him for anything as he walked in.

He went over to the bar while he scanned the rest of the room. The new juke box was playing, but there was no one else in the bar at all, the place was flat out empty. He felt awkward and out of place when he realized he was the only there not on the payroll.

He thought, 'The music playing on the juke box was good and the television had Sportscenter on, so it could be worse.' He sat down at a table close to the bar. The bartender looked up and said 'Hello, what are you having?'

Flynn paused. He actually hadn't thought about what he'd do when he was asked for a drink. He hadn't planned a response or thought of an alternative. He responded out of habit more so than anything else and said 'Bud light draft'. She rang him up and he paid her and left a dollar on the counter for a tip. He put the beer in the middle of the table and leaned his chin on his hands to stare at the condensation dripping down the cold glass. In his head he knew he didn't even want the beer, but now that it sat in front of him, it was calling for him. He continued staring at the full glass for over a minute. His concentration was so great he hadn't realized a very large man dressed in black come out from the bathroom and take a seat at the bar only an arms-length away from him.

It wasn't until the man got up from the bar stool and sat across from Flynn at the table that Flynn shook free from the hypnotic suds. He looked up at the man's face and thought he was pretty familiar, although he felt he would've remembered clearly any man with shoulders that broad and square, so he must not know him. He was confused about why the man had just taken a seat across from him, at his table, with not one other patron present in the bar. Flynn didn't scare easy however, and broad shoulders be damned, he would not be intimidated. He looked the man in the eye, but decided to let him speak first.

After a minute of non-verbal posturing, the large man broke his eye contact and showed a small smile. 'You like the Matrix?' he asked.

Flynn scrunched his eyebrows in confusion and replied,

'What? The fucking movie with Keanu Reeves?'

'Yeah. That's the one. You like it?'

'I guess it's alright.' Flynn answered still confused. 'Any reason? Or is that how you start all conversations with total strangers.'

'You were staring at that beer so hard I was waiting for the thing to bend like the spoon in the movie, that's all. Plus we're two local guys in Mackin's. We haven't met before, but we sure ain't strangers.'

'How do you know I'm local?' Flynn asked.

'You're in Mackin's and you don't have an Irish accent, where the fuck else would you be from?'

Flynn laughed at the man's response and decided he must just be old and lonely, here looking to socialize with the only other person in the place. 'Okay then, you got me. I'm a Quincy guy. My name's Flynn.' Flynn reached around his beer glass across the table to shake hands with his new acquaintance. 'Nice to meet you man.'

'Nice to meet you too Flynn' the man replied. 'I'm McNulty, Nick McNulty. Friends call me Nicky. Everyone else calls me McNulty.'

'What should I call you?' Flynn asked.

'How about Nick? You can call me Nick. Sound like a good compromise?'

'Sure does Nick.' Flynn answered. 'So . . . um . . . what brings you out tonight?'

'Isn't it obvious Flynn? I came out to meet some ladies.'

Flynn laughed again and thought he was really starting to like this guy.

'What about you?' McNulty asked. 'You're clearly not here to drink that beer, that's for certain.' McNulty pointed to Flynn's beer, which had become warm and flat in the brief time that they spoke.

'No' Flynn responded. 'Not here for the beer, not sure why I even ordered it. I guess old habits die hard. I'm hoping to meet someone here that's all. Need to talk to someone and clear something up for my sister. The guy's supposed to be in here tonight.'

'Sounds ominous my young companion, should I expect trouble?'

'No, no, not from me, I'm here to squash something not start something.' Flynn answered.

'Good' McNulty said 'I cower at the thought of physical violence.'

Flynn gave him a funny look accompanied with a smirk, 'I would've guessed otherwise Nick.'

'Well, appearances are not always as they seem, but perhaps I exaggerated a little.' McNulty answered. 'So is it 'One Day at a Time' then Flynn? You're in the program I take it?'

'What, AA? Um, yeah I guess I kinda am.'

'Sounds more complicated than that' McNulty said. 'Then again, it's usually something complicated, self-inflicted or otherwise that sends people to those meetings. It definitely ain't the coffee, that's for sure. Donuts maybe, but the coffee's consistently shit.'

Flynn laughed and asked, 'So are you in AA too then? Pretty shit luck for this bar huh? Only two people in the place, both are off the fucking sauce.'

McNulty laughed heartily, 'Good point Flynn, tough break for this place. I'm in the program. Well, sort of in the program. I dip in and dip out, been doing so for about 30 years.'

'Doesn't sound too successful, sorry to hear that. What's

your poison, if you don't mind me asking, is it booze or drugs?'

'Geez Flynn, don't even buy me dinner first huh?'

'Sorry man, I shouldn't have asked that. My bad.'

'No it's okay Flynn. I get it, you're new to this and you want to learn that's good. Truth is, for me it's neither. My involvement is more what you'd call . . . State imposed.'

'Oh. Okay, well if it makes you feel better Nick, you're in good company.'

'Young man like you, sorry to hear that Flynn. What'd you do time for?' McNulty asked.

'I . . . ahh . . . I don't think I want to talk about that actually. It was . . . not my finest moment and I don't want to relive it.'

'So you were guilty I take it?' McNulty asked.

'Yeah man. I was guilty alright . . . I still am.' Flynn answered. He reached over and put his hand around his beer. He lifted it up and looked into the glass, trying to catch his reflection in the liquid, but seeing only a distorted picture of McNulty's face across the table. He pushed his chair back and got up. He walked the couple steps over to the bar and handed the beer back to the bartender and asked for a coke instead. When he turned back around to take his chair again, he saw McNulty smile and give him a mock golf-clap.

'Fuck it, right Nick? Who needs it?'

McNulty nodded in agreement. 'That's willpower young Flynn, very impressive.'

'Thanks' Flynn replied

McNulty leaned forward on the table and rubbed his chin with his hand. 'A lot of things been done through willpower, amazing things, shit people thought impossible.

You want to hear a quick story about willpower Flynn?'

'Ah yeah man, I'm here anyway, got nothing but time.' Flynn answered.

'Good . . . when I was about your age, there was this bad motherfucker that ran a lot of the drugs through Dorchester, Quincy and the South Shore. Let's call him Jack. He wasn't the top guy or anything, but he had some weight locally. And, he loved to throw that weight around whenever possible. He loved fucking with average Joe's. It made him feel hard or something. I hated the fucking asshole. But, I didn't need to worry about him, ya know. I wasn't on anything and no one I hung with was either, so no need. A very close friend of mine however had a different situation. He was pretty straight edge himself, had two kids, head screwed on straight. He used to work for me in a shop I used to run back in the day. He had balls this guy and he was tough as nails, but most of all, anything he wanted, he went after it. He had willpower like no one I'd ever seen.

One night, my friend's two younger brothers wound up at a party with some of the wrong people, including Jack. The youngest brother apparently made a misguided pass at the wrong woman. A young chick who the dealer had a little crush on. Problem was, she didn't feel the same about him, but she did show interest in my friend's brother. Jack got jealous. Jack didn't like being jealous. So when my buddy's other brother asked Jack to set him up with an eight ball, Jack did it, but he spiked it heavy with something like rat poison. My buddy's youngest brother was talked into doing the first line by Jack himself. He gave it to him as a taster for free because it was his first time. That one time was all it took. That hot shot took hold within seconds. My friend and I were only minutes away, but it didn't matter. John was gone before he got to Carney hospital.'

McNulty paused from his story and walked up to the bar and got a glass of ice water. When the bartender handed it to him, he took a long gulp and then sat back down in the chair.

Flynn looked over at him questioningly 'So? What happened next man? What about your boy with the willpower, what did he do?'

McNulty smiled. 'What would you have done Flynn? Some motherfucker takes your younger brother's life away out of childish jealousy, what do you think? How does that end? How do you get him back?'

Flynn sat back in his chair. 'Shit. I don't know man. I guess . . . I mean, I don't have a brother or nothing, but I think I'd kill the motherfucker and anyone who tried to get in my way.' Flynn said emphatically.

'Yes! Young Flynn, you read my mind.' McNulty answered. 'And you're damn right too. My friend was an average Joe, just like any other hard working stiff. But, you know what he did? He walked right into that house and cleaned that place out. He fought through about five guys, five grown men, paid to guard this fucker, with weapons and all. I know this for a fact, because I was there with him. Then he dragged Jack to the roof of the triple decker and threw the bastard off it. That . . . I also witnessed.'

'Shit man' Flynn said in response. 'Was he caught? I mean, did the police catch him?'

'Police? Nah, not then. He burned that house to the ground though, so wasn't much linking him to the scene.

He sacrificed a lot though that night. From that point on, he was a ghost. Never around for more than a month at a time, cause someone or something was always after him. Plus he blamed himself for what happened to his brother. He blamed himself for not being there. The only thing he could do to dull the pain was to drown it in whiskey. And with that, the Ghost lost everything.'

'Fuck' Flynn said.

'Yeah. Fuck is right. The real victims though, unfortunately were the Carson boys. Those poor kids had to grow up with either their old man absent or drunk. Something I wish I never had to see.'

At the mention of the name Carson, Flynn slipped his foot off the bottom part of his chair and lurched forward knocking McNulty's water to the ground. 'Shit. Ahh . . . sorry Nick. I must've slipped.'

McNulty watched the water drip onto the ground, then looked coolly back at Flynn and smiled.

Flynn found the smile empty of humor and all of a sudden felt sick with nerves. He decided to take a walk outside and get some air. 'Hey, excuse me a minute Nick. I'm going to head out front and have a smoke. I'll be back in and I'll get that water cleaned up.'

McNulty shrugged and remained seated and continued looking unflinchingly at Flynn. Flynn practically ran out of the bar and stopped short out front and took a deep breath of cold air that burned his lungs. 'Carson' he thought 'How can that be?'

He took his cigarettes out from his pocket and put one to his lips. He pulled his lighter up to light the smoke but it blew out with the wind. He hugged the side of the building to obstruct the wind from the flame. He turned up toward the hill and looked up to see a familiar car that he placed right away. It was the same 80's style Buick he'd seen parked next to his truck much earlier in the day. 'Was that today' he thought 'Can that be a coincidence? No fucking way.'

Despite his fear, he slowly walked towards the parked Buick trying to see through the tint whether there was anyone inside of it. He approached it cautiously, and leaned closer to see into the window. As he leaned forward, the passenger door shot open and a man jumped out quickly. The man looked mean and experienced. He was older, 50's or so, with slicked back hair and a salt and pepper goatee. He looked directly at Flynn, then pointed behind him.

Flynn turned quickly around to see the massive frame of McNulty shadowing the light from the main street. He looked down at McNulty's hand and followed it until he saw the glimmer flash off the chrome gun. His eyes opened with fright as he looked into McNulty's. McNulty just pointed to the Buick and said, 'Get in the fucking car Flynn.' Flynn had no choice. With trepidation, Flynn opened the back door to the car and slid across into the seat.

Danny Carson

Danny's walk from the Braintree train station to Mike's house was short, but it was cold. The snow had stopped, but when it did the temperature dropped significantly. It had been years since he'd seen Mike's wife and kids. Even before Jim died, Danny hadn't taken much time on his trips home to visit the Riordan's.

He rang the doorbell and shivered on the front porch as he waited for an answer. From the porch, it looked like every light was on in the house and he could hear a commotion inside that sounded like little girls arguing. Danny saw a silhouette through the lace curtain covering the glass door. It was too petit to be Mike and when the door opened, Danny was greeted by Mike's wife Elaine. He hadn't seen her in what felt like a lifetime, but she still looked the same, like she hadn't aged at all.

She smiled at him when she opened the door to let him in. 'Danny' she said. 'Wow, it feels like forever.' She pulled him into a hug and gave him a kiss on the cheek. 'Get inside Danny, it's freezing'.

'Hi Elaine, good to see you, thanks for having me over.' Danny said as he kissed her back on the cheek and walked into the hallway. He took off his hat and pulled off his gloves and stuffed them in his coat pocket. He looked around the house as he took off his coat and draped it over the bannister at the bottom of the stairs. Nothing in the house looked familiar to him. Not just that he hadn't been in there really since the kids were babies, but also that the lifestyle was so foreign to him. He felt weak and alone, confronted with a life that he had once envisioned for himself, but never achieved.

Elaine appeared to notice his silence and took it as something else, 'Sorry Danny, the place is a mess. The girls leave toys everywhere.'

Danny turned to her and smiled. 'No, it's perfect, sorry for staring. Just looks so different since I was last around. I . . . um . . . I'm sorry I wasn't around more. I should've visited more often.' He apologized.

'You still can. We're not going anywhere Danny. You can visit whenever you'd like.' She answered. Here, come on in, Mike was fixing something out back. Head through the hall there to the kitchen, he should be back in shortly.' She led him in and pointed through the long hall to the kitchen.

Danny nodded in thanks and walked through the hall towards the back of the house. He walked past the living room and saw the two girls and smiled and said 'Hello'. Both little girls went silent, but stared closely at Danny not sure who or what he was.

'Don't be rude girls. Say hi to your cousin Danny.' Danny heard Mike yell from the back door as he walked into the kitchen. Danny was happy with the intrusion as it broke the awkward silence between him and the children. He walked into the kitchen and saw Mike shut the door and stamp his boots on the door mat before walking in. 'Danny boy' he said. 'Long time no see'. He walked over and the two men shook hands. 'You want a beer or something?' He asked as he took his coat off and hung on a hook next to the door.

Danny considered the offer for a second before answering. 'You got anything stronger lying around Mike?'

'Sit down' Mike said, 'I'll sort you out.' He reached up

to the top cabinet and pulled down two whiskey glasses, then went over to a tall liquor cabinet and took down a bottle of Jameson. 'This more like it?' he asked

'Yes. It is.' Danny answered and took a seat at a counter stool.

Mike poured two glasses, filling both more than halfway with the whiskey. He brought the glasses over to the counter and handed one to Danny. He put the other glass down, then walked over to get the bottle and took it over with him to the counter and put it down between the two glasses. Mike then sat down across from Danny and wrapped both hands around the drink.

Danny looked at Mike's large builder hands, then back up to his eyes. 'So, you learned how to sip the whiskey after all huh?' He said trying to smile.

Mike nodded slowly and also attempted a smile. 'I'm not in so much of a rush when I'm home already, ya know?'

'I guess you're right.' Danny answered. 'Elaine . . . she still looks great' he said awkwardly. 'And, the uh girls, they got big.'

'Thanks Dan. Yeah, it's been a while man. The girls'll be teenagers before I know it. I'll be chasing boys and shit away from the house I'm sure. Not looking forward to that one bit.'

Danny laughed. 'I think you've got a few years until that happens. Better stay sharp though just in case. You don't want to be shown up by some young punk.'

'I think we both know that ain't happening on my watch.' Mike answered. 'When the time comes, I'll be ready.'

'No, I think you're right. I think you have the

intimidation factor down alright.'

Danny saw Elaine lean into the kitchen out of the corner of his eye. 'Mike' she said 'I'm going to get the girls down and probably head to bed myself. I'll let you boys catch up. Don't fly off without saying goodbye Danny.' She said and blew them both a kiss goodnight.

Danny smiled at her and said 'goodnight'.

Danny waited until he heard footsteps upstairs, then turned back to Mike and raised his glass. Mike did the same back to him. 'What are we drinking to?' he asked.

Danny thought about the question for a second then answered 'To family'.

'Okay then' Mike said, 'To family.' He reached his glass across and clanked it against Danny's. Both men took the glass down in one gulp. Mike reached for the bottle and pulled the top off and poured the same again for each glass. When he finished pouring, he replaced the cap and put his large hands back around the glass. He looked up at Danny and said, 'I know why you're here Danny.'

Danny stared back at him for a moment, then answered. 'I'm here to say hello to you and your family.'

'Not here at my house' Mike said 'Here, as in back in Boston.'

Danny tapped the top of his glass with his index finger for a few seconds before answering. 'I'm not going to bullshit you Mike. Of all people, I won't bullshit you.'

'I know you won't Danny. So what's your plan?'

'I guess I don't have much of plan really. I just can't fucking walk around anymore like everything's cool. Jim's fucking killer is walking around free like shit never happened.'

'I didn't realize you were walking around playing things cool. Seems to me you've be hotter than Mel fucking Gibson since it happened. Michelle still calls Elaine every so often. She doesn't paint a good picture of you Danny.'

'Yeah well, she'd fucking know I guess Mike. Things just got out of hand I guess, I don't know.' Danny paused and took a gulp from his glass. He looked back up at Mike. 'I ain't asking you to help or anything man. I know you got bigger things to worry about.'

'Don't you Danny?' Mike answered 'What's going after McBride gonna solve? It sure as shit ain't bringing Jim back.'

Danny felt hopeless. He knew Mike was right, but he refused to accept it. He leaned his face against his folded hands on the table and bit down on his thumb. After a second, he popped his head back up and said. 'I have to fucking do something man. He was my brother. I owe it to him to do something.'

Mike didn't answer with words. He finished his drink and poured another into his own glass and topped off Danny's. Once it was poured, he put the bottle down again, picked up his glass and took it down in one gulp. He got up from his chair and started towards the hall door. He turned back towards Danny before leaving. 'The central heating upstairs is very loud, especially when the doors are shut Danny. It'd be a shame if someone was to ever bust through the back door and rob me.' He nodded again at Danny 'Goodnight brother.' He said, then turned and walked through the hallway.

Danny heard his footsteps as Mike climbed the stairs, then he heard the bedroom door shut. He knew Mike didn't want any part of what he planned to do, but at the same time, he knew Mike couldn't let him go empty handed either.

Danny finished his drink and washed out the glass in the kitchen sink. He tip-toed back through the house and grabbed his coat, hat and gloves then went back to the kitchen. He turned the lights off in the kitchen and turned off the back porch light. He then put his coat and gloves back on, and pulled the tight winter hat back over his head.

He walked out the backdoor and pulled the door shut. He checked that it was locked. He walked down the steps and looked into the bed of Mike's pickup truck. Inside he saw a black iron flat bar left loose next to a pile of empty cans. Making sure his gloves were pulled on tight, he reached over and grabbed the tool quickly. He walked right back up the steps to the back door. As quietly as possible he jammed the flat bar into the door jam and with one quick pop of the lock, the back door broke open. Once inside the kitchen, he opened a number of draws and cabinets to make it look like someone searching for cash. In a cabinet above the refrigerator he found a coffee can full of money, mainly rolled up twenty dollar bills and emptied out the contents. He stuffed the cash into his pocket and rolled the can onto the floor. Next he headed directly to the liquor cabinet. There was a dummy block of wood that served as a trapdoor to a secret compartment. He looked inside and there it was, same as always, Mike's 9mm pistol, which he often brought over to the Braintree gun club to fire off rounds to blow off steam. It wasn't loaded, but Danny reached up high over the top of the cabinet and found the stack of bullets. He popped the clip from the gun and loaded it with bullets as quickly as he could manage. He wasn't experienced with guns really, so he fumbled one or two shells and had to go onto his hands and knees to find them and pick them off the floor. Finally, he stuffed the gun into his deep coat pocket, then walked quickly out of the house through the back door and down towards the main street.

He moved as fast as possible without bringing obvious suspicion. If anyone saw him, he wanted to appear to be walking briskly to shrug off the cold. He was sweating pretty heavily with fear and with the increased body heat from his walk by the time he got back to the train station.

The train thankfully came within minutes and he walked onto the car and took a seat by himself, trying his best to look nonchalant. While sitting, he could feel the weight of the gun in his pocket sitting on his thigh. He prayed silently that the thing wouldn't go off by mistake and blow his dick off.

Wollaston T station was only 3 stops away, but the trip felt longer than his flight home to Boston. He stood just before the train stopped and walked onto the platform at Wollaston. The bright lights blinded him when he stepped off the train and he squinted until his eyes adjusted, moving slowly and trying to avoid bumping into anyone. He was filled with fear that if someone bumped into him, they'd feel the gun in his coat and he'd be forced to run, undoubtedly drawing attention to himself. He walked down the steps from the platform and through the exit barriers. He took a right at the bottom and headed up the steps towards Newport Ave, then stopped at the cross walk and waited for the lights to change to red.

He knew where McBride was staying. It was the same place many Quincy ex-cons stayed when they were paroled. It happened to be a block away from the house Danny grew up in. He'd visited his father there on a few occasions, so he knew the layout and how it operated.

When the light turned red, he crossed Newport Ave and continued onto Brook Street past the old DeeDee's lounge and a Carpet Warehouse. He took the second right and turned down a side street. The darkness of the street used to haunt him on walks home as a young teenager. For some reason the street lights in that part of Quincy were spaced too far apart. Many nights, he actually jogged home down this street because it gave him the creeps so badly. This night however, he needed the darkness, it covered his intentions from any neighbor up later than usual that happened to glance out the window and check for snow falling. He still felt the fear however. His heart was filled with fear and with doubt. Mike's words had meant something to him of course. 'Why shouldn't they?' he thought. 'He's right. Jim's not coming back no matter what happens to McBride.' But he made his decision and it was final, regardless of the consequences. Flynn McBride was going to die. Either he was going or Danny felt like he'd be the one to go. 'What difference does it make to anyone now?' he thought. 'They're all gone. I'm alone and that's not ever changing. Who would give a fuck if I'm gone?'

He bit his lip to chew back a sob. He felt tears well up in his eyes. They weren't for him however, they were for what should have been. They were for his younger brother, who didn't deserve what happened to him. They were also for those people he hurt from that point onwards. He thought just for a second that it'd be best to just turn back, but as he considered it, he saw the halfway house only yards away across the small street. The house was pitch dark as were all the other houses on the block. He jogged across the street through a dark area not captured by a street light and snuck between the house's fence and a series of bushes. He ducked down low behind the bushes and waited for a minute to listen for footsteps both inside the house and around the perimeter. He edged his way closer to the side entrance and ducked low against a couple of garbage bins. He paused again for a breath and to listen to his surroundings. All he could hear was his own heart pounding through his chest. He heard it and felt it going like a jackhammer.

He tried to get his breathing under control, in through the nose, out through the mouth, to slow his heart rate down. It worked after a minute and he slowly reached his hand into his coat pocket and pulled out the pistol. He heard a sudden bang behind him and turned quickly throwing his back against the wall and ducking his head behind the garbage can. His heart leapt back into overdrive. He saw a scar riddled cat move sleekly away from the garbage. 'It was the cat that caused the bang' he realized. 'Maybe only I heard it'.

He waited another minute for any other noises, but there was nothing. He decided to make his move. Staying crouched down, he slithered over to the side entrance and tried the door knob. To his surprise, it opened easily. 'Someone must've forgotten to lock it' he thought.

As had been the case when he'd come to visit his father there as a child, he saw the chart on the wall that outlined the 'guest' names and room numbers. He saw McBride's name near the top of the list and found the room number attached to it. He heard slight murmuring from upstairs, but figured that was normal, 'someone watching TV' he guessed. He slowly ascended the stairs, trying to keep the noise from the creaking steps to a minimum. He made it all the way up and paused outside McBride's room. He leaned his ear close to the door to listen. The murmuring was definitely coming from his room, but he felt like it wasn't the TV. He swore he heard voices. Then he heard a loud thump, like a fist hitting a person's cheekbone. He knew the sound well. Someone was definitely in there, but he'd come too far to back out now he decided.

Danny took one last long deep breath and counted to three. Then he jumped to his feet and booted the door in with a loud bang and stormed into the room with the pistol raised.

He'd entered the room so quickly that the door had banged off the wall and slammed shut again behind him. He didn't say anything at first . . . not freeze or gotcha or anything. He just stared at the man's face that calmly turned to him when he barged into the room. It was a face he'd known well and thought about often, more often than he'd ever wanted to. It was his father's face, the Ghost, in the flesh, alive and well and standing in front of him. Danny felt his legs weaken, but he didn't buckle. His outstretched arm however did buckle under the weight of the pistol and the gravity of his discovery. He slowly lowered the pistol to his side, but kept his finger close to the trigger. His eyes moved down from his Father's face to his hands which were covered in blood and wrapped in a chain. The chain, he realized, was also caked in serum. He noticed a broad shadow in the darkness that eclipsed the rest of the room and knew it could only be McNulty. Then he looked behind his father to see Flynn McBride, tied to a chair, covered in blood and God knows what else.

One look at his target was all it took. Right away, he knew McBride would never live to see the light of tomorrow's sun. He wasn't sure what else he felt, the scene he encountered was unexpected and it was too troubling to comprehend in that moment.

Finally, Danny spoke. 'What are you doing Dad?' he said with a voice that sounded much younger than his thirty-plus years.

Billy Carson responded simply, 'I'm saving my son.'

'What?' Danny responded confused. 'Jim's dead Dad, you're too late.'

Billy shook his head. 'I have two sons Danny. I am too late for Jim, but not for you.' He stared into Danny's eyes long enough to see Danny realize what he was saying. 'Go home Danny . . . it's over now.' Billy said, and then he turned his back on his son and waited.

Danny was overcome with feelings too raw to understand. He stood for what felt like an eternity staring at his Father's back and beyond to the heap of bloody mess that sat before him. Finally, he felt the gun slip from his gloved hand and heard it thump against the hard floor. He slid his feet backwards towards the door and reached for the doorknob twisting it open behind him. He turned at last and stepped into the dim hallway and staggered down the stairs and out the side door from which he'd entered. Outside, the darkness engulfed him like a quilt as he made his way briskly into the night.

Alex Dumitru

'Mommy' the little girl with the dark curls asked her mother, 'Where do the bunkies live again?'

'They're not bunkies baby, they're my *bunici*. It's the Romanian word for grandparents. Alex explained to her daughter. 'They live in Romania, near Bucharest.'

'Buuukaaaressst' the little girl repeated. 'Is that in America?' she asked.

'No, it's not honey, it's a different country. They moved back to Romania years ago.'

'Oh' the little girl said, nodding as if it was all coming together for her. 'We need to take an aero plane to go there right?'

'Yes baby, we do.'

'We're on an aero plane now Mommy. Does that mean we are going to Buuukaaaressst?'

Alex laughed gently and rubbed her hand through her daughter's wild hair. 'No Theresa, not this time. This time we're going to Dublin. Remember I told you we're going to visit your Daddy's brother Danny.'

'Oh yeah, I remember now Mommy.' The girl said and hugged her doll close to her chest.

Alex smiled sadly. She knew the awkwardness Theresa felt whenever the subject of her Daddy came up. Alex had done what she could to try to explain to the girl who her Daddy was and why he wasn't around. There's only so much you can explain to a 4 year old, even one so seemingly intelligent as Theresa. Alex knew that this would only get more difficult when Theresa began going to real school and making friends, most of which would have two parents.

'Come on baby' she said 'I want you to lay close to me now and get some rest.' She opened up the blanket and draped it over the child. 'We should sleep now and it will be morning when we land.'

'And we'll see Uncle Danny then?' The girl asked.

'Yes baby, that's right. We'll see Danny then.'

THE END

GREEN WINGS TO EDEN

Prologue

Andrew watched the tall reeds behind the school dance
back and forth in the light summer breeze. He held a
regulation sized basketball in between hands that looked
too small for the rest of his body. Others in his grade had
already seen growth spurts stretch out their limbs and
began to speak in voices that cracked with early signs of
puberty. Andrew's voice however, still had a child's pitch
and his hands along with the rest of him still waited
eagerly for any signs of extension. His father assured him
that he'd also thin out his pudgy frame once he did grow
taller.

He bounced the basketball off the ground in front of his
feet, then stretched backwards extending his neck so that
he could see everything behind him though his vision in
that position showed everything upside down. He caught
sight of the backboard and rim and judged their distance,
then brought his head back right side up again. The blood

had rushed to his head and he took a few seconds to regain his balance. When the dizziness wore off, he spun the ball gently in his hands and bounced it another time.

'Shoot the ball already!' his friend Stevie's voice yelled from underneath the basket. Andrew straightened up and took in a long breath, then blew it out slowly. He shut his eyes for a moment and tried to picture where the rim and basket were behind him. Then, he sailed the ball backwards over his head. He opened his eyes and turned towards the hoop in time to see the ball clank hard off the top of the backboard and out of bounds to the left. 'Shoot' he said to himself and kicked at a small patch of sandy pebbles that gathered in a crack at his feet.

Stevie chased the ball down laughing, 'ah ha' he yelled, 'you missed. That makes you H.O.R. You're a whore Andrew!'

'Yeah yeah Stevie. Okay' Andrew said back. He hated playing HORSE with Stevie because he had a knack for making trick shots that were nearly impossible to replicate.

'Nice try Andrew.' Bernie said from the swing set on the other side of the chain link fence. 'What do you mean?' Stevie yelled to her. 'He didn't even hit the rim!'

Andrew watched Bernie smile at him, then she turned and stuck her tongue out at Stevie. Stevie looked around him first to make sure no grown-ups were around then held up his middle finger. 'Ooooh' Bernie said 'I hope Ms. Cranston saw you from the window.' Then she turned and ran around the large slide and disappeared to the other end of the playground. Stevie didn't bother responding and walked back over to Andrew on the basketball court. 'I think somebody likes you Andrew.'

'Who? Bernie? No she doesn't.' Andrew said. He felt his

face start to grow hot as he blushed. 'You're scared!' Stevie said and laughed. 'Just take your next shot Stevie, it's getting late.'

'Fine' he said and dribbled the ball to the top of the three-point line. He paused and judged the distance to the hoop, then walked further away to the edge of the court and turned towards the basket again. 'Okay! Underhanded from here!' he yelled to Andrew. 'That's all, nothing else.' Stevie crouched down low and held the ball with both hands between his knees. He jumped up from his low position and strained to bring his hands up with force to reach the basket. He let go of the ball sending it high in the air.

Andrew followed the ball from Stevie's hands into the air above his head then all the way to the rim. It hit the back of the rim and bounced away. He chased after the rebound and grabbed the ball before it rolled into the long grass and reeds beside the court.

He picked the ball up in two hands and started walking back towards the court. He noticed three people walking from the other side of the court approaching Stevie from the parking lot. He grew nervous at the sight of them. There was a tall boy in the center that wore a Red Sox hat pulled low with the rim curved so that it cut the ends of his eyebrows from view. The boy looked at least a couple years older than he and Stevie. Andrew thought he had to be at least thirteen or fourteen. He was book-ended by two smaller boys that looked closer to Andrew's age. Each wore plain white t-shirts and shorts. One of the smaller boys called out to Stevie. Stevie looked back at Andrew and shook his head slightly. Andrew guessed Stevie didn't know them either. They stopped in front of Stevie, but

Andrew was too far away to hear if they were saying anything. He was nervous, but headed over towards them anyway, afraid to leave Stevie by himself. He'd heard of kids from neighboring parks going around to other schoolyards and starting trouble. It was only a matter of time before some ended up at theirs. Andrew had never been in a fight, but had heard stories from his older brother and his friends about how things happened. Although, it was still unclear to him why it happened at all.

Andrew continued towards the group and could hear them laughing as he approached. It was a mocking laughter, one he'd heard a few times in the schoolyard. 'Look at his shoes' one of the smaller boys said to the others while pointing at Stevie's sneakers. 'Little poor boy, can't afford real shell-toes! Look, he's got four stripes!' Andrew felt a pang of anger. It was not the first time he'd heard someone pick on Stevie for how he looked. He seemed to draw insults often from other kids whose parents could afford things that Stevie's mother couldn't, like brand name sneakers. He looked over at Stevie. He wasn't saying anything back. Andrew could see Stevie's flaring nostrils take in air slowly and saw his eyes start to fill with moisture. He could feel his own heart beating rapidly in his chest and his vision started to fade in and out with red clouds forming in his periphery. 'Leave him alone!' he yelled. He could hear his own high pitched voice echo in the empty schoolyard. He wished his voice had come out deeper, but he couldn't control it. He watched as the three boys turned to him. The tall one with the baseball hat stepped closer to him. Andrew shifted his feet back slightly. 'What are you gonna do, you fat monkey?' the tall boy said. The two smaller boys broke out in laughter. Stevie slid back a couple feet so that he was shoulder to shoulder with Andrew.

'Why can't you just leave us alone?' Andrew said in a lower voice this time. The tall boy leaned in and said to Andrew, 'I was talking to your friend here, until you butted in. I saw him give that little girl the finger. I want to see him be a tough guy to me.'

'That was a joke!' Stevie pleaded. 'Bernie's our friend.' The tall boy stepped quickly towards Stevie and shot a hand out and smacked him in the face. Stevie fell backwards and struggled to get back to his feet. Andrew's vision faded in and out faster this time and the red from the edges ran quickly towards the center. He watched the tall boy turn and give each of the smaller boys high-fives. 'Go get them one of the hockey sticks.' The tall boy said. 'maybe then it'll be a fair fight.' Andrew fought to control his breathing, but couldn't any longer. He gripped the basketball in his hands tightly. He stepped forward and yelled 'Run Stevie!' Then he threw the basketball hard, a chest pass, right at the tall boy's face. The boy didn't expect it and it hit him square on the nose and blood shot out from his nostrils immediately.

Stevie took off running when Andrew yelled. After he threw the ball, Andrew took off behind him. Stevie had always been faster than Andrew and the head start meant he had already created distance between them. He saw Stevie look back at him. Andrew waved his hand forward twice yelling 'go!' as he did. Stevie had reached the side walk and turned left up the street. Andrew was barely at the edge of the parking lot and he could hear the footsteps and yells behind him gaining on him quickly. He was about to step off the curb when he felt a hand grab hold of his shirt. That same hand pushed him forward and with momentum carrying him already, he fell forward hard and slid across the cement. His palms and knees burned as they scraped across the hard gravel. When he stopped sliding, he rolled over onto his back. In less than a second the boys were upon him. He pulled his knees closer to his body and brought his arms up over his head and face. He could feel punches and kicks all over his body. Some hurt, like those that made it to his ribs or his face. Others, he felt the impact, but the pain didn't register. He tried looking up, but saw only a sea of fists flying at him. After that he kept his eyes shut. The pain seemed to fall into the background and his body grew numb. He felt slimy liquid crawl down his face that left a metallic taste in his mouth. He was starting to slip away, in and out of consciousness. He struggled to keep his arms up, but knew he had to keep his head covered. The fists and kicks kept coming. It felt like days had past as he lay there, crouching, trying to make his body tight. Then suddenly, he heard a 'thump'. Then it all stopped.

The punches and kicks stopped coming. He laid there still. He was afraid to open his eyes for fear of what he'd find. Perhaps the tall boy wanted to make him watch his own demise. He felt a hand lightly shake his shoulder and a familiar voice call out. 'Andrew. Andrew, you okay?' it asked. Andrew opened his eyes. The boys were gone. Stevie was crouched down next to him, rubbing his shoulder. Stevie took his t-shirt off and wiped down Andrew's face gently. 'Hold it tight against your cheek Andrew. You're bleeding.'

Andrew sat up slowly with Stevie's help. He felt around

his face and could tell his eyes and lips were swollen. 'I thought you got away?' he asked Stevie. 'I did get away.'

'But, you came back?'

'Of course I did Andrew. They caught you. I thought they were gonna kill you. They wouldn't stop hitting you.'

'Where'd they go? How'd you get them to stop?'

Stevie took a seat on the ground next to Andrew and held his hands back to keep himself upright. He looked around the parking lot before answering. 'They ran off after I hit the big kid.'

'You punched him?' Andrew asked.

Stevie shook his head no. 'No. I didn't punch him. I didn't think that would work. I hit him with a stickball bat. The two other boys stopped hitting you then. The big kid tried to get up and come after me, so I hit him again. I hit him in the head Andrew . . . the others then, they dragged him away.'

'Jesus Stevie . . . you saved me.'

Stevie patted Andrew on the back gently. 'You stuck up for me. You would've done the same if they caught me.'

Andrew thought about it for a minute. He wasn't sure if he'd have done exactly the same, he was afraid. The fear might have frozen him, but he couldn't know for sure. He just nodded to Stevie. Stevie stood, then helped Andrew get to his feet slowly.

Andrew stood and began to walk slowly, leaning on Stevie's shoulder for support. He noticed the sky started to darken. It was late and he hoped he wouldn't get in trouble for staying out past dinner time. Then he thought about how he looked. He was obviously beat up. He began praying silently that his father and brother weren't home. He knew if they saw him in the condition he was now, they'd both drag him out to scour the streets for the boys that did it. All he wanted to do was get cleaned up and go to bed. They crossed the street and headed in the direction of Andrew's house. 'Where did you find the stickball bat?' Andrew asked Stevie after a couple minutes. 'It was leaning against the fence next to the playground.' Stevie answered. 'I saw it when I ran back to the parking lot.' 'Lucky for me.' Andrew said. 'Yeah, but not for that big kid.' Stevie said.

They didn't say much the rest of the walk to Andrew's house. When they reached the block before his, Andrew could sense Stevie's question coming. At least three or four nights a week during the summer Stevie would hint around or just flat out ask Andrew if he could ask his parents to let him stay the night. He never wanted to go home it seemed. Andrew didn't mind, but he could tell it irritated his parents sometimes, especially his father for some reason. It got to the stage that most of the time, Andrew would just go inside and pretend to ask his parents, then come out and tell Stevie that they said 'not tonight.' However, after Stevie had saved his life pretty much, he felt he owed him enough to actually ask his mother this time.

Stevie and Andrew walked into the house together. When Andrew's mother saw them first, she was obviously upset at Andrew's appearance and let both boys know it. She calmed after a minute however and went and got Stevie a spare t shirt and pair of shorts to change into. Then she took Andrew into the bathroom and washed down his face and cleaned his cuts with peroxide. Stevie waited in the living room and watched television.

'Who did this to you Andrew?' She asked several times,

but Andrew kept telling her that it was three boys, but he didn't know them, which was true. She finally gave up asking, but said, 'You're very lucky your father isn't home. Best stay out of his sight until the morning, or else he'll have you all around the city tonight hunting for these boys.' 'I know Mum' was all he could say. 'Do you mind if Stevie stays over tonight?' he asked. His mother finished dabbing his cuts with peroxide on a cotton ball and threw the cotton, now covered in blood, into the trash bin. 'Again Andrew?' she asked.

'I know Ma, but he did risk his neck for me today. Maybe next time I can stay at his house.'

His mother grabbed his shoulders firmly with both hands and looked straight at Andrew. She said in a hushed voice, 'He can stay tonight Andrew. But listen, I don't want you going over to Stevie's house. And I especially don't want you staying overnight there do you hear me?'

Andrew stared back at her and just nodded his head. 'Yeah, fine, okay Mum, but . . . why?' he asked. 'Just promise me you won't . . . someday you'll understand.' She answered. Andrew didn't know how to respond. He didn't know what she meant or why it mattered so much to her. He felt awkward all of a sudden and grew claustrophobic in the small bathroom. 'Fine.' He said.

He got up and walked out of the bathroom into the narrow hallway towards the living room. Outside the living room he stood in front of a mirror that hung at eye level on the wall. He squinted to look at his reflection using the dim light from the television. His face looked clean now, but his eyes and lips were both swollen badly. He thought he could already see a bruise forming around the outside of his left eye, all the way down the left side of his face. He looked away from the mirror and walked into the living room. 'You can stay over tonight Stevie' he said. There was no response. He saw the television flashing in the background with a sports highlight show playing. The television's volume was turned all the way down. He walked over to the set and switched it off. He looked down at the couch, which had Stevie stretched out across it, already lightly snoring in a deep sleep. Andrew stretched out the blanket that draped over the end of the couch and pulled it over Stevie's feet and up to his torso. 'Goodnight Stevie' he said softly, then reached behind the couch and switched off the last remaining lamp in the room.

1

Andrew Dawson sat in his truck listening to sports talk radio. Every weekday for years he sat in that very spot, struggling to keep his eyes open, waiting for his best friend, Stevie Black, to show up. They drove to work together every day. The meeting spot was always the same, the small front parking lot of West Elm Variety, a convenience store on a side street off of Wollaston Beach. The meeting time was always the same too, six thirty am. Although Stevie's zest for spontaneity often dictated exactly the time they met, sometimes earlier, but mostly later, unless it was pay day. The promise of a pay check always got Stevie out of bed before the alarm clock went off. West Elm Variety was the midpoint between Andrew and Stevie's childhood homes. It's where they met every morning before walking to school together. After high school, both men went to work as apprentice carpenters for the same company. They hung on to the habit of meeting outside the store, even though neither lived in his childhood home any longer.

Andrew waited patiently in his old Ford pickup truck. His eyes watered and nose was dried up from the defrost pumping hot air relentlessly at his face. Every time he turned it down, he struggled to fight off the chill that quickly settled in his bones. The cold air was let in by the rickety old truck's loose insulation. Also, the windscreen seemed to steam up immediately once the dial was turned off. The truck was weighted down with racks in the back and a retro-fitted lock box for tools, plus a solid foot of wet snow that had fallen overnight. Despite his six foot two,

two-hundred and thirty pound frame, Andrew never did grow accustomed to fifty hour weeks of physical labor. The toll his body had taken in his short career made him feel double his age.

He reached into the center cup holder and picked up a pill bottle. He held it up to the windscreen towards the street lights and gave it a shake to see if he could count how many pills remained. After a recent slip from a ladder that resulted in a pulled back muscle, a doctor prescribed him some high dosage Ibuprofen. He was nearly through his final refill, but the pain had yet to subside. The clock above his tape deck showed six forty-nine am. Andrew checked his phone to confirm. 'Yup, almost twenty minutes late, come on Stevie' he said to himself. Outside, the sky was still a charcoal grey and the snow remained steady, looking like specs of volcanic ash in contrast to the dim early day light. Andrew's Ford was the lone vehicle in the front lot, but he was surprised to see a slow trickle of pedestrians enter and exit the store in the last twenty minutes, each time hearing the chime of the door's bell faintly through the noise of the heat and the sound of the engine.

To give his tearing eyes a rest, he reached over and switched the heat off, slightly unnerved by the sudden silence once the monotonous hum was broken. He tried to breathe slowly so his windows wouldn't fog up, but within a minute the condensation blocked his view through the windscreen. He ducked his head and reached under the passenger seat for a sponge that he kept to wipe down the windows. When he finally got his hand on it, he stretched over the steering wheel and ran it across the windscreen. When his line of sight was cleared, something strange caught his eye inside the store. From the outside it looked like there was an animated conversation going on between the customer and the clerk. The clerk was a man Andrew grew up with called Chef Benson. Andrew cleared more of the window quickly with both hands now and peered through the glass. The customer wore a wool hat pulled low and a hooded sweatshirt. He was clearly pointing to something repeatedly, which appeared to be the register. Chef was only slightly visible from the street. Most of his frame was hidden behind promotional signs for Bud Light thirty packs plastered on the window. From what Andrew could see, he looked to be shaking his head frantically as if saying no.

Andrew's hands gripped the steering wheel tightly and without realizing, he'd pulled his body off the seat, tighter to the dash, his chest nearly resting at the wheel's twelve o'clock. He saw the customer lunge forward over the counter towards Chef, swinging at him with his right hand in a closed fist. Chef tried to jump back, but with limited space behind the counter, he couldn't move out of the way and the punch landed square on his temple. Andrew saw him fall to the ground. The thief then jumped forward again, this time reaching over the counter, for what Andrew assumed was the cash register. He pulled back his arm and his hand carried a fist full of bills. The man stuffed his hands into the pockets of his hoodie and turned and ran out of the front door.

Outside the door, the man paused at the top of the steps, startled to see Andrew standing in the parking lot staring at him. From instinct, Andrew had opened his door and jumped down from the truck to the pavement. Both men stopped in his tracks as they made eye contact with one another. They stood staring in silence for a few seconds, looking like a paused video game. Finally, the thief made a step towards the stairs only to quickly change direction and shoot the other way down the handicapped ramp. Andrew bit on the fake and slipped on the slushy ground when he tried to recover and change direction. The thief quickly made it down the ramp and with Andrew down in a pile of wet snow and slush, used the truck for leverage. He ran quickly around the truck bed and took off running towards Wollaston Beach.

Andrew got up clumsily and started in an attempted sprint after the man. As he did, he heard Chef Benson calling after him from outside the store. Andrew's feet moved as quickly as possible, pounding furiously through the snow on the un-shoveled sidewalk. He jumped off the curb and onto the street, which was slightly improved thanks to the early morning snow plows. He continued running through the street and after a final sprint towards the corner, he slid to a stop as if on ice skates. He looked across Quincy Shore Drive to the beach wall, unwilling to risk life and limb by darting aimlessly across the busy street. He pulled his wool hat off and looked left down the street, then right, searching in the distance for any sign of the thief or his footsteps. He saw nothing but white flakes in each direction as the snow continued to fall steadily like a shaken snow globe. He looked to the sky and let a couple flakes fall on his tongue before leaning forward with his hands on his knees while trying to slow his breathing and assess the level of pain now bursting from his back.

Andrew turned away from the beach after catching his breath for a minute and began a slow trod back down the street towards his truck. His walk was slow and deliberate with the piercing pain coming from his back muscles. Every step carried with it chronic discomfort. His hair had gotten wet with sweat from the run and mixed with the heavy snow flakes that continued to fall relentlessly. He shivered from the cold and put his wool hat back on his head as he trudged through the mess. He stared down the road surprised at the distance he had covered in his sprint. Through the peppering snow he saw a truck's familiar grill and headlights accompanied by its laboring engine. As the truck grew near, it grew more familiar as well. When it pulled to a stop next to him, Andrew shook his head at the driver in disapproval. 'Stevie' he said, 'I thought I was clear on my ground rules. You're not to drive my truck except for in cases of extreme emergencies.' Stevie had reached across the passenger seat to push the door open and heard him clearly. 'Listen guy, just be glad it's me driving this piece of shit.' Stevie answered, 'Who leaves their frigin car running anymore? You're lucky it's shitty out, this thing was a sitting duck outside the store. Forget unlocked, the damn door was wide open and the keys were in it. What's wrong with you?'

Andrew walked tenderly into the street, trying to keep his balance while stepping down from the curb to the glazed pavement. He reach the passenger door and pulled it open further. He lifted himself up onto the seat, grimacing in pain as he did.

Stevie noticed his change in facial expression and asked, 'Back still at you?'

'Yeah, a little. I think I might've tweaked it running down the street after that guy.'

'Well, serves you right chasing after school kids you creep.'

'Fuck you Stevie, I witnessed a robbery for chrissakes. I was chasing after the guy.'

'Yeah, I know' Stevie said 'I saw you take off down the street and Benson filled me in briefly as he made my coffee.' Stevie reached down and pulled up a white Styrofoam cup and held it to his lips, blowing gently at the steam coming out of the top as he did.

'You bastard' Andrew said 'you stopped for coffee when I was trying to make a citizen's arrest? What if I caught the dude and he had a weapon or something?'

Stevie took a delicate sip from the hot cup, then looked over back at Andrew. 'Seems like something you should've considered before you ran after him huh?'

Andrew just shrugged in reluctant agreement. 'Yeah you're probably right. But, still man.'

'Don't worry' Stevie answered as he finally put the truck back into drive and slowly rolled forward. 'You weren't ever going to catch that guy. That dude was a vampire man. He was all whacked out. You were running through that thick snow, he might as well have been floating across it. Plus, you ain't exactly known for your foot speed.'

Andrew just rolled his eyes and sat back into the passenger seat, willing to let Stevie drive since the pain in his back limited his reaction time anyway. 'Which I'd need in this weather' he thought. Although he began to reconsider as the unmistakeable waft of stale booze crept past his nostrils once the windows were up and doors were closed. 'You out somewhere last night Stevie?' he asked nervously while trying to sound casual. He wanted to avoid Stevie getting defensive, 'a mode he seemed to default to these days' Andrew thought.

'Might've been. Why, who's asking, my priest?'

'Nah man, just uh . . . making conversation that's all. But man, I hate to break it to you, you are giving off a werewolf scent.' Andrew answered and smiled trying to keep the inquisition light. 'You're cool to drive though right? Last thing we need is a DUI between us.'

Stevie's face flashed with irritation, much like that of a child being reminded of his homework. 'I'm perfect Andrew.' He answered 'You want me to pull over or something? Last thing I want is to crash your piece of shit truck.'

The air between the two men grew stale quickly. This was also becoming common place on their journeys to work and usually led to neither speaking to the other, at least not until boredom took its toll, which generally meant by lunchtime. Andrew decided to back down and try to salvage peace for the long day ahead of them. 'No Stevie, keep driving, you got it. Sorry I even brought it up.'

Stevie said nothing else in reply and seemed to just focus on the road. Andrew noticed his grip on the steering wheel tighten ever so slightly. He glanced up at Stevie's face trying not to be noticed while staring. He thought about the distance between them that seemed to develop out of nowhere in recent months, 'Maybe it was even longer than that' he considered, like a virus that had laid dormant and imperceptible until it was too late. 'Nah' he thought after a minute 'It's just a bad patch, even the closest of friends can get sick of each other. It's probably just over exposure.'

Andrew's thoughts drifted away from Stevie as he cleared the fog from his window with his sleeve. He watched the snow as it continued falling. It had gotten heavier than before and seemed to be mixing now with rain as the temperature started to rise with daybreak. He began to focus on the eight hours of work ahead of him. He felt dread thinking about the coldness that would embed itself into him by dinner time. With that thought he switched the heat back on high to let the noise from the radiator drum out his thoughts and laid his head back and shut his eyes to rest before facing the day.

2

Working on a house in South Boston was like the carpenter's equivalent of getting a grenade handed to you with the pin already pulled. For starters, the houses were either attached or at least too close together. That meant any job that involved outside work, had you wedged between buildings like a dinosaur trying to walk through the Gothic District in Barcelona. While any inside renovation had you equally cramped into spaces built for under-nourished nineteenth century immigrants. Add to the mix the steep staircases and snow falling outside and Andrew could barely move his limbs by the end of his day, let alone drive home.

His morning consisted of replacing windows on every floor of the narrow four-story town house, while the afternoon had him hanging vinyl siding in the crevice that was the side of the house. By the end of the day, every inch of his body ached and his hands burned from the over exposure to the wet snow and cold wind that swept through the alleyway. At home, he let the hot shower rain over him for twenty minutes. His skin flushed with red and stung with pain afterwards, but he felt it was worth it to rid the cold from his bones.

Andrew's apartment was small, but it was tidy. His bedroom seemed spacious, but that had more to do with his lack of furniture than the actual size of the room. There was a spare bedroom, but it looked more like a walk-in closet with a futon in it. His visitors were scarcely overnight guests. The living room was small, but functional with a basic couch and old television that echoed that same sentiment. His kitchen was what realtors called a kitchenette, but more realistically should be described as a closet with an oven in it.

Andrew dried off in the bathroom and got dressed in the spare room that housed most of his clean clothes. His laundry always got washed and dried, but for some reason he could never find the time, energy or inclination to put it away.

He took his time getting ready. He felt exhausted from the week's work and although he managed to shake off the chill from earlier, his face and hands still suffered from chaffing due to the unseasonable cold that plagued the east coast. He put on his best pair of going-out jeans and found a button-down shirt that didn't need ironing. He hadn't bothered to shave that morning, but usually he kept the grizzled look anyway, which he always felt took a few pounds off his face. He pulled out all the stops for his hair, broke out the expensive pomade that left a slightly slick shine through his dark mane. Lastly he gave his shirt and neck a mist of cologne before pulling on a brown pair of boots and grabbing his jacket.

He walked down his steps and outside to his truck. He put the keys into the driver-side door to unlock it, feeling awkward, even without an audience, a man trying to be spruced up, yet walking into a beat up old pickup. He imagined the sight of him dressed in his going out attire standing next to his sad truck was on par with putting cologne on a pig.

He slid into the driver's seat and started up the old Ford. The snow had stopped falling during the day and the evening was bright, which seemed to hasten the return of spring. The streets throughout the day also melted, but the road salt lingered, wreaking havoc on the undercarriage of unsuspecting automobiles, its presence on the road now at odds with the balmy evening.

Andrew's hands burned from splits that developed while working outside in the cold. He loosened his grip on the steering wheel to ease the pain that accompanied the cracks around his fingernails. Also, his back had continued to ache, surely exacerbated by the day's physical labor. When he got home from work, he wanted so badly to stay there in his apartment, shower, get the sweats on and just watch TV. However, Stevie had mentioned earlier that day that Bernadette was planning to be around that night.

All throughout high school and for the first few years afterwards, Bernadette had been his girlfriend. They were on again, off again, but for the most part during that time, they were together. She had been his first love and he was hers, at least he had hoped he was. In fact, Andrew knew she was the only girl he had ever loved. There was no one before and had been no one really after. He'd gone out with a few woman since, but no one consistent and no one that tugged at his heart strings like she did.

At times, he felt that he was under a spell, as if cupid himself followed him around and shot arrows in his ass every time he saw her. She was beyond gorgeous, especially in his eyes, though he never needed to ask anyone else's opinion. She looked like no one else he'd ever encountered, at least not in person. Her hair was red, well, more strawberry blonde, and her eyes were a dark blue. Her skin was fair, but seemed to always have a hint of color and her freckles, although faint, were unmistakable. Since the first time he laid eyes on her, he felt a stirring in his stomach whenever she was near. 'I can't even believe she was mine for years' Andrew thought, not in a sense that he owned her, but in a way they were connected, a ying to Andrew's yang.

As young love often did, theirs had grown apart over time. Once so connected and invested in each other, their lives both came to a point where it made sense to move on. She wanted to try somewhere new, a fresh start, so she went away to college. Andrew knew he couldn't live with himself if he'd held her back. Plus, after high school he ran into hard times with family issues, ones that he still couldn't bear to confront.

Bernadette went to Syracuse in New York. It wasn't a million miles away, but it was far enough. Eventually after school, she did move back to Massachusetts, but not Quincy. She moved in with a young business man from Philadelphia, to his house in a town called Boxford. It was a small town miles outside of Boston, almost in New Hampshire. Andrew had looked the place up when he'd heard. It was a tiny place north of Boston with less than ten thousand people. All he knew of it was that it was formerly farmland and it still had cows there. He'd heard it was nice and peaceful, it sounded so anyway.

Since then, her visits back to Quincy were not very frequent, and they were usually on Sundays just to visit her parents. The odd time she'd appear on a Friday or Saturday night in their local bar, Mackin's Saloon, or down in Marina Bay during the summer. If Andrew heard only after the fact that she was around and he'd missed her, he'd be miserable for weeks. Luckily Stevie saw a post on Facebook during the day and mentioned to him that she might be around that night. So Andrew, who originally just wanted his bed, decided to go out, just in case she was around. Time had passed and they were no longer an item, but there was still something between them, a flicker of hope maybe. Andrew felt it at least. He hoped he wasn't the only one.

3

Mackin's Saloon was a neighborhood bar. The small building sat on a street corner at the bottom of a residential hill that ran into a main street leading to the highway. Its location was outside of the town center, which lended to its reputation of a locals bar. It was enough out of the way that no one really went there by accident. The heavy wooden door at the entrance looked like some antique piece of drawbridge pulled from a castle's ruins. Inside that herculean door was an Irish bar in the purest sense, not made to look like one, but one which others would later be fashioned. The floors had to be changed every few years due to the foot traffic, and the drop ceiling had to be replaced after the smoking ban came into effect. However, everything else pretty much withstood the test of time.

Andrew liked the place because he could always rest assured he'd run into friends there or at least like-minded strangers he could blow off steam with. Plus, the first round on Fridays was on the house for regulars and the Guinness was probably as good as you'd find outside of Ireland.

Andrew walked in well after dark without fanfare. The doorman welcomed him with a nod to say 'you're all set' and he walked into the bar, slowly taking in his surroundings. He was looking for familiar faces, mainly Bernadette's. 'Way too overzealous' he thought 'no way she'd be in this early.' Andrew smiled and waved to the bartender and pointed to the Guinness taps with his index finger. She nodded in understanding and mouthed 'I'll bring it over.'

Despite a solid layering of people at the bar, the tables were mainly empty. Andrew grabbed a small round table in the center of the bar with a clear view to both the television, which had the Bruins games on, and the front door. The bartender brought his Guinness over after a few minutes. When she placed it down Andrew thanked her quickly, then watched as the foam within the glass finally settled to a perfect black with a fully formed white head.

He sipped away slowly, wanting to pace himself to keep his wits intact. It was hard to do however as he sat alone flicking his eyes constantly in a pendulum swing from the Bruins game on TV to down at his dust covered smart phone, a new model that was already speckled white with drywall dust. 'What's the point in buying anything new' he thought as he attempted to rub away the debris from the screen.

During the third period of the game, finally a familiar face walked through the door. It wasn't Bernadette, not even close, but it was someone who might talk to him for a while and take his mind off the waiting. Chef Benson owned the convenient store on West Elm Avenue. Andrew had seen him get whacked in the head just that morning 'though it felt like weeks ago after the day I had' he thought. Chef walked in with his head on a swivel, by himself, quite obviously looking for beer and a chat. Andrew knew him growing up as Mike, but over the years he'd picked up the nickname 'Chef'. Andrew wasn't sure exactly where he got it, but expected its origin was as murky as it was random since to his knowledge, Mike Benson wasn't known for his prowess in the kitchen. He was just south of average in height, but kept in good shape. His hair was always neatly combed, and his face was always smiling. Andrew wasn't sure if it was part of his persona as a local business owner, or if he was just genuinely happy, but it made him easy to like all the same. Andrew knew him mostly just from the store, mainly just small talk or waving hello in the mornings, but they had hung out a few times over the years. Andrew made a point to keep his eyes up and be noticeable. He made eye contact with Chef followed by a wave as he walked further into the bar room.

Andrew nodded another hello and pointed with his open hand over to a chair at his table in a gesture that asked 'join me?' Chef nodded in the affirmative and headed towards the table, but not before dropping a ten dollar bill on the bar and placing an order. He walked over then, with a bottle of Bud light in this left hand. He held out his right to shake hands as he got closer and Andrew did the same. Close up, Andrew noticed a slight bruise on Chef's temple where he'd been clipped that very morning.

'How's it going Chef?' Andrew asked 'Hope you put some ice to that' he said and pointed to Chef's temple.

'Hey Dawson' Chef answered 'Yeah, well I threw a bag of peas on it for a while this morning. It's fine though, stunned me for a second that's all, but he didn't get me that good.'

'It looked like a clean enough connection. Well, from outside it did anyway.'

'Yeah, well it definitely did hurt at the time. Hey, by the way, thanks for trying to chase after the guy for me. I was calling out to you from the store. I didn't want you to go to the trouble.' Chef said.

'Don't worry about it' Andrew answered 'Sorry I let him get away.'

Chef shook his head 'No problem man. I didn't want you to chase him cause I knew who it was anyway. Actually the cops picked him up later this morning.'

'No kidding? Who was it?' Andrew asked

'Actually a cousin of mine if you can believe it. Imagine that? Trying to rip off your own family like that?'

'No I can't actually' Andrew answered 'Sounds pretty low, sorry to say.'

'Yeah it was' Chef agreed 'Kid used to be alright, but he fell into hanging with the wrong crowd. I know that's what everyone says, but I feel like it's true for him. He got caught up with some of those dudes that hang around with John Bishop's crew. Have you heard of him? Bad dude by most accounts.'

Andrew shuttered with what could only be disgust at the mention of Bishop's name. 'Yeah, I know who he is' was all Andrew said.

'Well you know then.' Chef explained 'It's the same old story. My cousin started hanging around them, then next thing you know he's hooked on heroin and rolling over his cousin's convenient store for petty cash.'

Andrew nodded, 'Yeah, I know the type anyway.'

The bartender walked back over to the table again and put down another pint. She smiled and then backed away slowly. 'That from you?' Andrew asked Chef.

'Yeah man, cheers, least I could do after you tried to help.'

'Cheers' Andrew said and raised his glass slightly in thanks. 'Not a big deal really.'

'Hope you don't mind man' Chef continued, 'I gave the

cops your name when they showed up, just in case they needed a witness.'

'No problem. They know how to reach me?' Andrew asked

'Yeah I'm guessing they do. Hey speaking of which, why'd you guys take off so quick? The cops that showed up were hoping to talk to you on the spot. They waited for a while, but took off eventually.'

'Huh, yeah, it occurred to me actually.' Andrew said 'I guess when Stevie picked me up in my truck I just forgot and we headed off to work.'

'Stevie Black right?' Chef asked

'Yeah, you know him I'm sure, went to high school with us.'

'Yeah of course I do. He was kind of weird this morning actually, walked in real nonchalant, but very quick and got me to pour him a coffee. When I mentioned the cops were on their way, he just said that he figured as much, then paid and took off in your truck. I thought it was awkward. Kinda thought he'd pass the word to you to wait around.'

'Stevie can be like that sometimes. He's been on edge lately for some reason. To be honest, I smelled booze off him when he picked me up, so maybe that's why he bounced, I don't know.'

Chef shrugged in reluctant agreement, seemingly not convinced. 'Yeah, could be I guess. So anyway, don't be surprised to hear from them at some point.'

'Whenever man. Whatever I can do.' He answered then thought to himself, 'Especially if it in some way impacts John Bishop. And definitely if it hurts him.'

John Bishop had a reputation in the neighborhood as

someone to avoid at all costs. It was known that most of the drugs that found their way into Quincy and the surrounding area's streets passed through his hands first. The dirty money that accompanied it was cleaned through any number of local businesses that Bishop either owned or controlled. Andrew knew John Bishop well. He knew him better than probably anyone else. Unlike everyone else however, who whispered Bishop's name in either fear or reverence, anytime that name came across his lips he breathed it out with dragon fire.

Before the drugs, easy money, and reputation, John Bishop was just Johnny. He was a local kid who happened to be a best friend to Brian Dawson, Brian was Andrew's older brother. Bishop and Brian Dawson played in the same sandbox. They were friends since basically birth and remained best friends for a lifetime after that. Seven years his junior, Andrew spent much of his youth following behind or being bossed around by his brother Brian and by extension, John Bishop. Andrew went through his entire adolescence idolizing his brother and Bishop. He wanted to be like both of them in the worst way. He wanted to be noticed by them even more than that.

Hindsight is twenty-twenty, especially in this case. Whenever Andrew thought back to his early teen years and ran through those memories, he could spot the changes in Bishop like they appeared in slow motion. The rumors of Bishop's fist fights and other violent behavior became more and more frequent as Andrew reached high school. He could hear almost verbatim the words of warning accompanied by tears from his mother as she pleaded with her oldest son to break away from his friend. Andrew wasn't always clear on what she was upset about, but he felt the emotion in her tone even if her voice was muffled through walls and closed doors, not to mention the strengthening of her Irish accent that greatly intensified when she grew upset.

Eventually his brother did heed her advice to leave Bishop behind. Unfortunately he did so in a way that crushed his mother and brother greatly. He joined up. He enlisted in the military and within a year found himself on a Navy battleship in the Persian Gulf during the Iraq war. By the time he left the Navy and returned home Andrew had grown into a man. At 17, he was a young man, but a man nonetheless. Unfortunately, also by that time, the rumors of drunkenness and fights involving John Bishop were replaced by whispers of drug connections, money, power and more extreme displays of violence. Much to Andrew and his mother's dismay, Brian Dawson and John Bishop's friendship lasted the distance a war put between them and upon his return, they were quick to reconnect.

The Bruins game ended just before ten o'clock with a one-goal game going in Boston's favor. Andrew was glad to have Chef Benson sit with him, even if they did just watch the game and not say much. When the final buzzer rang, Andrew shifted in his chair poised to run for the men's room since he'd been holding in a piss while waiting for a whistle. As he stepped off the stool he caught a breaking news announcement flash on the TV screen from the corner of his eye. The screen then showed two young, sun-kissed and well-dressed news anchors. It wasn't the plastic former beauty queen that caught Andrew's eye however, it was the news headline that rolled across the bottom of the screen. It read, 'missing

Quincy woman found dead.'

'What happened there?' Andrew asked Chef Benson, while pointing up at the TV screen. Chef turned towards the television. When he read the headline he shook his head sadly. 'That's terrible man. I can't believe she was found dead.'

'I hadn't heard anyone was missing' Andrew answered.

'Yeah, well, you hear a lot of news and gossip behind the counter of a neighborhood store.

'I guess so. Who was she anyway? Did you know her?' Andrew asked.

'Yeah man, shit you're way out of the loop. You know her too. It's Gina O'Neil, she graduated with us.'

Andrew's eyes widened in surprise. 'Fuck' he muttered. 'Yeah I knew her well actually.' His mind lingered back to a young girl he knew years ago. He thought of her short brown hair that used to curl inwards towards her face and partially cover cute dimples. 'She hung around with us a bit. I haven't seen her in a long time though. What's that make then, three girls in three years?'

'More like three girls found dead in less than two years I think. I don't know what the hell happened to this place. I don't remember it ever being that dangerous.'

'It can't be random though can it? I mean . . . that's way too big of a coincidence. For fucksake they all went to the same high school and all about the same age.' Andrew said.

'Tell me about it' Chef said, 'It's fucking sick, that's what it is.'

'I wonder if they have any suspects.'

Chef leaned in closer towards the middle of the table before replying. 'You see that dude over there?' Chef asked, and nodded with his eyes and a slight lift of his chin towards the corner of the bar closest to the front door.

Andrew had matched Chef's lean forward with one of his own, then shifted slowly to peer through a group of people standing at a table that blocked his view of the bar. He noticed a well-dressed black man in his mid-to-late thirties talking quietly with the bar's owner while slowly scanning the room. Andrew looked back at Chef, just missing eye contact with the man.

'The black dude? What . . . is he a suspect?'

Chef shook his head no. 'No man, he's the police. He's a homicide detective with the Staties.'

'He looks really familiar' Andrew said.

'Yeah, he should. He's from here. Pretty sure he was a running back at Quincy high in his day. I think he still helps out with some of the coaching.

'You seem to know a lot about him Chef.'

'He's a customer, so he's in the store a few times a week. It's part of the job to small talk. Like I said before, plenty of gossip, I do very little beyond shooting the shit all day in that place. After a while you get to know people, especially in this city. Everyone knows everyone around here.'

'Yeah I guess so.' Andrew agreed. 'Still, what's he doing here? He doesn't look like a regular, he's in too good shape to hang out at a bar.'

'Yeah, well, like I said, he's from the area. I imagine he knows the Mackins. Plus . . . maybe he has a suspect in mind.'

Andrew felt a shiver run up his spine when he realized what Chef was suggesting. 'You think he's looking for someone in here?' he asked.

'Hey, I don't know man' Chef answered 'I'm just speculating, probably same as everyone else. Only thing I know is three girls are gone in two years, all from the city of presidents?'

'Yeah, I guess so Chef. Still, it's creepy as fuck to think about it.'

'It is definitely. It's surreal alright, but I wouldn't be surprised to hear it's a local dude doing this. That's all I'm saying.'

4

Andrew left Chef in Mackin's a short while later. He decided to leave his truck in the back behind the bar and walk home instead. The night actually grew warmer and more pleasant the later it got, the snow from that morning became a distant memory.

He walked steadily home, not rushing, but not strolling either. It was a good thirty minute walk back to his apartment, which was normally plenty of time to clear his head. Most nights it was, but not that night. He'd had a long day . . . a very long day. He was upset that Bernadette never showed up, but that drifted to the back of his mind for the moment, overshadowed by those three girls kidnapped and found dead. All were girls he knew pretty well in years past. 'God, even Gina O'Neil' he thought. 'He felt sad for her family, although he knew deep down, despite the sorrow, it meant very little to his day to day life. Gina had been a friend. In fact, there was a time he thought of her as a good friend, but that had long since passed and they were no longer in touch. He probably would've gone the remainder of his life without a single thought in her direction. He was pretty sure they weren't even Facebook friends. Maybe it was just human nature to be able to block out things that didn't impact your daily life. Perhaps it was some internal, instinctive defense mechanism allowing humans to wake up every day and keep moving forward despite all the shit that's wrong with the world. Logically it even made sense to let some things go in the background. Otherwise, each day there could be reasons to get upset. People could walk around with a permanent dread looming over them.

That's not much of a life if that's the case. Most people want to just live their lives and be left the hell alone. 'If only it were that simple' Andrew thought 'If only the world and people in it had the capacity to live and let live. Unfortunately badness knows no bounds and the world has plenty of it, whether it's obvious or lays dormant in wait. It permeates mankind, taking host in every dark shadowed corner of the world. Look at the Catholic Church for fucksake' he thought, 'if only that were an extreme example, but it's really not.' Evil could be more subtle too, invisible much of the time only to rear its head at opportune moments through some influence or even mere suggestion.

Andrew felt it was this subtle, slow and deliberate evil that chipped away at his brother until it eventually overcame him. He knew intellectually that his brother's downfall and death was not as black and white as he made it out to be. There were several factors and twists of fate at play. Instinctively though he blamed John Bishop. No one ever said pain and grief had to be rational. John Bishop was evil incarnate as far as Andrew was concerned. He was the lowest of the low, the personification of subtle badness. He was the driving force behind the current drug epidemic in the area. Surely if there was no Bishop, there'd be someone else driving it, there always is. But, there is a John Bishop, so in Andrew's eyes it's all on him. Andrew shook his head hoping to cast away his train of thought. Always, his mind went back to his brother Brian, and all dark roads in his head led to John Bishop.

'God, what happened to me?' he asked himself out loud as he walked. 'I swear I use to smile. I use to laugh even.'

He dug his hands into his pockets and picked up his

pace as he turned a corner and headed up a steep hill that led to his apartment. 'It's been a long day that's all' he thought 'And Bernie didn't even show up. I'll be better tomorrow.'

His legs started to ache along with his back again as he climbed the hill towards his apartment. He made it to the side steps off the driveway. It was dark, near blackout on his porch, and it was quiet. The neighbors had all gone to bed, and the night was still except for the sound of water steadily dripping down the loose drain pipe that hung on its last remaining hinge. 'I'll have to mention that to the landlord before spring arrives and it keeps me up all night with the windows open.' He thought.

He reached the top step and the porch light came on suddenly and blinded him momentarily. Startled, he shifted quickly to his left dragging his right foot back to brace his weight. His vision cleared up quickly when his eyes adjusted to the light. He smiled at his intruder and settled his fighting stance down, bringing his hands back down to his sides with it.

'Something must have you on edge.' Bernadette said with a smile. 'I thought for a second you were going to attack me.'

'Jesus Christ Bernie,' he answered while letting out a breath he noticed he'd been holding. 'I very nearly did. You really know how to get a guy's heart rate up.'

'I try, thanks.' She said smiling.

'Don't thank me, I'll invoice you my medical bill. Shit you nearly gave me a heart attack.'

Andrew took a step back and looked Bernadette over. She had startled him and with good reason. 'Why was she here?' he thought. 'Of all places, she stakes out my porch.

This is either really good or really bad.' Something instinctive told him it was more likely the latter.

She was dressed in skinny jeans with boots and a navy overcoat. She wore a hat as well, also navy, a cross between a beret and something a sailor might wear during the winter. Strands of her red hair crept out from under the hat and dangled fashionably around her face. Despite the rise in temperature, it was still brisk for the season, which showed on her flushed cheeks. 'She must've been here for quite some time' Andrew figured 'waiting in the cold for me. This doesn't feel right.'

After staring at her for what seemed an eternity, Andrew finally realized he hadn't asked her in. 'You must be cold' he said 'Do you want to come inside?'

Bernadette looked up, her blue eyes glistening in the moonlight. She slid over on the bench where she was sitting and motioned with her hand for him to join her. 'Let's sit out here for a while. It's nice out finally.'

Andrew shrugged slightly, then eased onto the bench next to her. She must have noticed his gingerly approach and gave him a look of concern. 'Your back still hurting you these days?' she asked.

'It's fine' Andrew answered 'Just tweaked it this morning again, that's all.'

'Maybe it's time to find a desk job ya think?' You'll be older than your years if you keep it up.'

'I don't see me lasting long or doing much good with a pencil or sitting behind a computer screen, but I get your point. Maybe I should've listened to my mother and went to college.'

'It's not too late for that Andrew. You know how many people go back to school these days? And I mean much older than you.'

'Maybe . . . probably not though. I still kick around joining up though. Maybe Army, maybe Navy.'

She gave him a disapproving look. 'Please Andrew, think long and hard about that choice.'

'I've thought of little else actually.' He answered. 'Give me a reason not to then. Give me a reason to stick around here.' He said almost pleading.

'Come on Andrew, you know I . . .' she hesitated. 'Your mother, she'd surely be upset, after, you know . . . your brother and everything.'

'Probably' Andrew agreed, clearly deflated by her response or lack thereof. 'Not that I see her now anyway.'

'That's right, sorry I forgot she moved back. Where is she now, still in Dublin?'

'No, not anymore she isn't. She moved home to Donegal.'

'Does she visit at all?' Bernadette asked

'She hasn't, no, but we Skype the odd time and really that's all.'

Andrew's mother suffered a nervous breakdown the year his brother died. She'd been battling depression since forever. It grew noticeable after Andrew's father died when Andrew was twelve. She'd nearly come out of it, or at least seemed to emerge from the darkness briefly. But, when Andrew's brother Brian went to war, she couldn't cope with the stress of worrying about him. He survived the war alright, at least physically. Emotionally however, he was never the same. Next came the drinking. After that came the drugs. His mother's cries for help fell on deaf or tormented ears so they went unheeded for a long while. Heroin finally took him. The pressure of it all successfully took her. He died, she didn't. She did, however, melt. Living in America for thirty years was finally too much for her. She hopped on a plane to Dublin and stayed with relatives at first. After a while, she finally managed to move back to her family's home in a small town in Donegal. When the smoke cleared, Andrew found himself alone. Well, he had Bernadette then. And he had Stevie.

Andrew's mind drifted momentarily with the thought of his mother, but he quickly came back to the present. 'Enough' he thought, 'there's a reason she's here.'

'Bernie.' He said and shifted his body to face her directly. I spent the entire evening at Mackin's hoping for the chance to see you. After you didn't show, I resigned myself to that, only to come home and find you waiting for me on my porch. I need to know now. What are you doing here?'

'There, it's out there, on the line' he thought 'cards are on the table.'

He watched her stiffen slightly and noticed she looked nervous. She was biting down the corner of her lip. 'always when she's nervous' he thought and fear loomed over him.

He watched as she slowly, hesitantly pulled off her left glove with her right hand, finger by finger, one at a time. When it was off she held it towards him. He looked down at her hand, then up into her eyes which now shone with the beginning of tears.

'Does that mean what I think it means?' he asked while trying to swallow the lump in his throat.

'It does Andrew. I'm getting married.' She answered.

Andrew leaned back against the bench and brought his hands up to his head and locked his fingers behind it. He let out a slow breath. He said nothing. She noticed.

'I had to tell you in person Andrew, that's why I'm here. I. . .'

'It's okay' he said and slowly stood up, putting his hand up in a gesture to stop her from elaborating.

'You're leaving?' she asked, clearly hurt.

'I want to happy for you Bernie . . . it's just . . . I need time.'

She stood up and put her glove back on quickly. 'I'm sorry if I hurt you Andrew. It's just not something I could've lived with telling you over the phone or having you find out any other way. I'm going now.'

She reached over and hugged him, then kissed him on the cheek. Andrew stood frozen like a statue, thinking for a second that her touch, her final touch, had turned him to stone. In a way, he'd guessed that it actually had. He watched her get to her car and drive off safely. His mind raced. He let himself into the apartment and double-locked the door behind him then planted himself face first down onto his couch. After a minute, sleep finally took him.

5

The next morning came quickly for Andrew. He woke up right where he laid down the night before. His body ached with a night of uncomfortable sleep on a sofa not big enough to hold a man of his size lying horizontal for that length of time. He stood up and stretched grazing his fingertips at full reach against the ceiling. His clothes felt too loose on his body after being slept in. He threw on running pants and a sweatshirt and headed for the kitchen. He chased down the last of his ibuprofen with some orange juice and threw a bagel in the toaster. Waiting for it to pop, he dialed Stevie's cell phone number. Stevie picked up after four rings sounding groggy, but awake.

'Any luck last night?' he asked.

'Only bad luck actually. Let me wake up a bit and I'll walk you through it later.' Andrew answered, then asked, 'We're on for today right?'

'Yeah fuck it, might as well, we ain't working.'

'Good, I need to burn off some beers, not to mention blow off steam.'

'Outside the store in an hour? I have to go get my truck first.'

'Sounds perfect, I'll get my gear ready.'

'Later Stevie.' He said then hung up. Any weekend that Andrew and Stevie didn't work was used for training. Over the years between the two of them they had done some boxing, kung fu, jiu jitsu, even Krav Maga. Through a little experience and a lot of drive, they jointly put together a series of different workouts incorporating things each had learned over the years, both in relation to self-defense and general working out. A lot of what they did involved running, sometimes calisthenics, but all involved some form of hand to hand fight training or weapons defense.

Each had gone through his coming of age fist fights, but this wasn't really about that. It was more about preparation. Preparation for what, Andrew could never figure out, but for one reason or another he always carried a niggling dread that his days of physical altercation were not over. Maybe it was the stress of physical labor and working in close quarters with other stressed out men on different building sites. Maybe it had something to do with his past, his father dying on foot of a road rage incident or watching his brother go off to war. 'Or maybe, it was just too much fucking television.' He thought. Regardless of the driving force, like everything else, after years of doing it, it became somewhat of a custom. It was never for show and never something either Andrew or Stevie talked about to others. It was just something they did together. Like going to the gym, it was part of their normal routine.

Andrew pulled into his usual spot in the shop's front parking lot. He looked around after he put the truck in park, but didn't see any sign of Stevie yet. 'No surprise there' He thought.

He entered the shop through the front, nodding to the teenager behind the counter, while he headed towards the back for the large refrigerator. He grabbed a gallon of water and two large Gatorades from the fridge. He walked to the front of the small shop and put the items on the counter. 'I thought Chef opened up every morning?' he asked the young man. 'He does usually' the man answered. 'He texted me last night to see if I'd cover for him on the early shift. I work it sometimes, usually the mornings after he's been out on the sauce.'

'He must trust you, that's good.'

'Yeah, I guess so. Brothers can be like that.'

'Oh, sorry I didn't realize Chef had a brother. I'm Andrew.'

'He does and I'm him. I know who you are, you're friends with that dude Stevie right?'

'Yes, I am.' Andrew answered. 'How do you know Stevie?'

'Just from around' He answered, 'plus he comes in here a lot. He's kind of a dick if you don't mind me saying. He's always calling me Sous chef.'

Andrew smiled and laughed briefly. 'Yeah, I guess he can be. What's your real name?'

'It's David'

'Okay David, good talking to you.' He said and handed over a five dollar bill for the drinks. He grabbed the bottles between his knuckles and lifted the gallon with his free hand and backed through the door on his way out, nodding good bye as the door chimed behind him.

'Top of the morning bud' Stevie yelled from over next to the passenger door as Andrew walked down the steps.

'What's up Stevie' Andrew answered.

'One of those for me?' Stevie asked pointing to the Gatorade.

'Yup' Andrew said and stuck one bottle under his armpit and under-handed the other to his friend. He reached over the bed of the truck and put the gallon of water into the back. When he did, he saw Stevie's old North Quincy High School hockey bag lying next to it.

'You brought some props I take it?'

'Of course. I got a few new things in there to try out.'

Andrew opened the driver's door and stepped up into the truck, he reached over and flung the passenger door open from the inside. Stevie climbed in and stuck his Gatorade in the center cup holder.

'What'd you bring this time?' Andrew asked.

'Not much new really. Brought wooden short swords and knives, some markers . . . oh and a couple of real blades I picked up recently.'

'Real blades huh?'

'You know, for authenticity.' Stevie answered and smiled.

Every time they went training, Stevie stuffed his old hockey bag with weapons, some real, some fake. Mostly what they practiced with were wooden replicas of weapons that Stevie spent time fashioning himself. That way, the motions were true to life and they could go full force without really killing each other. The markers were a poor substitute for weapons, because the size and shape were all wrong. But, they were a good way to decide who won the fight. He with the least purple swipes of Crayola was generally deemed the winner, unless the other came away with a strip across the neck or something similar.

Most of what they practiced was hand to hand combat. They used padded gloves a lot. Other than that, they practiced a hell of a lot on knife disarms. Stevie also sanded down a set of wooden pistols to practice gun disarms, but realistically unless you were within arms-length or closer to someone pointing a gun, conventional wisdom was to run like hell and scream.

Andrew hated knives and felt sick at the thought of

what blades did to human flesh. He feared them. He feared guns too, but felt like knives were easier to access and therefore more likely to come across. Although the ease and likelihood gap between knives and guns grew more narrow each day. Still, it was knife fighting, particularly, learning to disarm someone wielding one that he worked hardest to perfect.

There was one disarm in particular he and Stevie referred to as "the move". The move was what they practiced most. Andrew could pull it off in his sleep. Stevie however was very much against it as a viable technique. This was for a few reasons. Firstly, it wasn't something either of them were taught by a trained martial arts or self-defense coach. In fact, they saw it first in a low budget Steven Segal movie before either of them entered puberty. They had been practicing it since then. The other reason Stevie spoke against the move was because in order to pull it off, the attacker's arm would have to strike with the knife straight forward at about neck level or higher. Stevie always said that it was more likely that an attacker stab low and straight or slash with a high swipe. He argued vigorously and often against anyone knowingly trying to stab someone in the bony chin. Nevertheless, it looked bad ass when Segal did it and they worked on it since they were young, so they stuck with it out of habit.

The move itself was simple on paper. It was much more difficult in practice. When an attacker struck out straight forward so that his arm is elevated at the victim's height or higher, the intended victim bounces back from his lead foot, tilting his head to the outside and sweeping the knife hand in the opposite direction. Next, his strong hand tightly clutches the attacker's knife wielding wrist and he pivots the lead foot bringing the weak side shoulder upwards hard into the attacker's elbow. The aim is to break the elbow, not just hyper extend it, so force is key. The last part is circumstantial and fortuitous at best, but what should happen is that the elbow break and corresponding shriek of pain should free the knife. It should at least loosen it, making it possible to grab with the strong hand, pivot with the back foot and plunge the knife straight forward into the attacker's own heart.

Andrew agreed it was unlikely to ever be useful, but felt at least it was an exercise in coordination and speed. Plus, he was a sucker for nostalgia.

A short drive later and Andrew and Stevie pulled into Marina Bay. Marina Bay is a plot of water front land on Dorchester Bay overlooking Boston's city skyline seven miles to the north. Years of development and an influx of cash turned it into a hot waterfront town, with Condo's, bars and restaurants, night clubs and office buildings. Like any old beach town however, it was virtually dead during winter months and severely overcrowded in the summer. With winter dragging on into March, the place gave off a desolate air.

Andrew weaved his truck through the newly minted roads and drove into the large parking lot towards the back of the marina. He parked at the very end of the lot where cement and concrete gave way to dirt and wild brush before the uninhabited section of the property. He killed the ignition and helped Stevie grab the bag from the back of the truck. They began walking down a dirt path, towards the bay about a mile in the distance. They had discovered this semi-secluded beach back in high school. A few times they had been to small parties on the beach.

Eventually however the local police caught on to the underage drinking taking place and put a stop to the festivities. That was years ago. Since then the small hidden sand patch overlooking the city remained untouched. They started working out there around the same time Stevie started bringing out more and more obviously dangerous weapons to practice with. When that happened, co-users of the local baseball fields were no longer so welcoming. Apparently playgrounds and martial arts weaponry were not a great mix.

The walk down the dirt path was more or less silent. Having been friends for so long and still spending plenty of time together meant that periods of silence or long pauses in conversations were not awkward. In fact, they were often a nice break from arguing with each other.

Stevie stepped forward and ducked his head under a low hanging branch to enter the grounds of the beach. Andrew followed behind him. The sand was dark and tightly packed with moisture. The small surf had left branches and other debris where the water met the sand. The morning still had a dull edge, but the sky was bright despite the cloud cover.

'So, you ready to talk yet?' Stevie asked as he hoisted the bag onto a small dune protected by a large rock. 'You haven't said shit about last night.'

Andrew had already begun stretching out and answered Stevie as he pulled his arm across his body and twisted his waist. 'She's getting married I guess. That's pretty much all there is to say.'

Stevie pushed out his bottom lip and nodded his head slowly several times. 'So she's gonna settle for that douche bag she's been going out with?'

'Apparently, yes. I don't know why I'm surprised. I guess . . . just some part of me always felt we'd end up together, you know.'

'What a bitch.' Stevie said.

'Dude, come on I'm not sure I'm ready to bad mouth her. It's her decision really. It's not like we were going out.'

'Yeah, well, you're a faggot then. Let her marry some fucking accountant from Pennsylvania, what do I care?'

'He probably isn't a bad guy. I'm pretty sure of that actually.' Andrew replied.

'Dude, I've seen him before.' Stevie said shaking his head. 'He wears Dockers and clips his fucking cell phone to his belt.'

Andrew just shrugged. 'Alright . . . maybe he does sound like a douche bag.'

'Yeah, and that d bag is banging your girl.'

'Real nice.' Andrew said.

'Just speaking the truth my man, and you know it.' Stevie said and dropped to a knee to tie his sneakers.

'Hey, did you hear about Gina O'Neil?' Andrew asked.

Stevie finished tying his lace and stood back up. 'Yeah, I did actually. Too bad.'

'Yeah, to say the least.'

'I heard they found her body under the Neponset bridge.'

'Really? Well . . . maybe she was dumped there.'

'I wouldn't think so.' Stevie said.

'Why not? '

'Place is swimming with cops, that's why. They always park under the bridge. Probably just to prevent that shit from happening outside the hotel beside there ya know, and other stuff like drug deals and shit. She was probably dumped upstream and the current took her.'

'I guess. You appear to be the expert.'

'No expert buddy, just logic. Anyway here, let's get started before I decide to go back to bed.' Stevie said, then took off in a sprint across the small beach. Andrew, a few steps behind, followed after.

They ran a few laps, then rested, then ran a few more. Once the heart rate was up, they hit some stretches, then straight into rounds with the gloves and pads. Once it got to a point where Andrew felt his arms would fall off, he asked 'Want to switch it up?' To answer his own question, he tore the Velcro strap from the outside of his glove with his teeth and pulled off the mitt using his arm pit for leverage.

Stevie threw the pads down and crouched down to look into the hockey bag. He rummaged through it for a few seconds, then pulled out something about the size of a wooden serving spoon that was wrapped in a cloth. He lobbed it underhanded to Andrew. 'Here' he said.

Andrew caught the object in both hands and carefully unwrapped the towel around it. Inside was a knife with a polished wooden handle and a long blade with small serrated peaks that thinned to a sharp point at the top. 'It looks like a steak knife on steroids.' Andrew said.

He gripped the handle with his right hand and carefully held the blade across the palm of his left. 'It definitely doesn't look legal.' He scraped his thumbnail across the knife edge in the way a hockey player checks his skates for sharpness. Unconvinced, he put his finger tip on the top of the knife, which cut it immediately drawing blood from his finger, which dripped down the blade. 'Fuck!' he said and shook his hand loose then brought the fingertip to his mouth. 'It's wicked sharp, thanks for the warning.'

'It's a knife Andrew, what'd you expect?' Stevie answered. Andrew smiled and nodded. 'Where'd you find it anyway?' he asked. 'You know I've been trying to pick up some side work? Anyway, I was helping this guy Mike Doyle sheetrock his basement. When we were clearing it out, he gave it to me along with a set of old golf clubs.'

'Not bad' Andrew said and nodded. 'Hope he paid you with more than just his old shit.' Andrew dropped it back into the towel and got up to put it back in the bag. He picked up a wooden knife instead. 'I'm not practicing with that thing. Here get up, we'll use the wooden fakes.'

'Pussy' Stevie answered and smiled as he jumped back to his feet.

'Yeah okay, whatever, a pussy cause I don't want to gut my best friend like a fish.' He stepped towards the clearing, then quickly started swiping at Stevie with the wooden blade.

6

They worked out for over an hour before calling it quits. Both dripped with sweat as the spring sun arrived at last and burnt off the early cloud cover with it. Andrew carried the bag back to the truck and flung it over the side when they reached it. He put his hands out and grasped the side of the truck bed then squatted down as far as he could. He felt his lower back stretching and it felt good, a vast improvement from the days before. 'Want me to drop you back home?' he asked Stevie.

'No actually. But can you swing me by Wollaston train station? I need to run into Dee Dee's.' Andrew slowly stood up and leaned over the truck bed to look at his friend. He paused before responding, confused because Dee Dee's lounge was a small dive bar across the street from the train station. No one really went there, except for John Bishop's crew. Rumor was Bishop acquired it at some stage. It was a debt payoff. He kept it open so he could conduct business in a legitimate establishment. 'Yeah, sure I'll drop you there.' Andrew answered 'but that's Bishop's place.'

'I know who's place it is Andrew.'

'So, you're in with Bishop now?'

'What? Come on man. Of course I'm not working for Bishop. I just know some of his people. That guy Doyle I mentioned. He's apparently one of Bishop's crew . . . I didn't know that when I took the job Andrew, I swear.'

'Fine' Andrew said and opened the door and got into the truck. Stevie followed suit on the passenger side. 'You don't need to come in or anything. Plus I heard that Bishop's hardly ever there, so you won't run into him.'

'You think I'm scared of Bishop?' Andrew asked

'Aren't you?'

'Please.' Andrew said.

'No.' Stevie said and laughed, 'You're not scared of Bishop. I saw you bounce him off of every car on Kingston Street. But . . . you are scared of trouble.'

'Fuck you Stevie. I'll drop you off there, don't worry. You can stop selling it to me.'

'Thanks Andrew. Ya know . . . you're my hero.'

'Prick' Andrew said. He fought to hold back a smile, then started the truck and pulled away.

The drive to the train station was silent from that point onwards. Andrew drove the truck around the back of Wollaston train station's parking lot to avoid the main street's traffic. He pulled up close to the curb and Stevie jumped out. Each managed a 'see ya later' before Stevie slammed the door and headed down the steps to the station's swinging doors.

Andrew's cell phone started ringing while he was still sitting idle. He looked at the screen. The number was local, but he didn't recognize it since it wasn't programmed into his phone. 'Hello' he answered.

A man's voice said 'Hi, Andrew?'

'Yeah it is' Andrew answered

'Hey man, it's Chef Benson. Is this a good time?'

'Ah, yeah, hey Chef, what's going on?'

'Remember I mentioned that those cops might need to talk to you? Well they were here again today and wanted to see if you could drop into the police station and give an official statement.'

'Oh. Okay, I didn't realize I'd have to go to them.'

'Yeah, sorry man, I didn't either, my bad.'

'Nah, don't worry about it Chef, I can do it today no problem, I'm not working.'

'Thanks Andrew, I appreciate it.'

'No problem, anything to help man.'

Andrew hit end on the cell phone and dropped it into the center console. He put the truck into drive and pulled away from the curb slowly, joining traffic just before the intersection. It was mildly irritating that the cops needed him to go into the station for a statement, but he had told Chef he'd do whatever he could to help, so he felt obligated.

He arrived at the police headquarters quickly. The building sat on a corner overlooking the YMCA and a baseball field on the left and a cemetery to the right. He drove into the parking lot next to the building which was manned by one officer and had a gate as a barrier. Andrew rolled down the window and spoke to the officer. 'Hi, I was asked to come in and give a statement. Do I need to sign in or anything?'

'No' he yelled from the hut 'just park over next to the building and give your information to the officer at the front desk.'

'Thanks' Andrew said and waved. He continued into the parking lot and parked at a spot against the building as instructed. He walked around the building to the front entrance. Inside it was dark and appeared dusty like someone just shook out a carpet. A large metal door closed off the public to the rest of the department. The remainder of the room was plexi-glassed. Andrew noticed a female officer sitting behind the glass. He waved and smiled. She gave him the 'one minute' sign with her finger.

Andrew looked around while he waited. There wasn't much else to the room, just some official forms slotted next to a bulletin board that held posters for several hotline numbers. He felt self-conscious suddenly, and put on his best nonchalant stance. He had that irrationally guilty feeling like the one that arrives when approaching the passport control counter.

He heard the window slide open and turned towards it. 'Good morning' the policewoman said. Andrew stepped over towards the window and answered. 'Hi. Good morning. I'm here to give a statement.'

'Okay, do you know the detective in charge of the case?'

'I don't actually. It's related to a robbery I witnessed in a store. West Elm variety. It's a convenience store near Wollaston beach.'

'Okay' she answered, 'I can take your statement, I'm familiar with the case. Detective Maloney's in charge of that one and he's not in. Just give me a minute.'

She then shut the window and disappeared into the back.

A minute later another officer sat at the window and at the same time, the large metal door opened and the police woman waved Andrew in. He followed her through the door and eventually into a room that was furnished with a table and four folding chairs. 'Have a seat' she said as she shut the door then took a seat herself. 'I'm Officer Donovan.'

Andrew looked at her. He recognized her. 'I'm Andrew Dawson. I think we were in high school together.' He said. 'You were a few years ahead of me.'

'You're right. Sorry, I did recognize you, but couldn't

place you until now. You had a brother . . . Brian, right?'

'Yes. I did.' Andrew answered.

'So, anyway, your statement . . . why don't you walk me through what happened first, then I'll have you write it down and we'll sign it. That sound okay?'

'Um, yeah.' Andrew said 'That's fine with me.'

He gave her a play by play breakdown of what he saw. She asked some questions to help him remember details and also that helped him filter out anything he might have inferred but hadn't actually seen. The whole process took under an hour. When he finished, he wrote out the statement verbatim, then she read it aloud back to him. Next each signed the bottom of the form.

'Thanks for coming in' she said as she led him out through the hall. I'll walk you out.'

He followed her down the same path she had led him in and back through the heavy door into the waiting area. 'Here, I'll walk you outside to make sure the officer at the gate sees that we're done and you're good to go.'

Andrew left the building and held the door for her. 'How long have you been a cop?' he asked.

'I've been on the force for over three years now.'

'You like it?'

'I love it actually.'

Andrew nodded, 'That's great. Wish I did something I loved.'

'What are you up to these days?'

'I'm a carpenter. I do mostly residential work now, like putting windows in and hanging vinyl siding.'

'That doesn't sound so bad.'

'Yeah, I know. It's not bad really. It's just not something I jump out of bed for every morning. I guess

I'm lucky to have work these last few years.'

'I hear you, there are plenty of people without it, that's for sure.'

'Anyway, here's my truck.' Andrew said and slapped the bed of his Ford. He looked up at her and noticed she was looking into the back of his truck.

'Ah, hey Andrew? What do you have in the back here?' She asked.

Andrew followed her gaze to the open hockey bag with assorted weaponry in full view. 'Oh, shit' he thought. 'I forgot Stevie left the bag with me.' He paused, not sure what to say. He felt . . . indefensible and dumb as shit.

Finally, he spoke up, 'Those are . . . well, they're weapons actually. Mostly knives, swords and clubs, but it's not what it looks like.'

'Oh yeah? Tell me what it looks like?'

'I guess it looks like a bag of weapons.'

'And is it a bag of weapons?'

'Well, yes.'

'So it sounds like it's exactly how it looks.'

'Yeah' he said 'I guess it does. They're for training . . . martial arts training.'

'Andrew?'

'Yes?'

'I figured as much, but honestly, I can't let you drive out of here with those.'

'Okay' he answered 'I understand. Am I in trouble here?'

'Honestly, I don't think so, but I'll need to take them for now. I should actually take you in . . . but, listen let me take the bag. I need to speak with my sergeant.'

Andrew just waited. He was afraid to move. He kept

away from the driver's door and kept his hands visible just in case. He watched Officer Donovan as she stepped backwards a few feet away, out of earshot, but kept her eyes up. She was alert to head off any sudden movement, which Andrew had no plans to make. He watched her lips moving as she spoke into the radio near her shoulder, then held it near her ear as she listened for the response while nodding. Andrew couldn't tell what that nodding meant for his fate. She walked back over finally.

'I need to take the bag for now Andrew. Considering you came in on your own accord, you're free to go. We'll need to inspect what you have here. Anything that may be illegal will likely be confiscated, but you should get the rest back.

'Okay, I understand.' He said. Andrew watched her reach over and carefully haul the bag over the truck bed. She laid it on the ground at her feet, then waved at the officer guarding the gate.

'We'll call you and let you know what you can pick up. Bye for now Andrew.'

'Officer Donovan' he yelled.

'Yes?'

'Um . . . thank you.'

She waved again, a hesitant goodbye. Andrew let out a deep breath he'd been holding. He fired up the Ford and when the barrier lifted he drove out slowly, fighting the urge to peel out. 'Idiot' he thought as he took a left towards the beach.

7

Stevie's cell phone kept going direct to voicemail. Andrew dialed it three times in the span of twenty minutes. He drove back to Dee Dee's lounge in Wollaston and parked on a side street looking towards the bar on the corner facing the train station across the street. He debated whether he should just walk in, but he wanted to avoid any trouble if it was possible. He turned the ignition key backwards to let the radio play lightly without burning through a tank of gas. He was angry at himself for getting Stevie's stuff confiscated, but he found himself strangely calm and relaxed sitting in his truck watching the cars breeze past on the busy street in front of him. He watched as people entered and exited the train station. He noticed mostly young people, probably early twenties going in, and mainly workers, carpenters likely or laborers, coming out. He imagined the tradeoff was the young ones heading into Boston to party, while the working men made their way home after a short shift on Saturday at the building site. The former looking spritely and energetic, the latter looking weary yet satisfied with the opportunity to work an extra shift.

He lost himself people watching, and before he realized thirty minutes had passed. 'I'll try him one last time' he thought, and picked up his phone from the console. He ran his thumb across the screen to open his recent calls. He tapped Stevie's name to start the call. He put the phone to his ear in time to hear the start of the voicemail greeting. He didn't bother with a message, just hit call end on the screen and tossed the phone into the passenger seat. He peered across at the bar and noticed the door swing slowly open. Two men walked out. One was Stevie, still wearing a zipper up hoodie with his hands dug into the front pockets. The other man walked out behind him with a cigarette in his mouth. He used both hands to light it, blocking the flame from a slight breeze from the passing cars. Andrew recognized him as one of Bishop's guys, but he wasn't sure of his name.

He felt awkward suddenly as it dawned on him that he was spying on his best friend. He considered whether he could pull away without being noticed. He slid down an inch or two to hide his face behind the steering wheel, knowing full well it was pointless since Stevie knew his truck. As he thought it, Stevie happened to look over in his direction. He appeared to pause his conversation as he stepped forward towards the curb and crouched slightly to peer over with a hand up to shield the glare.

'Caught' Andrew thought. He waved and Stevie stood straight again and returned the wave. Andrew had no choice but to join them. He took his keys from the ignition and jumped down from the truck. He brushed the wrinkles from his shirt as he walked towards the two men. He cut across the street in front of a couple of cars stopped at a red light.

'Andrew' Stevie said and nodded.

'Hey Stevie' Andrew answered, 'Figured you'd still be here.'

'Yeah, I am. This is Mike Doyle?' he said pointing to the other man. The man pulled the cigarette from his mouth with his left hand and stretched out his right. Andrew took a slow step towards the man and shook his hand briefly.

'I'm Andrew.'

'How's it going? You look familiar. I've seen you around I think.'

'Likewise' Andrew said. He turned back towards Stevie. 'Hey, can I talk to you for a minute?'

Mike Doyle took a drag from his cigarette and flicked it into the street. 'I'm heading inside anyways.' He turned and walked back into the bar room.

The doors swung open and closed behind him. Andrew couldn't help but think of an old western movie. He caught a glimpse of inside the barroom when the door opened. It was dark. The only light seemingly from the Budweiser sign lit up behind the bar. He saw at least three others inside including the bartender. He recognized none of them.

He turned back towards Stevie now that his friend was out of ear shot. 'Hey man.' He said.

'Hey. Weird, you showing up here, waiting out front like some pervert watching a playground from a distance.'

'Yeah. Sorry. I called a few times. I didn't really want to barge in there you know.'

'Yeah okay.' He said. 'What's the emergency anyway?'

'There's no emergency. I just wanted to give you a heads up. I went to the police station to give a statement to the cops for Chef Benson. When I was leaving, the cop noticed the bag of weapons in the back of the truck. She made me leave them with her. I don't know what I'll be able to get back. I got the vibe they're gonna confiscate most of it.'

Andrew looked up at Stevie. He read irritation on Stevie's face, but he didn't say anything for a few seconds. 'Anyway. I just wanted to let you know, in case you were looking for them.'

'Fuck.' Stevie said after a moment. His eyes went bright and distant at the same time. He looked to be considering something internally. After a few seconds, he looked back at Andrew, smiled and shrugged. 'That sucks . . . okay, well, don't worry about it. It's not the end of the world.' He said. 'Did you let them know it was my bag?' he asked.

Andrew shook his head no. 'Nah, didn't occur to me.' He said. 'She assumed it was mine I'm guessing, no reason not to.'

Stevie stepped back and stood up straight. He looked up the street at nothing in particular. When he looked back at Andrew, he said 'Alright . . . let me get back in there. I need to finish up with this guy Doyle. I assume you don't want to come in.'

'No, I'm all set. Like I said, I just wanted to give you a heads up. I'll catch up with you later.'

Andrew turned to walk back to his truck. As he started across the street he heard the swinging bar doors creak behind him.

'Hey!' he heard someone yell out. He turned to see Mike Doyle walking back out towards him. 'I do know you don't I? You're Dawson's brother. I've heard about you.'

Andrew paused in the street. He shrugged then turned to Stevie silently requesting an intervention. Stevie must have understood the look because he cut in front of Doyle and began to corral him back inside.

'Later Andrew' He said and held his hand up in a wave. Andrew answered 'see ya later Stevie' and continued back to his Ford.

8

Andrew's Saturday night consisted of pizza and beers by himself in front of the television. As punishment for his indulgence he headed out Sunday morning for a long run. He ran through Quincy's Wollaston and Montclair neighborhoods and continued north for a couple miles until he reached Dorchester. Then he turned and ran back on the same route. He kicked himself as he struggled up the several hills on the return path.

A shower and shave later he found himself bored and lonely in his apartment. Shortly thereafter, he found himself behind a piece of electrical tape on the floor of Mackin's Saloon. The tape on the ground marked the legal distance from the dartboard. Andrew stood behind the marker and repeatedly threw darts at the board. He threw six darts, walked to the board, pulled them out, and repeated. He wasn't alone in the bar. There were two men sitting at the bar trading complaints and a table of women in the corner drinking wine. The women looked like the after church crowd and were at odds with the bar's surroundings.

Andrew chatted periodically with the lone bartender in between throws, but he seemed too preoccupied with cleaning behind the bar and sweeping floors for idle chit chat. 'For what' Andrew thought. 'This place will be lucky to see fifteen people between now and Thursday.' He held the weight of the three darts remaining in his hand. He quickly fired the last three one at a time at the board, harder than was necessary.

'You mad at something?' a female voice said behind him.

He scrunched his eyebrows at the question and turned around slowly, surprised to see Bernadette standing less than two feet behind him. He smiled at her. She smiled back.

'Honestly, we need to get you a bell or something.' He said.

'I'm stealthy huh?'

'You're ninja-esque alright. What brings you here? Last I checked you weren't a Sunday drinker.'

'Look who's talking. Come on Andrew, it's not even football season.'

He laughed. 'You sound worried about me.'

'Maybe a little bit.' She said.

'Is that why you're here?'

'It's not the ambiance.'

'Seriously.'

'Seriously. I wanted to see if you were still mad. Considering how hard you threw the last few darts, I'd say yes, you are.'

'Oh that . . . No, I'm more accurate when I throw fast.'

She looked at the dart board. Six darts were stuck in the board, but none were remotely close to the center. 'Really?' she asked.

He shrugged his shoulders. 'They're not stuck in the wall right?'

'True I guess.' So which is it? Mad?'

He bit his lip and took a few seconds to respond. 'I can't stay mad at you. Let's call it disappointed.'

'Very parental thing to say.'

'I was thinking more school teacher, maybe principal. But you get it.'

Well. Do you want to talk for real?'

'I didn't realize we weren't.'

'Come on Andrew.'

'Okay. But . . . you know, what's it been, a day? I think I need some more time to deal with it before . . .'

'Before what?'

'You know, before we can be friends I guess.'

She bit her lip now and looked like she had more to say, but she just answered with 'I know you do. Well, I just wanted to see you before I headed back to Boxford. I'm on my way now.'

'Back to the cows?'

'Yup, and the deer . . . and don't forget the pigs. So, I'll see you when I see you?'

'Sure. See you when I see you.' He answered.

She smiled back and turned to walk out the side door of the bar. Before she left, Andrew yelled over to her, 'Bernie!'

'Yeah' she answered

'Congratulations. Really. I am happy for you.'

'Thanks Andrew.' She waved again then stepped out the door.

'See you' he said to himself finally after she walked out.

9

The body and mind are amazing tool sets. Many things they accomplish are done without having conscious knowledge of it. A loud bang can cause the heart to beat quickly sending blood flowing rapidly to limbs preparing the body for fight or flight. The unconscious mind spots problems or errors before the brain can put meaning or words to it. Using data gathered by all available senses, the brain compiles an assessment of a situation and sends the body into action, while conscious understanding of those actions arrives much later, as an afterthought really.

So, before Andrew knew why he was running, his legs were pumping like pistons. As he ran, his mind began to catch up and put pieces of information together. He woke up late for work on Monday, which meant he was late to the store to pick up Stevie. He parked his truck and climbed out, planning to pick up a coffee in the store. He noticed then that two very similar blue sedans were parked equidistant from the shop's entrance. Despite being late there was no sign of Stevie waiting in the parking lot. The lot itself was empty. As he stood there, he saw Chef Benson through the window. Chef was always smiling. He smiled when he sneezed. He probably smiled in his sleep too. But this morning, Chef was not smiling. He pictured Chef's face and the slight turn of his head when they made eye contact. He knew then that something was wrong. So, he ran. He didn't think about it really at the time. He didn't consider whether he had any reason to take off. He just set off in a sprint down the street towards the beach.

He didn't stop at the beach. He turned left at the corner

and continued north running down Quincy Shore Drive. It was early morning, but there were plenty of cars on the road. A grown man running in work boots and jeans must've looked awkward. Had he time to look, he would have noticed plenty of double takes and lingering looks from commuters driving by.

As he reached the main intersection, he felt his lungs beginning to burn and his legs grew weary, no doubt due to his heavy boots and the initial adrenaline wearing off. He slowed to a jog at the corner, pausing only to gauge his timing before running across the street. He saw the Dunkin Donuts in front of him and headed for it, hoping to melt into the crowd. He needed to catch his breath and more importantly, he needed to think for a minute. He reacted. He wasn't sure what was actually happening. Chances were, he thought, 'no one's even chasing after me.'

He slid past a series of customers that were on their way out of the coffee shop. The place was full, which was typical on any weekday morning. Andrew walked to the back and took one of the few small tables. There was debris still on the table from the previous inhabitants, but at least it looked like he bought something. He put the palms of his hands up to his face and rubbed his eyes.

He tried to piece together in his head what he knew, or really, what he believed based on what he saw. The convenience store was definitely surrounded by cops. The two cars on either side were unmistakably cop cars. No one drives navy blue Crown Victoria's. At least very few did. That made it unlikely to have two randomly parked so close together. Then there was Chef's demeanor. He could see it from the street. Chef wasn't being Chef, no

277

smile, no animation in his movements. He was stiff. He looked nervous. Then there was the look he gave Andrew through the glass. It was strange. Andrew interpreted it as a warning. There was no sign of Stevie, but that alone could be coincidence. It was Monday morning after all. What Andrew couldn't figure was, 'Why the need for a setup?'

'Why stage a pickup like that? Was it just over some small weapons that he willingly turned over? They were more like props than anything. Then again' he thought, 'why would I run for that?' His nerves began to kick in. 'How must that look? Why would I take off like that? It had to have been fear, but would anyone buy that? I surely look guilty of something now.'

A voice spoke from across the table and broke Andrew's train of thought. He hadn't heard what the voice said, just registered the noise and felt the shadow of someone standing over him. As the man stood, he blocked out the sunlight from the window. Andrew looked up and acknowledged him. 'Excuse me?' he asked.

'I asked if this seat was taken.' the man said.

'No, go ahead.' Andrew answered.

The man pulled out the chair and sat down across from Andrew. He left the chair out a little from the table so he could cross a leg over his knee.

Andrew watched him dig into his inside pocket. When he pulled his hand out, a leather wallet came with it. He flipped it open to reveal a police badge. It was then that Andrew recognized the man from Mackin's Saloon. He was the state police detective that Chef pointed out a few nights ago.

'Do you know who I am?' the man asked.

'Ah . . . not by name. You're obviously a cop.'

'That I am son. I'm Detective Harris with the state police. And you're Andrew Dawson.'

'Yes sir I am.'

'Have a nice jog?'

'Not really, no.'

'Do you often take off on morning sprints?'

'No sir. I . . . got spooked I guess.'

'Okay, well, you're here now. There's a few ways we can go about this. The easiest is if we slowly get up and walk down to my car and we take a ride down the street and you can answer a few questions. Do you have an issue with that?'

'Ah, no, but, questions about what?'

'Why don't we save it for the station? Too many ears around here.'

'Okay, but, what about my truck? And, I'm supposed to be at work.'

'Come with me and don't worry, you can call your boss on the way. And don't worry about your truck. I'm sure it's safe at the store.'

He got up then and tucked his badge back into his jacket. Andrew stood up with him. He moved slowly, unsure of himself. Walking out, Andrew noticed a couple of officers in plain clothes had been hanging around out front. Both of them joined Andrew and the Detective for the journey. One sat next to Andrew in the backseat, but neither spoke to him.

At Quincy police headquarters Andrew was led into a different entrance from that which he'd gone through just days before. The room however was eerily similar to that which he'd given his statement. From the uniforms and small pieces of conversation he heard, it was the Quincy police that walked him in, and one Quincy cop stayed behind in the room. But, it was Detective Harris that did most of the talking, including the chit chat on the car ride in. Andrew felt confused, and was more than a little nervous. It was unclear why he was brought there. A man came into the room and explained to Andrew that he was currently there on his own accord and was not yet under arrest. That little spiel only further clouded his understanding. Finally, he and Detective Harris were alone. Although Andrew was skeptical about just how alone they actually were. He'd seen enough cop shows to know there'd be one or two people monitoring behind the glass at least.

'So, you're an interesting guy I have to say Andrew. From what I gathered, you were born in Dublin. Is that right?' the Detective asked

'Ah, yes, I was. My mother's Irish.'

'You live there long?'

'I don't think I lived there at all really. Like I said, my mother's Irish. My father was American. They lived there for a while, but it was only up to the time I was born.'

'So what's that make you, American or Irish?'

'Both I guess.'

'Where's your mother now?'

'She's moved back.'

'Back to Dublin?'

'Well, back to Ireland. But she's not in Dublin. She's in Donegal. Anyway, why do you want to know this? No offense, but I'm confused.'

'No it's okay. I just wanted to understand more about you than what's already on my file.'

Andrew sat back and paused. He was surprised to hear he had anything to do with the Detective's file. 'Well then, why don't you tell me what you already have on file Detective, then I can fill in the gaps.'

Detective Harris shrugged. 'Okay, we can do that.' He flipped over a manila folder that was sitting on the desk and looked through its contents briefly.

He spoke in a conversational tone, though his head remained down as he continued reading. 'Your father, an alcoholic, was beaten to death in a road rage assault in front of your eyes. How old were you when that happened?'

Andrew tried not to flinch and answered calmly. 'I was around twelve I think. Possibly younger.'

The Detective just shook his head. 'And you had a brother die from a heroin overdose. You were nineteen?'

'Sounds right.' He answered.

'I'll admit, you definitely had it rough. Andrew shrugged and averted his eyes.

'If you say so.'

'What? Are you saying those things didn't affect you?'

'No. I'm not saying that. It's just that . . . I'm saying what I've been through is not that uncommon around here. Shit, half the people I know have alcoholic fathers and brothers or sisters with drug problems.'

'Is that right? Well at least there's the other half that are doing okay.'

'Nah, the other half are on drugs themselves.'

'Oh yeah? Why do you think that is?'

'Honestly, I think the city . . . no, the entire country turns a blind eye to the drug trade. Why's it so easy to get prescription drugs? There's not enough aunties with cancer to pilfer from, so they're coming from somewhere.'

'Sounds like an indictment on law enforcement. You sure you're in the right place to make a statement like that?'

'I'm sorry sir, but you asked me my opinion Detective.'

'Detective Harris shuffled his feet under the table and leaned forward on his elbows.

'That's right, I did. And let me ask you another question now too.'

He reached down and pulled another folder from his case. 'Was Gina O'Neil on drugs?'

'Gina? How should I know?' Andrew asked.

'You knew her didn't you? You two were close I heard.'

'Well yeah, back in school I guess we were close enough, but I hadn't spoken to her in a long time.

'Until the other night you mean?'

'What?'

'You hadn't spoken to her until the other night.'

'What?' Andrew said again. 'I didn't speak to her. I haven't seen her. I haven't seen her in years actually.'

'Not what I heard.'

'You heard wrong I'm afraid, Detective.'

'Maybe, maybe not.'

Andrew paused. He didn't know what else to say. He was racking his brain to remember seeing Gina, but just couldn't recall. 'How could the Detective have his facts so wrong' he thought.

He spoke again after a minute. 'The officer earlier said I wasn't under arrest.'

'That's right, as of now you're free.'

'Then I'm free to leave?'

'If you want to, then yes.'

'Then Detective, I'm leaving now.'

'Okay Andrew, that's your decision.' He said. He began gathering up his papers on the desk. He looked up at Andrew and gave him a stern fatherly look. 'Stay Local Andrew.'

Andrew walked quickly down the hall, tailed the whole way by a uniformed officer. He weaved through the corridors, which had become familiar to him at this stage.

He headed out the front door and walked in the direction of Wollaston Beach. It dawned on him outside that his truck wasn't with him, it stayed parked in front of the store at least a mile away. He started walking quickly up the street, taking long strides despite digging his hands in his pockets.

He made it half a mile when one of the two unmarked police cars pulled up next to him again. It slowed to a stop. Andrew knew who it was even before the door swung open and Detective Harris climbed out flashing his badge again, as if they hadn't spent the last hour together.

'Andrew Dawson' he said as he reached around his waist. Andrew paused, unsure what to say or whether to move. He watched the Detective's hand move back to the front, carrying a set of handcuffs. 'You're under arrest Andrew, for the murder of Gina O'Neil.'

He continued speaking, Andrew could hear him and knew his rights were being read, but he wasn't really listening. His mind had glazed over. He felt weak. He pictured himself floating above the actual scene looking down at his body, watching the motions, his hands on the hood of the Crown Victoria. An officer patting him down for any weapons he might have acquired in the ten minutes since he left the station. The whole time, the

Detective's lips were moving, but the words were soundless. Andrew shut his eyes and could feel wetness on his lashes as tears rimmed his eyelids, not falling yet, but gathering heavy around them. And for the first time in recent memory, maybe since childhood, Andrew began to pray.

10

Andrew sat staring at a heavy beige door, willing it to open. He waited twenty minutes already in a small rectangular room with no windows. Meanwhile his court appointed attorney signed some paperwork and spoke with the prison officer just outside the room. His patience had long since left him. In a whirlwind forty-eight hours he had been arrested and arraigned on murder charges. It was exhausting. Emotionally, he was breaking down. Physically, he was following shortly behind that. 'Murderer' he thought. 'I've never so much as hurt a fly in my entire life.'

The police apparently had evidence that linked him to the crime. He imagined the investigation carried on at full scale, people in haz-mat suits furiously searching for physical evidence to tie him to the murder, to strengthen a case that at its foundation had to be wrong. 'Doyle's knife' was the only thought that kept running through his head. 'It had to be this guy Doyle.'

He was arraigned and entered a 'not-guilty' plea. A request for bail was denied. The court appointed attorney said it was due to the seriousness of the charge and also that he was seen as a flight risk. 'If I wasn't before, I definitely am now' he thought. He spent the last thirty-six hours locked up in Wyngate Correctional Facility. He was given orange scrubs to wear that signified he was a pre-trial inmate. Jurisdictional rules required that pre-trial inmates be isolated from convicted inmates at all times. Whether or not that was the intention, the jail's excessive population made it a difficult requirement to enforce. When Andrew arrived he was shown to a cell built for one person, but already holding two. He was given a pop-up mattress that the inmates called 'canoes' to sleep in. He laid there the last two nights, but on the whole, sleep evaded him. It helped him a little to think that most County inmates were short-timers, serving for misdemeanor offenses. It was the state facilities that held the more severe prisoners.

He heard voices outside the door grow louder and heard the door buzz and then click open. A Correctional Officer opened the door and held it for the young attorney that the court appointed to handle Andrew's case. He entered the room and pulled out the chair across from Andrew at the small table. 'Hi Andrew.'

'Hi Barry.'

Barry put his brief case on the table top but left it closed. 'Did you sleep any better last night?'

'Not really, no. Would you be able to sleep if you were me?' he asked.

'Okay Andrew, that's too bad. I spoke with one of the warden's representatives about the arrangement.' They assured me that you'll be moved to a double bunk room as soon as one is available.'

'Okay. Thanks then. Is there any update on my case?'

'There's no significant updates, no. The district attorney's office is making sure they're handling it slowly and by the book because of its . . . profile.'

'So they still think I'm guilty then?'

'It's my understanding that they believe you're guilty. They're in the process of handing over all available evidence for the defense to review, but they're also continuing with the investigation to try and cover all angles. They'll likely try and speak with you again.'

'But you'll be here for any future meetings right?'

'Yes. You shouldn't be talking to anyone without me.'

'Okay.' Andrew said. 'So, what are the papers saying? Does everyone think I've done this?'

'I wouldn't worry too much about what the media's saying right now Andrew.'

'But, do they have my name?' he asked.

The lawyer brought his hand up to his face and brushed the hair from his forehead with his thumb before answering. 'They have your name, yes. People are talking. It's best for now that you don't listen.' He answered.

Andrew put his face into his hands and rubbed his eyes hard with his palms. He felt the blood drain from his face and his head was light.

'Are you going to puke?'

Andrew couldn't answer with words, but waved him off as he turned to the side and tried to regain control of his breathing. After a minute, he restored his composure and turned back towards the attorney.

'There's one other thing I wanted to run by you Andrew. I'm getting some questions about your relationship with John Bishop. It's small, but it may be a bargaining chip. Not on sentencing, considering the charge, but we may be able to negotiate small concessions if you can give helpful information on Bishop, you know, like anything you might have about his operations.'

Andrew forced himself to straighten his posture. The implication that he and Bishop were connected bothered him. 'I think there's a misunderstanding Barry. I don't have a relationship with Bishop.'

'The police don't think that's the case.'

'Listen, he was brother's friend when I was a child. I

haven't even seen him in probably two or three years. If I had something on Bishop, believe me, I'd gladly hand it over to them. And I'd do it for free.' He said.

'Okay Andrew. Just keep it mind. Like I said, it could be useful.'

'What about Mike Doyle?' Andrew asked. 'Have the police even bothered following that up?' The attorney slid back in his chair and snipped the top button of his suit jacket closed. 'I communicated to them everything you shared with me Andrew. I've been told they'll look into it, but honestly, and I mean this in the most constructive way possible . . . you're not the first person in here to start naming names after an arrest.'

Andrew shrugged. The more time he spent with the young attorney, the more resentful he grew towards him. He was beginning to find everything he said and did patronizing and was nearly certain the man did not believe that he was innocent. He wasn't sure if that mattered in court, but it mattered to Andrew and it bothered him.

'So are we done for now then?' Andrew asked.

'Yes. I'll be in touch soon with any progress. Remember, don't talk to anyone without me present. Oh, and I'll follow up on that whole bed situation.'

'Yeah thanks Barry.' Andrew said. He heard the door buzz again and click open. The same officer opened it and let the attorney out. Andrew waited again, knowing the guard would be in shortly to take him back to his cell. He felt truly alone and overwhelming dread took hold of him as he pictured Bernadette sitting at her kitchen table, looking at his face in the newspaper under some daunting headline splashed across the page to get a passive reader's attention. He hoped that she knew him well enough to know it couldn't be him. He hoped she, at least, believed it wasn't true.

11

Andrew's eyes fully adjusted to the darkness within his cell in the early morning hours. He'd been awake most of the night for the third day in a row. The prison produced its own noises in the dark. Those sounds frightened him deeply and grew no less ominous as they became more familiar. The prison was built in the 1950's. Andrew overheard other inmates' conversations of rumors that it originally housed a mental institution and was extended and repurposed in the 1970's to combat the overcrowding in existing jails. As ghost stories went, Wyngate's was a good one. The sounds throughout the night were attributed to voices and screams echoing from earlier times as opposed to hissing and grating from bad pipework and rusting metal. Stories or not, the place was unnerving to Andrew.

He heard a sound against the cell door and listened to the latch unhinge as he lay in the makeshift cot. It didn't feel quite like the wake up time, but it was difficult to judge with the rectangular door window the only view from within the cell. An officer entered and whispered 'Dawson'.

Andrew sat up quickly to show he was awake. 'I'm here.'

'No shit. Here get up and get anything that might be yours, including your shit tickets. We have a bed for you in another cell.'

Andrew got up quickly. He didn't have much with him since he didn't like venturing to the canteen. He grabbed the small blue recycling bin that was issued to him. In it was his toothbrush, toothpaste, his one roll of toilet paper and a stick of deodorant. He picked it up and followed the prison officer out of the cell. There were two others outside the cell with him. He walked behind the main one and in front of the two others down a long hall to the end, then down a set of stairs. They went through another set of doors into a different wing of the facility. Andrew was unsure of himself. Not that he'd enjoyed the first area they put him, but there was some level of comfort in the separation that the pre-trial wing held from convicted inmates. The officer stopped outside a cell that was close to the entrance of the wing and radioed to a supervisor to confirm the cell's location. He unlocked the latch with a key that looked to belong in medieval times and opened the large steel door. 'Here Dawson' he pointed. 'The bottom bunk has freed up.'

Andrew walked into the cell. It was close to a mirror image of the previous one except there was no canoe set up on the floor. He looked around the small room. He saw the top bunk's occupant was stirring awake. He noticed the color of the scrubs folded over the edge of the bed differed from his own. 'Excuse me sir' Andrew asked the officer 'I thought pre-trial inmates were supposed to be kept separate from convicted inmates?' He pointed over at the different colored uniform.

The officer raised his eyebrows and stiffened his lips before answering. He pointed up at the man in the bunk. 'He's not a convicted inmate. He's an ICE inmate. Consider him in transit.'

'What's an ICE inmate?' Andrew asked.

'Ask him. I'm sure he'll tell you all about it.' The officer answered. He stepped out of the cell and started to close the door. Before he did, he said 'Be glad I didn't throw you in with a skinner. But don't worry you'll meet plenty of them in Walpole once you're convicted.' Lastly he said 'You probably have an hour 'til chow.'

'Okay.' Andrew said.

The door slammed shut loudly and Andrew heard the large key turn the lock back into place. He walked over to the bottom bunk and slid into it. 'An hour until chow' he thought. 'Okay, so it's five am.' In his short time, he was beginning to understand that the prison was built on routine. Everyday every activity followed a strict schedule.

From six to six thirty they got breakfast. Meals where wheeled down in giant carts by inmate workers. They lined up, picked up the food trays from the cart and ate in the cells. From seven to nine am, they were locked down. At nine, there was rec time either in the common room in the housing unit or the adjoining rec yard that held a weight bench, half-court basketball and a handball court. Then lunch was brought in the same manner as breakfast, let out again at one for rec, back in lock down at two, dinner at four, back in lock down until six, then free to roam around in the rec area until lights out at ten. He had been warned to stay cautious during this evening free time. The inmates had four hours to play with. If something was going down, it was likely happening during that period. Andrew didn't feel he needed warnings to remain cautious. His shoulders felt permanently tensed and his eyes darted around rapidly since he'd arrived. He didn't go out of his way to make conversation and for the most part no one spoke to him. He guessed much of that had to do with word getting around about what he was being charged with.

Others did make some small talk, seemingly just to pass

the time. He was in no hurry for time to pass. In fact, he wished it froze days ago while he sat on his porch with Bernadette. His new cell mate didn't say much that morning. He basically avoided eye contact altogether. By the time they were locked down after lunch however, he had started to chip in a few words. Andrew figured boredom had probably gotten the best of him. He assumed most people broke down and talked to their cell mates eventually, regardless of what each was being held for. It wasn't natural to be in a confined place with another human being. Something had to break that awkwardness.

'You're pre-trial right?' the man asked.

'Yeah, I am.' Andrew answered.

'I guess that's obvious with the orange suit.'

Andrew nodded 'What's the blue mean? The CO said you were ice or something. I didn't know what he was talking about.'

'You never heard of ICE?'

'No, should I have?'

'I don't know. You would if you were illegal here. It stands for Immigration and Customs Enforcement.'

'So you're illegal.'

'Well, yeah. I've lived here over ten years, but I don't have a green card. They picked me up in Dallas trying to get on a plane back to Logan. I was on holidays in Texas.'

'Shit. What'd they pick you up for?'

'Just for being in the country, no other crime or anything.'

'And what, they sent you back to Massachusetts to sort it out.'

The man laughed, but Andrew felt it wasn't one of

amusement. 'I wish. I sat in a Texas prison cell for a month while they kicked my case around the county, state and federal courts.'

'Sounds a little extreme.'

'More than a little. It's safe to say ICE is a federal power that's at best, unchecked. Fucksake, they spend millions each year just to move us back and forth. This place is getting some of those dollars for every day that I'm held here. It's like they're renting jail space until they can figure out whether to leave me be or ship me back to Mayo.'

Andrew nodded in understanding. 'Yeah, well, sorry to hear that.'

The man climbed back up to the top bunk and laid back down 'Thanks.'

Andrew took this to mean the conversation was over. He guessed that lock down time was winding down and stood up to peak out the door slat. When he turned back around, he noticed the man cautiously watching him. He averted his eyes when Andrew turned back, but he'd seen the look the man gave him. He also felt it. He sensed fear from that look and realized his cell mate must've heard from other inmates or the officers about what charge Andrew was being held on. He felt shame just thinking about the accusation. Although, he was somewhat glad that no one had asked him about it. He knew in his heart that he was innocent. Whenever he felt the urge to try and convince others of this, he thought of how shallow a stranger's words would come across to them. 'How many more before me screamed their innocence from the rooftops? How many of them were actually guilt free?' So he held back. He said nothing, because talking about it to inmates and convicts wasn't going to help. He needed help, and he needed it fast. As to how he could find it, it was too bad his mind continually drew a blank.

At six pm the cell doors were unlocked for the last time that day and the inmates poured out from their units into the block's common areas. Andrew remained in his cell with the door open. He stayed lying on the bed just staring at the metal springs on the bottom of the bunk above him. For twenty minutes he laid there, listening to the voices outside the cell. Some were deep murmurs, others were pitchy, but none were very clear. He made out a few conversations in that time. One he heard was an inmate complaining to another about being forced to wear bobos. Bobos, he gleaned, were the standard issue jail shoes that were more like Velcro slippers with plastic bottoms. The inmate was pissed off because his mother hadn't put cash on his canteen account. That meant he couldn't pick up a pair of the white Reebok classics, which they sold in the commissary. The bobos made his feet sweat apparently. He heard another man with a nasally voice calling one of the inmates a banker, which Andrew picked out of context had something to do with feeding information to the prison officers.

After a while, straining to listen to conversations grew tiresome. He sat up on the bed, careful not to hit his head on the bunk above and planted his feet on the ground. He stood up and walked slowly over to the cell's doorway and looked out. He took in the scene around him. There were small groups scattered around the common area in conversations. Others lounged in communal chairs alone, either flicking through books or just staring into space. He watched several men walk in from the outdoor area and join some of the already formed groups. There were a mix of uniform colors, but most were brown. Andrew wasn't sure what those or the other's signified. Part of him wanted to know, part could live without finding out. There were a few others in orange, but not many and those there appeared to be alone like him.

Andrew walked out of the cell slowly and made his way down a small set of stairs. Through quick glances, he saw some people take notice of him as he passed, but none acknowledged him outwardly. He assumed it was a defense mechanism that was learned in these places quickly. Look, but be fast and avoid eye contact. He felt that in three days, he needed eyes in the back of his head to survive in there. He walked outside and took a seat in a small set of benches in between the weights area and the handball court. A few inmates worked out, while a couple others looked to be playing HORSE on the basketball court. Others just stood around, Andrew imagined, taking the time to breathe in fresh air while the opportunity existed.

Andrew was looking at his own pair of bobos down on his feet when a shadow passed over him and he felt the bench shift slightly as a man sat close to him. 'Too close' Andrew thought. He looked young and old at the same time. He was really thin Andrew noticed, and had a close cropped bowl cut that made him look like a teenager. His face was gaunt however, and it cast a vampiric hue. That face made him appear older than his thin frame suggested.

'Hey new blood' the man asked. 'You carrying? Hook me up?'

Andrew didn't know what to say so just shook his head

no and shrugged.

'Come on dude, I know you got that stop sign. Hook a brother up, I'm fucking fiending here.'

'Sorry man, I don't what you're talking about.' Andrew said and tried to shift away slowly to his left.

'Aw fuck you then dude.'

Andrew heard another, deeper voice from behind him. 'Get lost Pete!'

The skinny guy looked over toward the voice, then got up and walked back inside. The other man came around and took his spot on the bench. 'Don't mind Pete, he's just one of the junkies. They're like part of the furniture in here and always looking for handouts.'

Andrew nodded. He was glad Pete took off, but not exactly comfortable with his new visitor either. The man was much larger than Pete, close to Andrew's size, but broader and Andrew thought 'Denser?' He had a healthy complexion compared to Pete too. He wore a neatly trimmed beard and had a set of forearms that went straight into his palms, which Andrew noticed. The lack of wrists suggested great strength and looked dangerous.

Andrew swallowed saliva that had built up in his throat and gathered enough courage to speak. He asked, 'What's 'stop sign'? That guy said I had to have stop sign on me.'

'Stop sign is suboxone.' The man answered.

Andrew was confused. 'The rehab drug?'

'Exactly, except it ain't for rehab in here. It's used for getting high.'

Andrew asked 'Is it allowed in here?'

'Fuck no kid, but it's here. The skids will smuggle it anyway they can. They crush it into paste and have their kids use it for art projects and send daddy pictures made from the shit to hang on his cell wall. CO's are even stripping stamps off the mail cause it can be used to seal them on the envelopes.'

'Wow . . . shit.' Andrew said. He was amazed, but not surprised by the ingenuity and brazen tactics that drug addicts employed. He had seen some of it firsthand.

He noticed suddenly that the sun had been swept aside for much dimmer moonlight, though the air remained warm in the dark. He looked around the yard and saw that most of those inmates that were outside had headed indoors except for two stragglers plus the man next to him on the bench. It dawned on him that the two men kept looking over in his direction. Every few seconds they looked over, then away, then at the doorway, and then back again.

He felt the hair on the back of his neck stand up and a tingling feeling ran down his arms. 'Something's wrong' he thought. As he thought it, he saw a brief flash of light in his periphery when the moonlight caught metal that shimmered in the man's hand next to him.

Andrew jumped to his feet just in time to dodge a swipe that came across the man's body. The man was off balance from the miss and Andrew took the advantage and kicked the bench as hard as he could, knocking it backwards and sending the man falling over with it. He turned to find the two stragglers almost upon him. He had no time to move, so he tightened his body and absorbed the blows as both men hit him at the same time tackling him to the ground. The three of them hit the pavement with momentum and rolled. Andrew kicked out at both of them from the ground, while covering his head with his arms. His kicks were wild, but accurate enough to land, catching one man in the face and the other in his testicles. Both fell away, but not before landing several punches to Andrew's face. The adrenaline blocked any immediate pain from the blows, but he tasted blood that ran down from his nose, over his lips and into his mouth. He scrambled to get up, landing a heavy kick to the man's head that had fallen closest to him as he rose. He spun around frantically searching for his original attacker. Andrew knew that he was the main worry.

He turned just in time to see the man lunge at him with the blade again. This time Andrew dove out of the way and rolled over next to the weight bench. He reached around on the ground, searching for anything he could use to defend himself. The man ran at him again. Andrew reached for a short metal dumbbell, a detached pole the length of his forearm with no weights connected. He stood up and braced himself, feeling the weight of steel in his hand. The man plunged forward with the knife. Andrew side stepped it this time, brushing it aside with his left hand, then came down hard with the steel pole onto the man's forearm. He heard a crack and saw the knife fall from his hand. It was small and looked homemade, more a shiv than a knife. Andrew paused only for a second. He heard commotion behind him as the officers on duty rushed out and grabbed hold of the other assailants. In that second he saw into his attackers eyes. First he saw pain, from what Andrew assumed was a broken wrist. He hoped to see fear next. He was wrong. Anger overtook the pain in the man's eyes in that second. Andrew only knew one way to stop it and he swung the steel pole hard again. Officers tackled him to the ground at the same time, but not before he heard the crunch of a jaw breaking and watched shards of broken teeth fall before him like snowflakes as his face was shoved hard into the ground.

12

A staff doctor worked each day during normal daytime hours. In evenings and overnight however, there generally wasn't a need at Wyngate. There were tough guys in there, but most were serving short time. That alone seemed to stem some of the violence that ran rampant in other longer term state and federal facilities. Plus, with Boston about thirty minutes away, not to mention several other hospitals within ten to fifteen miles, the prison budget couldn't afford doctors working twenty four hour shifts. There was a medic on every shift however. Also, it was required that at all times a certain number of correctional officers with medical certifications were scheduled.

The infirmary was more like an office. It reminded Andrew of a nurse's office at his old high school except the medic was male and the supplies were a grade above Tylenol and Midol. Since the attack in the prison yard, his heart beat like a bass drum. It was loud enough to effect his hearing. No number of breathing exercises or reassurances from the medic seemed to calm him down. Initially, he worried that the men that came after him would strike again, especially if they also ended up in the infirmary. He asked multiple officers about this and each had the same answer. One of the men was in isolation, while the other two were taken to Massachusetts General Hospital. One man had a concussion. The other man was hurt more seriously, with a broken wrist and broken jaw, not to mention several broken teeth. Andrew also kept pressing the officers to explain why the men attacked him. The only answer he got was that those guys were short-timers. They were local men, with daughters of their own. Andrew knew men like them. He knew that they weren't trying to send a message. Their only aim was to take him down. He could see it from their side. He could nearly empathize with them. At the same time, he knew they had the wrong man, although there'd never be the opportunity to explain that to them.

Andrew wanted to believe that under normal circumstances he'd feel bad for what he'd done. He thought he'd experience at least trace levels of guilt. However, current circumstances were well beyond normal. He felt his actions were justified and necessary. Mostly, he was just glad that he wasn't also lying in a hospital bed. 'It very nearly could've been the morgue.' He thought. His injuries weren't serious. His nose had been bloodied and it swelled badly along with both eyes, but luckily, nothing was broken. He imagined he looked much worse than he felt. His head was in some pain, but that was probably more related to coming down after a stressful situation.

After he was cleaned up, he was walked down to a different area of the prison. It wasn't openly stated to him, but he guessed the prison now considered him a target. 'Should have known that already.' He thought. He assumed he was now in protective custody as they miraculously found him a cell for himself in a separate wing and officers seemed to be around him much more frequently than the previous three days.

Whether it was the body's release after the fight or just being alone finally in a cell on his own, he slept much better that night. He made it straight through the night without waking once. Also, he had no dreams, good or bad, that he remembered. That morning he felt refreshed. There were aches and pains of course, but he felt well rested at least and believed his mind was sharper than it had been for days. It was like a fog that cloaked his thinking had finally dissipated with the rising sun.

Breakfast was brought to him and he ate in his cell. He was locked down longer in the morning than usual. When he was let out, he was allowed to walk around the common area, but he was flanked by two officers the entire time. Andrew noticed a slight change with the officers who were around him. Something about their demeanor towards him was different than it had been before. He was unsure why. 'Surely, it had nothing to do with the fight.' He thought. He considered whether it was all in his head. He asked himself whether it was just his perception of how they acted towards him, had that changed since now his mind was functioning more clearly.

As the morning passed and the day wore on however, he put aside the notion that it was all in his head. While they weren't exactly nice to him, they were no longer as cold towards him. Some were more talkative it seemed and others appeared more relaxed around him now. There was no mistaken that there was a difference overnight.

After lunch an officer came and got him from the cell and said he had a visitor. He was led down a series of corridors until he came to a locked-down room in between the attorney meeting rooms and the contact visit area. He was informed by one of the officers that he was allowed visitors, but that pre-trial inmates could only talk to visitors behind glass. Next, he was led to a seat in one of the booths at the end and told he needed to speak and listen through the phone.

He sat down and picked up the receiver. He cradled it on his shoulder while he waited. Through the phone's ear, he heard a buzzing noise as a visitor was let into the room and led to the booth on the chair opposite him, protected by glass.

Bernadette picked up the phone and looked at Andrew. He could see her eyes search his face and take in his injuries. He watched helplessly as she started to cry. Tears filled his eyes as well. Seeing her at all was a shock to him. Seeing her crying across from him, behind a protective glass barrier was nearly too painful to bear. He spoke into the receiver.

'Bernie.' He said

She looked up at him and tried to choke back the sobs. Finally she managed to hold them back and she wiped the tears from both sides of her face with her free hand. 'I'm sorry.' She said.

Andrew wasn't really sure how to continue. He wasn't certain what she knew or whether she thought he did what the papers said he did. He stayed silent. She continued finally. 'I had to come . . . I had to see you. Just . . . your face. You're hurt.'

Slowly he answered. 'I'm glad you came . . . this' he said and pointed to his face, 'don't worry about this. Honestly it looks much worse than it feels.

'I sure hope so. I mean, it looks really bad.' She gave him a small smile through her flushed cheeks.

Andrew laughed lightly and smiled back. He felt pain from the bruises on his face when he did. 'So, that's why you came here? To insult my looks?'

'No. But that doesn't mean I'd pass up the opportunity.'

'Of course.' He said. 'So . . . how are you?'

'Andrew'

'What?'

'That's not why I'm here either. I don't want to small talk.'

'Okay. Well then, what is it?'

'You know my uncle, the attorney.'

'Um. Yeah, I don't know him, but I remember meeting him before.'

'You did, I'm sure of it. Anyway, he's a defense attorney. Like, a really good one. He's taken over your case.'

'What? How . . . why?'

'I . . . um, I spent the last few days crying at his feet to get him to do it. That's how.'

'Really?' He felt awkward, but grateful nonetheless. 'Thank you. But, I guess . . . why would you do that?'

'Andrew' she said sternly 'You're my friend for one, and you're innocent. I asked about your court appointed attorney. He's not bad, just not as experienced.'

'Wait, you know I'm innocent. You didn't believe what was in the news?' he asked.

'Of course I know you're innocent Andrew, I know you, plus . . .'

'Plus what?'

'I saw you Andrew. I'm your eye witness, or, your alibi.'

Andrew looked around him to see if the officer was listening. He wasn't sure if the conversation was being recorded, but he said it anyway. 'Bernie, I am innocent. But, Gina was killed Thursday. I saw you on Friday night, not Thursday.'

'You don't understand.'

'What don't I understand? Please, explain it to me. I don't want to see you taking a fall for me.'

'You didn't see me Thursday, but I saw you.'

Andrew sat up straighter, pushing his eyebrows close together in confusion.

Bernadette continued talking, 'I came to see you Thursday night too. I knocked on your door. I could see you. You must've fallen asleep watching television on the couch. I waited. I waited for over an hour on your porch, deciding what to do. When the snow started falling heavily, I decided to leave.' She paused. 'I'm sorry, it's embarrassing.'

'Bernie' he said and leaned forward towards the glass 'it's not embarrassing. You just saved my life. So the cops, you've gone to them with this?'

'My uncle and I did yes. Well to them and the District Attorney. The timeline fits Andrew. They're letting you go.'

Andrew was stunned. He felt weak and light headed from excitement. Had he been standing, he thought, he would've fallen over. He ran his palm over his eyes to hold back tears that welled up, and then ran his hand through his hair. 'I can't believe it.' He said 'when?'

'I think there's some paperwork and stuff they've been working on all morning, but it should be soon, at least within twenty four hours.'

'I don't know what to say. Thank you Bernie, I can't believe it.'

'There's one other thing though Andrew. It's not good, but there's another factor to why you're getting out.'

'What is it?' he said concerned suddenly that he'd been dreaming and this was all part of a sick joke.

'There's been another one.' She said.

'Another what?' he asked

She paused for moment before speaking into the phone 'Another girl found. Lisa Stark.'

Andrew looked up at Bernadette, but didn't say anything for a moment. Memories flashed into his head of another precocious, smiling young girl he had known in his youth. 'Lisa Stark' he said. 'She was in school with us too.'

13

Andrew walked out of Wyngate Correctional Facility the following Monday morning. The day that greeted him was wet, but warm. He walked out in his work boots, jeans and hooded sweatshirt, the same way he walked in. The rest of his belongings were handed to him in a big brown envelope, which he emptied out and tossed outside of the gate. Stevie greeted him outside. Andrew was glad to see a friend's face the moment he was freed. Stevie drove in with Andrew's truck, which he picked up from impound a day earlier after it had been combed through for evidence. He offered the keys to Andrew, but he wasn't interested in getting behind the wheel. Andrew got comfortable in the passenger's seat and watched the trees blur by out the window on the highway as they drove back to Quincy. Stevie tried to make small talk, but didn't force it. Andrew noticed and appreciated that he kept the topics light, like recapping the Bruins games he missed during the week.

They pulled up outside of Andrew's apartment. Stevie handed the keys over to him and Andrew asked, 'You need the truck to get home?' 'Actually' Stevie answered 'I thought I'd stay with you a few days and help you get settled. If you're cool with it.'

Andrew stood for a moment swinging the keys around his finger in short intervals considering the request. 'Yeah Stevie.' He said 'it'd be good to have a friend around, thanks.' Andrew walked into the apartment to find it clean. The spare room had already been cleared out for Stevie and he found fresh milk in the refrigerator and a loaf of bread on the counter. Stevie watched him look around for a moment, then took a seat on the couch. 'I had your spare key. So when Bernie told me you'd be getting out, I wanted to make sure the place was clean and everything, ya know.'

'Thanks Stevie, I appreciate it. You ah . . . you talk to Bernie since?' Stevie shook his head. 'Afraid not brother. She called me to let me know when you were getting out. That's all. I think she got a bit of shit from her fiancé for . . . you know, getting involved and everything.'

'I take it they're still together though right?' Andrew asked. A glimmer of hope crept into his chest followed sharply by guilt. Stevie looked at him with an apologetic smile and nudged his shoulders. 'I know man.' Andrew said, 'don't know what I was thinking.' He stood in the doorway between the kitchen and living room and reached his arms up to stretch them against the frame. 'You heard about Lisa Stark I take it.' He asked. 'I did.' Stevie answered. 'You wanna . . . talk about that stuff now?'

'No actually, I don't. Just that, this dude's out there still you know?' He paused for a few seconds, then continued, 'Hey you uh, you been around this Doyle guy since?' He asked. 'It was his fucking knife that jammed me up, I know it. Well, I don't know it-know it, like for a fact I mean, but . . . I can feel it.'

Stevie shook his head slowly. 'I haven't seen or heard from him since that day you saw us outside Bishop's place. To be honest, he and I squared up on the work I did for him then and there. It's not like we were buddies or anything, you know.'

Andrew nodded his head and took his arms down from the wall. 'Yeah man. I know. Listen, I can't even think about it right now. I'm gonna take a shower and stuff.

You good here for a few on your own?'

'I've made myself at home Andrew as you can see. Do what you need to do, I'll hang here.'

Having Stevie in the apartment with him helped Andrew to start to feel himself again. They danced around the topic of Lisa Stark, Gina O'Neil and the others several times over the next couple days, especially when something would show up in the news in the evenings. Andrew couldn't really stomach the topic for longer than a minute. He stopped watching any channel on television that even remotely showed news and he tossed his cell phone off the back porch into the trees behind the house after making the mistake of checking his Facebook page and looking at the newspaper online. His release made the news, but with much less fanfare than his capture. He was page five material at best when he walked out of Wyngate.

He was still waiting to hear if his old boss would take him back to work, which felt less likely with every passing day. He insisted that Stevie should go to work that week instead of moping around the apartment with him. There was still a stigma around him, especially with another girl found dead and no one else in custody for that or the other murders. He felt the eyes him when he walked into the shop or went to the gas station. Basically anytime he stepped out of the house he got looks. Innocent until proven guilty might work in the courts, but not in the media and not in the public's eyes.

He was emotionally worn down by Saturday. Stevie wasn't working on the weekend, so he talked Andrew into going out for some food around lunch time. It was the first time in over a day that Andrew agreed to go outside.

They drove down to a local deli that they frequented since teenagers and grabbed a small table in the corner of the dining room. Andrew grabbed the seat with his back to the wall. There weren't many people in for a Saturday, but he still felt eyes on him when he entered. He thought to himself 'it'd be better if it was jammed with people, no one would probably notice me then.' He could see the lingering stares in his periphery. He wasn't sure if it was real or his imagination, but he could sense hostility in the air. He stayed seated as Stevie walked up to the counter, ordered their lunch and paid. The line was short, so Stevie was back over in less than five minutes. In that time, Andrew sat hunched over, trying his best to look small and unnoticeable. He kept bringing his hands up over his face, rubbing his chin or scratching his forehead. Stevie sat down in his chair and looked over at him. 'What's up man? You look like a cornered squirrel. You okay?'

'I don't know Stevie. I'm tired of people shooting daggers through me with their eyes. Can't take this shit much longer.'

'Hang in there man. You didn't do anything wrong. It'll just take time, that's all.' Stevie said. Andrew took in a deep breath and let it out slowly. He leaned forward across the table and said in a quiet voice, 'You think time is gonna make people forget that I was arrested and charged with fucking murder Stevie? Really?' Stevie just shrugged. Andrew sat back a little in his chair. 'Sorry Stevie. I'm not trying take anything out on you.' 'Hey man' Stevie said. 'Don't worry about me, you're going through some shit, I get that.'

'Where's the food anyway?' Andrew asked. Stevie started playing with the napkin holder. Andrew thought he wanted to say more, but didn't press him. 'What? Oh, yeah, they'll bring it over.' Stevie answered. A second later they both turned to look up at a man standing over their table, casting a shadow over the middle of it. Neither had seen him approaching, but both noticed him now. He was tall and wore a dark button down shirt with the top few buttons undone so that chest hair and a thin gold chain peeked out over the cloth. Andrew and Stevie both sat looking up at him, but he didn't say anything right away. He reached into his pocket and pulled out a receipt, which he slapped onto the table. Then he pulled out a roll of bills and counted out the amount from the receipt and laid it on top.

'What the fuck is that?' Stevie asked and pointed to the cash on the table. 'That's your money back.' The man answered. 'I know it's my money back, I'm more curious of the why?'

'I'm the manager here and I'm refusing to serve you two that's why.'

'What? Are you fucking kidding me? We've been coming here for years.' Stevie said.

'I know perfectly well who you are. He's not welcome in here.' He said and pointed to Andrew. 'Now, I'm asking you nicely to leave.'

'This is asking us fucking nicely?' Stevie said. The man put his hands on the table and leaned closer towards them. 'I don't want a scene here. So just take off. Go somewhere else please.' Stevie swiped his own hand quickly across the surface and picked up a fork and jammed it into the table. The man pulled his hand back off the table just in time. Stevie jumped up from his seat and lunged forward with an elbow towards the man's chest. Andrew jumped up too and grabbed Stevie across the table holding him back, but just barely. 'Leave it Stevie.' Andrew said. 'Let's just go.' Stevie was breathing heavy. His eyes were locked on the tall man, who was trying to stand his ground, but looked weak all of sudden and Andrew saw fear in his eyes. 'Stevie!' Andrew said more firmly. Stevie shook his head finally and broke his stare from the man. He looked over to Andrew. After a few seconds he nodded. 'Yeah Andrew. Fuck this place.' He grabbed the cash off the table and stuffed it into his pocket. Stevie shoved the chair hard under the table. The loud 'bang' drew the remaining looks from the few that hadn't already turned their attention to the altercation. Stevie brushed past the manager as he walked out and gave him one last fervent stare. Andrew followed closely behind Stevie. He was braced to interfere with any sudden rush Stevie might attempt just in case. They walked out the door slowly, but without further incident and went around back to get the truck.

Stevie lightened when they were back in traffic. 'You wanna try someplace else?' Andrew looked over at him and shook his head. 'Nah man. I think I'll just head back. Order a pizza or something, I don't care.'

They lounged back at Andrew's apartment watching television and not really saying much for the rest of the day. Andrew kept running over the last week in his head. He couldn't focus on anything else. 'Time might change things, sure' he thought. 'but how much time.' The more he considered it, the more appealing it became to him. He needed to disappear. He couldn't take the looks, the sneers, the judgment any longer, at least not now. 'I need to just go' he thought.

'Just start fresh somewhere else, somewhere that no one knows my face.'

He got up and walked to the refrigerator and grabbed two bottles of beer and opened them. He threw the caps in the trash and walked into the living room. He sat on the couch adjacent to Stevie and reached over and handed him one of the beers. Stevie took it from his hand and gave him a questioning look as he sat down. 'I need to go Stevie.'

Stevie gave Andrew a puzzled look. 'Now? Where?' Andrew shook his head. 'No, you're not getting me. I mean, I need to go somewhere else. Get away for a while, you know what I mean? Like, start fresh somewhere else.'

Stevie leaned forwards and put the beer down on the coffee table in front of him. 'Come on Andrew. I told you, time is all. It'll take time, but this shit will blow over.'

'I don't think so Stevie. And, I can't just hide in my apartment here until it does man. I'm a fucking prisoner still, afraid to walk out of this place.'

'Who gives a shit what these people think man? Really, they don't know you.' Stevie said.

'Stevie, I give a shit! Everyone in this fucking city, shit, probably even the state has seen my face and associates me with one thing. I can't live in fucking shame any longer!'

'So . . . your gonna leave. Just leave everything you know?'

'Yeah. I think I am.'

'Where you gonna go then?'

'I don't know really. But . . . when my mother took off, she made me get my Irish passport renewed. I think I might go there. Fuck it. I think I will.'

'And do what man? You need money and shit to even do something like that.'

'Stevie, I've got money. I've been fucking busting my ass working since I was eighteen. I've got enough in the bank.'

'You're all set then huh? I mean what the fuck. What about me?'

Andrew took a long sip from his beer and put it down on the coffee table. 'Stevie, man. You're my best friend. You know that. But really, this ain't about you.' Stevie got up and walked into the spare room. Andrew could hear rustling from the room. A minute later Stevie walked back out with his backpack on his back. 'Dude, come on Stevie. Don't be like that.'

'I'm not being like anything man. You made your mind up Andrew, I can see that.' He walked over towards the doorway. He turned back towards Andrew. 'Just tell me though. You won't stick around for me. What about Bernie? You'd stick around for her I'm sure.'

Andrew leaned forward, then stood up and turned to face Stevie. He knew the answer was yes. Stevie knew it too. But, it's not something he could ever admit to Stevie, as close as they were. Andrew knew his leaving would hit Stevie hard. The guy had no one else, but Andrew. He never knew a father and his mother had disappeared off the face of the earth years ago. Where she'd gone or who with was something Stevie never discussed. Andrew remembered bringing it up to try and comfort him, but a dark cloud seemed to descend over Stevie when he did so Andrew dropped it. 'Too painful.' Andrew thought at the time. He knew the feeling. He had his own pain to contend with. Andrew guessed it was that silently shared pain that drew them to each other and kept them such good friends over the years. He looked over at Stevie. He thought he saw the beginning of tears forming around his eyes. 'I'm sorry Stevie.' He said. Stevie kept his face hard and swallowed. 'Yeah, me too.' he said and turned and walked out the door.

14

Andrew carried a large box from the back of his truck to the storage locker. It was the last of several large boxes he'd packed and loaded into the space. Mostly he packed away clothes and tools. He'd signed his old Ford over to Chef Benson who said he could find use for it and planned to leave it behind the shop on West Elm before heading off. He offered it to Stevie first, but he said he didn't want it. They barely spoke at all since Andrew made his decision to leave. He had some furniture packed away in the storage locker along with the clothes and tools, but not much. Half of what furnished his apartment was borrowed. Most of the rest wasn't worth storing. When he thought about it, he was surprised to find his stuff still in his apartment at all when he was released. He had half assumed that the landlord would have gotten rid of everything to avoid having him on his property. 'Perhaps they were afraid of what they might find there.' He considered.

He thought more about his decision after Stevie had left his apartment upset and in the days following as he began to get everything together. The factors for his decision hadn't changed one bit and that further solidified his resolve. Stevie would miss him, he knew that, but Bernie was still getting married to another man and his boss had to let him go in order to avoid losing most of his customers.

He didn't want to be recognized every time he stepped from his stoop. 'Not for the current reasons anyway' he thought. 'It would kill me to live like that.'

He reached up and grabbed the metal grate and pulled the shutters down on the locker. He took a knee to close the lock at the notch on the floor. As he was crouched down, he heard a car pull up behind him and turned his body to see it. It was a navy blue sedan and without looking further, he knew who it was. He finished locking the shutters and stood up. He turned around and brushed his hands off on his jeans.

Detective Harris was walking towards him. When Andrew turned to him, the Detective put his hands up and said 'I come in peace.'

Andrew just nodded, but waited for the man to get closer before talking. When he approached Andrew said 'Detective. Can I do something for you?'

'No Andrew, you can't. I just came by to see you off. I heard you were leaving town.'

'Wouldn't you if you were me?' Andrew asked.

The Detective nodded in agreement. 'Yes, I suppose I would if I were you. So, where you headed?'

'Does it matter?' Andrew asked, making it obvious to the Detective that he wasn't up for talking.

'No . . . no, I guess not. Well, I'll let you off then. I genuinely only came by to say hello and goodbye before you took off. Good luck Andrew.' He said.

Andrew sighed. 'One question Detective. Why did you let me walk out that day only to pick me up minutes later?' It was a question that weighed on Andrew heavily. He had initially asked his lawyer about it, but never got clarity as to why. Once he was in prison, other things had taken over his mind. It was only after he knew he was being released that the question began to eat away at him again.

The Detective paused and considered the question for a few seconds before answering. 'I cut you loose because I thought we had the wrong guy Andrew. Soon after I did, the evidence said otherwise . . . looks like I was right after all.'

The Detective started walking away. Andrew wanted to ask more. He wanted to know whether they were any closer to finding the real killer. He wanted to know had they found Doyle. He wondered if they took him serious or just assumed he was giving out any name he could to get the scent off himself. 'No' Andrew thought. He wasn't sure why, but he had a strong feeling that Detective Harris was not one to leave any tip or bit of information un-pursued. He wanted to talk more, to find out and to help. But, his urge to run, to get out while he still could was stronger. 'I'm free.' He said internally, 'Stay that way.' Andrew watched the Detective take a few more steps towards his car, then called after him, 'Dublin.'

'What's that?' Detective Harris asked and turned back towards Andrew.

'I'm going to Dublin. Figured I'd put my Irish passport to use. It's been gathering dust for a while.'

He nodded. 'Good. Dublin's a good city . . . good. Take care Andrew.' He said, then waved and continued towards his car. Andrew waved goodbye, then walked to his truck. 'Nope' he thought. 'I won't miss this place. Not one bit.'

15

There were a handful of memories locked away in the vault of Andrew's mind. Many were painful and those stayed deep within that vault at all costs. Some were embarrassing, which made him blush whenever they rose to the surface. The rest however were just dormant for the reason that they didn't seem important at the time. The Dawson's had visited back and forth to Ireland a few times when Andrew was young, but not since before his father was killed. Everything got harder after that. Vacations grew fewer and further apart. He didn't remember Dublin really, nor should he since most of their trips started with landing at Dublin airport, then driving three hours straight to Donegal. Cities were natural to him after growing up in the Boston area, but Dublin city was still unchartered territory. He wasn't sure what to expect except through bits of information he'd heard from others, mostly his mother, over the years. Although she painted the picture of the 'Big Smoke', a dirty Dublin that probably existed more in her imagination at that time than anywhere else.

Though unfamiliar with Dublin city center, he remembered the airport except that the old terminal building was now overshadowed by a modern state of the art second terminal. The air outside the airport made him nostalgic when he breathed it in. It tasted of damp grass and smoked peat that reminded him of winter visits to Donegal. The early morning was still dark and a mist hung in the air like a cloud in slow descent. Also, it was crisp, jacket weather, as expected in early spring.

He lined up for a taxi and was seated in one on the way into the city within minutes. The journey through Dublin city ran at odds with the serenity offered outside of the airport. In the north inner city many revelers were still out and active, spilling out of nightclubs or fast food restaurants called chip shops. He looked on in amusement counting the rhythm of the street's design, chip shop, pub, chip shop, pub, chip shop, pub. It was an odd city planning strategy, but was not without a certain charm.

O'Connell Street was heavily littered with discarded food wrappers and empty beer cans, mostly Budweiser and Dutch Gold. The trash lessened the impressiveness of the statues that lined the center of the street, while the tall metal poll that the taxi driver called the spire just looked out of place with its historic surroundings. Several statues also had a number of twenty-something men and scantily clad young women loitering around the base. Many looked worn out from a booze-filled night out, while others were locked in loud disagreements. When the driver hit the central lock button, the sharp slam of the knobs had a disconcerting effect that Andrew thought was the opposite of his intention.

They crossed the River Liffey in the cab and Andrew thought to the naked eye it looked to be more of the same, despite what he'd heard of the city's north-south divide. The driver talked the entire journey, explaining much of the route in real time as they drove it. They drove past Trinity College and turned left past a late night burger place and signs for a men's hair clinic shortly after that. The driver explained they needed to take Georges Street, Aungier Street and then Camden Street. Andrew was surprised to learn it was three street names for one road that seemed to be named at arbitrary sections. The road itself was not very long, but the sea of taxi cabs made it nearly impenetrable.

At the corner, the taxi swung around left to Harcourt Street, where Andrew's early morning tour of Dublin ended. Harcourt Street looked to be a business district with Georgian buildings lining both sides of the street. The buildings housed everything from offices, bars, restaurants, hotels, night clubs, coffee shops, art galleries and a police headquarters. Andrew crossed the street to the small hotel that the taxi driver had pointed out to him. He stumbled over a set of tram tracks that he hadn't noticed until he crossed them. He had chosen that hotel online, mainly because of its central location and its affordability. He needed somewhere he could live for up to a week or two until he could find a place to settle. He noticed as he approached, his hotel doubled as a bar and also housed a nightclub on its below street level landing. A couple of doormen still lingered around the entrance, but appeared to only be shepherding out the last remaining stragglers from the club. He slipped past two staggering young men in cheap suits with no ties and started up the steps to the reception area's entrance. As he reached for the door, it flung open quickly and without regard for his face. He blocked it with his arm just in time and noticed a blur charge past him. The door-swinging blur was a woman and she stopped at the bottom of the steps and turned back to him. He must've yelled 'shit' or 'woah' or something like that without realizing. The girl looked at him and asked 'Excuse me?' Andrew thought it came out a little too aggressively.

He gathered himself and turned towards her. She had

dark hair that looked nearly black in the night, yet glimmered with a hint of red or auburn from the shine off the orange streetlights. Her skin was very white, not pale or unhealthy white, more porcelain, except for her cheeks, which held a healthy rose blush. Her eyes were red like she had recently been rubbing them and her nose ran slightly like she had been crying. Andrew assumed she had been. He realized he was staring only when she spoke to him again. 'Well?' she said.

'Nothing' he said back and shifted his feet uncomfortably and averted his gaze from her red eyes. 'Just . . . you alright?'

'I'm grand. You're the one staring.' She answered.

Andrew shrugged, 'Sorry' he said 'I'm a little dazed, I just flew in.' Andrew looked down at his bags and kicked one lightly with his foot to draw her attention to them. His discomfort made him feel he needed to point out the obvious.

She followed his eyes down to the bags that sat at his feet. 'Right' she said.

Andrew reached down for his luggage and said. 'Well . . . goodnight.'

She turned then and sat on the stoop. Her fingers held a cigarette she pulled from nowhere and she put it to her lips. She pulled it out again and said up the steps, 'it's morning actually.'

Andrew paused again with the door now held open with his hip. 'Yeah, I guess it is.' He walked into reception, puzzled by the girl's demeanor, but strangely intrigued with her as well. He gave the man at reception his name and credit card. The man swiped his card and handed him back a room key and pointed out the way to the room. 'Will you be looking for breakfast?'

Andrew considered the request. 'Doubt it' he answered 'I'm looking to sleep.'

'Okay, hang the sign on the door then if you plan on sleeping, it'll keep the cleaners out of the room.'

'Got it, thanks.' He said and walked off with a wave.

His room was on the second floor and he found it easily and opened it with his key. It was smaller than the pictures on the website, but he accepted that was usually the case. He threw his luggage in the corner and pulled his toiletry bag out from the front slot. He brushed his teeth quickly, then stripped down to his boxers and climbed into bed. He laid awake for a minute or two, but not any longer, as weariness overcame him. The journey in was not really what he expected, but he felt that at last his troubles were behind him, at least for the moment. His last thoughts before sleep took him were not of prison cells, murder or death. They weren't even of Bernadette. After he shut his eyes, he thought only of the girl with dark hair on the stoop. Something about her was alluring and it was her image that was burned into his brain.

16

The hours faded by as Andrew's slumber continued. He'd wake periodically from a dream, but fall asleep again within moments, each dream dissolving into more sleep, no longer discernible from any other forgotten memory. When he woke for good, it was dark again. He'd passed an entire day under the sheets with his eyes shut, but strangely felt worse physically than he did before it, as if his body had grown accustomed to laying down and showed no interest in any other position.

It was hunger that finally forced him from his mattress. It attacked him fiercely, but only after he'd realized just how long he'd been out. He climbed out of bed begrudgingly and found refuge in a cold shower. He let the water pour down on his face for a quarter of an hour before he finally felt refreshed. The cold from the water eventually woke his limbs as the blood was shocked back into circulation, making him feel more awake both physically and mentally. He dug into his case and pulled out a pair of jeans and a shirt that he felt could be worn without ironing. His options were slim on that front considering his belongings had been shoved in a bag for over twenty-four hours at that stage.

He shaved after looking in the mirror and seeing a homeless guy staring back at him, then brushed his teeth to chase the dry cotton taste from his mouth. After getting ready, he grabbed his wallet and headed down to reception to get some information.

He used an ATM machine in the corner to withdraw some euros, then walked over to the front desk and greeted the same man he'd met that morning. 'You must be on a long shift.' He said as he approached.

'My relief phoned in sick. Glad to see you're up Mr. Dawson. The cleaning staff were worried you'd never let them in.'

'Yeah I was tired' Andrew said. 'Sorry, hope I didn't cause them any trouble.'

'Them, no. They're only afraid you'll not let them in only to complain later about not having fresh towels.'

'Is that right?'

'Well, either that or they were just afraid they might have to clean up after a dead guy. Either way, not to worry. What can I help you with? Planning on heading out?'

'I'm hungry. I could eat a horse. Can you recommend somewhere close to eat?'

The man looked over at the clock. Andrew followed his gaze. The hands showed it was nearing eleven pm. 'Wow, they really were probably worried' he thought, 'that's about seventeen hours.'

'There's usually plenty of places to eat, but it's pretty late and you might have missed the good places, they've probably stopped seating by now.'

'Oh, you got me wrong. I want something decent, but not looking for expensive anyhow. Is anyone open?

'You like kebabs?' he asked.

Andrew considered the question. 'Not sure I've ever even had one.'

'Do you eat chicken?'

'Yeah of course.'

'And garlic?'

'Uh . . . yes.'

'Then I'd guess you like kebabs. There's a place on the

corner down the street.' He said and pointed in the direction across the street from the hotel. 'Order the chicken sheesh.'

'Thanks' Andrew said, 'I'll try it out.'

'I'd go now if I were you, then get out. If you wait much longer, you'll be the only sober fella in there.'

'Got it. Thanks again.'

Andrew walked down the front steps in the direction the man at reception pointed to. He crossed the street and disappeared around the corner. At the next corner, he caught a waft of meat and garlic and knew he was close. He saw the meat on a spit from the window and walked into the restaurant. The place was plenty busy, but not fully packed. Mostly, it was young men in suits with loosened or no ties. Andrew thought it must be the office workers in the area that flooded the surrounding streets, the after work crowd. Andrew walked to the counter and ordered the chicken sheesh as suggested. He paid and got a number from the clerk and was told to grab a seat and wait, which he did. The tables were heavy and wooden and the décor Mediterranean. Andrew took a seat near the back of the restaurant. He sat facing a mirror, which he instantly regretted, feeling strange enough by himself, he didn't need his own reflection for company. Part of him moving countries was in order to escape his past and he wasn't prepared to face the man in mirror quite yet. Not literally anyway. He got up from his chair and moved to the other side of the table, doing so as nonchalantly as possible. His number was called within minutes and he walked to the counter to pick up his food. When he got back to his table, he ate the food voraciously, as his hunger had grown greater each minute since waking. He finished the plate quickly and without once looking up. The food was delicious and he decided he'd done himself a disservice waiting so long to try a kebab. He felt self-conscious afterwards concerned that people saw him tear into his food like a starved hyena. When he finished and looked around at others sitting around enjoying their own dinners or engaged in conversation, he realized he might as well have been invisible. That was a welcomed change from the mean-eyed stares from strangers that filled his last few days at home. He sat slowly drinking his can of coke, people watching, happy once again to be a wall flower. Minutes after devouring his food, his brain finally registered the calories and he went from starved to very full and sleepy once again, despite his near marathon slumber.

He kept looking over at one particular group that sat talking loudly and laughing over their plates. Again it was a group of men in suits, though these gentlemen looked a few years older than most and wore more sophisticated attire. One or two even managed to keep their ties straight. There was a man at the edge of the table who Andrew thought looked very familiar. He looked to be in his thirties with dark hair that went slightly speckled with grey in places. He was engaging in the conversation, but appeared to be either more reserved than the others or at least looked preoccupied or distracted. Andrew guessed he was the boss from his demeanor. He appeared relaxed and amused, but not overly so. He conversed with the others, but let the louder ones do most of the talking, chiming in only once in a while for support. Plus, Andrew saw him walk over and pick up the check for the table. Something about the way he looked reminded Andrew of home, but he couldn't place him.

After the man returned from paying the bill, the others at the table all rose, gathered jackets and started to disperse. Most walked loudly by the table where Andrew sat finishing his coke and picked at the last one or two fries, including the man who looked familiar. He was the last to walk by and when he did, he paused in front of Andrew as he put on his jacket. Andrew was surprised when the man spoke to him, even more so when he realized the voice had a similar accent to his own. 'I saw you looking over, do you know some of my guys?'

'Me?' Andrew asked, 'No, sorry, I don't know any of them, I just got in yesterday.'

'Oh yeah, where from?' the man asked.

'I flew in from Boston.'

'Yeah, I was gonna say, I noticed your accent. You look familiar.' The man said. 'Where are you from?'

Andrew paused, not sure he was ready to relinquish his new found anonymity yet. He decided it wasn't worth hiding anything. 'Plus, what's one person.' He thought.

'I grew up in Quincy.' He said.

'No kidding' the man said 'me too.' and pulled out the chair across from Andrew. He started to sit down, but stopped and yelled over to his crowd of colleagues at the door first 'I'll catch up.'

'You mind if I sit? It's not often I run into people here from my hometown. Actually, this is the first time it's ever happened.'

'Really. You been here long?' Andrew asked.

'Over ten years, though it went by a lot faster than it sounds. I guess that's common.' The man sat across from Andrew and stared into his face. Andrew was unnerved by the man's gaze and continuous eye contact, but tried to hold his stare.

Finally, the man seemed to relax and lean back in his chair, crossing his leg over his knee. A hint of a smile came to his face as he seemed to ponder a question. He leaned forward on the table with his elbow keeping his leg crossed. Andrew found himself lean in as well in response.

The man asked in a low voice 'So what is it you're running from?'

Andrew was unsure how to respond. After a pause he asked 'What makes you think I'm running?'

'Well . . . you don't look happy enough to be on vacation. If you were, you'd probably not be alone and I'm pretty sure you wouldn't spend your first night eating dinner in this place. Also, I don't see any maps on you or near you. Or, any other evidence of an itinerary for that matter. If you've lived here as long as I have you pick up on habits of American tourists. Believe me . . . they're usually smiling, carrying at least one map and for the most part mildly irritating'

'So, you drew your conclusion from that?' Andrew asked.

'Yes, mostly anyway. Plus, I can't remember the last time I watched someone eat alone in a restaurant without at least one glance at a mobile phone. You either don't have one on you or you're showing great will power. I've assumed you don't have one. And what young man doesn't have a cell phone these days? My guess is it's really only those that don't want to be in contact with anyone they knew before today. How am I doing? Getting warmer at least?'

'So, I have to be running away from something?'

'Or running towards something. But in the end, what's the fucking difference if we're all running to the same place.'

'Okay, okay' Andrew said admitting defeat. 'Let's say I'm running from something. But, to be honest, I'm not ready to talk about it.'

'Naturally. If you were, you wouldn't be running.'

Andrew shrugged. 'True I guess.'

'Hey listen, I'm just busting your chops. Believe me brother, you're not the first yank with problems to jump on an Aer Lingus jet and believe he's flying those green wings to Eden. Shit, there's two sitting at this table.' He said and laughed lightly. The man got up from the chair slowly and stood up straight, stretching his arms out then shaking them out by his side.

He was as tall as Andrew and as broad, but he carried a few more years around the waist. 'It was good talking to you anyway bud. You planning on sticking around for a while.' The man asked.

'That's the plan' Andrew answered 'But so far, that's the extent of it.'

'So you're looking for work then?'

'Yes actually, though I haven't started looking yet.'

'What did you do back home?'

'A carpenter.' Andrew answered.

'You and everyone else. I think you might have missed the boat on that here I'm afraid, those jobs disappeared when the Celtic Tiger took his catnap. Can you do anything else?'

Andrew held up his hands. 'I'll shovel shit against the tide if it means I get a fresh start.'

The man laughed hard and slapped the table. 'Good! I

like to hear it.' He reached into his inside jacket pocket and pulled out a pen. Then he took out his wallet and pulled out a business card. He flipped it to the blank side and dropped it on the table and began writing. 'A friend of mine owns a restaurant close by here. He owes me. Go see him and tell him I sent you. It's just up the street past Stephen's Green.' He slid his card across the table. Andrew picked it up and read the handwritten name on the back. It read 'Dawson Street Grille'. He laughed.

'What's funny?' the man asked.

'Not funny just coincidental. My name is Dawson. Andrew Dawson.'

The man paused and gave him a look with squinted eyes. 'That is funny Dawson. Maybe it was meant to be.' He held out his hand across the table. 'My name and number are on the back. Give me a call if there's any issues or you can't get a hold of the owner, his name's Donal Coughlin.'

Andrew stood and took the man's hand and shook it. 'Thanks. Wow, man, I really appreciate it. Okay, Donal Coughlin, I'll remember that.'

'Nice to meet you Andrew. My name's Danny Carson. Go see Donal. Oh, and don't fuck it up.' With a smirk he took his hand back. Andrew watched him walk out and leave a tip in a jar by the register, then disappear from view out the front door.

As soon as the man said his name, Andrew's brain kicked in. 'That's why he's so familiar' he thought. He had seen Danny Carson before, likely met him at some stage in his life. He was around the same age as Andrew's brother and from the same neighborhood. He knew of him anyway. There was some mystery attached to Danny

Carson, which he added to by apparently never returning to the Boston area. His reputation was that of a really good person, but dangerous to cross. Like Andrew, Carson had lost a brother. The difference was that Carson's brother was killed. Within a couple years after that, the people involved in his murder, which occurred during a robbery of the younger Carson's restaurant, started disappearing. Danny Carson's name was thrown around as a suspect. Whether he did it or not, his absence from Quincy ever since added to the mystique. 'I'll have to play this pretty close' Andrew thought 'Real close.'

17

Andrew figured there was no point in waiting to check out Dawson Street Grille. The sooner he found work, the better off he'd be, no matter what it was. His savings would only last him a short while, especially with the exchange rate and incurring cross border fees. He headed up towards Saint Stephen's Green the next morning after a light breakfast. A girl working at reception in the hotel was able to explain to him the directions, which were straightforward, walk to Grafton Street, take a right, then take a left. The walk took him less than ten minutes. He arrived at the restaurant, which was part of a strand of bars and restaurants that spanned a few blocks on Dawson Street. Unfortunately, the place wasn't opened when he showed up. He peered through the window to see if there was staff inside preparing, but could see no one. There was a menu on a pedestal just inside the door and he could make out from where he stood that there was a lunch section. That was promising, since he'd only have to occupy himself for a few hours before anyone showed up.

He walked around for a while getting his bearings in the daylight finally. He walked a loop around Dawson and back up Grafton Street then crossed into the Green, which he did a lap through. He thought Grafton Street was pleasant at first, but it grew nerve wracking trying to get through the packs of tourists crowding around various street performers and buskers, each ranging in skill, most were either just okay or awful. That didn't seem to matter however as crowds gathered regardless of the performance quality. After he finished his walk through the Green, he found a pharmacy for a few essentials. Also, he found a phone shop and bought the cheapest smart phone off the rack and picked up a prepaid sim card. He figured as someone hunting for a job he needed a better contact method then saying 'call my cheap hotel and ask for my room.' He wasn't even sure if his room had a phone in it. He assumed it had one, but it never occurred to him to check and he hadn't noticed if it did or not.

After his walk and his shopping, he went into a small internet cafe and paid the man running it two euros to use a slow, old computer to check his email. He checked his account, but it was nothing but junk mail. He wanted to check Facebook, but he had closed his account the second he was able to after his acquittal. He opted for his own sanity not to scroll through the various comments that were venomously splattered across his homepage. Suffice to say when he got out, he had a fraction the number of friends he had the day he went in, both real and virtual. With no social media to peruse and an unwillingness to read any Boston online newspaper, he spent most of the remaining twenty minutes he purchased to read up on the menu of the Dawson Street Grille. 'At least I will have appeared to do some research' he thought. He did a search for the restaurant name and found they had a website. He clicked on the link and brought up the page. He scrolled through some of the reviews on the side, they were all glowing, but what else could be expected from the restaurant's own webpage. He clicked into the 'contact us' section. He found the breakdown of serving times above the frequently asked questions section. They opened for lunch daily at one o'clock until four, then served dinner from five thirty until eleven. He thought if they opened at one for lunch, then it was nearing the time the staff would likely have to be in. He only had a few minutes left on the computer's timer and opened up the a la carte menu section. It opened in a pdf and he scrolled down the list, first starters, then a grill section, then seafood. The list of food looked a cut above what he was used to, both from a quality and price perspective. He guessed he probably heard of about fifty percent of the items included in the dinner menu. He had actually tasted probably closer to thirty percent. He read through the rest of the menus and finished just before the timer ran out and his computer went on standby.

He picked up his shopping bag and headed back out onto the street towards the restaurant. It was still not one o'clock, but he figured he'd get more attention if he showed up before opening hours anyhow. The front door was closed and the menu pedestal was still inside the door, but when he tried the handle it opened and he walked into the room. The ceilings inside were taller than he expected and it made the restaurant quite airy. There were different pieces of art, mostly paintings, hanging on the wall. The tables were wooden and looked heavy and expensive. Several tables lined the middle of the dining area and there were elevated sections with round leather booths that appeared to be areas for pre-booked groups. Andrew could hear music from somewhere. He guessed it was coming from the kitchen as the staff prepared for lunch and prepped for the later dinner service. He walked deeper into the room and called out 'Hello?' Hoping to get someone's attention.

He was startled to hear a man's voice answer from behind him. 'How's it going? Help you with something?' it said.

Andrew turned around and saw a man sitting at a low table near the entrance. He was going through some papers that were spread out on the table itself. He must've walked right by the man when he entered. 'Hi, sorry, I didn't see you there.' He said. 'I'm looking for Donal. I believe he's the owner or manager.'

The man stopped sifting through his paperwork and pulled down his glasses from his eyes and looked over at Andrew. Andrew put him at or around forty five or fifty years old.

'I'm Donal.' He said and picked up the papers he had across the table and stacked them into a neater pile. 'What can I do for you?'

'Um, Danny Carson sent me up. He mentioned you might have some work for me. I'm new to the area.'

'Danny sent you huh? Okay, here sit down.' He said and kicked out the chair across from him so Andrew could take a seat, which he did.

'What are you looking to do?' Donal asked.

'Really anything sir. I just flew in a couple nights ago from Boston. I've moved over here and I'm trying to settle in. I'm willing to take on anything you've got for work.'

'Okay, have you waited tables before?' he asked.

'No sir, I haven't.' Andrew replied.

'Alright, what about worked in a bar, either serving or assisting?'

'No, sorry, I'm afraid not.'

'Okay, so then . . . have you worked in a restaurant ever before in your life? Washing dishes even?'

'Uh . . . No I haven't.' Andrew answered. He was beginning to feel that this was a dead end.

Donal put his hand to his face for a minute. He shook his head after a few seconds and said to himself, 'Fucking Danny.'

'Listen sir, it's safe to say, I have very little experience working in a restaurant. In fact, I have none. Probably the closest I've come to working in a restaurant is actually eating in one. And, I must say, I'm not sure I've eaten in one this nice ever.' Andrew said.

Donal didn't say anything. He just smiled and shook his head.

Andrew continued talking to plead his case, 'I don't mean to offend, but when I met Danny yesterday, he seemed pretty confident you'd find something for me. Should I have taken him with a grain of salt? Is there nothing for me here?'

Donal stopped and considered his response. 'There's plenty of shit I could have you do, sure. It would just make my life easier if you'd done any of them before. Danny sent you, so I'll put you to work. Wouldn't be the first time he sent me an employee so green he had roots. How do you know Danny anyway?'

'I don't I guess.' Andrew answered. 'I met him randomly yesterday for the first time. We're from the same neighborhood though.'

Donal nodded his head. 'I don't think Danny Carson meets anyone randomly, but anyway, we'll get you doing something. What's your name?'

'My name's Andrew. Andrew Dawson.'

'Dawson is it? Well you're in the right spot then. Okay Andrew Dawson, when can you start working?'

Andrew looked around before he answered, 'I can start right this second.'

Donal put his hands up in a slowdown gesture. 'Listen, why don't you come back tonight at half five. I'll be here, so just come in and ask for me if I'm not out front. I'll see if I can think of what to do with you between now and then. Sound alright?'

'Yes it does, it sounds great, thanks Donal. I really appreciate it. Do I need anything with me?'

'If you have a black t shirt or something close to it, just wear that and a pair of jeans. That's basically the uniform here. Other than that, we'll see you later on.'

'Black t shirt and jeans, got it.' Andrew said. He got up and tucked the chair back under the table. While standing with his hands gripping the chair he said 'Danny said you owed him a favor. Must have been some favor he did for you.'

Donal looked up from the table at Andrew as he put his reading glasses back on. 'You could say that I guess. It's no secret, this place is his favor to me. He invested in the restaurant.'

'Oh okay, so he's like a silent partner.' Andrew asked.

Donal shrugged, 'Loudest silent partner I've ever known, but yes, I guess you could say that.'

Andrew nodded his head. He let go of the chair and stood up straight. 'I'll be back this afternoon, five thirty. Thank you again.'

'See you then Andrew. Don't mention it.' Donal waved him goodbye as Andrew weaved through the tables in the dining room and left the restaurant.

18

A black t shirt was easy to come by. Andrew found one for basically no money in a store inside the shopping center at Stephen's Green. Jeans were more difficult to find. They seemed to be sized differently than in America and he wasted more time than he planned trying to find a pair that fit him right. Finally happy that he had his uniform sorted out, he walked back to the same internet café he was in before. This time he paid the man five euros and was granted an hour on the computer. Now that he had a job on the horizon at least, he had to get serious about finding a place to live. There seemed to be one or two websites that were pretty good and he searched through a number of places. His plan was to stay as close to the city center as possible for as cheap as possible. A few places looked right for him and he sent off requests to the contacts by email. He printed off those apartments plus a few others and took them with him back to the hotel.

He still had time to kill when he got back upstairs to his hotel room so he pulled his running sneakers from his bag along with a pair of shorts. He asked at reception if there was any decent routes for jogging around the hotel, but the girl working the desk gave no real insight. She mentioned a canal down the street that he could run beside and at least then not lose his way back. It seemed a reasonable suggestion, so he headed south for it and found it minutes later. He turned west and ran alongside the canal. He felt good to be doing something active, but the route wasn't great and several times he needed to stop before crossing the street. The road along the canal was packed with cars and cyclists. The cars were barely moving with the traffic. He was surprised at how aggressive the cyclists were on their small path. Most seemed to pedal without regard for danger. He ran for a couple miles he judged. The further west he ran, the dingier the surroundings seemed to grow. When he reached a set of flats that looked too much like the projects in South Boston, he turned and began his jog back.

The canal wasn't a great running route, but the receptionist was on to something since he found his way back to the hotel without any hesitation. He took a shower and got ready to go back to the restaurant. He double and triple checked his t shirt and jeans for hidden tags in the mirror then started back up the street. He was a little early and slowed his pace and took a short detour through the Green before walking down Dawson Street. He kept a close eye on the clock on his new phone and at twenty minutes past five he decided it was reasonably early to arrive.

He walked in to a much busier place than he'd seen earlier that day. There seemed to be a full wait staff dressed and ready. There were four of them that he could see, walking around the dining room cleaning off tables and straightening chairs and table ornaments preparing for the dinner crowd. Donal walked out through the kitchen. He saw Andrew right away and waved him over. Andrew crossed the dining room and joined Donal outside the door to the kitchen. They shook hands once again. Donal said, 'let me show you around quickly and introduce you to a few people.'

'Sounds good.' Andrew answered. He followed Donal

into the back. The kitchen was smaller than he expected, not that he'd spent time in any restaurant kitchens before, but he still pictured it bigger. It was hot back there, and it was loud. He could hear fans going, music playing and a lot of banging noises coming from somewhere. They walked around a corner and he could see the entire place. It was a rectangular room, separated by a counter in the middle, making it look like two chicken runs. There were stoves in each area and the center seemed to be the prep area and looked to have refrigerators underneath the counter. There were three people steadily working away at different things. One looked to be putting garnishes into silver pots and placing them into slots within the counter. Another was rough chopping vegetables for a soup.

'I don't want to get in the guys' way here, so I won't walk you through. This is the kitchen staff, 'hey guys!' he yelled. The kitchen staff looked up. 'This is Andrew. He's starting work with us tonight. When you're done prepping, introduce yourself to him.' They nodded in unison at the request.

'Here' Donal said 'Follow me, I think the Chef is around here somewhere. Usually he goes over the menu with the wait staff one by one to make sure they're clear on everything on there.' He continued walking. Andrew followed along nodding his head. They entered a smaller room that housed dry goods. Donal paused and looked back at Andrew, 'We do one or two specials usually per night that change quite a bit. Oh, and fair warning, Chefs can be temperamental in my experience. Our's is no different. Poor Ivan thinks he's an artist sometimes, so he gets moody about certain things. His favorite things to bitch about are well-done steaks and pretty much any changes requested from what's on the menu. Just stay out of his way when he has his period and you'll be fine.' Donal looked at Andrew. He looked down at his feet, then up across his shoulders. 'Plus, you're a big enough guy that he probably won't say a thing to you. He's more the type to bitch at those that can't physically intimidate him. Ask the waitresses about him, I'm sure they each have a horror story or two.'

'Great. Okay, think I'll just stay out of his way to be safe.' Andrew answered.

There was a large walk-in freezer and refrigerator out the back that Donal pointed out. Then he opened a door that had a set of steps that led up to a second level. 'Up there we keep a lot of the business files, some other paper supplies, shit like that. If you can't find me I'm usually up there trying to reconcile credit card receipts with the night's intake or trying to figure out which employee might be skimming off the top. Ivan and the others go up there to type up the specials and print the inserts out for the menus.' Donal craned his neck up the stairway, 'Ivan, you up there?' he yelled.

Andrew heard a voice yell down. 'Coming down now.' It said and Andrew could hear heavy footsteps walking down the stairs. Seconds later, Ivan got to the bottom of the steps and joined the two men in the hall. 'Ivan, this is Andrew, he's gonna be working here starting tonight.'

Andrew held out his hand and Ivan took it. He wasn't quite six feet, but he was close. He had dark hair, but it was buzzed down close to his head. He wore a five o'clock shadow that Andrew took for European designer stubble and he was much thinner than Andrew thought any chef should be. 'Nice to meet you' Andrew said.

Ivan looked down at Andrew's hand, then followed his arm with his eyes up to Andrew's shoulder. 'What, do we need security now?' he asked.

'Funny Ivan.' Donal said, 'if anyone does here, it's you, so keep young Andrew here on side would ya?'

'Welcome.' Ivan said and took his hand back from Andrew'. 'Ask me any questions about the menu. It's better you know from me, not these others.' He said flailing his hand out towards the dining room to indicate anyone else that worked there besides himself Andrew guessed.

'Will do. Thanks Ivan.'

'You're welcome.' Ivan said, then nodded and walked off into the kitchen.

Andrew looked at Donal and said, 'seems alright.'

'Ah, he's alright. Great in the kitchen anyway. Ivan's from Budapest. A couple drinks after dinner service and he'll be telling you how the best Palinka in Hungary is from his hometown and listing off Nobel Prize winners and famous inventors from Hungary, just wait for it. The first time it's interesting. It grows less so every time after that. But, you wait until goulash or goose leg is on the special board and for fucksake, you'll fall in love with the man.'

Andrew laughed. 'I'll keep an eye out for it then, great.'

'Okay Andrew, that's pretty much it back here. Let's head out to the dining room.'

Andrew nodded and followed Donal after he started walking out. They walked back through the kitchen area and out the same door into the dining room. Leaving the kitchen was a relief and Andrew could feel the sweat on his torso. He got a chill from it when they were back out in the dining room. 'So, Donal?' he asked.

'Yup' Donal said and stopped walking.

'I'm just wondering. What are your plans? I mean, what do you think you'll have me do tonight?'

'Oh right, okay. Well, I've been short on wait staff recently, so I'd like you to learn to wait tables. But to let you run out there on your own tonight would probably lose me more money than anything else . . . no offense.'

Andrew shook his head. 'None taken.'

'Good. So, I want to get one of the girls to train you as a waiter. You'll have to do some busing of tables and clean up stuff as well, but for the most part tonight you'll stick with Vicky. She's one of the waitresses here. She'll show you what to do, you know, let you take orders from tables, tell you what you did wrong. Shit like that. That alright?'

'Yeah, great, perfect. Like I said, whatever you need.'

A girl walked out of the door carrying a tray of small candles that she started putting on each table. 'Ah, there's Vicky there.' Donal said. 'Vicky! Come over here a second.'

The girl left the tray on a table and walked over to where Donal and Andrew stood talking. She had dark hair that was somewhere between wavy and curly. Her skin was white and unblemished. She wore dark eyeliner and had thick lashes that covered eyes that looked royal blue in the light. Andrew thought they were so blue they had to be fake. 'Hi' he said and held out his hand.

She took his hand lightly and shook it once. 'Hi.' Andrew squinted slightly and suddenly recognized the girl. She had almost knocked him down the stairs the morning he arrived at the hotel. He wondered if she recognized him, but didn't want to bring it up. 'I'm Andrew.' He said.

'Vicky' she answered. They stood in silence for a few seconds until Donal broke up the moment. 'Okay, Vicky, like I explained earlier, can you show Andrew the ropes tonight.'

'Yeah okay sure.' She said.

'Alright then, I'll leave you to it, I've got work to do myself now believe it or not. Andrew you're in good hands. Vicky's another of Danny Carson's blow-ins. She came in as green as you and now she's the best I've got.'

'Aren't you sweet?' she said to Donal

'I try to be. Okay Andrew, good luck.'

'Okay, great.' Andrew said, 'thanks Donal.'

When Donal walked away Andrew turned back towards Vicky. 'So . . . where can I start?' he asked. In response she walked over to where she left the tray of candles and carried it over to Andrew then stuck it into his hands. It was heavier than expected and he had to adjust his balance quickly so that he didn't drop it. 'Here' she said. 'Start by holding these.'

When he regained control over the wobbly tray he answered. 'no problem' and followed behind her as she walked into the dining room.

19

'What's Ranelagh like? Is it better than like Rathgar or Terenure?' Andrew asked the man working reception at the hotel. After days of exchanging banter, Andrew grew to like the man called George who seemed to work nonstop at the hotel.

'Ranelagh, Rathgar, Terenure, Rathmines, they're all grand villages. It depends what you're looking for. Ranelagh's the closest. You could probably kick a football to it from here. It's probably considered the most posh too, besides Ballsbridge or Donnybrook. They're all nice. I'd say you're fine with any of them, just stay clear of places like Inichicore and Dolphin's Barn.' George answered.

'Why does Dolphin's Barn sound familiar? I can picture the name for some reason, I must have past it at some stage.'

'I don't know. It's a straight shot west down the Canal, it's not too far from here. It's not the worst, but there's a lot of flats around there that's all. They can be rough.'

'Flats? You mean like what I'd call projects right?'

'I think so, close enough anyway.'

'Ah, okay, I know why I know it. I took a jog down the Canal and must have made it down the far. I remember seeing the flats and then I turned around.'

'Probably the right move.'

'I thought it was at the time.'

'So you're going to view this place in Ranelagh then?' George asked pointing to one of the printouts that Andrew laid on the counter.'

'Yeah, well there's two places in Ranelagh. I'm gonna

see 'em both this morning and get it out of the way. Are they walking distance?'

'You could take the Luas if you're lazy, but yeah, it's probably a ten to fifteen minute walk at most. This first one' he slide the print out in front of Andrew, 'that's on Ranelagh road. So you're literally walking down to the Canal, crossing the street and it's on that road. The other one is a little further down. If you walk to the village and turn right at the Triangle, its right by there, you can't miss it.'

'Thanks George' Andrew said 'Appreciate the help once again.'

'Don't mention it. Add a nice review on tripadvisor or something.' He said smiling. 'I'd hope for the same if I was ever moving to Boston.'

'I think you'd find that in Boston, there's still plenty of first generation Irish. You'd probably know more people there than I would.'

'I've had friends that had been over. Maybe I'll check it out at some stage.'

'You should, definitely.' Andrew said, then thought to himself, 'Just don't tell anyone you know me.'

'Alright George' he said and folded up the printouts and put them into his pocket. 'I better go check these places out. Gotta work again later on.'

'Good luck Andrew.' George said.

Andrew left in the direction that George had sent him. The small hotel had grown on him in the few days he stayed there. He attributed this to the friendly familiarity that the staff showed towards him. He'd miss having someone come in and clean up after him every day too. He knew it wasn't economical for him to stay there any longer than he had to. If he was really going to give his fresh start his best effort, he couldn't live like he was on vacation. Plus, he wanted to feel settled, and hoped an apartment would help do that. Only a few days away from home and he already was beginning to feel free again. He hoped a few more weeks and he'd feel close to normal, if that would ever be possible. Things had happened that he couldn't just forget. He had been accused and arrested for murder. He was sure that's a memory that wouldn't go away easily. It was only a short time ago and he felt the ghost of that memory linger between him and any person he met for the first time. Always in the back of his mind, 'What happens if this person hears what I had allegedly done? Will they believe me or will they run like hell?' The inevitable coming out of those skeletons haunted him, never more so than the previous night as he followed Vicky around, making small talk as she walked him through how to do his new job. He liked her. He liked everyone he'd met there. Would they see him any differently if they knew?

He spent so much energy worrying about getting on with his own life, he felt selfish every time he climbed out of his own self-centered well and remembered that as far as victims go, he got off the easiest. The count was up to four girls now that were dealt a much more punishing and final fate than him. These were four young women that were innocent. He had gone to school with them, had known two of them well enough to call them friends. Now they were gone. Whoever dealt them that fate was still in the wind. With that perspective, he'd gotten off light. 'It should be Gina O'Neil and Lisa Stark that occupy my mind.' He thought, 'Not my own fractured shadow.' Fear gripped him with the realization that there could be more. There were only four girls that had been found. 'Also, what's to stop the real killer from doing it again? He's free, there's no incentive to stop now. If anything, he probably feels more in control.'

Andrew shook the thoughts to the back of his head as he approached a building that housed the address on his printout. He pulled out the form from his pocket to double check the apartment number and rang the doorbell. A second later, he heard a buzzing noise and he pushed the large door forward. The buzz and click sounds reminded him of the prison. He pushed the memory away. The door opened into the hall and he walked in. The ceilings were high and a set of cement steps lay in front of him. The lighting was poor as the surrounding walls had no windows and therefore no natural light. On the wall a bulletin board was hung and cluttered with pieces of papers that varied from pizza delivery menus, trash day reminders and phone numbers of house cleaners that could be hired by the hour.

A dingy carpet covered much of the painted cement floor. It was discolored in many random places and worn heavily in a line leading to the stairs. The apartment for rent was on the first floor. Andrew looked around for the right apartment door number and found it behind a heavy fire proof door that snapped shut loudly behind him after he walked into a smaller, darker hallway. The inner hall gave him an eerie tingle down his spine. He didn't envy the late night fast food delivery man, having to spend many evenings knocking on doors in these claustrophobic hallways.

He knocked on the apartment door and a man in his

sixty's or seventy's answered and let him in. The man was gruff and seemed put out by the visit as if Andrew was intruding. 'Not exactly a sales man.' Andrew thought. The apartment was unappealing. It had large windows that let in plenty of light, though much of it struggled to penetrate an ageless layer of grime on the glass, giving the room a speckled, hazy effect. This ended up being the apartment's best feature. The rooms were untidy and the carpet in the apartment was more worn and spot-laden than that in the main hall. The heating system consisted of two storage heaters, one in a corner in the sitting room, the other in the bedroom, which Andrew was informed often didn't work very well and smelled of burning hair when it did. The kitchen was the smallest he'd ever seen, but mostly it was the layer of grease around the stove top that turned him off it. Within thirty seconds, he knew the place was not for him and every second after that he had to hold back the urge to run out of there. Some ingrained respect for his elders made him continue to be courteous despite not receiving the same in return. He was glad to leave minutes later and headed off down the street, feeling dirty for having spent longer than a minute inside that dump.

He was slightly discouraged, but only because his hopes had been so high going in. When he reached the second viewing, his expectations had level set to reality. The lowered expectations served him better and the second apartment on the whole, though more snug, was much nicer. It had clean floors and was freshly painted. The windows could be seen through, which was what he'd grown to expect from glass. The sitting room was smaller, but the furniture looked relatively new and comfortable. The apartment had a kitchenette as opposed to a kitchen, but at a glance there were no obvious signs of aged grease stuck to the countertop around the stove. Best of all, he could picture himself living there. He told the owner as much and said that he'd take it. The owner seemed glad to give it to him and promised to draw up the lease provided Andrew could get Donal to confirm his employment and pick up a bank draft for a deposit. They exchanged numbers and shook hands.

Andrew felt lighter leaving there and walked back up the street towards his hotel feeling he had accomplished something that morning. He looked forward to getting his own place and hoped to have it secured in the next couple of days. Moving across the Atlantic had always seemed daunting to him, but within a week he had a job secured, in a stalled economy no less, and now was close to having a place to live. Never an optimist, he still felt a nugget of caution looming in his stomach. But for the moment, for the night at least, he was going to consider the day a success. 'Now, to buy a few more black t shirts so I can be clean going to work.' He thought and headed past the hotel and up to the shops on Grafton Street.

20

Andrew walked out of the kitchen carrying three hot dinner plates the way that Vicky showed him. One was in his left hand which he held with three fingers underneath, then his pinky and thumb extended to balance another on top, braced on his forearm. His right hand grasped the remaining plate tightly and he kept it close to his left in case he needed to use it to regain balance. His forearm stung with pain from the hot plate resting on top of it. No one else working the tables seemed to notice, apparently anyone with more than six months experience working in a restaurant grew impervious to burns. At two days, he wasn't yet and he noticed his forearm was red raw when he looked at it after he delivered the plates to the table across the dining room. He shook it out as he walked. He headed out back to see if there were more plates to go out.

'Ivan's looking for you.' Vicky said as she breezed past him carrying plates of food to another table. Andrew was walking that way anyhow and ventured back into the kitchen. He stood on the edge where the wait staff dropped off order slips. He could feel the heat from the kitchen as soon as he walked in from the dining room. With the stoves on full blast, the room was hotter than a crematorium. The kitchen staff were all required to wear hats specially made to absorb sweat from the forehead. They had a rotating break system during the night to make sure each had the opportunity to cool down for three to five minutes at a time during the evening rush. Everyone took the breaks except for Ivan. Andrew figured it was time spent in that heat that was likely why the man was as thin as he was. He manned the kitchen at all times and was very hands on. Donal had mentioned to Andrew that Ivan thought himself an artist. After watching him work only twice, Andrew had to agree. He was a perfectionist and could be temperamental, but he appeared to work harder than anyone Andrew had met before. Also, he seemed to truly love what he did for a living. 'Ivan!' Andrew yelled over the noise of the active kitchen. Ivan looked up, saw Andrew and pointed for him to walk around the back. Andrew did and Ivan went around the other way so as to not cross through the kitchen. He had two slips in his hand, which he roughly shoved into Andrew's palm. 'Young Andrew' he said. 'There's no temp on the ribeye for the first one and I can't read your hand writing on the other. I need you to do better.' He stood looking Andrew in the eye. He didn't appear angry, just really matter of fact.

Andrew looked at the slips, then back at Ivan. The man was right. Andrew's hand writing was atrocious. It was barely legible even to himself as he tried to read it back. He'd hardly hand written anything since he was in school. Many restaurants had wait staff carry tablets that relay orders directly to the kitchen. Dawson Street Grille wasn't quite there yet. Pen and paper remained the communication medium. Pens were like gold dust around there. Each waiter had his or her own stash. The slips were sequentially numbered and handed out by Donal at the beginning of each night. He had to write neater, that was obvious. Forgetting the steak's temperature was just an oversight, a rookie mistake. He looked back up at Ivan's face.

'Okay?' Ivan said. 'You bring them right back.' He said and pointed to the slips in Andrew's hand.

'Yes sir.' Andrew said. 'Sorry Ivan.'

'No time for sorry Andrew, too busy. Just do better next time.' Ivan said and started back around to the busy kitchen.

'Will do.' Andrew said and headed back to the dining room. He confirmed the steak order and sent that slip back into the kitchen, then rewrote the other in a neater hand. He looked at the clock, wrote the time down on the slip and yelled 'Fire it!' That was the system for letting the kitchen know to get the main courses started. Vicky told him you had to judge the table to know when to fire an order. A group that gathered to have drinks and talk, might want to take their time. So there was no point in firing that main course until everyone finished with their appetizers. It was the booze that made the money really, so it was worth letting a table linger that had the drinks flowing. Other tables may have two people on a first date and the conversation might look slow and awkward. If they're flying through their appetizers or salad, then it was wise to fire it as soon as you got back to the kitchen after dropping off the starters. Judging the tables like this proved difficult to Andrew on the first night when Vicky was testing him and making a game out of it. On his second night, it was nearly impossible for him as the staff was short-handed so he handled quite a few tables alone. His timing was off at least a few times. He hoped no one really noticed, but they likely did.

Donal was there greeting people at the door and seating them at tables. There was a small bar and waiting area by the front entrance, he could usually be found around there talking to some of the regulars that came in for dinner, but had a drink first. There were also several regulars that seemed to arrive later in the evening just for drinks.

Donal approached him a couple times earlier in the night to make sure he was doing alright. 'You managing?' he'd asked a few times.

Andrew didn't want to appear overwhelmed, so he always responded something like, 'yeah boss, I'm doing alright.' They both knew he was struggling, but when there was a lull after the seven o'clock crowd finished up before the later crowd came in, Donal chatted to him for a few minutes and let him know he was doing okay and told him not to get too stressed. 'You're brand new he said. 'Don't get too stressed. I expect a few mistakes. You'll get it soon.'

The other wait staff pitched in and helped him out whenever possible. A few times he'd hustle to the kitchen to pick up plates only to find one of the others had already run the food out to the tables. The same would happen when he'd remember he hadn't bussed a table or dropped dessert menus off or refreshed a round of drinks. 'That's not because you're new' Vicky had told him, 'That's just something we all do to help each other out.'

It was all new to him really. He worked the last decade or so on building sites or doing home renovations. Those days were typically long with frequent lulls in activity, especially as an apprentice when his lack of knowledge and experience meant he couldn't do anything on his own. He had to move at the pace the journeyman set and that varied depending on who it was and how ambitious they were. Two nights in the restaurant and doing nothing was not an option. Everyone had to be moving. They were either taking orders, dropping off food, carrying drinks, dropping checks or cleaning. Cleaning seemed to be constant and it was something Donal seemed to take seriously. 'People don't come here to eat from a trough' was a line he'd already used at least five times in two nights. Andrew found the evenings flew by and it was all down to pace. After two nights, he decided that for the moment at least, he really enjoyed the pace. He could just work. He needed to be organized and to learn what he was doing, but it seemed from observing the others, that once those basics were down, it was all experience and reaction. Concious thought barely seemed to come into it when the entire restaurant was moving at the speed of light.

He liked the comradery that the restaurant seemed to offer as well. The place was busy and Donal wanted every customer taken care of like they were the only ones there eating. It took everyone there working together to make that happen. Every person there, from the bus boy to the head chef had a role to play to meet that ultimate end. Each had to give it their best effort and pitch in beyond their own role when needed. That's what Donal wanted and so that's what he rewarded. He saw restaurants as not just a place to eat good food, but as a place to meet people, socialize and enjoy good food and surroundings. He told Andrew on his first night, that the food was very important. But, if the food was really good and the service or atmosphere was shit, then most people these days wouldn't bother coming back. There were too many options, so to stay competitive, they had to focus on getting the full package right. In that spirit, any and all tips were pooled between the wait staff and the bartender, bus boys and kitchen staff were all tipped out at the end of the night.

Once the final dinner orders were out and most of the checks dropped and paid for, the restaurant became a different place. It went from hectic and breakneck speed to one of relaxation. As everyone pitched in to clean up and finish up any last dessert or drink orders the kitchen staff would throw on some kind of snack for the staff, usually pizza's or calamari. Donal went around to each of the staff and took the staff drink order, the first one at the end of shift was on the house.

Andrew really enjoyed this part of the night. In his first two shifts, he didn't say much. He just listened to a lot of the joking back and forth between some of the other staff and sipped his beer slowly. Finishing the night's service made them feel like they collectively accomplished something. At least that was the impression Andrew got those first two nights. He'd heard they'd often head out after work and go for a few drinks, but he was happy enough for the time being to enjoy his staff drink, then head back to his room. Both nights he walked back to the hotel by himself. Hustling from the service worked up a sweat and left him too wired to go to bed, so he took his time each night walking back, taking in the surroundings including the cool spring air. The refreshing air cooled him off on his walk and dialed his engine down, so that both of his first two nights after working he fell into bed and slept a comfortable, dreamless sleep.

21

Over a month past in front of Andrew's eyes in a blur. A month into his journey and he still felt that he'd only just arrived in Dublin. Day after day flew by, it was as if time ticked away in the background without him having any perception of its passing. His month in Dublin felt half as long as his few days locked in a Massachusetts prison. 'That's likely part of the punishment' he guessed. Time was supposed to crawl by slowly inside prison. Most new things he encountered thus far had occurred within that first week, including a new job, new friends and coworkers and a new apartment. After that first week, where he felt things were hectic despite being energized by its speed, a routine began to develop. He wasn't exactly sure, but he guessed he had worked twenty five or twenty six out of thirty days at the restaurant since arriving in the country. There was a span of two straight weeks were he couldn't recall if he'd taken a day off. He liked it that way at the minute. Perhaps that pace wasn't sustainable and it probably wasn't healthy either given the late night drinks and food after closing hours, but he believed it kept him focused and sane at least in the first month in Dublin. He enjoyed the job. He liked the work and going to work each afternoon or evening became more part of his social life than a nine to five job every could.

He'd settled into his new place as well. Only days after his viewing, he found himself unpacking his one large suitcase full of belongings in his new apartment. The area where he rented grew on him quickly because of its convenience to the city center and its local amenities. The village seemed to be full of people always, even when walking home late at night after a shift. There was something comforting about that to Andrew, like the presence of others made the night less threatening.

The downside was however, whenever he looked himself in the mirror, guilt ate at him. He'd been there a month and still hadn't even contacted his mother, never mind go to see her. Each day he'd wake up and say to himself, 'today's the day' only to find a reason shortly after to put it off. There was something holding him back, but he didn't know what. He wanted to see her. He missed her badly. But, some unseen barrier still existed. And for that, he felt guilty, which was yet another reason just to bury himself in his work.

Each shift at the restaurant came with incremental improvement in his work. He became more comfortable and his mistakes grew less frequent. He noticed a corresponding rise in his tips, which steadily began to increase with each passing day. The people working at the restaurant seemed to accept him pretty quickly into their fold. Within the first week, he thought they lightened towards him on the whole and Andrew responded by trying to be more open with them. He chipped in with the workplace banter whenever he could, though he was still pretty shy about it and was careful not to cross the line with anyone he didn't have a good read on yet. A few times in the last couple weeks, he'd even tagged along for a couple drinks after work. He felt awkward doing so at first, but the others often insisted and made sure he felt welcome when he joined. Still, despite all that, he kept a large part of himself reserved. He believed he developed a good relationship with Donal. It was easy to do so because Donal was genuinely a nice person. Plus, each time he watched him diffuse a conflict or just do something hands-on to manage his people, his level of respect for the man increased. Also, he kept close to Vicky whenever he could. Out of everyone, she talked to him the most and seemed to be the most tolerant of his incompetence at the beginning. He knew a fondness for her was slowly building within him. He wasn't sure he was ready for anything like that or if she even looked at him that way, so he did his best to keep it in check. He also made a conscious effort to avoid making it obvious to everyone else how he felt.

Besides that, the rest of the wait staff were friendly and seemed to like him, the kitchen staff too. Ivan the chef appeared to take a liking to him and they chatted often after work over staff drinks. He came to realize that Donal was right about his goulash and goose leg, they were special and were unlike anything Andrew had ever eaten before. Donal still made it clear to Andrew that it was his size and stature that kept Ivan from picking on him, something he joked about quite often with both employees.

Donal was also right about Danny Carson. For a 'silent' partner, Andrew felt he sure showed up a lot. He'd shown up at least every Friday to be exact. Also, he'd pop in once or twice during the week to say hello. He arrived usually Friday evenings around nine, ate dinner then hung out in the front bar and hassled Donal for the evening. Andrew still wasn't sure what to make of him. He seemed friendly when he wasn't coming across as arrogant. He talked a lot and about everything, but at the same time always gave the impression he knew more than he actually said. His opinions were many, forceful and varied, but each seemed equally important to voice with clarity, making sure his logic was understood by all. Andrew thought he was borderline offensive at first, but found he was one of those people that grew on you the more time you spent with him. He decided he liked him at the very least. Once he realized half of what he said was for comedic effect, Andrew found he was much easier to get along with than he originally thought. Also, the more he got to know him, the more he began to think the dangerous man he'd heard of through whispers back home existed more in stories than anything else. Still, he wasn't going to rush to find out the truth. He'd grown comfortable being around him and that was enough for now.

Considering his consistent visits, it was no surprise when Danny Carson walked in after nine pm that Friday. He took a seat at the bar that was closest to where Donal stood greeting people at the door. He usually took that seat so he could chat to Donal while he worked, but also it meant he wasn't taking up space for any other customers. 'Taking up a table is like throwing money out of my own pocket.' He had said. Also, the bar area was more casual and conducive to having conversations with many people at once. A table in the dining room would have him confined to speaking to only his waiter.

Andrew watched him walk in through the door and head into the bar. He started over towards him to say hello. He made a point of going over and saying hi every time he was in provided it didn't disrupt his work very much. He owed him for getting him the job, so it was part of how he said thanks. He watched him pull off his light jacket and wrap it around the back of one of the tall chairs in the bar. He saw him say hi to Donal and watched him point to the Guinness tap and hold up his index finger to order a pint. Andrew slid into the bar area and walked up to Danny's table. 'Hey Danny. How's it going?'

'Andrew. Going good. Glad it's Friday, I had a busy week.' Danny said as he let the buttons out of his shirt cuffs and flipped up his sleeves to his forearms. 'How about you? Donal tells me you're working hard and you've picked up a lot quickly. Glad you didn't drag my good name through the mud.'

Andrew nodded. 'Yeah, I think I'm doing okay. Everyone here's been great. They've taken time to show me anything I've asked, so yeah, I'm feeling good about it. I'm picking it up at least.'

'Good.' He said. Andrew followed Danny's eyes as he looked around the restaurant. He pushed out his bottom lip and looked back at Andrew after scanning the dining room. 'Looks like a pretty slow night. Too bad.'

'It's slow now I guess, but it's nearly nine thirty. We had a good crowd in earlier on, but not much of a late crowd.' Andrew said.

Donal walked in from the kitchen and joined them at the bar table. 'Distracting my waiters I see Carson.' He said.

'Not busy enough to matter Donal. Where the hell is the Friday rush? The place looks dead.'

Donal looked around the dining room then back at the two men. He nodded and said, 'You're right. Is there a match on I'm not aware of or something? It's too slow for a Friday.'

'Don't think so' Danny said. Andrew just shrugged, he hadn't gotten into the Irish sports in the month he'd been there, so he wouldn't know if there was an important game on anyway.

'We can't take too many Friday nights like this anyway.' Donal said. 'Pretty soon, we'd all be in the bread line.' He looked at Danny, 'You get a drink?'

Danny nodded and pointed at the bartender who had the Guinness in his hand walking it over. He put it gently onto the table. 'Thanks' Danny said. The bartender brought over a menu too and Danny opened it up and flipped to the middle looking for the insert that Ivan put in there for the specials. With his head down he asked, 'Ivan making goulash?'

'No, it's not on there tonight.' Andrew said.

'Damn it.' Danny said. 'Really wish he kept it on the standard menu.'

'It's summer Danny' Donal said. 'Who the hell eats spicy soup in the summertime?'

Danny held up his hands, 'Not for lack of effort.' He said.

'What's he got on there?'

'It's a seafood risotto' Andrew answered for Donal and before Danny could find the insert.

'Look at you showing your skills.' Danny said. 'Okay Andrew. Sell it to me, what's it like.'

Andrew looked at Donal. Donal shrugged and said 'Let's hear it.'

'Okay. It's delicious. It's made in a butter base and with Chicken Stock. Ivan adds chopped parmesan cheese and mixes it in to give it a fuller texture. He mixes in chopped courgettes, prawns and chunks of salmon that he lightly fries first in olive oil and garlic. He serves it with a small triangle toast. It's very rich, but very nice.' Andrew said, then waited for a response.

Donal gave him an approving nod. 'Not bad Andrew' Danny said. 'Okay, you sold it to me, give me that.'

'What about wine?' Andrew asked. 'It goes well with pinot grigio.'

Danny laughed. 'What are you running sales training drills here Donal?' he said.

'No, but the kid does spend a lot of time with Ivan.' Donal answered.

'I guess I do' Andrew said. 'But Ivan's pretty explicit with us about highlighting what he wants us to focus on in our specials' description.'

'I guess so. Anyway, it sounds good, put it through for me. And tell Attila the Hun I'm out here and to come have a drink when the last order's out.' Danny said.

'Will do Danny.' Andrew said and walked out back to drop the slip. Outback the kitchen was slower than usual. The staff were still working and Ivan was finding things to yell about, but Andrew could definitely see that Danny and Donal were right. For a Friday night, it was dead. 'Less tips to share out' he thought, but wasn't too concerned. He decided that, as long as he had enough to live on currently, having a job he enjoyed for a change was the important thing. He wrote the time on the slip and yelled 'Fire it' when he dropped it down for the kitchen staff. 'It's for Danny' he said 'Ivan he's looking for you for a drink when you're finished up back here.'

Ivan looked over and yelled back 'Tell him, he buys, I drink.'

'I will' Andrew said. He headed back out to the dining room and did a loop around his tables, seeing if anyone needed anything, which they didn't. Most tables were finishing their main courses or already done and having dessert and coffee. He walked past a couple of Vicky's tables and noticed the people had finished. He asked if they needed anything and both indicated they were ready for the bill. He continued moving around and started doing some cleaning around the wait station. He was looking around the dining room for Vicky when one of the other waiters walked by and Andrew asked 'Hey Conor, you seen Vicky?'

'Saw her a while ago, pretty sure she walked outside' he said and continued walking past. Andrew realized it had been a while since he'd last seen her, which was curious since she was always good with staying close to her tables. He walked over towards the front door and looked outside, but he couldn't see her. He walked around to the front window and peered out, trying not to lean over any of the tables that sat tight to the glass.

He couldn't see her at first, but spotted her eventually. She was a few yards away from the restaurant. She was talking to a man who looked about Andrew's age. Andrew looked closely and could see they were arguing. He saw Vicky was crying. That was twice he'd seen her cry in a month. He watched for a minute, not sure whether he should worry about her. Then he felt for a moment that he was invading her privacy and decided to turn away. Just before he did, he saw the man shove her and she fell back onto the ground.

Andrew's mind went blank. Before realizing he'd moved, he was out the front door and walking quickly down the street towards her. He saw she had gotten up and was walking towards him. The man who shoved her started after her again. She picked up her pace and ran past Andrew. The man started jogging and calling after her. Andrew put his hand to the man's chest to stop him as he tried to shove past. 'Get your fucking hand off me!' he said to Andrew. Andrew gripped the man's shirt and stiffened his arm. The man tried to twist Andrew's arm loose forcefully. Andrew shoved him backwards. 'Take a walk.' Andrew said and pointed down the street. 'Fuck you, this has nothing to do with you.' The man said.

'I watched you shove Vicky, so now it does.' Andrew replied.

'Who the fuck do you think you are?' the man said and tried to push past Andrew again. Andrew shoved him back with two hands this time. 'I'm her friend and I said take a fucking walk.' Andrew felt the air deaden around him. Pedestrians rushed quickly around them to avoid walking through any conflict.

'Ya bud.' The man said 'Before what? You think you make me fucking nervous?'

Andrew saw the man tense up at the shoulders and shift his feet to steady his balance.

Andrew tried to keep his breathing steady and his limbs loose and relaxed, he said. 'I don't give a shit what I make you. But you're not going after her again.'

'Fine' the man said and turned like he was going to begin walking away. Andrew didn't buy it. He could see the man's blood was up and that he wasn't backing down so easily. The man pivoted on his left foot and came around with this right fist swinging for Andrew's face. Andrew saw the pivot of his foot and the man's weight shift like it was delivered in slow motion. By the time his fist came close to where Andrew's face had been, Andrew had already bounced back half a foot and watched the punch sail by in front of him hitting nothing but air. The man put everything he had into the swing and fell forward with the momentum. Andrew snatched out quickly with his left hand and grabbed the man's shirt in the middle of his back. He kicked out hard with the side of his left foot into the back of the man's knee, bringing him down on the same knee. With his free hand, Andrew grabbed the back of the man's belt and gripped it tightly. He spun the man around and using his weight and the spin's momentum, stepped forward and rolled the man onto the cement.

The man hit the ground hard and rolled a few feet forward on the cement. He got up as quickly as possible. Andrew could see he was in pain both from the fall and from his damaged ego. He looked up at Andrew. Andrew shook his head slowly, urging the man to reconsider. He didn't. He dropped his head and ran hard at Andrew. He attempted to tackle him, but Andrew stepped aside and tripped the man. He fell back onto the ground, but jumped up quickly and started swinging wildly. He hit Andrew a couple times with punches, but nothing landed square. Andrew covered up and most either landed on his arms or missed him completely. As he covered his head Andrew read the timing of the swings and began to time his ducks to move away from the punches. Within seconds, the swings started coming in slower. Andrew used the opportunity to push the man back and create space between them. The man paused for a moment then rushed him again. This time Andrew didn't bother jumping out of the way. He timed the rush and lashed out with a quick left jab, then right cross. On the tail end of the right cross, he dipped low, then pivoted and came up with a left hook to the man's cheek. The man was stung by the first two blows and too slow to avoid the last. His knees buckled and he hit the ground within seconds. Andrew stopped himself from coming across with a boot at the last second. The man was moving on the ground but it was slowly and Andrew saw he was done. A strong arm came across his chest from behind and grabbed him. Andrew was caught off guard and tensed in response. 'It's Danny.' Danny Carson said in his ear as he pulled Andrew towards him back through the door of the restaurant. 'That dude's done, get your ass in inside before the guards pick you up.'

Minutes later, the Guards did show up. But by the time they did, the man had left. He took a number of statements from people leaving the restaurant who had seen what happened through the window. He also spoke with Donal and Danny, then with Vicky and finally with Andrew himself.

They seemed convinced Andrew had acted in self-defense and left within an hour. By that time, the slow night at the restaurant had grown even slower and Donal decided to flip the closed sign on the door twenty minutes early. The other staff were abuzz with the excitement from the evening's events, but Andrew was sullen. He noticed Vicky was too. Donal must have understood the body language because he decided that he'd buy the staff drink in the bar next door instead of in the restaurant. He gave Vicky the key and asked her to lock up. Andrew stayed behind with Vicky to finish cleaning up and also so she wouldn't be by herself.

When the others left, Andrew and Vicky continued cleaning for a few minutes. Andrew felt awkward and wasn't sure what to say. Finally, he said. 'I'm sorry Vicky.'

Vicky looked at him with scrunched eyebrows in reply. 'What do you have to be sorry for?'

He shrugged, 'I mean . . . I guess I'm sorry if I put my nose somewhere it shouldn't have been. You know, if I got into your business.'

'Don't be ridiculous.' She said 'I'm the one who's sorry. You could've gotten hurt. He went after you because you were sticking up for me.'

'I guess so.' Andrew said. 'Still.' He shrugged his shoulders again.

Vicky stopped cleaning and walked closer to where he stood. She paused for a moment looking at Andrew, 'It's not what you think though Andrew.' She said.

'I'm not sure what you mean.'

'I guess, I mean, I'm not one of those girls who goes after bad boys or something. I only went on a few dates with that guy, then broke it off cause he's an asshole. He's crazy or something, I guess that's why he couldn't take it. Now every time I see him he makes a scene.'

Andrew pulled up a chair at one of the bar tables and took a seat. The cleaning was done to begin with as they both were thinking about how to start the conversation. Vicky walked into the bar and reached behind it and underneath into the refrigerator. She pulled out two bottles of beer and opened them. Then she came over to the table and handed one to Andrew. He took it and said, 'thanks.' Vicky walked around the table and took the seat across from him.

'You know, I saw you the first morning I arrived in Dublin.' He said. He took a sip from the beer. She took one from her own beer too.

'I know you did.' She said. 'I remembered you.'

'You did?' he asked.

'Of course I did. I just wasn't sure if you remembered me, so I didn't want to say it to you.'

Andrew laughed. 'Me too. Same reason I didn't say it to you.'

Vicky smiled and laughed as well. Andrew thought often about her smile. She had dimples that only showed up when she smiled. Andrew loved to see her smile and laugh because it made her even more beautiful whenever she did. He found himself staring and dropped his eyes to his hands, both of which held the beer bottle on the table. 'So that night, or morning I guess. Was that why you were crying.' He asked.

'Was I crying that night?' She said as if to herself. 'Yes, I guess I was. I ran into him and he wouldn't leave me alone all night, so I left the nightclub where I was with some friends, but he kept following me.'

'This guy sounds dangerous.' Andrew said.

'Yeah, I guess he was.' She said and slid her chair back an inch and stood up, stepping closer to where Andrew was sitting.

'What do you mean he was Vicky? He probably still is.'

'I doubt it now.' She said.

'Why's that? What's changed?'

'Well . . . now I have you to protect me . . . Don't I?'

She looked at Andrew and appeared to be trying to keep a straight face. He leaned back slightly at first, but then relaxed in his seat again and smiled. 'Yeah, okay Vicky. I'll protect you.' He said.

'Good.' She said and slid closer to Andrew. Andrew turned in his chair towards her. His hands dropped too, away from the beer bottle he'd been holding. She edged closer to him again, so that she was inches from his face.

Andrew looked in her eyes first, then dropped his gaze down to her lips. He could smell her perfume and her shampoo. Her dark hair glistened under the dim restaurant lighting. He could feel her body heat and could hear his heart beating loudly as it thumped faster in his chest. Then he smiled slightly again at her, looking back into her eyes. 'Good.' He said and leaned in and kissed her.

22

Andrew was restless that night in bed. Though he'd fallen asleep in near bliss, at some point during the night he slipped into a nightmare. His dream had him transported back to America. He saw himself standing in the woods along the edge of a golf course he knew well as a teenager in Quincy. He stood in a clearing. It was covered with pine needles that cut his shoeless feet. The surrounding trees were bare and the air wintry cold though he stood in a t shirt and jeans only. Fear gripped him in the dream. Along the edge of the clearing he could see the bodies. They were the four missing girls from Quincy all found dead. He recognized Gina, she lay lifeless at the foot of a barkless tree with eyelids open though her pupils were fogged over. Then everything grew blurry. His brother Brian appeared, though it only looked vaguely like Brian, his hazy memory distorting his features so that he was paler and elongated like a walking El Greco painting. The distorted Brian only said one thing, but said it over and over. It was a question. 'Couldn't you have done something?' he asked, continuously stressing the word *something*. In his dream, Andrew could hear things, but was mute so could not reply. Brian slowly faded into invisibility. Next the man who had gone after Vicky appeared and came after Andrew. Andrew was running but every glance back saw the man gaining on him. His final glance behind him showed that the man after him was no longer that from outside the restaurant, but the three men who attacked him in prison. Andrew tried to pick up speed, but his legs dragged in his dream as if running in a shallow pool. He stumbled through a block of trees and spilled into another clearing. Inside the clearing, the trees thickened around him. He looked around frantically for a way out. He walked into the center then heard the brush shift behind him. He turned and saw Vicky. She was kneeling down and her eyes were red from crying. Next to her was a younger John Bishop. He stood looking at Andrew and laughing. He grabbed Vicky's hair and held up in his other hand a large knife.

That was all Andrew remembered when he awoke with a start, which was plenty. It was morning already and he went over to the window and lifted the shade. Outside was dull and it looked like a light rain fell overnight as the ground looked to be damp, though not newly soaked. He walked into the kitchenette and poured himself a large glass of orange juice. He flicked the television on in the living room for some background noise. He pondered whether to eat breakfast or do some exercise first. It was one of his few days off, in fact there were a rare two days in a row that he had to himself. He decided a jog might do his mind some good. Going for a run helped him focus his thoughts, as long as he left the Ipod at home. He wanted to forget his dream and wanted to clear his head so he could accurately assess what the night before meant. He really liked Vicky and got the impression she felt the same for him. They had kissed. That was all they'd done, but it was long and to him felt like it meant something. 'But, there's so much she needs to know first.' He thought. 'And if I tell her everything . . . she might run.'

He put on his gym shorts and a rugby tech shirt with a t shirt over it. He tied his sneakers while he watched a Top

Gear repeat in the background. He took a few minutes to stretch out then headed outside. He turned west toward Rathmines village and started jogging. By the time he reached the small shopping center just minutes away, he already felt better. His blood was flowing and his muscles warm. Both helped to clear his mind, melting his concerns into the background at least while his legs and arms pumped. He continued running and eventually looped around several other South City Dublin villages, each a near mirror image of the other. Each had their own small restaurants, various pubs, butchers and a bookmakers. He finished the loop and ended up back at the Triangle in Ranelagh. It was a few miles at least and he ran it at a good rate so that he was sweating heavily by the time he reached the Triangle. He stopped there and stood for a minute with his fingers locked on top of his head. He continued to pace back and forth as he got his breathing back under control and his body began to cool down. He took his time walking slowly back to his apartment. With nothing much on his agenda for the day, there was no reason to rush.

Back at the apartment, he stood for a long while under the electric shower and let the hot water pour over him. The steam build up created a sauna in the bathroom. He got out and slowly got dressed. Physically, the jog did him well and he felt refreshed and energetic. Mentally, the workout shook off the morning cob webs and he was able to think more clearly.

He poured a bowl of cereal and took a seat on the couch. Halfway through his bowl his doorbell rang. He walked over to the front window, pulled the curtain aside and looked outside. He could see the street below, but couldn't make out who had rang the doorbell. The apartment building had an intercom system recently installed. Andrew walked to the buzzer and held the talk button. 'Who is it?' he said then held down the second button to listen. 'Hey bodyguard' the voice said 'let us in. It's Danny, I'm here with Vicky.'

Andrew paused for a moment. 'That's odd, why are they here?' he thought. He pushed in the talk button again. 'I'll buzz you in' he said, 'I'm the top floor.' then let held down the buzzer He waited by the door, but wasn't comfortable leaving the door ajar until he heard Danny's voice close up. A minute later there was a knock on the door. 'What gives Dawson?' Danny's voice said from outside. Andrew turned the locked and opened up the door. He opened it a crack at first and peeked out. He saw Danny standing there with a confused look on his face. Vicky was behind him smiling. He opened the door fully, 'come on in.' he said.

'Jesus, Dawson, you nervous prick. Who are you expecting?' Danny said as he walked in and took off his jacket. 'I wasn't expecting anyone. Can't say I get many people dropping by.'

'I get it kid. Not everyone's a fan of the pop in.'

'It's not that' Andrew said. 'Anyway, come on in. Make yourself at home.' Danny continued into the living room and walked into the kitchenette. Vicky lingered behind him. She smiled at Andrew when he locked the door and turned back towards them.

'Sorry, it's a small place.' He said.

'I think it's nice.' Vicky said. 'You could do much worse than this.'

Andrew laughed, 'yeah I know, I've seen worse.'

'I believe it. Even the nice parts of Dublin aren't without some slumlords.'

'Here' he said and walked over and cleared a sweatshirt and loose blanket off the couch. 'sit down, make yourself comfortable.'

'Thanks Andrew' she said and dropped into the couch.

'Can I get you a coffee or tea or something?' he asked.

'Coffee!' Danny yelled from the kitchenette. 'I see you've got a French press. I'd love a coffee.' He walked over to a small table with two chairs in between the living room and kitchenette and sat in one of the chairs.

'Okay' Andrew said. He walked over to the sink and filled the kettle. He flicked the switch on for the kettle. He pulled the coffee out of the cabinet and scooped it into the French press.

'It is a decent place Dawson. No parking though. I left the car in the supermarket in the village.'

'Sorry Danny. I don't drive here anyway.' He said as he poured out the water into the French press. He brought it over to the table with a few cups and some milk.

'So what can I do for you guys? I'm guessing there's a reason you dropped over.'

Danny poured two cups and walked one over to Vicky on the couch. 'Well Dawson.' He said. 'How long you been living here now?'

Andrew took a sip from his cup before answering while he tried to count the weeks in his head. 'It's over a month now anyway.' He said. 'Went by fast.'

'Yeah I bet.' Danny answered. 'So, you've been here a month already and you haven't even gone to see your mother yet.'

Andrew looked over at Danny, then at Vicky. The

comment took him by surprise. Then again, the entire visit did too. 'Did I tell you my mother lived here?' he asked, leaving the question open to both of them. He couldn't remember ever talking about her, but decided he might have said it at some stage and not recalled.

Vicky shrugged and shook her head. Andrew looked at Danny who did the same. 'Not that I remember. But, you gotta know this. We live in a small world sure, but in that world, you're living in a really small country.' Danny said.

'Okay, but what does that mean, really?' Andrew asked.

'It means we have mutual friends Andrew.'

'Really?'

'Yeah, really. My wife's in Donegal. Same town as your mother.'

'Oh' Andrew said.

'What?'

'It's just that . . . I didn't realize you were even married.'

'Well, you never asked.' Danny said. 'I am. But, I work in Dublin, my wife Michelle lives in Donegal. It's complicated, but yeah, I'm married.'

'So it wasn't really a coincidence then.'

'What's that? Me and you meeting?'

'Yeah, did you know who I was then?'

'Ah, come on kid, I had an idea.' Danny said. He let his eye contact with Andrew linger for a few seconds. 'I'd heard of you at least. Plus, you look just like him.' he said.

Andrew gave him a funny look. 'You . . . knew my brother?'

Danny shrugged 'I knew him Andrew yeah . . . But that was many years ago.'

Andrew nodded. He wanted to know more, but he

wasn't sure now was the time. He looked over at Vicky and asked 'What about you Vicky? You have family in Donegal too?'

'Me? God no. I've never even been there, I'm from Dublin. I just thought it would be fun to tag along . . . if you'll have me?'

He considered the question for a moment before replying. 'I don't see why not. So, what? We're heading to Donegal? The three of us?' Andrew asked.

'Why not Dawson? I'm going that way anyway. I'll take you. You have a few days off right? That's what Vicky said. I'll go see my wife. You can let your mother know you're alive. Seems like a no brainer.'

Andrew looked at Danny, then back at Vicky again. He considered the offer for a minute, but knew he had to go. 'Okay' he said. 'Yeah, what the hell, I'll put some clothes in a bag and we'll go.'

'Good' Danny said and stood up. 'Thanks for the coffee.' He walked over to the front door and opened it. 'I'll get the car and meet you both out front in five minutes.'

23

It had been several years since Andrew had stepped foot in Donegal. He was still really a child the last time he was there. The route that Danny drove there seemed different from that he remembered. Back then he remembered passing through many more towns and driving for longer on smaller roads. The road network had expanded through some of the Celtic tiger years it appeared, although the motorways never seemed to last as long as they should and the journey northwest still took them through several towns and more than a few periods of one lane roads where one slow driver could result in a traffic backup that stretched for miles. Andrew took the front passenger seat. He wasn't used to being in a situation where he needed to pass other drivers out by pulling into the oncoming lane. Every time Danny did so, Andrew felt his heart rate increase, though by the time they hit Sligo, he'd grown accustomed to it and no longer had to clamp his eyes shut until they were safely back in the correct lane.

After passing Sligo's city center, the surroundings grew familiar to Andrew. He remembered the stretch of beach that ran along the west of the county line, the sandy shoreline was a landscape made for postcards. Also, he remembered the name of the mountain when he saw it, Benbulben. The odd shaped mountain was carved by glaciers during the ice age. It was an impressive spectacle even as a child, but what he remembered more clearly was laughing with his brother at the sound of its funny name.

They drove on through Sligo, passing through Leitrim

and onto a newly constructed bypass into Donegal. Danny turned off a short distance later and took them through the town of Ballyshannon. Andrew thought it looked similar to how he remembered it. It was still quaint, though there were more bookmaker shop fronts than he remembered. Also, the center of the town now held a statue of the Irish blues and rock legend Rory Gallagher, who was born in the town. They continued through the town and out past the road leading towards Rossnowlagh beach. Danny slowed to a stop a few miles away from the beach entrance in front of a small cottage. The house looked old and badly in need of painting. Also, the front grass was not well kept and several shrubs were overgrown and blocked much of the walkway leading to the front door. The view from the house however was beautiful. Andrew stepped out of the car and walked to the front, he turned with his back facing the house and could see Rossnowlagh and the ocean in the distance. Green cliffs dropped steep into a long sandy beach that stretched out for over a mile in the distance, eventually wrapping around grasslands and small sand dunes. He could see a few cars moving slowly on the sand itself and when he looked more closely could spot surfers in the water around the beach. He breathed in the sea air that blew across the land from the Atlantic Ocean. He held it in his lungs for a ten count before releasing his breath. 'Well?' he said to Danny, as Danny opened the driver's door and climbed out. 'Well nothing.' He pointed up to the front door. 'This is your Mom's place.' She's expecting you.

Andrew looked over at Vicky as she also stepped out from the car and stretched her arms over her head. She had fallen asleep in the back for the last part of the journey. Before she was in ear shot, he asked Danny quietly, 'Are you both coming in too?'

Danny shook his head slowly. 'I'm not, but she is.'

'Okay' Andrew said. 'You sure you won't come in, even for a second?'

'Sorry, got my own agenda buddy. I got you here, but that's as much as I can do. I'll give you a call tomorrow morning and see how you're fixed.' Danny said.

'Alright' Andrew said. 'Thanks for bringing me Danny.'

'Forget about it, it was my pleasure.' He held out his hand and Andrew shook it. He walked back over to the car and grabbed his and Vicky's overnight bags from the back. Vicky walked around the car and joined him at the walkway. Danny turned the ignition and waved one last time before he slowly pulled away. Andrew turned towards Vicky. He felt awkward and put his head down. 'So . . . just us then.'

She smiled 'looks that way, yeah. Will we knock now or are you still procrastinating?'

Andrew looked up at her. He smiled back and said 'you're right, I'm stalling. Come on let's go.' They continued down the walkway leading to the front door. There was a small step up to a platform. Andrew stepped onto it and knocked heavily on the door. He turned back towards Vicky and smiled again and shrugged his shoulders. He heard steps making their way to the door on the other side of it. He heard a lock click and the door opened. His mother pulled the door open and stepped back in to let him enter. 'Hi Ma' he said and she hugged him, squeezing tightly around his back. 'My baby's finally come to visit. Took you long enough for fuck sake.'

'Sorry Ma, I meant to come up sooner, but it's been

busy in Dublin, with my job and getting settled and everything.'

'I know it has' she said 'here come in, come in.' She stepped aside and let him walk further into the hall. Vicky followed, slowly behind.

Andrew grew suddenly aware of the tightness in the hallway while the three of them stood in it. 'Sorry Ma, this is my . . . uh, friend, Vicky. She works with me at this restaurant in Dublin.'

Andrew's mother looked at Vicky then slowly raised her hand. Vicky held it and shook it lightly. 'Nice to meet you Mrs. Dawson.' Vicky said.

'When I heard Andrew was bringing a friend up with him, I didn't expect one so . . . young and beautiful. Please call me Rita.'

'I'm Vicky.'

'Well, come in please. I'll put the kettle on.' Rita said and led them into a small kitchen at the end of the hall. She filled the kettle under the tap and hit the button to start it boiling. She took down three cups from the cupboard along with a clay tea pot.

Andrew dropped his and Vicky's bags outside in the hallway. He circled the small kitchen table and stopped in front of the refrigerator. The face of the fridge was bare for the most part except for a small magnet white board that had nothing written on it. He was surprised to see the refrigerator door so empty. As a young boy, he remembered it overflowed so often with graded tests, pictures drawn during school or photos taken of his brother and himself. It was usually so full that when he shut the refrigerator door, one or two items fell to the floor from the impact. He turned to the table and sat in one of the chairs in the small kitchen. Vicky waited for Andrew to sit down before joining him. 'Is there anything I can help you with?' she asked Rita.

'No thank you Vicky, please make yourself at home.'

Rita finished making the tea and brought the pot and cups to the table and brought out a packet of digestive biscuits and other chocolate bars from a cabinet. She then joined Andrew and Vicky sitting down. They made small talk for a while at the table. Andrew told her all he could think of about the job at the restaurant, including how he came to meet Danny Carson and end up working there in the first place. Rita spoke whimsically, Andrew assumed for Vicky's benefit, about what Andrew was like as a child. 'He was much less reserved.' She had said 'In fact, he was very funny as a child and often the family depended on him for jokes and laughter.'

Andrew didn't like the direction that the conversation was headed or the implication that he no longer had as good a sense of humor. So, he steered the conversation back to his mother. He asked about how she was settling in Donegal and about the health of his Grandmother, who was nearing ninety years old. The obvious topic he stayed clear from was anything to do with his lock up or the unsolved murder of the girls in Quincy. He read into his Mother's body language that she was also purposely staying away from those topics, though he couldn't tell from her manner whether it was for Vicky's benefit or if it was genuinely still too painful or embarrassing to think about.

After a few hours, she made them a small dinner and showed them where they could sleep, awkwardly presenting options that included them staying in the same bed if that was what they were used to. Andrew and Vicky both blushed with embarrassment before Andrew said he'd stay in the sitting room on the couch and Vicky could sleep in the spare bedroom. Rita urged them to take a walk down to the beach while the evening had a stretch of sunlight in the early summer. She insisted they walk by themselves and she would stay behind and clean up after dinner.

They left the house and walked along the edge of the road in the direction of the beach. There was a small laneway that they cut through that halved their journey. They came to a small inn that had a bar and restaurant attached. It was perched at the top of a steep hill that led down a path to the beach. Vicky sat down at a picnic table out front of the restaurant, while Andrew walked inside to see about getting drinks. He ordered two beers from the bar and took them back outside. He sat down next to Vicky on the picnic table and put the drinks down in front of them. They both faced out towards the sea. The sun was still out, but it was a cool evening and there was a breeze coming off the ocean. 'Some view.' Vicky said and took a sip from her drink. 'It is.' Andrew said. 'I don't think I've ever seen anything like it.' Across from them the wind coming off the ocean made the water ripple and the late evening sun glistened off the waves as they formed. They were closer now to the beach and could see everything more clearly than before in front of the house. A few cars still remained on the sand mostly in front of the hotel that sat at the beach's edge. The vehicle owners were likely made up of either those individuals surfing in wetsuits or those jogging or walking pets along the sand.

'It's a nice break from Dublin definitely. I can't believe

you waited a month to come out here. With all this' she swept her hand across the landscape. 'Not even considering your poor Mother.' Vicky said.

'You've never been here at all I thought. So I don't think you can talk.'

'Okay I guess so, but I never had any reason to come here before. Now I have a good one.' She said.

'I'm assuming you mean me and not just the scenery.' He said and smiled.

'Maybe.' She said 'Maybe not.'

He laughed at her. 'Good. So, you're glad you came along then.' Andrew asked.

'Of course I am. It's beautiful out here. Plus, it was nice to meet your Mother, she seems really nice. Really, she's not like any other Irish mother I've met. She's very . . . accepting of me. Not sure that's typical of mother's meeting girls that their sons bring home.' She said and smiled.

'Really?' Andrew asked. 'Could be the years in America, but I don't ever remember her being any different.'

'I mean it as a good thing.' Vicky said. 'Also, I feel like I know you a little better now.'

'Really? Is that a good thing?' he asked.

'I think so.' She answered. 'I was glad to learn you weren't always just this big guy that walked around all quiet and nervous all the time.'

'Is that how I come across? Quiet and nervous?' Andrew asked.

'Don't forget the big part.' Vicky said.

Andrew smiled. 'Right, and big of course.'

'Truthfully though Andrew, you are so quiet and you

do seem nervous often . . . or something like it I guess. I just feel like you're always holding something back.'

Andrew didn't say anything. He took a sip of his drink and looked away for a moment over towards the ocean.

'Sorry Andrew' Vicky said. 'I didn't mean to offend you or anything. I think what I meant is that . . . well, I like you when you're outgoing. You're funnier than I expected and nicer. I think you shouldn't hold back as much. You know. Like the other night. I'm pretty sure that arsehole who you chased off didn't find you quiet or nervous.'

Andrew laughed. 'No, I reckon he did not.' he said. 'Listen, I'm not offended or anything. It's just . . . there's, um, reasons I am the way I am these days. I don't think I was always like that. I guess I'm glad to hear you like me at all.'

She laughed at him and pushed his chest back lightly. 'Of course I do, you eejit. Why else would I be here in fucking Donegal with you? And meeting your Mother no less?'

Andrew brushed her hand away and smiled. 'What about Danny then? To be honest, I'm confused by your whole relationship with him. I thought for a while you too were together. But now, I'm guessing you're not . . . right?'

'Danny? No, of course not. He's a friend alright, but that's all. Danny worked for my father for a pretty long time in Dublin. My father got sick a few years ago and I think I started acting out a bit from the stress of it all. He asked Danny to keep an eye out for me from time to time. I think setting me up with a job that had me working most evenings instead of going out partying was his way of doing that you know . . . and I enjoyed it, so I've been there ever since.'

'Oh, okay, that makes it clearer I guess. I'd been meaning to ask that for a while.' Andrew said.

'Well now you know. Feel better?'

'I think I do actually.'

'So what about you then Andrew? Are you ever going to tell me your story?' she asked.

Andrew paused. He felt his heart start to race and could feel his face was beginning to blush.

'With the exception of a little bit tonight at your Mother's dinner table, I don't think I've ever heard you talk about anything remotely personal from your past. It's like you were born the day you landed in Dublin. Either that or you have amnesia or something.'

'Sometimes I wish I could forget' he thought, then he said 'There's things . . . reasons I guess, for why I left. I just don't talk about them . . . because I don't know how anyone would react to hearing them.'

'Andrew' she said.

'Yeah?'

'I know about you.'

Andrew leaned back and looked at her, confused. 'What do you mean? What do you know?'

'Well, I know some things. I know you were thrown in jail for some disgusting crimes that you didn't commit. And I know that you were friends with some of those girls that were killed.'

Andrew's eyebrows raised in surprise. 'What? How? Who told you that?' he asked in a high pitched voice.

'Danny did.' She answered. 'When are you going to realize that Danny may not live there anymore, but he's still connected with what goes on in his hometown. By all accounts, you weren't exactly small news either. I'm surprised there wasn't much coverage over here.'

'Who else knows? Who else has he told?'

'I don't know for certain, but I assume everyone at the restaurant knows. Donal definitely does and I'm guessing Ivan too.'

Andrew was flustered. His mind raced and a dozen personal interactions with his co-workers ran through his head. He'd always judged those interactions on the basis that no one knew anything about him. He was overwhelmed by learning that he'd need to reassess everything that happened in the last month, every last exchange he experienced.

'Andrew' Vicky said. 'Just relax.'

He listened to her, 'she must've read the concern on my face' he thought and tried to slow down his breathing and pull himself together.

'Weren't you . . . I mean, aren't you scared off then?' he asked after a minute of catching his breath.

'Sure, I think everyone was a little nervous at first, but it's not like you actually did those things Andrew. You were wrongly accused. '

'I know I was.' He said. 'I think I just got so used to being judged by anyone who looked at me. Even though I was innocent, people still see you differently once you're accused of something like that. There's always doubt I guess. It's not something that anyone can erase from their memory and I can't really blame them. I was tarnished for life. So, really, I had no choice but to leave. There's no way I could've stayed there and faced that judgment down every last day of my life.'

'So' Vicky asked 'Really, is that why you hadn't come

to see your mother? I mean, was that like, part of the reason?'

Andrew looked at her. In a short period of time, he felt like she could read him so well. He wasn't sure how he felt about that, but he was leaning towards he liked it. 'I was afraid.' He answered.

'Afraid to see your own mother?'

'Afraid to look into my mother's eyes and realize that for a time . . . even a fleeting second, she actually believed that I was who they said I was. That I . . . did those things.'

Vicky nodded at his explanation. 'I guess that makes sense.' She said. 'And? Is that what you saw when you looked at her today?'

He shook his head. 'No Vicky. All I saw today was joy.'

'Good' Vicky said and edged her way closer to Andrew so that she was inches from his face. She reached over and took his hand in hers. 'Listen to me Andrew. You did nothing wrong, you hear me? Stop apologizing for everything, you shouldn't do it and you don't need to. And for fucksake, stop walking around with your head drooped down, buried in your shoulders. You have nothing to be ashamed of. You need to keep that big head of yours held up high to show them that, especially if you want people to believe it.' She leaned over and kissed him gently, then laid her head on his shoulder and looked out across the ocean. She slid her fingers past his and interlocked their hands.

He smiled at her and squeezed her hand tightly. 'You're something else.' He said to her.

'Is that right?'

'Yes, I believe it is. You're like medicine.' He said.

She laughed. 'Lousy analogy, but I'll take it assuming it was meant to be a compliment.'

'It's a compliment.' He assured her. 'A very big one.'

24

The countryside's remote silence and utter darkness could be unsettling to those unaccustomed to such things. Andrew had forgotten just how dark the night was, although during the summer months it didn't last very long as the sun returned only a few hours after the twilight turned to black. The heavy curtains in his mother's living room helped to keep the early morning sunrise at bay, however there was no defense from the cows mooing from the neighboring farm outside the window. The animals woke Andrew from a deep, yet uncomfortable sleep on a sofa that was a foot too short length-wise. He stood up and stretched his arms out, then twisted his back left to right quickly to force it to crack. The clock on the wall behind the television showed it was close to eleven am, which was much later than Andrew expected. He and Vicky took a taxi back to the house around one am after they decided it was safer than venturing down the small dark roads with no sidewalks. They stayed up talking in the kitchen for an hour or so when they returned and finished off a bottle of wine that had been opened earlier. Andrew had dry mouth from the wine and his back ached from the awkward sofa, but besides that he felt good from the decent night's rest. Also, there was that lingering joy he had for the opportunity to spend the evening with Vicky. He had that feeling of excitement that comes at the start of new relationships. The more time he spent with her, the stronger his feelings seemed to grow.

He walked from the living room out into the hallway. He could hear voices from the kitchen and walked in their direction. He entered to find Vicky up and dressed, having coffee with his mother at the table. They both looked up to him when he walked in. 'Morning.' He said.

'Morning' they said in unison. Andrew walked over to the counter and found a coffee cup on it and poured himself a cup from the French press and stirred in some milk. He took a sip and turned around to Vicky and his Mother.

'Wasn't sure if you'd ever get up.' Rita said. 'I didn't think you were back that late.'

Andrew reached into the cabinet and pulled down a cereal bowl. 'No, it wasn't that late.' He said. 'I was just tired I guess, been working a lot. Plus I think that's how my body functions now with the restaurant hours. I'm finally adjusting.'

'You sleep alright on that couch?' she asked.

'It was okay Ma. I've stayed on worse.' He said.

'Danny's been by this morning already.' Vicky said. 'He said he'll grab us at one or so to head back.'

'Okay', he said 'thanks'. He took a seat at the table and poured himself some cereal. He looked over to his Mother and said 'Sorry it's such a short trip Ma. Maybe next time I can get a few more days off and stay awhile.'

'Maybe, or I can come see you in Dublin. We were just talking about that.' She said and pointed to Vicky.

'It would be fun.' Vicky said. 'Andrew can take you to the restaurant and show you where we work.'

'Yeah sure, I can do that.' Andrew said with a mouth full of cereal. 'Let me know when Ma.'

They chatted around the table a little longer while they finished breakfast. They made loose plans for Rita's Dublin visit and pegged the timeframe for within the month. Vicky insisted on cleaning up after breakfast and cleared the dishes and started washing them in the sink. Andrew took the opportunity to get dressed and pack up his bag. He showered and shaved then threw on jeans and a t shirt. He folded up the blankets he had in the living room and put them and the spare pillows in his Mother's bedroom. Danny Carson showed up promptly at one o'clock to pick them up. They said goodbye to Rita just outside the door. She gave Andrew a hug. Andrew saw that her eyelids were lined with tears when she let go of him. 'I'm sorry I didn't come sooner Ma. I'll make sure I come up more often.' He said.

She smiled and wiped the slow falling tears from her cheeks. 'I'm glad you're okay Andrew.' She said and hugged him again. 'Me too.' He said softly.

'She's a good one. Worth sticking around for I hope.' she said to him as she waved to Vicky before she got into the back of the car. 'Take care of her Andrew.'

'I know she is.' He said nodding his head. 'I'll try. Bye Ma.'

He turned and walked around to the passenger door and got into the car. Danny waved goodbye out the window, then he did a U-turn in the road to head back towards town. Andrew waved as they drove away, looking back until the house was finally out of view. They drove back the way they came, back through Ballyshannon, then on through Sligo, Roscommon then Longford. Within three hours Danny pulled up in front of Andrew's apartment in Ranelagh. Andrew thanked him and the two men shook hands before he opened the door and climbed out of the car. He stood for a minute with a hand lingering on the car's hood. He looked in the back window at Vicky. He decided he wasn't ready to say goodbye to her just yet. He knocked on the back window lightly with his index finger. She leaned over and pushed the button to bring the window down. When it was half open she stopped and looked out at him. 'Can you stay for a while?' he asked. She smiled at him and put her hand on the bag in seat next to her. 'Of course I can.' She said. She got out of the car and said 'bye Danny' and waved after she shut the door. She joined Andrew on the sidewalk as Danny pulled the car away from the curb. He drove away, tapping the horn once as he did.

25

Andrew peeled apart two slices of bacon and dropped both onto a hot pan. The pork sizzled immediately and a second later spit hot grease at his wrist as he reached over the pan to light the back burner. 'You're up early.' He heard Vicky say from behind him. He turned around to find her standing in the living room wearing nothing but one of his t shirts, which looked like a fat man's poncho draped over her. He smiled at her and said, 'good morning. I thought I'd make you breakfast.'

'Thanks' she said and slid into one of the chairs at the table by the kitchenette. 'What are you making?'

'An omelette' he answered as he whisked two eggs in a bowl with a fork quickly, then poured it onto the round frying pan at the back of the stove top. 'Some bacon too.'

'Sounds great.' She said. 'I didn't know you could cook. Honestly, I wouldn't have pictured it.'

'I'm not sure that I can.' He said. 'I'll let you be the judge. I figured I spend enough time with Ivan listening to him talk about food and watching him work, I'm hoping some of his skills in the kitchen have rubbed off on me.'

'Sure, we'll see.' She said. 'He did take a shine to you.'

'He's a complicated man that Ivan. I listen to him that's all.'

'Is that the trick?' she asked.

'Seems to work for me.' He got a plate down and flipped the omelette in half on the pan, creating a perfect semi-circle. After a couple seconds he transferred it carefully to the plate using a spatula and dropped the bacon next to it. 'Here you go' he said as he put it in front of Vicky with some silverware and a glass of orange juice.

'Thanks Andrew' she said. 'Are you not having anything?'

'No I am. Just don't have a pan big enough to do two at a time. Go ahead and start, there's nothing nice about a cold omelette.' He cracked two more eggs and whisk them quickly, then poured them into the pan to start the process over again. He smiled as he did it. He found that recently he enjoyed trying new things in the kitchen. He never did much cooking before, but in the last month he seemed to do it often. He really liked it and was developing a knack for it. He suspected his interest was mostly drawn from working around good food all the time at the restaurant. His palate was spoiled by the staff meals served before each shift. He was starting to think he may have found his calling. As he prepared his own breakfast, his mind drifted to the night before. He smiled at the images as they played back through his head. Vicky had stayed with him and they made love for the first time. He woke up early and couldn't wipe the smile off of his face. He couldn't sit and wait for her to wake up either, so he decided to start cooking, trusting in the smell of frying bacon to rouse her from her sleep, a method he figured worked for most of the western world.

He made his own plate quickly, without the same finesse or attention to detail he'd shown on Vicky's breakfast. He took the seat across from her. 'Any good?' he asked.

She smiled at him. 'Really good actually. Careful or I might make a habit of this.' She said.

He laughed, 'good, I was hoping that'd be the case.' He started into his omelette when he heard a knock at the door. He looked up at Vicky. She looked back at him and shrugged, 'I don't know' she said. Andrew stood up and took a sip of his juice to wash down the first bite of his breakfast. He slowly walked over to the door. He hesitated before reaching for the lock. It was odd to have anyone stop by really. It was odder that whoever it was didn't ring the doorbell from downstairs first. That meant they were already in the building. He leaned slowly toward the door with his ear, listening for any voices. There was another knock, followed by a man's voice, 'Dawson, come on man, I know you're in there, I can smell your breakfast.'

'Danny? Is that you . . . again?' He looked over at Vicky. She nodded then got up from the table and walked into the bedroom. Andrew opened the lock and opened the door a few inches. Outside Danny Carson stood, with Donal next to him. 'Come on man, let us in. Got something important to talk about.'

Andrew was confused, but opened the door to let them in. Danny walked in first and Donal followed behind him. 'Come on in. Twice in the same week Danny, what's up?' Both men walked into the living room and over to the table. Danny sat down first and Donal sat across from him. He looked down at the table, noticing the two place settings. 'You here with someone?' he asked looking up at Andrew as he walked over and sat on the armchair of the couch. Vicky walked out just then from the bedroom. She managed to throw on jeans and her own shirt. 'Morning Donal. Danny.' Donal smiled and waved back. 'Sorry to intrude' he said and held his hands up.

Danny turned to Andrew, 'Yeah, we're both sorry, but listen Andrew, there's a reason we came by.' He said.

Andrew looked at Danny, he looked more serious than usual. His face had a stern gaze instead of the jocular smirk it usually wore. He looked anxious, which in turn made Andrew anxious. He slid down from the armchair to the seat of the couch. 'What is it?' he asked looking back and forth from Danny to Donal.

Danny spoke first. 'Bernadette Gleason. You know her?'

'Bernie, yeah of course I know her.' Andrew answered. 'She's my . . . uh, good friend. Why, what's this about?'

Danny crouched down in the chair, leaning towards Andrew. He brought his elbows to his knees and his hands together, resting his chin on top of them. 'There's no easy way to say this Andrew, so I'll just say it. She's missing. There's talk that she's been nabbed by whoever's snatching those Quincy girls.'

Andrew slid further into his couch and pushed his back against the cushion. His mind raced too quickly to isolate any one thought. He brought his hands up to his face and ran them through his hair. 'Oh no Bernie.' He thought. When he didn't say anything for a minute. Danny continued. 'Andrew?'

Andrew looked at him. His eyes were wide open and his jaw slack. 'You understand what I'm saying to you?' Danny asked. 'You know what that means if the same dude does have her?'

The life crawled back into Andrew with a sudden burst of adrenaline. He jumped from his seat. 'I have to go.' He said quickly bouncing on his feet. 'I need to get back there.'

'Andrew' Donal chimed in. 'Think it through for a minute. How much could you even do going back there? I'm not sure there's anything good for you there.'

Andrew looked at Donal, surprised by his interjection.

He shook off the tingle of irritation that ran up his spine. 'It doesn't matter Donal. I can't sit here. I need to do something. I don't know what. But, whatever it is I can't do it from here.'

Andrew looked over towards Vicky. He saw a painful look develop in her eyes. He wanted to explain, but he felt there wasn't time, plus he wasn't sure what to say. He reached into his pocket and pulled out his phone. He pressed a button on the side to bring up the time. He turned back to Danny. 'Can you get me to the airport Danny? I have time, but I need to move now.'

Danny stood up and nodded. 'Yeah, Andrew, I'll take you.' Andrew ran into his room and grabbed a backpack and his passport. He stuffed a change of clothes into the bag, then ran into the bathroom and grabbed his toothbrush and deodorant and threw them in also. 'Let's go.' He said.

All four of them went on the journey to the airport. No one said anything during the trip. Andrew sat in the back with Vicky, but he looked out of the window for much of the duration. They pulled up to departures just over twenty minutes later. Andrew reached down and grabbed his backpack. 'Thanks Danny.' He said and pushed the door open. He paused, then reached his hand over and took Vicky's wrist in a light grasp. 'I'm sorry.' He said.

Her eye's looked watery, but no tears had fallen. 'Be safe Andrew.' She said then looked away, out her own window.

Andrew got out of the car and started walking away, but heard the car door open. Danny climbed out and leaned over the top. Andrew looked across at him. 'Are you sure I can't talk you out of this Andrew?' he asked.

'Are you sure you're the right person to try Danny?'

'No matter how it ends Andrew . . . no matter what happens, there'll be . . . regrets. That's if you make it out alright yourself.' Danny said.

Andrew considered his words for a moment. Then he said, 'If you're me right now Danny . . . do you stay?' Danny let out a breath and smiled slightly. 'I hope you make it back here safe Andrew. I've decided I like having you around.' He said and tapped the roof twice.

'Take care Danny.' He said and turned and walked away. He broke into a brisk walk, nearly a run after he cleared the automatic doors and headed straight for the Aer Lingus ticket desk. He made it just in time to purchase a seat on the next flight to Boston.

26

When he purchased the plane ticket and made his way through security to the gate, Andrew felt like a six hour plane journey would be sufficient time to align his thoughts and devise some kind of plan of action. When the airplane touched down in East Boston however, Andrew still couldn't figure his next move, never mind having a plan of any description. 'Maybe they were right', he thought. 'What the hell good can I do being here? Who will even talk to me?'

The flight was the longest six hours of Andrew's life. It made his days in prison feel brief and insignificant in comparison. He felt helpless waiting on the plane. He couldn't eat, he couldn't sleep, he didn't want to talk to anyone, and he couldn't listen to music, watch movies or read anything at all. His mind ran circles around itself, most thoughts disappearing in a puff of smoke as soon as they arrived in his head. He just stayed sitting up straight and kept his face buried into the window looking out across the blue sky, then the sea, until eventually he started recognizing neighborhoods from above. Then he began to feel sick, his stomach twisted in knots from a combination of minor turbulence and a familiar unease that he mistakenly thought he had rid himself of in the last month. He thought of Bernie. He could picture her face, in his mind's eye she was smiling. He knew wherever she was now however, she would not be smiling. 'If she's even breathing at all.' He considered, then shuttered at the thought. He couldn't fathom why someone would take her. 'What could they want with her? Why her?' It dawned on him that those close to the other ones, those other girls that were taken, must have felt the same way he did now. He knew the weight of their angst finally and felt guilty for not feeling much of anything before, until it was really someone he loved that was taken. 'Have I become so callous?' he considered.

He didn't check a bag in. He carried his backpack with him on the flight and walked straight from the landing gate through passport control, then downstairs through customs. The customs official looked him up and down sternly. Andrew figured he was likely noting the lack of luggage and deciding whether it was a threat. Finally, he let him through. Andrew used his U.S. passport to travel back, which he assumed quickened the silent interrogation. He walked out into the arrivals hall in Logan Airport's International terminal. He sifted through the crowds of people waiting for loved ones and spilled out until the sidewalk. He crossed over the street to the taxi stand and was inside a cab within two minutes. The taxi driver didn't say much to Andrew. He was too busy on his cell phone speaking in another language through a blue tooth connector in his ear. Andrew guessed he was Haitian based on the tone of the language that sounded vaguely French. Even stepping into the taxi, he wasn't sure where exactly he was headed and just said 'Quincy.'

As they weaved slowly through traffic down route 93 south Andrew decided he needed access to a vehicle. If he was planning to act with any semblance of speed, he couldn't be depending on taxis and public transport. The driver took a Dorchester exit and swung around towards Quincy. Andrew directed him towards Wollaston Beach, then down the side street to West Elm variety convenience store. Andrew paid the man and climbed out of the taxi.

He stood for a moment on the sidewalk outside the shop, staring in through the window. Nostalgia took him momentarily as he considered the cumulative hours, days, probably weeks of his life he'd spent sitting outside that shop staring into the window. The memories were so many and so mundane, that they seemed to melt into one long waiting period. There were no cars in the lot out front, which he was glad to see. 'Not ready yet to be recognized by random people.' He thought. He gathered himself, then walked up the front steps and reached his hand out to grab the handle. He wasn't sure if Chef would even be working, but he had to try.

The door chimed when he opened it. He stepped inside and felt a blast of cold air from the cooling system that hung just inside the door. He shivered from the unexpected breeze. He looked over at the register, but couldn't see anyone behind it. He walked deeper into the small shop, but there was no sign of anyone. 'Hello?' he said loudly. 'Chef, you around?'

He heard a noise from somewhere and a voice called out. 'Just a minute.' Seconds later, Chef Benson walked out of a small doorway that led to a storage room. He carried a box of potato chips, which he fumbled and nearly dropped when he walked out and saw Andrew. He regained control before placing it down softly at his feet. 'Shit, Andrew. I wasn't expecting to see you.' He said.

Andrew watched him walk around the back of the counter and duck under a door flap. 'Hi Chef.' He said. 'Didn't mean to surprise you. Honestly, I wasn't expecting to be back . . . not so soon anyway.'

'So you've heard?' Chef asked. He leaned against the outside of the counter. He looked tired and more unkempt than Andrew could remember ever seeing him.

Andrew nodded at Chef's question. 'Bernie? Yeah Chef, I heard.'

'I should've guessed you'd be back. You and her were close I know.' Chef crossed his arms nervously in front of his body. 'What are you planning to do?' he asked.

'I'm still thinking on it. But . . . I mean, I have to do something. I think I'll start by talking to that Detective. Does he still come in here?' he asked.

'Harris? Uh, yeah, from time to time he does, sure.' Chef answered. He shifted his hands from across his body and stuffed his fingertips into his jeans' pocket, leaving the thumbs out.

'Do you know how to contact him?' Andrew asked. 'I mean, can you get in touch.'

Chef considered the request for a moment before answering. 'I, uh, I don't have his number. But, listen, I can probably get it. Just might need some time.'

'Okay.' Andrew said. 'How much time to do you need?'

'I don't know, a few hours maybe.'

Andrew paused and put his index finger to his teeth and bit down on the nail. After a few seconds he took it out from his mouth. 'It's gotta be faster than that Chef. This is fucking important. I don't have time to waste man.'

Chef nodded his head in reluctant agreement. 'Yeah, okay. You're right. Give me an hour though, I need to track down a few people to try and get in touch. Is there a number he can call you on?'

'Shit, not really. Just have my Irish phone. Here' he said and walked over to the counter. He picked up a Keno pencil and took one of the lottery forms and wrote his cell number down. I'll give it to you anyway, but tell him I'm waiting at Mackin's pub for him. I'll wait an hour.' He handed the piece of paper over to Chef, then dropped the pencil back into the holder. He stood standing in front of Chef silently for a minute.

Chef looked at the paper and took in the number. He looked back up at Andrew to see him staring at him. 'Is there something else?' he asked.

'Yeah, one thing.' Andrew said. 'Is my old truck out back? I need to be able to get around.'

Chef dug his left hand into his pocket and fished around for a moment. He pulled out a set of keys and lobbed them underhanded to Andrew. Andrew caught them to his chest, then grasped them in his hand. 'Thanks Chef. You can have it back when I leave.'

'Hey, it's your truck Andrew. I have my car out back there too, so keep the truck as long as you need.'

'Thanks Chef.' He said. He stuffed the keys in his pocket and started to walk over to the door. He looked back as he grabbed the handle. 'Remember. Mackin's. One hour from now.' He said.

'I'll do my best.' Chef said.

'That's all I'm asking.' Andrew said. He paused a moment longer then turned back to Chef. 'Hey Chef.'

'Yeah Andrew?'

'Have you seen Stevie around? I mean recently.'

Chef thought for a moment then said. 'I've seen him since you've been gone, I'm pretty sure. I haven't seen him for a couple weeks though. Aren't you still in touch?'

Andrew shook his head. 'No . . . not currently. If he happens to come by, tell him I'm back.' He said. He turned then and walked out through the chiming door.

27

Outside of Mackin's pub, Andrew waited for a few minutes in the truck before going in. Sitting in his truck brought back more memories. The smell of the leather seats was still the same. It drove the same and the noises it produced hadn't changed. If there was one thing he did miss from home, it was that truck. It was on its last legs and had been for some time. He could've afforded a new one at any stage, but could never part with it until he was finally forced to. The truck had been his Father's. He had purchased it brand new a year or two before he was killed. To Andrew, it was really one of the only remaining connections to the man. He struggled even to picture his face a lot of the time, but whenever he sat inside the truck and took in its sounds and smells for some reason, he could see his father's face clear as day. He let thirty minutes roll by since he left Chef's store, then decided he'd go into the bar room and wait. He walked inside through the large door and took a seat at one of the tall stools at the corner of the bar. The bartender had to look twice when he saw Andrew. He obviously recognized him, but didn't make a big deal of it. 'What can I get ya?' he asked.

'You have coffee?' Andrew asked.

'I can put some on, sure.' He answered.

'Okay, good, please do.' The bartender walked over to the coffee machine and started fiddling with its dials. Andrew turned around to the clock that hung high up on the wall in the center of the bar room. He noted the time. He wasn't sure what he'd do next if Detective Harris didn't show up, but he wasn't prepared to wait much longer. He knew Bernie was out there, he could feel it. But, every second that ticked by, he sensed she was one step closer to hell. He felt confident that Harris would show up however. Despite their run in, Andrew found himself liking the man. 'Well, at least I respect him.' He thought.

The bartender brought over a coffee. Andrew pulled out his wallet and sifted through it to luckily find a twenty dollar bill stuck in one of the folds. He slid it across the bar. The bartender's fingers snatched it up and he quickly returned with the change. Andrew watched him count out the bills and lay them on the bar, then drop the coins on top of them. When he finished, he walked away to another customer that lined up at the other end of the bar.

A sliding chair grated the floor behind Andrew and he turned around to find the Detective pulling up a seat next to him. 'Andrew Dawson.' The Detective said and held out his hand.

'Hello Detective.' Andrew said and shook hands with him.

'Didn't think I'd see you again so soon, but considering the circumstances, I'm not surprised.' Detective Harris said.

Andrew nodded. 'So you know why I'm here then?' he asked.

The Detective sat up straight on the tall chair and undid the zipper on his light jacket and shook it out. 'Well, I know the catalyst for why you're here. As to what you're here to do. No, I don't know that.' He answered. 'The question is, do you know?'

'I just can't sit idly by Detective. Bernie . . . she means a lot to me.'

Detective Harris nodded. 'I'm sure she does Andrew. I know a little bit of the history there. Does her fiancé know that?'

Andrew shrugged and held his hands up. 'Don't get the wrong impression Detective. That's not what I'm here about. Bernie's a friend, a good friend. Never mind our history. That's just what it is . . . history.' He said. 'I just want to help. What can you tell me about the case, anything?'

'It's an open investigation Andrew.' He said. 'I think you know I can't tell you much. I'm not leading the missing person's case, that's another division. But, I am looped in considering . . . . Well you know, considering there's a chance, a very good chance that my cases are related.'

'But do you have leads?' Andrew pleaded. 'Are you out there searching for her?'

Detective Harris looked tired and his tone was sharp. 'Right now, I'm here talking to you Andrew.'

Andrew could see the Detective's patience was worn thin likely from the lack of success in finding the killer, but he wasn't about to be bullied by anyone just now. 'What's that supposed to mean?' Andrew asked.

'Come on. You know the line. Any second I'm talking to you means I'm not out looking for her . . . unless you know something that can help that is. Do you Andrew? Do you know something that could help?' he asked.

Andrew tapped the side of the coffee cup with his fingers. He was growing more impatient each second. His frustration was building at the Detective's unwillingness or inability to share any details. He knew there were protocols the man needed to follow, but was blinded by his anguish. 'No.' he said. 'I don't have any new information.'

The Detective slid his chair back slowly and stood up. He reached into his pocket and pulled out a card. 'Here' he said and slid it across the counter to Andrew. 'I have your number. Now you have mine in case anything does occur to you.'

Andrew lifted the card and stuffed it into his pocket. 'You'll let me know if there's anything I can do to help?' he asked.

'I will.' He answered. He softened his facial expression for a moment and said 'Hey, I know it's tough, but there are good cops on this. We're doing our best to find your friend Andrew.'

Andrew nodded. 'I know Detective.'

'Okay' he said and patted Andrew firmly on the shoulder then he turned towards the door and briskly walked out. Andrew watched him leave. He turned and propped his elbows on the bar and brought he hands up to his head, hugging his ears with his forearms. 'What next?' he said to himself. 'What else?'

He sat that way, with his arms around his head for a couple minutes. He leaned back in his chair and rubbed his eyes. He felt anger start to build within him and could feel his body heat rise with the increased blood flow. 'Fuck this.' He said quietly to himself. He stood up quickly and kicked the chair back behind him. It scraped loudly across the floor and he saw heads turn in his direction. He turned and walked out of the bar quickly and over to his truck. He pulled the door open and jumped in, slamming it shut after him. He fired up the engine and pulled the transmission into drive. He pushed down on the gas so the truck's engine roared as he drove away. He turned a tight left down Newport Avenue, past the back of the Quincy Center train station. He sped down the road, stopping only minutes later at the Beale Street intersection. It was closing in on evening time and the traffic started building. He tapped the steering wheel waiting in a line of cars for the light to change color. Up ahead he could see Dee Dee's lounge. The small bar sat on the corner of Newport Avenue and Brook Street across from Wollaston train station. A line of budget Asian massage parlors lined the pathway to the bar's dilapidated shop front. He remembered a much more vibrant neighborhood in his youth. It had given way to depravity after years of economic downturn.

The light turned green and he hit the gas to move. The cars in front moved slowly off the start line. He felt the pause in the traffic helped him to get his nerves under control. At the next block, he turned down the side street and pulled up to the curb. He killed the engine and pulled the keys out of the ignition. He took in a deep breath, then let it out slowly before pushing the driver's door open and jumping down from the truck. There were very few cars parked on the block. At a glance, it was difficult to tell whether the bar was even open, but he knew it was. Mike Doyle might be in there. Bishop at least, was in there, he could sense it.

He put his hand softly on the door and pushed it in. It swung in easily and he walked inside. The room was dark. The beer signs behind the bar weren't lit, but a small lamp at the corner of the bar was. Two men were standing near it, one on either side of the bar. Their shadows from the lamp stretched long across the wall behind them. The one on the outside of the bar turned around in his seat, then stood up slowly, peering across at Andrew through the dark room.

Andrew stood still for a moment after walking in, waiting for his eyes to adjust to the drastic change in lighting. Once they did, he continued walking across the room towards the two men. As he approached, he could make out their faces. Neither one was John Bishop. The one that was standing closest to him however he recognized as Mike Doyle. Andrew froze for a moment, though it felt longer to him. He fought to control his breathing, but struggled to do so. He could feel his temples begin to pulse rapidly and his vision blurred and sharpened several times in a matter of seconds, red clouds growing more poignant with each interval. The man took a couple step towards Andrew as he entered the room. Andrew had the lighting in his favor as Doyle walked closer, staring to get a look at his face. 'Help you with something?' Doyle asked.

Andrew took a few more steps, then stopped. He saw in Doyle's face that he recognized him at last. 'I know you . . . Dawson. What the fuck do you want?'

'You know what the fuck I want Doyle. Where is she?' he yelled.

Doyle postured his shoulders and brought his hands slowly towards his waist. Andrew's eyes followed his hands, keeping note of any sudden change in the man's stance. 'Get lost Dawson.' Doyle said.

'Fuck you Doyle. Last chance. Tell me where the fuck you have Bernadette!'

Doyle took another step towards Andrew. Andrew slid his right foot back a couple inches. He kept his eyes trained on Doyle's right hand. 'I won't say it again Dawson. Fuck off!' Then he quickly reached under his shirt near his belt.

Andrew didn't wait to see any metal gleam. He wouldn't have caught it in the poor lighting anyway. He brought his right foot up quickly and kicked straight out at Doyle's groin. He connected flush and Doyle fell backwards into the bar. He bounced off the bar, which kept him upright and managed to get a handle on the grip of his revolver. Andrew jumped forward and grabbed his wrist with his left hand and swung a heavy elbow with his right, catching Doyle in the face, but falling over in the process. Blood shot from Doyle's nose and splattered red across Andrew's face. He wrestled the gun from Doyle's hand on the ground. He heard a loud 'pop' and his hand jerked back as the gun went off in the struggle. The bullet missed both of them, and dug into the wood floor, shooting splinters in the air when it hit.

Andrew freed his right hand and managed to grab the gun away with both hands, burning his palm on the nozzle when he gripped it. He raised both hands and came down hard on Doyle's head with the butt of the weapon. Doyle stopped struggling. Andrew saw a flash of movement from his left just in time to duck out of the way of a whiskey bottle. The man behind the bar had come around the other side and just missed him with the bottle. It broke in pieces off the side of the bar and shards hit Andrew in the face. One long piece of glass broke off and buried itself in the bartender's wrist. He fell back and let out a howl. Andrew jumped to his feet and pointed the revolver at the man. He held it up for a moment to make sure the man wouldn't rush him again, then he spun around back to where Doyle had fallen. He was no longer there. Andrew slowly edged over the bar and scanned behind it to find nothing, he looked around the room but Doyle was nowhere in sight.

He was winded from the fight and had to take a couple breaths before he could get a word out. 'where did he go?' he muttered between breaths 'Where?'

The man sat bleeding before him. He looked to be in pain. He didn't reply with words, but he glanced across the room at a heavy green door hidden in a dark corner. It was enough for Andrew to understand. He backed over towards the door, keeping the gun raised with a shaky hand as he did. When he reached it, he grabbed the knob and twisted. It opened with a creak. He turned and walked into a dark room. He shut the door behind him. A shelf stood beside the door and he tipped it over to obstruct the entrance. He continued into the room and over to another door. The door was ajar and a dim light shone through it. Andrew walked slowly towards it. He kept the gun at his side and pushed the door open slowly with his left hand.

John Bishop sat behind a desk next to a few small television screens. He sat back in his chair and held out his palms when Andrew opened the door fully. Andrew stood in the doorway and looked at the man. He had changed quite a lot since he had last seen him. His hair had gone from black to a stark grey, making him look much older than a man in his thirties. He wore a black fitted military jacket that made it obvious he still took care of himself physically. His face showed weathered lines, especially on either side of his eyes. His skin looked taught and he was tanned, except for a thick white scar that ran under his left eye. It was a reminder of their last encounter. Andrew looked from him over to the television screens. It was CCTV linked to cameras that he must've had in the front bar. Bishop saw him looking at the screens. 'Doyle's gone.' He said calmly.

The adrenaline from the fight with Doyle and the bartender was starting to wear off and Andrew felt weak. He could feel his hands shaking, but for the most part, he seemed to have his emotions back under control. He held the gun in his palm out for Bishop to see. It was slick with blood that also stained Andrew's forearms, wrists and hands. 'Do I need this here?'

'Tell you what Andrew. Hang on to it if it makes you feel safe.' Andrew considered it, then tucked the revolver into the back of his pants.

'You looking for a job?' Bishop asked then pointed to the screens. 'Two positions in my crew just opened up.'

Andrew shook his head. 'We both know that's not why I'm here John.'

'Well then Andrew. Can you enlighten me? Why are you here then? Just to put a beating on my men and shoot off guns in my barroom?'

'The girls John. I need to know what happened to those girls. I need to know where to find Doyle. Where did he run to?'

'Ohh' Bishop said, drawing out the word. 'Your girl goes missing. So now you care is that right? Now you're desperate. So desperate that you come to me.' He smiled and started laughing, the creases in his face growing more pronounced when he did. 'Now you're looking for help?'

'I guess I am.' Andrew said.

'You got a strange fucking way of asking for help.' He

said. 'Tell me why I should help you.'

'You owe me John. That's why.' Andrew said.

'I owe you?' Bishop said and pointed at the scar under his eye. 'Remember this?' he asked.

Andrew just nodded.

'I think we could debate about who owes who here.' Bishop said.

'So you won't help me?' Andrew asked.

'No, I would Andrew. Despite that hatred I see in your eyes, I'd definitely help you. Well, I would if I could.' He said. 'But I doubt I can offer anything more to you than you already know.'

'That's bullshit John. This is your city remember. Yours. Not a damn thing goes on in this slime bucket that you don't at least know a little about.'

'Listen Andrew. I don't know shit about any missing girls. I don't know shit about any dead girls either.' He said.

'Come on John.' He pleaded. 'You have to.'

'I have to Andrew? I fucking have to?' he puffed out a breath then he leaned forward onto the desk and stood up. He was as tall as Andrew and their eyes were level. He stared for a minute at Andrew. Andrew didn't understand his expression, but continued to hold his eye contact.

Bishop let out a breath, then finally spoke 'You still working out a lot to keep that temper of yours under control?' he asked.

Andrew tilted his head slightly and continued looking at Bishop. He waited for more. He didn't know what he was getting at. 'There's a mirror in the bathroom Andrew' Bishop continued, 'I suggest you go take a good long look in it.'

Andrew shook his head. He could feel his blood rising to his head once again, but fought hard to keep his anger down. 'What the fuck does that mean?' he asked through gritted teeth.

'It means you should start looking a little closer to home, if you really want to know who did those things and who has your girl.'

'You implying I did this?' Andrew asked.

'No, you fucking asshole. I'm implying you're either dumb, blind or in denial. Jesus Christ Andrew, the cops had a knife they believed was the one that gutted Gina O'Neil like a fucking fish. They pulled it from your truck, it had your fingerprints and both yours and her DNA. How the fuck could that happen huh? Who could do all that if it wasn't you? I'd say the pool of candidates is pretty fucking small or your tolerance for coincidence is pretty fucking big.'

'I fucking know what the cops had John. It's Doyle's knife. Now tell me where I can find him!'

'Way I see it bud, there's only one piece of information the cops didn't have and that's cause you never offered it.'

'What Johnny, enough with your cryptic bullshit! Fucking get to the point.'

'Where did *you* get the knife Andrew?'

'From Doyle! You know this.' Andrew said.

'You're not hearing me kid. Listen to me, there's a reason Doyle was never brought in. He was in fucking northern New Hampshire with me buying a fucking ski lodge the night Gina O'Neil was killed. So think! Not who owned the knife. I'm asking where did you get it? Who put that knife in your hands? I think I know. But, I *know* that you know.'

Andrew stood up straight. He was stunned to hear what Bishop had to say. He felt weak. He was light headed and his knees began to wobble. He felt his stomach turning and could taste bile rising in his throat. It was obvious. It was obvious to Bishop. Bishop knew Andrew well. He knew there was only one person Andrew worked out with. It was obvious to him now too. When the words left Bishop's mouth, Andrew knew it was true. That niggling thought always in the very depths of his mind, every ounce of logic and intuition stifled by utter denial that penetrated deep into his mind, body and soul. He had always known it. If it wasn't the only possible explanation, it was at least the most likely. 'How else could they ever had mistaken me as the killer?' He knew who had Bernie. It was clearer than any thought he'd had in a lifetime. There was no doubt. He knew it to be gospel. And, he knew where she was too.

He regained control of his legs by putting a hand on the desk that separated him and Bishop to support his weight. He looked up at Bishop, who stood silently witnessing Andrew's dawning realization. He walked around his desk and over to the side of the room. He pushed aside a curtain to show another door. It was a back exit. 'Here' he said. 'Go this way Andrew. I don't think you have much time to waste.' He held the curtain back with one hand and twisted the knob with the other, opening up the door that led to a back alleyway. Andrew said nothing else to Bishop. He slowly stepped over towards the exit and ducked under the curtain. He looked at Bishop one last time in the doorway before turning his head away and heading out into the darkness.

28

The sun had just about disappeared when Andrew stumbled out of the back alleyway from Dee Dee's lounge and walked quickly, yet unsteadily around the corner back to his truck. He reached Marina Bay in only minutes. There were lights around the marina and the front parking lot was lit up brightly with street lamps and bustling with cars. He drove around the large lot and passed through to a much quieter and darker lot that led up to the dirt pathway. He entered the brush on foot. After a few steps the light from the parking lot was suffocated by the shrubs that hid much of the entrance. He walked down the path, but stayed close to the edge to maintain cover. The air was warm and he began to sweat. There was a breeze off the water that he felt every couple of steps. The cool air against his clammy skin made him shiver. The ground beneath him was soft mud that clamped around his shoes in many spots. He could hear his own footsteps in those moments as it popped when he pulled his feet out to step forward. The pathway was a mile long to the small beach at the end. He tried to keep a quick pace, but was slowed by the need for stealth. He knew the spot's isolation meant that any unaccustomed sound could signal his approach.

It felt like an eternity had passed by the time he could see the entrance to the beach. He ducked behind a row of rough bushes a short distance away and peered out to where the mud turned into sand. He could just about make out the wrinkle of waves in the distance, though the sea itself mirrored the dark sky. He thought he heard a rustling noise behind him and held his breath to listen for more sounds though the echoed heart beat in his ears made it difficult. He waited a minute and decided it was the wind. He slowly emerged from behind his shelter and edged his way along the brush, closer to the sand. He reached the entrance to the sand and peeked his head around the corner. He had a clear view of the beach. It appeared empty as he glanced over to his left then right. He slowly walked onto the sand. He felt his feet sink down as he stepped into the dry sand at the top of the beach. It grew more firm as he walked closer to the water's edge. The area was quiet, except from the noise of the wind that blew harder now across his face as small waves ran up to the tip of his shoes. The beach looked empty, but he couldn't be wrong. He could sense the presence of eyes on him. He turned around and started to walk back to the top of the beach. He paused when he saw a series of grassy dunes that ran along the sand below it for the length of the beach. 'The perfect spot' he thought to himself. Slowly he took a step towards the dunes. He saw the flash of a shadow in his periphery, but was too slow to move. Stevie had bolted from his hiding spot and tackled Andrew hard into the sand. The tackle took him off his feet. They hit the ground locked together and slid to the edge of the water. Andrew's eyes burned from the sand and salt water that shot into his face. His head slapped hard off the firm sand sending a shockwave through his body. He was disoriented and Stevie took the advantage to lock Andrew's arm across his chest. Andrew struggled to free himself while Stevie landed direct blows to his head and face. Andrew tried to avoid them, but his movement was limited. He shut his eyes and dug his chin into his chest. The blows kept coming. He managed to lift his knees, then thrust his hips upward with as much force as he could muster. The force knocked Stevie off balance and Andrew managed to roll to his left quickly and crawled in the sand to create some distance between them. His head ached and he was dizzy. He managed to climb to his feet, but his legs were rubbery. Stevie rushed him again. Andrew rolled with the charge and shifted out of the way at the last second, tripping Stevie with his ankle. He jumped up quickly, while the momentum sent Stevie stumbling into the shallow water. He scrambled to his feet and turned to rush Andrew again. Andrew reached behind him and felt the revolver handle sticking out from his belt. He gripped the handle and pulled the gun out from behind him. Stevie paused, his chest heaving to catch his breath. Andrew stood with his arm outstretched, at the end of it was the revolver. Stevie's eyes moved from the gun up to Andrew's eyes. 'You won't do it Andrew.' He said.

'Tell me where she is Stevie.' Andrew said.

'She's around.' He said. His face turned into a smile.

Andrew winced. 'It was you.' He said. 'It was all you . . . Why Stevie?'

Stevie shook his head. 'What the fuck do you want to hear Andrew?'

Andrew gripped the gun tighter. His index finger danced around the trigger. 'There has to be a reason. You were gonna let me rot in there?' He said.

Stevie shook his head. He took a hesitant step forward. Andrew responded by straightening his arm out further. 'You want to know how I do it Andrew. You want to know all about it? Well I'll tell you. I like to strangle them first to the point where I can just about see the life get ready to leave their eyes. If they shit themselves I cut their throat on the spot and watch them slowly bleed to death. If they only piss themselves, then I fuck 'em first.' He smiled wider and leaned his head forward. He then whispered. 'That the shit you want to hear, you chicken shit. Plus . . . I'm the reason they let you out.'

Andrew felt sick to his stomach. His outstretched arm began to ache. 'He killed Lisa Stark, so the police would know it was wasn't me.' He thought. He felt like he was about to explode. His eyes pleaded with Stevie's. 'Why Stevie? It's me man. We're like brothers.'

Andrew watched Stevie's eyes slowly begin to water. For a moment, he was his longtime best friend again. 'Brothers' Stevie whispered, 'and you left me.' He blinked his watery eyes and looked back at Andrew. 'You knew. You knew who she was. What she did to me . . . over and over. Everyone knew.'

Andrew fought to keep his arm up. He wanted to drop the gun and reach out to Stevie, but he knew that was a mistake. Stevie was right though. Deep down, Andrew did know. He thought of the dark cloud that would come over Stevie whenever she was brought up. 'Stevie . . . your mother?'

Stevie nodded and the tears came back into his eyes, stronger this time. He sniffled, 'no one even asked any questions when she disappeared. That's when I realized for certain . . . everyone knew.'

'Stevie, these girls . . . they are not your mother' Andrew said in soft tone, 'Gina, Lisa, they were our friends. Not your mother.'

'You don't get Andrew. You can't get it. You never will. They all were her . . . to me . . . all of 'em.'

Andrew's arm finally gave in to the strain and he lowered the gun to his side for the moment. 'Not Bernie. She's not.' 'No' Stevie said. 'Bernie's something else entirely.'

They both remained standing, neither one was prepared to move just yet. Andrew heard rustling noises around him suddenly, but refused to take his eyes off of Stevie. In a panic, he raised the gun up again and kept it fixed on Stevie. He heard a voice yell. 'Dawson! Put the gun down and step aside!' he recognized it immediately. It was Detective Harris's voice.

Andrew kept his gaze fixed on Stevie. 'Harris must have followed my truck. Probably since I left Mackin's' he thought. He yelled back 'You don't know what he's done Detective!'

'I do Andrew. I do know. And he'll pay. Just step aside and put that gun down son.'

Andrew considered what to do next, but made no movement.

'I'm not going with them Andrew.' Stevie whispered to him through gritted teeth. 'I die here today. It might as well be you.'

'Fuck you Stevie.' Andrew said back.

'Fine, be like that, but as soon as you move, they'll shoot. Believe me, they'll shoot.' He said. 'Or I'll make 'em shoot.'

Detective Harris yelled to Andrew again. 'Andrew, please. Listen . . . we have Bernadette Andrew. We found her. She's safe . . . it's over now. Put the gun down.'

'A trick?' Andrew thought. Then a moment later he heard it. Her voice. 'Andrew!' Bernadette yelled. 'Put the gun down please.' She said, her voice straining. 'I'm here . . . I'm safe now. Please!'

Andrew felt his sinuses loosen. He felt his eyes swell with tears that blurred his vision. 'Her voice' he thought. 'Sweeter than any music on earth.' He looked at Stevie. Stevie smiled at Andrew, willing him to do something, pull the trigger most likely.

Andrew slowly brought his arm down again. He kept his eyes on Stevie while he lowered it. Finally he gripped the gun in his palm, turned and threw it as hard as he could into the water. He heard voices behind him and could hear movement. He assumed the cops staked out with the Detective were moving in. He let out a breath and felt a moment of relief. He dropped his gaze from Stevie for only a moment. It was in that moment, that Stevie stopped smiling. His face turned hard and grew a gross snarl. Andrew looked up at him to see his right hand now held in it a long knife. Andrew shifted his right foot back quickly. He heard shouts from behind him and could feel the sandy ground thunder with pounding footsteps. Had it not happened so fast, he would've had time to think. But, Stevie was always fast, much faster than Andrew at least. Stevie had initiated the action, all Andrew could do was give over control to his body and let his muscles react in the way they had been trained.

Stevie stepped forward quickly. Andrew braced himself. Stevie plunged forward with the knife straight and high, aiming for Andrew's neck. Andrew bounced back from his lead foot shifting his weight to the back and quickly moved his head to the left. He swept the attempted blow past him with his left hand. The forward motion threw Stevie off balance. Andrew shot his right hand out and grabbed Stevie's wrist, which held the knife. He dipped down and drove up with his left shoulder striking underneath Stevie's elbow. The arm hyperextended and Andrew heard a 'pop'. He could feel the strength leave Stevie's arm. He slid his hand from the wrist upwards and pulled the knife away. Andrew gripped the knife tightly, then pivoted with the back foot and plunged the knife straight forward, landing it directly into Stevie's chest.

He looked up and saw Stevie's eyes widen in momentary pain, then go dull as he stumbled backwards. He watched him slowly fall into the sand. Andrew felt hands grabbing him and pulling him back. Voices were talking to him, but he was in a daze and couldn't make out the words. The last thing he saw before he dropped to his knees to get sick was the ring of red slowly starting to form around the handle of the knife that was protruding out of best friend's chest.

29

Andrew stood holding onto a pole in the middle of the tram. It was a Friday afternoon and the tram going towards Stephen's Green was wedged with people heading into town. It slid to approach Stephen's Green at the top of Grafton Street and slowed to a stop at the end of the track. The doors chimed twice, and then opened. The people inside flowed out of the doors like water from a broken damn, while still avoiding blocks of people bunched together waiting to climb on going the other way. Andrew squeezed through the people, pushing his way past the tightly packed commuters and spilled out at the entrance to Stephen's Green. He crossed the street and walked the short distance to Dawson Street.

He walked the few blocks and stopped outside of Dawson Street Grille. He stood back and took in the shop front. He had missed the place over the last few weeks. He'd wanted to race back sooner. He would have as soon as he knew Bernie was safe, but Detective Harris insisted he stick around for what he termed 'administrative purposes.' Finally after a few weeks of waiting that included several meetings with cops and lawyers, he was left to continue on with his life. He took in a deep breath then walked up to the door. He twisted the knob and opened it, then slowly entered the restaurant. He could smell food coming from the kitchen that made his mouth water. He looked around the room quickly and saw Donal standing in the bar. He was leaning his elbow against one of the tall tables, talking to Danny Carson who was seated there with a pint of Guinness in front of him. Andrew walked over towards them and nonchalantly cleared his throat. Each man turned and looked over when they heard him. Andrew nodded to them both. Danny Carson smiled and nodded back. Donal waved and said 'Well well. The prodigal son returns. How're you keeping Andrew?'

'I'm good, thanks. I'm uh . . . glad to be back.' He said. Danny pointed at his own face in question, silently asking Andrew about the scars on his cheek. 'You're alright I take it?' he asked.

'This' Andrew pointed. 'Yeah, might scar a little, but I'm fine.'

Both men nodded. By the lack of questions, Andrew assumed they both were aware of what happened in Quincy and that Bernadette was found. She was badly beaten, but she was alive, and now she was safe. He couldn't really say the same for Stevie Black. He was taken into custody and operated on under armed guard at Massachusetts General Hospital. The surgeons were able to save his life. But, there isn't much of a life to be saved. If Detective Harris is to be believed, he'll never again see natural light.

'So . . . Donal' Andrew said. 'I was really hoping I could, you know, get my job back. I know I kind of disappeared on you and let you down. I want you to know I'm sorry.'

Donal looked at him and kept smiling. He shook his head and said, 'Suit up Andrew. We could use you tonight. Go grab an apron and start setting up.'

'Thanks Donal. You don't know what this means to me. I won't let you down again, I promise you that.' He said.

Danny Carson slid his chair back and stood up. 'If you're giving out apologies Andrew, I'm not sure it's Donal you need to start with buddy. If I were you, I'd start with her.' He said pointing into the dining room.

Andrew looked across the room. He saw Vicky. She was busying herself getting ready for the shift. He stared across at her. Her hair was pulled back, and tied up, but the dark curls fell loose in the back. Andrew felt a stir in his stomach. He had forgotten, however briefly, just how powerful her spell over him was. Only now did he truly feel the pain of how much he'd missed her in just those few weeks. She looked up and saw him. Andrew smiled and waved to her. Her face stayed straight. It did not smile. In fact, it showed no emotion at all. She looked down quickly, then walked directly back through the kitchen doors.

Andrew looked back over to Donal and Danny Carson. Both men smiled and shrugged.

'I think you're right Danny.' Andrew said. 'That's where I need to start.'

THE END

ROOK TO BISHOP

LIAM MAGUIRE

Liam Maguire took a final haul from his cigarette and flicked it into the wet street. He stood across from Saint Ann's Church and waited patiently for the traffic on Neponset Avenue to ease. His hood was up with the strings pulled tight to his face to keep out the rain and cold. The brim of his Red Sox hat stuck out from the hood like a duck's beak and heavy rain drops pounded loudly off the wool-covered plastic. The rain had penetrated the hood and soaked into his hat on the walk up the street from the parking lot. He could smell the wet wool and cursed himself for wearing it, knowing it would never be shaped the same after getting wet.

A pick-up truck roared past as Liam looked up towards the church's steeple. Its back wheel caught a pothole close to the curb sending black water towards his sneakers and jeans. He jumped back at the sound but was too late to dodge the debris. The traffic lights turned red and Liam jogged across the street and leapt over the tall curb at the other end. He walked around the church's stone staircase over to a hidden side entrance. He slowly opened the door and peaked inside. The Alcoholics Anonymous meetings were held in the church's lower level. It was a small chapel, less ornate than its upstairs neighbor, but still nice in its own way.

The room was dimly lit by the lights behind the altar. There was a table at the back of the room with two large coffee containers and a tray of pastries. Liam walked in slowly towards the table in the back. He tried his best to be quiet, but the creaky door and squeak from his wet sneakers on the ceramic flooring gave away his tardiness.

He pulled off his hood and the hat along with it. He opened up his jacket but kept it on. The room had a draft coming from somewhere. He slid into the pew just in front of the table next to a blonde woman he guessed was twice his age. She smiled at him with yellow teeth and too much make up. A stale cigarette scent emanated from her clothing. He thought it was strange that he noticed considering he smoked as well and the smell reminded him that he wanted to quit. He smiled back and settled his spine against the wooden bench. He scanned the room, looking around at those in the rows in front of him, though he could only really see the backs of heads and sides of faces. There were several men with grey hair, some with earrings, and others with forearm tattoos. He noticed a flaming tire tattooed on one man's neck. He was staring for a few seconds to figure out what it was when the man turned his head towards him sharply with a scowl. Liam dropped his gaze quickly and hoped the man's glaring eyes would look away. After a minute he cautiously looked up to find they did. His cousin Brendan had known McNulty somehow, though Liam didn't dare ask for more details. He had said to look for a man about fifty-five to sixty years old that appeared as wide as he was tall and looked like he might snap an ordinary sized man in half. His cousin said McNulty is an intimidating guy, but he also told him that behind his insults and four-letter words was his own brand of reluctant kindness. Liam thought it was a strange way to speak about someone known locally to break legs. Those were the rumors Liam had heard anyway.

After looking over body shapes sitting in front of him, no one seemed to fit the description he'd been given.

Brendan said it would be obvious. Liam was about to give up and make his way quietly out when a man stepped up to a small wooden podium just in front of the first row of people. His broad frame cast an eclipse on the room as it cut out the lights on the altar. He was an older man with close-cropped silver hair and matching sideburns that cut down sharply towards a neatly shaved chin. He wore dark jeans and a waist length leather jacket that looked like it cost a poor cow every inch of its hide. He appeared tall, probably over six feet, but it was difficult to judge his height considering his girth, which overshadowed any other physical attribute. The word 'dense' came to Liam's mind when he saw him. Not in the mental sense, but in that he looked thick and strong, not fat, though not with show muscle either. Liam thought he was built more like someone who swings sledgehammers for a living rather than someone who lifts weights in a gym. He stood silently in front while a much smaller man, at least relatively, stood next to him speaking. Liam hadn't been listening to what the man said, but he watched him. The smaller man pulled a shiny token out of his pocket. It looked like a very large coin. McNulty held out both large hands. The man placed the token in his left palm and shook McNulty's right hand. The people sitting began to clap and Liam joined in, though he wasn't sure what he was applauding. While the clapping continued, the smaller man took a seat in the front row. The applause died down a few seconds later. When it did, McNulty took another step closer to the front row and quietly said thanks as the last applause still echoed in Liam's ears.

Liam found himself leaning forward eagerly waiting to hear this giant speak. He imagined a voice like James Earl

Jones' would echo through the hall. He watched McNulty's face closely as he stared down at the shiny bronze token held now between his thumb and forefinger. His face was one of a man deep in thought, pondering something more profound than just one moment alone. Finally he broke his trance and looked out to those seated in front of him. At last he spoke, 'Bad decisions' he said, then paused for a few seconds and scratched his temple with his forefinger. 'Sometimes made for the right reasons. Other times not.' He ran a hand through his silver hair and continued. 'That's what got me here.' He said then another pause. 'I have kids . . . two of them. My daughter . . . she turned thirty-two last month. My son, he's twenty-seven today. The last time I saw either of them I was ten years younger and it was from behind a pane of glass. My wife . . . she made the right decisions. And, she made them for the right reasons . . . good for her. This chip' he said and flicked the token up with his thumb and let it land in his palm. 'This is my third five year chip. You all know what that means.' He said. Liam heard muffled agreement from the crowd. 'One way or another, this will be my last.' He said and stuffed the chip into his pocket. He waved to the people in front, then walked over and took a seat in the front pew among subdued applause.

Liam was struck by the emotion showed by the large man. His words, though brief, sounded sincere. There was sorrow in his voice, 'or a longing' Liam thought. They were not at all what he expected to hear from the hard man known only as McNulty. When McNulty sat down, the same smaller man stood up again and walked to the front of the room. 'We'll finish off with a prayer.' He said, then began, while most of those seated joined in unison, 'God grant me the serenity to accept the things I cannot change, the courage to change the things I can, and the wisdom to know the difference. Amen.' they all said. People started to stand and the man up front said 'there's coffee and danishes in the back. Thanks everyone for coming.' Liam slid out of the pew to let the other people exit. He needed to approach McNulty and try to talk to him, but he didn't want to risk doing so with a crowd around. He needed to try and get him alone. He lingered towards the back and joined the line at the table for coffee. The line moved quickly and within a few minutes he found himself holding a foam cup with black coffee. He ripped open a sugar packet with his teeth and stirred it in with a thin pink straw. He skipped the pastries and walked towards an open space closer to the door. He waited for a minute alone trying to watch for McNulty without appearing to do so. The big man was surrounded by others however, most came over and quickly said hello or gave him a hand shake, though a few stayed close by him engaging in conversation. Liam looked away from McNulty and towards the thinning sea of other faces. Many passed by him to get out of the door. As the crowd inside the chapel thinned he grew self-conscious, no longer masked by numbers. He felt awkward, like he was intruding all of a sudden and slowly slipped out the exit himself. Outside he felt he could breathe again, though the rain hadn't tapered off much and began pelting him in the face with cold droplets. He put his hat on and tightened his hood again and found a little relief in a neighboring doorway. He pulled a pack of cigarettes from his jacket pocket and fished one out along with this lighter.

He cupped his hand around it and lit the end, doing his best to keep it from getting soaked. 'I'll give him five minutes' he thought, 'then I'll call the whole thing off.' He thought of the faces he'd seen inside the chapel, so many and so varied. Some were old and weathered, others young and drawn, some looked just normal or no different than him. In each he could sense pain however, or a weariness, like an endless battle of attrition was taking place in each mind. He knew what addiction could do to people and to those around them, the change in personality, the deceit, the violence. He hadn't struggled with it himself, though he had seen it firsthand, been a victim to it in some sense he guessed, 'that's what brought me here' he thought.

He had crouched down to take further cover from the rain, but stood up when he took the last haul from his cigarette to flick it into the street. He had just decided to leave when he saw McNulty walk out from the church. He walked out alone and zippered his jacket up to his chin as he walked to the edge of the curb. Liam hesitated for a moment. After waiting he'd grown accustomed to the idea that he was just going to go home and forget about everything. Seeing McNulty walk out and his chance to speak with him alone ended up catching him by surprise, which in turn made him nervous. He regained his composure after a second and walked towards McNulty. He was a step or two away and he cleared his throat loudly to signal his approach. McNulty turned towards him but didn't say anything. Liam took another step towards him and said 'Hi, you're McNulty right?' He watched McNulty look him up and down without speaking for a moment, then he answered 'Hmm, I thought you'd be taller.'

Liam was confused by his response and asked 'You were expecting me?'

'Of course I was, I've been expecting you for fucking years.' McNulty said.

'I don't understand.' Liam said. 'Who told you I was coming?'

'No one told me shit, just figured you'd show up one day, looking to take me away, you know, pay for my sins and all that.'

'What? I . . . what?'

'Where the fuck's your sickle?'

'My what?' Liam asked.

'Your sickle. Or is it a scythe? Whatever the fuck, you know, tall stick with a pointed blade. You got some kind of speech impediment or something?'

'What?'

'That all you can say, fucking what?'

'No . . . just . . . well, who do you think I am? I think you might be mistaking me for someone else. That's all.'

'Dark hood, dark coat, bag of fucking bones, you're the Grim Reaper I suspect. Who the fuck else could you be?'

'What? No . . .'

'Again with the what. Listen Junior, I'm done fucking with ya. Have a good night.' McNulty said, then took a step into the street.

'Wait!' Liam said loudly, then said 'please' in a quieter voice.

'Oh right, you need something right? What do you want a fucking packie run? Can't do it bud. Not sure if you noticed, I just walked out of an AA meeting. Bad decisions I can deal with, but hypocrisy I cannot.'

'No . . . I don't want a packie run. I'm twenty-two.'

'You look fifteen.'

'I'm skinny that's all.'

'I see that, remember the fucking Grim Reaper thing?'

'Right.' Liam said. He reached up and pulled his hood back from his face and took his hat off. The rain had tapered off to a slow drizzle at last. 'My name is Liam. Liam Maguire. You knew my cousin Brendan. I think you might be able to help me.'

McNulty shook his head and smiled. 'That fucking kid' he muttered. 'He'll never stop giving my name out will he? That son of a bitch still writing books down in Philly?' He asked. Liam shuffled his feet and dropped his eyes for a moment. 'Nah. He's not.'

'What's he up to then? He hasn't shown up and bothered me for a while.'

Liam paused then raised his eyes slowly and met McNulty's 'He's dead actually.' Liam said. McNulty tilted his chin and looked at Liam. Liam guessed he was trying to figure whether it was part of a joke or not. 'Shit' he said. 'Sorry to hear that kid. Brendan . . . well . . . he was good.'

'Thanks.' Liam said.

'What happened anyway?'

'He was teaching kids . . . well teenagers. It was a special program for troubled teens. One of his students got into it with some gangbangers or something. Brendan tried breaking up a fight. He ah . . . got stabbed for his troubles. He died a few days later. That was two months ago.' Liam said. He watched McNulty's face as it appeared to chew back some emotional response. After a few seconds McNulty ran a hand quickly through his short silver hair then wiped away the rain that had gathered where his hairline met his forehead. 'I really am sorry kid.' He said, then looked quickly at his wrist then back at Liam. 'Thanks for telling me. I have to get going now. Good luck.'

'That's not why I came to see you though.' Liam said.

'Oh?' McNulty asked.

'Brendan mentioned to me a few months ago, that if I was ever in a jam, well, like really in a jam, that I should go find you and you'd be able to help.'

'And he told you to look here huh?'

'Yeah. Well actually, he told me if I couldn't find you at the evening meeting at Saint Ann's that you probably weren't worth finding at all.'

McNulty chuckled to himself 'fucking kid' he said quietly. 'So?' He said looking at Liam. 'What is it then?'

'I'm in a jam.'

'Yeah, I fucking got that part.'

'I need some . . . protection.'

'Sorry kid, not sure what you heard, but I'm no fucking body guard.'

'Not that' he said. Then he leaned forward and looked around him quickly. Quietly he said, 'I need a gun.'

'What?' McNulty said. 'Fucking go buy one kid, Second Amendment and all.'

'I need one faster than that.'

'What makes you think I can even help with that?'

'I don't know. I guess . . . well, you're . . . you know those type of people.'

'What type of people is that?'

'You know . . . criminal types I guess.'

McNulty made a face like he just bit into a lemon. 'I

don't like what you're insinuating.'

'Sorry' Liam said. 'I didn't mean to.'

'Didn't mean to what?'

'Didn't mean to . . . insinuate.'

'No?'

'No . . . sir'

'Good.'

'Sorry. I'll ah . . . I'll go.' Liam said.

'How much money you have?' McNulty asked.

'I don't know, like ten bucks.'

'Not on you asshole, in your fucking bank or top drawer or wherever the fuck you keep it.'

'Oh, like four or five hundred or so.'

'Go get it and bring it to me.'

'Ah. For what?' Liam asked.

'The fucking gun kid, you want one or not. Jesus Christ.'

'Yeah, yes, I do.' Liam answered 'Wait, bring it here? Now?'

'You know the skating rink behind Garvey Park?'

'Yeah, of course.'

'Meet me there. One hour.'

'Yes, sure. Thanks McNulty.' Liam said and turned to head towards the crosswalk.

'You can stop using my name anytime now kid. Dead or not, this is my last favor for Brendan.'

'Sure. Thanks again. One hour.' Liam said.

McNulty left abruptly, disappearing into traffic across a side street. Liam watched him for a moment, until he lost him through passing vehicles. He then headed off quickly in a fast walk towards his car. The rain had stopped completely but the night air grew colder than it had been.

The cold air and damp clothes gave Liam a chill and he tried to hurry the car's heat along by revving the gas, a method that never seemed to work, but felt right to try. He drove back across the Neponset Bridge to his apartment in North Quincy. He parked tight to the curb in front of his place and climbed out of his car. The street was quiet, though he could hear sirens in the distance. His nose caught a waft of Chinese food cooking from a nearby restaurant and it made his mouth water. He walked over to the side entrance that brought him up to the second floor and into his small apartment. He jiggled the keys for a few seconds to get the lock to open. Inside he tossed his keys into a dish on top of the radiator next to his front door and switched the hall light on. He walked down the tight corridor towards his kitchen and his shadow followed him along the floor. There was a wooden shelf built into a bench in the kitchen. He took a knee and opened it, then removed a loose board to expose his hiding place underneath. He had lied to McNulty, 'sort of' he thought. He had some money in the bank, but he wasn't about to tell him that. He had a few hundred dollars stashed away in his hiding spot, his rainy day fund. He'd use that up first. 'Jesus Christ' he thought. 'Am I really going through with this?'

Liam was never in any trouble in his life. Maybe he missed the odd homework assignment or was late to school once or twice as a kid, but really that was it. He had a couple of good friends growing up, but he let himself fall out of touch. He wasn't close to anyone anymore. He didn't really play sports. His lack of coordination ruled out any skill positions and his slight build just wouldn't withstand any repeated contact. He graduated from high school and then went on to college at UMass Boston, now he was working full time at State Street. He was pretty ordinary he thought, 'even harmless' he considered, though he loathed to be referred to as 'harmless'. 'McNulty said I look fifteen' he thought, 'probably not far off that.' He'd kept to himself his whole life, never pissed anyone off or gave anyone trouble. He never really stood up to anyone either. 'That had to change now' he thought, 'it needs too. For Penny's sake.' His sister Penelope, 'Penny' for short, was eleven months older than him, 'Irish twins' his mother called it. Penny walked a different path in life than he did. People knew Penny, she had a reputation. In high school, teachers would wince when they found out Liam was Penny's brother, expecting the worse. 'She wasn't that bad' he told himself, 'just outspoken and hard-headed.' Although in the last year or two, ever since their mother died of breast cancer, it grew more difficult to even believe that himself. Despite her behavioral issues she was without a doubt the smartest person Liam knew. She was courted by several big name colleges and eventually landed at Brown University in Providence. She left halfway through her sophomore year when their mother started getting really sick. Everything changed from then on. She never went back and only worked odd jobs at restaurants or coffee shops, but even that work tapered off. More recently, she lived off of what Liam made along with the small life insurance payment they got after their mother died.

They shared the small two bedroom apartment near the train station, though Liam could go days at a time without seeing her or hearing from her. Whenever he tried to confront her, she'd either clam up or fly off the handle. It got to the stage that he would just try to avoid her when he sensed her mood darken. He had known for a while that she was seeing someone new, but he wasn't sure who it was and it wasn't exactly a topic she opened up to him about. Over time he had heard things from other people, concerned mutual friends mostly. She was going out with a guy named Jeff Conrad. From what he'd heard, Conrad was closer to thirty-five than twenty-five. He worked as a laborer or painter, Liam wasn't too sure, but he knew for a fact that he was also involved with a man named John Bishop. Bishop was well known locally. He was not someone that people knowingly crossed. He was dangerous and had the local heroin and cocaine market cornered, at least in Quincy and much of Dorchester. Most of what Liam heard about either Jeff Conrad or John Bishop was hearsay and likely some rumor, but there was enough of it that made him think there was some truth to it. Liam figured if Conrad ran around with Bishop, then he was definitely tied up in the drug game in some way. In his mind, that meant that Penny was too. It was after he learned who she was going out with that he started noticing things about her, small changes mostly, but they were noticeable. She would eat less, if at all, and grew very thin, which was saying a lot since she was slight to begin with. She was around less often too and when she was there, often times she was asleep. Liam worried about her day and night, especially when twenty-four hours would pass and he hadn't heard from her at all. He half expected to see her face on the news some morning, but she always came home eventually. Then, one morning as he sat eating his cereal and watching the morning weather report, she arrived home in a panic. It had been thirty-six hours since he'd seen or heard from her. She was borderline hysterical when she arrived and Liam assumed she was on something, though he didn't know what. He called in sick to work that morning and stayed home with her. She calmed eventually and fell off to sleep. She slept for a long time. Liam wasn't sure exactly how long, but it felt like forever as he paced back and forth near her bedroom door, listening in and checking every few minutes to make sure she was still breathing. When she woke eventually, Liam was surprised to find her lucid and more like her old self than he'd seen her in months. He noticed bruises around her eye and on her upper arms and shoulders. They looked pretty fresh and he wondered how he hadn't noticed them before, perhaps he did, but they didn't register with him while he was preoccupied making sure she continued to breathe.

She was slow to give him any details and held back as much as she could. He could tell that she was openly afraid of something. She revealed that she had seen something that spooked her involving Conrad and John Bishop. She wouldn't tell Liam exactly what that was and she cried when he pressed her for details. 'Bottom line is they're looking for me' she had said. 'I saw something I shouldn't have and now they want to shut me up. They think they need to shut me up.' She told Liam that she managed to talk Jeff Conrad into letting her go, but the rest of Bishop's crew wouldn't stand for it. A fight between Conrad and two more of Bishop's cronies broke out and she managed to slip away in the mist of the mayhem. They were in a house overlooking one of New Hampshire's lakes. It was one of Bishop's hideouts. She ran flat out for what she said was miles. She hit a small town and managed to hitch a ride back to Boston from a young couple in their late twenties or earlier thirties that had Massachusetts license plates. They dropped her at South Station and she took the Redline back to North Quincy. That was one day ago. Since then she had been holed up in her and Liam's apartment trying to figure out what to do. She went to take a nap and Liam said he'd run out for some food and come right back. That's when he went to find McNulty. He hoped Brendan had been right and that McNulty could help him out somehow, though he wasn't ready to tell him too much. For all he knew, McNulty and John Bishop could know each other. But, he had to do something.

Liam reached into the hiding spot under the loose board. There was always a lingering fear that some rodent would find its way into the space and be waiting there to take a chunk out of his finger. He fished around with his hand for a few seconds and pulled out a large ziplock freezer bag with loose bills in it. He counted out three hundred dollars, mostly in twenties and tens. He folded the bills over as cleanly as he could and stuffed them into his pocket. He resealed the bag, which had a few loose bills remaining and placed it back into the hole. He felt cold metal touch his hand and remembered that he had dropped a knife in there as a weight to hold down the bag of dollar bills. He grasped it with his hand and pulled it out. It was a fold over knife. The handle was an ivory white material that he thought might be plastic but made to look like marble. In the center was a bronze bald eagle. He rubbed his thumb over the eagle and felt the grooves. The knife was cheap really, but for him it held some sentimental value. His father had given it to him when he was fifteen, right about the time when he ran off. He shook away the thought of his old man, but stuck the knife in his back pocket. He closed up the hole with the loose board and stood up and brushed his knees. He walked out of the kitchen and back into the dim hallway. Penny's bedroom door was slightly ajar and Liam slowly opened it. He clenched his teeth when the door creaked loudly, but Penny didn't move in the bed. He tip-toed over to get a closer look. He could see the covers over her chest slowly rise and fall, which confirmed that she was still breathing. He backed away towards the door and slipped back out of the room, pulling the door with him as he did. He left the apartment and double locked the door behind him. 'Not quite an hour' he thought, 'but no point in waiting.' He got back into his car and headed back in the direction of Dorchester.

MCNULTY

McNulty didn't have far to go. He lived a five minute walk from Saint Ann's Church on the same street. His home was a third floor apartment of a triple-decker house that he owned outright. He lived most of his life on the first floor apartment but now preferred the top floor so he didn't have to hear footsteps above him all day and night. Although now he had to deal with the noise from jets passing overhead, with the neighborhood sitting under a flight path into Logan airport. It was down in the basement however where he kept a workshop that housed his supplies, which is how he referred to them. No other tenants had access to the basement and he kept it well secured due to the nature of its contents. He entered through a bulkhead at the side of the house and walked into a damp room with cement walls and flooring. He went through another locked door into a smaller room where he kept a legitimate workshop and some tools. There was also a man-sized safe. It was insulated and fire and explosion proof, or so he was told when he bought it. Inside were several types of firearms and even a couple of manmade explosives. They were pipe bombs acquired recently on one of his collection assignments. The guy that gave them to him was in debt. He was short on cash, but disturbingly flush with explosives, firearms and samurai swords. He carefully opened the safe and reached just above eye level and pulled down a small box. He opened it and inside it were several revolvers, all loaded and with serial numbers filed off. He picked up one and reached in again for a box of bullets. He put both on the worktop and put away the compartment. Then he locked up the safe. In a drawer he pulled out a heavy padded envelope and opened it. He lifted the gun, which looked like a toy in his hand. He felt the weight of it and chuckled slightly to himself. 'Hope this kid can fucking hold this upright.' He thought, 'else it ain't gonna protect shit.' He stuffed the gun into the envelope along with the box of bullets and sealed it. He clipped it to an inside pocket of his leather jacket, a mechanism he had fashioned himself for just such a purpose. He bolted everything up and left out the same bulkhead door he entered.

He walked through Garvey Park a minute later and crossed a sopping baseball diamond towards the hockey rink at the other end. He entered the rink through the front door, which opened into a room with foam matted floors and several wooden benches painted in Dorchester Youth Hockey blue and white. The room was empty except for one man behind the skate shop window. McNulty nodded at him and the man did the same back, but they didn't speak. Everyone knew McNulty in that place and he was not bothered, approached or ever spoken to unless he initiated it. It was an unwritten rule and a longstanding one at that. He had been coming to watch hockey games there for over thirty years 'probably longer than that' he thought. He loved the sport and found out long ago that the noises the game produced, the sound of skates digging into the ice, the crunch of body checks and yells from the coaches and crowds, all echoing loudly throughout the rink, brought him solace. Being engulfed in those sounds he could either focus or drown out his thoughts. No other place else on earth gave him that sensation. He continued walking towards the back of the room and headed through a set of doors that led to the rink itself. The cold air from the fans hit him in the face as he walked in. He felt goose bumps form on his skin and he shivered when the cold air touched his damp neck. The familiar smell of the rink calmed him immediately. Its scent was a mixture of sweat, burnt pizza and foam rubber and always brought him back to his youth when he played hockey for his high school team. No two rinks in Massachusetts were alike, but McNulty remembered that they all smelled the same. It wasn't a pleasant smell by any means, but it was strangely comforting to him.

There was a bantam travel team practice already in full swing when he entered. McNulty walked down to the very end of the stands, just before the back emergency exit. He climbed up the stone steps and took a seat on a cold metal bench. He kept his hands in his pockets the entire walk. It was cold anyway, but he really kept them there since it was best to make sure he could hug the gun in its envelope at all times. He took a long thoughtful glance around him, then quickly pulled the envelope out from underneath his jacket and slid it into the space between the metal bench and cement base under his knees. He breathed deeply with a feeling of relief that a loaded gun was no longer resting so close to his ribs. He passed some time watching the practice, which was good since the team had split into two sides and were scrimmaging. They usually did this for the last twenty minutes of any practice. McNulty had seen the team play before and knew who a few of the players were. He knew the good ones anyway and the tough ones, the guys with grit, he knew them by name. He glanced at his watch and saw that about forty-five minutes had passed since he parted ways with the Maguire kid. It was strange, some scrawny young punk seeking him out like that, but when he mentioned Brendan Maguire's name it all made sense. 'That kid never could grasp the concept of boundaries' he thought. He felt a wave a sorrow pass over him as he thought of Brendan again, 'good kid' he thought, 'shame what happened.' He'd do this last favor for Brendan and that was it. He felt like he had to, but the longer he thought about it, the less clear it became. 'I don't know this kid from Adam' he thought 'and I'm about to arm him, against what? Who knows?' Granted, handing a gun over to a guy who happened to drop the right name wasn't even close to the top ten worse things he'd done. 'Still' he thought 'it feels wrong.' Normally this type of transaction barely registered a moment's thought. They had grown to be standard over the years. 'Guilt' McNulty thought, 'what a fucking waste of time.'

Minutes later McNulty watched Liam Maguire slowly walk through the doors and enter the rink. He walked close to the glass and slowly looked around the ice surface and then up towards the stands. He had taken off his hood and his hat, which meant McNulty could see him clearly again. He had noticed him walking into the AA meeting before. It was his youthful face that struck McNulty as odd. His hair was parted neatly and patted down from his hat. He really did look young, 'probably looks no older than sixteen at most' McNulty thought. That's why he noticed him before, he just looked out of place at a meeting for alcoholics. Also, McNulty knew many addicts over the years and Liam Maguire didn't look like one. He was skinny, but his skin tone in his face and hands looked too healthy, 'though I've been fooled before' McNulty thought. He watched Liam's eyes scan the stands starting with the area closest to him and stretching out until his gaze finally fell upon McNulty. Liam gave a slight, almost imperceptible nod and started walking in the direction of where he sat. 'At least he didn't do something stupid like put a big grin on and wave to me.' McNulty thought. As he approached him, McNulty pointed at the bench to the right of where he sat. Liam understood the gesture and climbed the stone steps and sat down next to him, slightly less than an arm's length away. McNulty waited a few seconds after he sat down, then spoke to Liam without turning his head towards him, 'How much you find, four or five?'

'I have three-fifty' Liam answered, trying to keep his voice down, though there was no one else in the stands to hear him. 'Will that be enough?'

'Yeah, that'll work. It's in an envelope?' McNulty asked.

'Ah . . . no, just in my pocket.'

McNulty shrugged in irritation, then turned slightly towards him to look him in the eye. 'Let's have it then, hand it over.' He said and held out his hand palm first.

'Okay, but, well . . . no offense sir, but can I see the gun first? I mean, do you have it here?'

McNulty grew irritated. 'Fucking amateur' he thought. 'Listen Son, there's a loaded thirty-eight in a padded envelope between the bench and the cement under my right knee. There's extra ammunition in a small box in there too. What's gonna happen is you're gonna stop being a pussy and put your fucking lunch money in my hand. Then I'm going to stand up and walk down those steps and out that fucking door. You're going to wait ten whole minutes after I leave, which you can time using that huge fucking scoreboard clock. Then, and only then, you're gonna slide over, put your hand nonchalantly under the seat like you're a kid wiping a fucking snot under the couch. You're gonna pick up the envelope, stuff it inside that ridiculous size coat of yours, walk out the door you came in, get in your car and drive home. When you're home safe and in your pajamas and no sooner, then you can open the envelope and take a look. Is that clear?' McNulty asked. He kept his eyes on Liam's the whole time. The kid looked genuinely overwhelmed and more than a little nervous. McNulty saw the look and softened for a moment, 'It's the way it goes down kid. That's standard operating procedure. You've heard of honor amongst thieves right?'

'Yeah, sure' Liam answered and shook his head slightly. 'I got it, no problem. I'll do it just like you said.'

'Good. That's good kid.' McNulty said. He stood up slowly and took a step towards the stairs. He turned back with a dawning realization and asked 'you don't know how to use that thing do you?'

Liam shrugged. 'I haven't before, but I'll figure it out.'

'Figure it out? Shit. Listen. It's loaded. It gets pointed at no one unless you mean to use it. And if you do, cock it first, then pull the trigger.'

'It'll be okay.' Liam said.

'Defense only right? Protection you said.'

'Protection only.'

'You're not gonna shoot up a fucking school or something are you? I don't think I could handle that.'

'What? No, of course not, it's for . . .'

'Good enough kid. On second thought, I don't want to know. You didn't get it from me and you've never seen or heard of me before.'

'Of course.' Liam said.

'Good' McNulty said. He dug his hands in his pockets, then continued down the steps and walked briskly out the emergency door without looking back. The door emptied into a parking lot. It was bare except for an immaculately refurbished eighty-two Buick Regal. McNulty walked in the direction of the car. The engine started up and the car's headlights switched on as he approached. McNulty opened the passenger door and slid down into the seat. 'What's up Billy?' He said to the driver, his partner, Billy Carson.

'Nothing much. You gonna tell me what that meet was all about?' He asked. Billy Carson was McNulty's long standing best friend. They knew each other since their school days and worked together for over thirty years in one capacity or another, not usually on the right side of the law, 'but the lines were often blurred' McNulty thought. Billy was from the same neighborhood as McNulty. They were thought of by most in the business as a team, and quite a good one at that, unless one or the other happened to be spending some alone time in a state or county facility. 'What, you need to know every aspect of my business now Bill?' McNulty asked.

Billy shook his head, 'No, just when it's cutting into my schedule or is something out of the ordinary, something rushed. This feels like both.'

'Don't worry about it, it was just a simple transaction. Nothing crazy.' McNulty said.

'Your transactions are never something I'd call simple Nicky. Who was that kid anyway? I saw him waiting out front for a while then watched him gather up the courage to finally walk into the rink. He looked pretty young, he's not gonna shoot up a school or something is he?'

McNulty laughed. 'No, he's not Billy. I thought the same thing for a moment. I can tell though, he's a genuinely good kid. That much I know at least.'

'Does a good kid randomly buy a firearm off Nick McNulty under circumstances that seem fucking cloudy at best?'

McNulty shrugged. 'Good kids get jammed up too Billy, just like the rest of us. He said it was for protection, he said it was exactly that, he was in a jam.'

'You didn't want to pry or something?'

'Fuck that, I just didn't want to know. Besides, I wouldn't say the circumstances are random. He's related to someone I . . . no, we know, or, knew I should say.'

'Yeah, who's that?'

'You remember Brendan Maguire?' McNulty asked knowing the name could invoke any number of responses from his good friend.

Billy turned to McNulty. He was holding his chin in his hands, the hair from his goatee had gotten long and unkempt and protruded out from between his fingers. McNulty kept eye contact with him. In his periphery, he could see how grey the hair on top of Billy's head had turned, though his goatee was still speckled heavily black and grey. 'Where's the time go' he thought. After a few seconds Billy stopped rubbing his chin and answered. 'Well Nicky, I tend to remember people well enough, especially if those people were heavily involved in my son's death.'

McNulty nodded in agreement. 'Figured you'd say something along those lines. Listen, Maguire's dead Billy.

Killed by some scumbag teenager a month or two ago, that's what his cousin told me anyhow. I believe him.'

'Hmm.' Billy answered. 'Unfortunate kid, guess karma got him after all.'

McNulty nodded 'I think it catches up with everyone eventually. Just hope I have a head start on the old bitch.' McNulty said.

'If anyone has a step on her it's you Nicky.' Billy reached into his inside pocket and pulled out a folded piece of paper. 'Here' he said and handed it to McNulty. 'O'Brien asked if you could take care of this in the next few days. Just pay some guy a visit and remind him he's overdue. Nothing heavy.'

McNulty took the paper and squinted to read it in the dark. He struggled to hold it straight as Billy pulled out of the parking lot and headed south. 'This an address?' McNulty asked.

'Can't you make it out?'

'Yeah, but I don't know it. Does that say Revere?' He held the paper over for Billy to take a look.

'Seems to, yeah.'

'Tell O'Brien to find someone else for it.'

'What? Why? It's easy money.'

'It's a fucking pain in my ass is what it is. You think I'm gonna drive an hour and sit through traffic in the city so some fucking north shore guido can take a run at me.'

'Why would anyone take a run at you? I don't know if you've noticed, but this type of work has been the most steady and well-paying we've seen for the last few years. O'Brien's been pretty good to us. Wouldn't you say? Come on Nicky just take the job.'

'Can't do it Billy. Listen, I told O'Brien before, I'll do

anywhere in the city and south of it. Well . . . except Charlestown. Soon as I go north of the Garden people don't know me up there. Everywhere around here, people know me, they see me, they get the point, no harm done, O'Brien gets paid, I get paid. As soon as some fuckers don't know me, they want to shoot their mouth off, push some limits . . . you know, it gets messy. I'm getting too old for that shit.'

'Okay whatever, you call him tomorrow and tell him. I already said you'd do it.'

'Fuck him. I'll call him tomorrow, don't worry. I'll smooth it over. What do you have for tonight, anyone's memory in need of jogging?'

'One or two stops, nothing major. Hey . . . what's up with you big man?' Billy asked. 'You're off beat tonight. First the meeting at the rink, then pussying out on an easy job cause it's in Revere. Something's up with you.'

McNulty shrugged his shoulders. He let out a sigh and sat deeper into the passenger seat. He looked out the window at the night. It was dark, but there were plenty of cars lighting up the road. He could still see his faint reflection in the window. 'I don't know man. Something funny's up with me.'

'Yeah. Like what, you sick or something. Everyone gets sick or has bad weeks, you'll be alright.'

'Nah Billy, that's just the thing. You know . . . I was never really sick in my life. Not one day sick that I can remember, in my whole entire fucking life. That's crazy isn't it?'

'Come on Nick. Course you have been.'

'I'm telling you straight up, I haven't. At the very least, I don't ever remember being sick.'

'Okay then, for argument's sake, you were never sick before. Isn't that a good thing?'

'It is, or . . . it was I mean. See just last week I went to the gym for a swim and a soak. Same as usual. After my workout, I was in the locker room, about to walk into the shower and suddenly my legs gave out. Like, they just gave the fuck out, stopped working completely. I was down for at least twenty minutes, begging them to work, but they didn't. So I just sat there. I mean fucking hell, if the place caught on fire, I'd be a pile of ashes by now. I wasn't moving. I mean, eventually I got my strength back and everything and I've felt fine since, but for that while, I thought it might be it. I thought my number was called Billy.'

Billy held a serious face for a moment, but after a few seconds he smiled and started laughing.

'What the fuck Billy? I tell you I was sitting there thinking I'm about to die and you're laughing. Some fucking friend you are.'

Billy tried to breathe and let the laughing die down before he responded. 'Sorry Nicky. It's just . . . you're telling me your fat ass was sitting on the gym locker room floor naked for twenty minutes unable to move?'

McNulty paused for a moment and thought about the scene. Then he smiled and laughed a little. 'Some roid head might've had his way with me and not a damn thing I could've done about it.'

Billy pulled the car to a stop and put it in park. 'My guess is you would've liked it old man. Here, stay here, I'll make this house call. Just keep an eye out. And keep your fucking clothes on.' He jumped out and walked up the steps toward a multi-family house and pressed the doorbell. He turned and gave McNulty a sarcastic wave. 'Asshole' McNulty thought, 'serves me right for confiding in him. On second thought, I should've left out the part about being on my way to the shower.'

JOHN BISHOP

Lake Winnipesaukee is the largest lake in New Hampshire. Formed by glaciers a millennium ago, it has been a vacation destination for Bostonians for more than a century. John Bishop had been going to the lake since he was a child. Some of his earliest memories involved sitting around a fire pit next to the lake in early autumn. His parents loved to get away one last time in late September before winter took hold and they always brought John and his sisters with them. In his mind's eye the onset of the New England autumn brought on the most vivid colors imaginable. The smell from a fire place nowadays transported him right back to his childhood, sitting so close to the fire that he could feel the heat on his face, his exposed legs cold as the night brought a cool moon with it, while his top half was buried in a hooded sweatshirt. He knew from a young age that someday he'd own a house overlooking the lake. It was inevitable, something that was just a matter of time. He bought a monster of a cottage with three floors, six bedrooms and even more fireplaces. Perched on a height overlooking the lake, it had private access to the water and a large boathouse with multiple moorings. It was the house he dreamed of having as a kid when he used to imagine himself, his sisters and all his cousins running around a cottage the size of a mansion, playing hide and seek inside or swimming in the lake outside. It was all he could've asked for when he was ten years old. When he bought it as an adult however, he had done so for much more practical, less nostalgic reasons. He needed a safe house outside of the city, somewhere

458

that was close enough to travel back and forth quickly. The house's location was perfect. It was also minutes from Laconia, which had a small airport and was frequented each summer by motorcycle enthusiasts, many of which Bishop was currently in business with in one degree or another. Having a perk like access to a cottage mansion during Bike Week would always serve him in good stead. The reasons for buying that house may have changed since he was a ten year old kid, but it was no less rewarding knowing that it was all his, every last inch of the place.

That had all changed however in the last seventy-two hours. His 'safe house' was safe no longer. The house was compromised, 'my freedom is compromised' he thought 'all for a booze and coke filled weekend.' Lefty Sturgis, one of his older guys, a guy that had been with him when he was just making inroads into Dorchester, was supposed to make a pick-up in Laconia and then head straight back to Quincy. Instead he short-changed Bishop's connection up north and treated himself and a couple of friends to a weekend of debauchery in Bishop's own house, not to mention on his dime. It was Lefty's doing, Bishop knew that. He knew something was up when he sat at his bar in Quincy and checked his watch to confirm that Lefty was thirty minutes late and hadn't checked in. No more than a minute later, Bishop got a call from an angry associate from the Tooth & Nail Motorcycle Club wondering how he wanted him to approach the distribution of the Gold Medal flour he was sold at the agreed asking price. Bishop did his best to appease the angry biker, promising to make good on all purchases. He managed to save face thanks to a previously untarnished reputation, but he knew now there was a strike against his name in their books. They were a dangerous bunch to get on the wrong side of, not to mention a major revenue stream for Bishop's operation. Twenty-five years was how long he knew Lefty Sturgis. They played on the same basketball team in middle school. Who could have guessed two and half decades later he'd be standing over the man's corpse with his blood and brain matter running up his right arm. He did what he had to do, 'the only thing I could do' he considered. In his business, failure to act when someone ripped you off was a death sentence. It could be slow, it could be immediate, but either way, it was the end unless there was proactive intervention. He never thought of himself as a killer. He still didn't. He never even thought of himself as a drug dealer really. He had never set out to be either. 'Shit happens and you react' he thought. 'Opportunity knocks, you either answer it or let it move on to a neighbor's house.' When the opportunity presented itself, he took advantage of it. At seventeen years old, he helped out a friend who told a mid-level connection that he'd take a couple ounces of Moroccan hash. When his friend couldn't come up with the money to pay him, Bishop fronted the money so his buddy could avoid an ass-kicking. The kid proved irresponsible with his handling, so Bishop stepped in to secure his investment. Everything snow balled from there, he figured. It became about fulfilling a demand, pure economics. People wanted what he had, so they came to him and he got them set up. As his reputation grew, so did the stakes. Eventually, it became only about money. Once Bishop had a taste of the green stuff, it was impossible to turn back. He didn't use drugs himself, in fact he considered himself a health nut, taking only an exceptional drink here or there. He figured that was what made him a perfect dealer, he had no interest in sampling his own product. The deeper he got into it, the more intense the violence grew with it. It moved in direct correlation to his financial success. More money, more suffering. That's what the drug game proved to be for Bishop. It was a spiral that he knew now he could not control. There was a time when he thought he was in charge and that he could control it, but he knew now he was wrong. 'That was naive' he considered 'or worse, it was hubris.' The violence he witnessed firsthand and often took part in, he could almost live with. However, it was the realization of what he was doing and its impact on his neighborhood and society more broadly that he found sickening now. For years, he was able to successfully block out the fact that he was dispensing poison to men and women that was basically eating them alive. It was killing them and destroying the lives of those around them. He hadn't kicked it off, but he was feeding the opiate epidemic in the North East. Bishop knew deep down this was happening the whole way along but he managed to stop it from penetrating his conscious mind. Then a few years back his best friend, 'hell, my only friend' he thought, succumbed to his demons. He died of a heroin overdose. Bishop found him in the upstairs apartment of the bar he owned in Quincy. Brian Dawson was his name. Bishop let him live there while he was down on his luck. He should've known the inevitable would happen, though he felt powerless to stop it. He'd given word to his own people that Dawson was off limits and no one was to sell to him. That's when he realized just how resourceful opiate addicts could be. Faced with the stark reality that he was now a victim of his own greed, he had wanted to give it all up. 'It's just not that easy' he thought. 'This is not a business you just cash in your chips and walk away from. So here I am.'

The sun began to rise in the early morning and it shimmered its orange reflection off the glassy lake. John Bishop stood on the top floor balcony overlooking the sun's spectacle. He had his hands around a coffee mug as he leaned his forearms on the bannister. 'Fucking Lefty, you son of a bitch' he thought. He had pulled his gun out and put it to Lefty's temple just over two days ago. He had done it with some level of self-control to begin with. However, when he threatened Lefty, gun to his head and all, Lefty just laughed. Well, he insulted him then laughed. That's when Bishop lost his cool. In a blind rage he shot him. Lefty's girl, a junkie that he let feed off his connections, screamed and came after Bishop, so he turned and shot her. He shot him in the head. For her, he aimed at the chest and pierced her heart. Seconds later, with Lefty's blood and brains still staining his fitted jacket, he took off with another associate to Laconia to try and make amends. What he didn't know was that Jeff Conrad, one of his other employees, and Jeff's young girlfriend had seen and heard everything from the closet where they had run and hid just before Bishop got to the room. While Bishop was away, Conrad was able to fight off a couple of his men momentarily and the girl escaped. Conrad took off himself as well, but he didn't get far before he was found in the woods and dragged back to the house. He was still in the house now. And, he was still alive for the moment. Bishop and his last remaining trustworthy soldier, Mike Doyle, had worked him over for more than a day. Bishop was up all night. It had happened so fast with Lefty. He wouldn't let it end with Jeff Conrad too quickly. Perhaps he was compensating one with the other. Conrad wasn't the real guilty party, Lefty was. However, he was definitely complacent. 'And he has to go.' Bishop thought. 'Both for what he took part in and for what he had seen. The girl too.' That's the real reason it took so long with Conrad. He really did love the girl. That was apparent. 'No one withstands that much pain over that length of time for anything less than love.' Bishop thought. Finally, just before sunset, Conrad had finally given her name up. 'Penny Maguire' Bishop said her name out loud to the sun's reflection off the lake. 'I'm sorry Penny.' He said. He wished he didn't have to do it. 'She's just a kid.' He thought 'But I have no other options . . . well no other good options. She's a loose end. It's her or me now.'

A knock on the glass door behind him broke his concentration. Bishop turned to see Mike Doyle through the glass. Doyle slowly opened the door a crack and stuck his head out. 'We should wrap this up don't you think Johnny?' He asked.

Bishop stood up straight and ran a hand over his face. He rubbed his eyes for a few seconds to try and rid them of tiredness. 'Yeah Mike. Let's get it done.' Doyle opened the door wider and let Bishop walk back into the room. He then led Bishop through to a smaller room tucked in the back of the attic. It was a small box room that was left unfinished by the previous occupants. Bishop walked in slowly. The room was dark and it took a moment for his eyes to adjust to the dimmer lighting. When they did he could see Jeff Conrad clearly. He was seated in the same chair that he had been for hours. His face was bloodied and bruised from the hours of persuasion needed to pump him for the right information. Bishop crinkled his nose in disgust as an unmistakable waft of urine found its way to his senses. The ammonia smell was mixed with a rusty iron scent, which Bishop knew was human blood. He imagined that the scent of the room was similar to that of a slaughterhouse, which it was. 'How you doing Connie?' He asked the messy pulp seated in front of him. Jeff Conrad slowly managed to turn his head to the front and raise his one unswollen eye upwards in Bishop's direction. He muttered something that Bishop couldn't really make out, but assumed it was a request for a drink. 'Mike, bring him some water would ya?' Bishop said without turning back towards Doyle. He heard Mike Doyle's footsteps leave the room and then he heard the faucet running. The sounds from the pipes in the old house were only slightly muffled by the walls and ceilings. Doyle walked back in seconds later and stood next to Bishop. Bishop nodded towards Jeff Conrad and Doyle brought the water over and held it up to his lips. Jeff Conrad took a large gulp from the cup, but coughed most of it back up. 'Easy now Connie.' Bishop said.

After a couple of smaller sips of the water, Jeff Conrad seemed slightly more alert. 'You just gonna do it Johnny? If so, just get it done.'

'It'll happen Connie. Soon enough.'

'You know I would never say anything John. You don't have to do it.'

'It's not you I'm worried about Connie. We both know that.'

'She's just a kid John. Let me go and I'll talk to her. I'll straighten things out.'

Bishop shook his head. 'It doesn't work like that and you know it. The girl saw too much. She's a liability. And, you're smitten with this chick. There's no way if I free you, you don't become a liability too. Isn't that right?'

Jeff Conrad didn't say anything in response. He dropped his gaze from Bishop and let his chin rest into his chest. 'I don't take any pleasure in this Connie.' Bishop said. 'I want you to know that. This is business, I wish there was a way around it.' At that, Bishop slowly slid his right hand along his belt towards his back. He felt the gun handle sticking out from the waist of his jeans and he wrapped his hand around it. Jeff Conrad stirred for a moment and Bishop paused and waited to hear if there were any last words. 'Fucking Lefty' Jeff Conrad muttered. Bishop swung his arm around quickly and fired before Jeff Conrad could say anything else. The sound of the shot was deafening as it echoed in the unfinished room. Bishop saw Doyle tense up next to him at the explosion. Bishop dropped his arm after a moment, but kept his hand on the gun. He could hear ringing in his own ears that drowned out the sudden silence. He turned to Doyle and asked 'You have the number of the clean-up crew that Tooth & Nail use?'

'Yeah I have it in my phone. I'll call them now. You want me to stick around and wait for them.'

'No, leave them to it, I trust them. They're paid well enough. I need you with me.'

'We heading somewhere?'

'Yeah, we're heading back to Quincy. Let's close this shit down.'

'You're really gonna take the girl down?'

'You see any other way?' Bishop asked.

Doyle shrugged, 'No I guess I don't.' He said.

Bishop tucked the gun into the back of his belt and turned towards the door. 'Make the call and let's go.' He said, then he disappeared into the adjoining room and down the stairs.

LIAM MAGUIRE

Liam decided to blow off work the rest of the week. He needed time to think and plan. Plan for what, he wasn't too sure. Penny was adamant that she was in danger, though her unwillingness to share details kept him in the dark on the extent of danger she was in and how long it would last. She was equally adamant that they could not, under any circumstances, go to the police. He pleaded with her on this, but she swore up and down that doing so would have even worse consequences. That's the main reason he had sought out McNulty. He was short on options and short on time. McNulty's demeanor towards him was odd and inconsistent to say the least. In the couple of short interactions with the man, Liam could sense he was prone to quick and drastic mood changes. He could also sense that something was always eating away at him. For a large man with a big reputation, he appeared uncomfortable in his skin, like something was itching him somewhere just out of reach of his scratch. He wondered if he'd ever meet McNulty again. Part of him was glad to be out of his company. Although, another part of him was interested to learn more about the man. He seemed to be more than just the wise-cracking muscle that his image portrayed. For now, he was just glad he was able to secure something that he felt he could protect Penny with, and himself if it came to it. He stood at the sink and filled up a glass of water from the faucet. He looked down at the counter top and over at the top drawer next to the sink. That's where he dropped the gun when he got home the night before, but now he had an eerie sensation that it was no longer there. He put the glass down next to the sink and shook the excess water from his hand. Slowly he reached his right hand towards the handle of the drawer. He paused for a moment and took in a deep breath. He released the air from his lungs, then snapped out quickly with his hand and pulled open the drawer. He was relieved to find the gun still in the drawer exactly where he left it. He heard a chair scrape off the tiled floor and was startled by the sudden noise. He closed the drawer quickly and swung around towards the kitchen door. Penny walked towards him, squinting her eyes in suspicion as she did. 'What's that you're hiding?' She asked and tried to reach past him and open the drawer. 'Don't' he said and blocked her path and tried to hold her hand away by grabbing her wrist. She smiled cheekily and pulled her hand forcefully away from his, then reached out with both hands and started pinching him in the chest. He tensed up and yelled 'Ahh! What the hell Penny!' He pulled his body away from the pinches long enough for Penny to reach over and pull open the drawer. 'What the hell is right' she said looking at the gun. 'You think that's the answer to my problems?'

He reached past her quickly and slammed the drawer shut again. 'Penny, I'm not even sure what our problem is. Why don't you enlighten me?' He said. Then he stood back and stared at Penny, his eyes demanding more details. 'We're in it . . . deep.' She said 'But that's all I'll say. The details . . . they can only hurt you now.'

'So you won't tell me? You'll just let me sit here and wait for whatever is coming to happen? Is that it?'

Penny pulled out a chair from under the kitchen table and sat down. She put her elbows on the table and her face in her hands. She sighed deeply into her palms.

'We're laying low. That's what we're doing.'

'Okay' Liam said, 'I get that part, but what are we laying low for? Or at least, what should I be looking out for?'

'I'm waiting on . . . someone to ah . . . get in touch and tell me whether it's okay to raise my head or to . . . I don't know, run I guess.'

'Great. Run. Real great Penny.' Liam said. He sat down in the seat across from her at the table. He looked across at her and they stared at each other for a few seconds. He looked over her face. She looked better than she had. Her face was still so thin you could see her bone structure clearly, but the color had returned and her hair looked healthier. 'The twenty-four hour or so nap really made a difference' he thought. He was still surprised when he looked at her how much she reminded him of himself. 'We could've been actual twins.' He thought. He was reminded of when they were kids and used to sit across from each other at breakfast like they were now. She always complained at the way he chewed his cereal and used to slide the cereal box between them so she wouldn't have to watch him eat. He smiled thinking about it for a moment 'little bitch' he thought. 'It's Jeff you're waiting on to call, right?' He asked.

She squinted at him. Liam thought she looked unsure as to whether or not she should be surprised. 'Yes.' She said.

Liam nodded. 'And he said he would?'

'Not exactly' she said. 'He said if I didn't hear from him by five pm today that I should worry, because he'd most likely be dead.'

Liam straightened at the word 'dead'. He felt goose

469

bumps grow on his arms and a tingle at the back of his neck. 'Dead' he thought, knowing that his worst fear was true, he may need to use that gun after all. He looked up at the clock on the wall. 'Penny' he said 'it's five minutes to five. Do you realize that?' Penny swallowed deeply and nodded slowly 'I know Liam. That's what has me nervous.'

Liam put his hand to his face and rubbed the stubble that had grown on his chin. 'He's not calling is he?' Liam asked.

Penny stared back at him for a few seconds, then shook her head slowly. 'I don't think so, no.'

'So, what do we do? Run?'

'I guess so.' She answered.

'But . . . run where? And how?' He asked.

Penny shrugged her shoulders but didn't respond. Liam noticed that her eyelids were now rimmed in tears. 'We should go to the bank before it closes' Liam said. 'I can get some money at least. Then, I guess we can try to get away . . . go stay somewhere, I don't know.'

'Where did you get the gun?' Penny asked.

'A friend of Brendan's' he said. 'A guy called McNulty sold it to me. I found him at an AA meeting at Saint Ann's in Dorchester.'

Penny nodded. 'I think I've heard of him. Do you think he'd help us?'

'Penny. Why not the police? If this is life or death, we need to go to the cops like right now.'

'I'm telling you we can't. That's it, flat out, not an option.'

'But . . . why! Tell me that at least!' He yelled.

'Jeff said we can't. He said that John has a lot of the

cops on his payroll, so going to the cops would only get us found faster.'

'And this is . . . John Bishop?'

'Yeah.'

'Shit' Liam said. 'He's not someone to cross from what I hear, if that's true I mean.' Liam could see fear in Penny's eyes suddenly. She shook her head quickly. 'It's true Liam. Take my word for it.'

'Shit' he said again. He stood up from the table and walked over to the kitchen sink. He ran the water and filled his glass up again and took a big gulp of the cold liquid. When he finished, he held onto the glass. He looked down and could see his hand shaking, the movement causing the remaining water to wave in the glass. 'I'm scared Penny.' He said without facing her. He heard the chair scrape the floor again and seconds later felt Penny's hand touch his shoulder. 'I'm sorry Liam.' She said. 'I never meant for . . . well for anything.' Liam turned towards her and looked into her eyes. Tears grew heavy around her lids and the water lumped together her long eyelashes. 'I know' Liam said and gently squeezed the side of her arm. 'We'll figure it out.' He walked past her and knelt down in front of the wooden bench. He opened it and removed the loose board. He pulled out the contents, which included his remaining loose cash in a zipped up plastic bag. He took out the bills and reached into his wallet and pulled out a credit card. 'Hang onto these' he said and handed them to Penny. 'It's in case we get split up at any stage'. She took the dollar bills and credit card and looked at them for a moment, then stuffed them into her jeans pocket. 'I don't plan to get split up though.' She said.

'Neither do I.' He said. 'But you never know.'

JOHN BISHOP

There's a small, dreary bar across from Wollaston Train Station in Quincy. At one stage, years ago, John Bishop acquired it as part of a debt repayment. At the time he didn't want to own a bar or any other business, but soon after it was in his hands he knew he wouldn't part with it. It was the first business he began cleaning his money through, but it wasn't his last. As the scale of his operation grew, the small neighborhood bar could no longer mask its infrequent customers or inconsistent opening times. Bishop branched out to other cash-based businesses like massage parlors and tanning salons. He even owned a small gym franchise. Despite its decline in strategic importance, Bishop still used his small office at the bar as his principal place of business. It was where he felt most comfortable and most protected since he was never without at least two armed men holding down the fort. Also, he had the place rigged with cameras and his office was lined with several CCTV screens. He knew who was in the barroom at all times and basically had visibility on the street in front of his walls and fifty feet down each block. The only downside was that people knew they could typically find him there, which is why he spent most of his time out of sight in the back office. The barroom itself was dark and rundown. The aim wasn't to be inviting, it was quite the opposite. There were swinging doors at one entrance that looked like something from the Wyatt Earp days. When it was nice out, the swinging doors would let in rays of sunshine, though light didn't suit the place. All the sunshine achieved was that it made the room look dusty and accentuated the areas needing immediate upkeep.

John Bishop sat at the bar itself for a change as opposed to being hunkered down in his office with the door shut to avoid anyone that may come looking for him. That day though he was anxious. He and Mike Doyle arrived back from New Hampshire hours ago, but Bishop knew it was best to wait until dark before making any move. Doyle took the opportunity to sleep much of the day on the couch in the upstairs apartment. Bishop however couldn't sleep. He couldn't relax either. His mind raced constantly while he waited out the daylight. He was both angered and saddened by recent events. Before a few days ago, Lefty Sturgis and Jeff Conrad had been his friends. At least, that's how he thought of them. Now he felt the weight of their ghosts and the increased gravity was making him weary. 'Now there's the girl' he thought. 'I don't know her, but it's me that has to cut her down.' The longer he waited, the more he had to fight to not lose his resolve. Luckily for him the late winter had yet to yield a stretch to any evening. Just after five o'clock the sun was closing in on the horizon. He roused Doyle from his slumber through a phone call that he followed up with a bang or two on the ceiling with a hard end of a broom. Doyle came down minutes later rubbing the sleep out of his eyes and trying to pat down a stubborn cowlick. 'We doing this?' Doyle asked.

'Yeah, it's time' Bishop said. 'Mickey here's coming along too so we have some cover.' He pointed to a young guy carrying a case of beer towards the bar. 'Get your shit Mick, we're heading out.' He yelled down the end of the bar. Bishop got up from the barstool and was joined seconds later by the young kid named Mick. The three men walked out the back entrance through Bishop's office to a hidden driveway. Bishop tossed his truck keys to Mike Doyle. 'Doyle, you can drive.'

'No problem' he said and walked over to the driver's door of the Ford Expedition. On the way back from New Hampshire earlier, Bishop and Mike Doyle took a slow drive by the address that Jeff Conrad gave them. It was the second floor of an apartment, just across from the North Quincy Train Station. The drive from the bar took less than five minutes. Mike Doyle parked in a commercial lot a few minutes away on foot. The plan was for the three men to make their way into the apartment quietly if possible, but by any means necessary they needed to secure the girl. Then they'd send Mick back for the truck. They parked the truck and walked nonchalantly up the street. Each man was concealing a firearm. Jeff Conrad gave them no reason to expect any real resistance. The girl lived with her brother in the apartment, but neither were really deemed a threat. Doyle had done a little digging on the brother, but no one really knew anything about him. He was young, only recently out of state college. He went to North Quincy High School, but no one from North that Doyle connected with remembered much about him.

They slowed their pace as they approached the house. Bishop said, 'Mick, I want you around back just in case. Don't go waving your gun around unless it's a last resort. We need to get this girl out of here and out of town, not create a trail of evidence here in Quincy.'

'Got it John.' Mick said and jogged up to the side of the house and hugged the wall as he made his way down the driveway and into the back.

Bishop and Mike Doyle slowly climbed the front steps and walked over to the side entrance as Jeff Conrad had explained. Bishop double checked the house and apartment number just in case. He gave Mike Doyle a nod and Doyle tried the door knob. 'Locked.' He said. 'Should I try the bell?'

Bishop gave him a questioning look and said 'You think she'll answer?'

Doyle smiled briefly and reached inside his long jacket. He pulled out a flat iron bar that hooked at the end. He carefully wedged the pointed edge in between the door and the wood frame next to the lock. He looked up at Bishop before proceeding. Bishop gave him a nod and said. 'Do it.'

Doyle slammed the cornered end of the flatbar with the palm of his hand to wedge the sharp point in further, then jerked the bar hard towards his body. The door splintered immediately and popped loose from the lock. 'Go!' Bishop said sternly as he pulled his gun from behind his back. 'If they're in there, they heard that.' He thought. They took the stairs quickly and were met at the top by another locked door that appeared to lead into the apartment. The door was at the top of the stairs without a landing, which made it difficult to get any leverage to kick it in. Doyle pushed on it hard with his shoulder, but it didn't budge. 'Move!' Bishop yelled and Doyle slid up next to the wall. Bishop jumped down to the landing at the bottom again, then charged at full strength to the top. He lost some momentum from the climb, but still hit the door with force. The charge pushed the door away from the lock, but not all the way open. 'There's something holding it shut' Bishop said. 'Get up here and help me out!' Doyle took a step down then charged and put his shoulder into the door. It opened another six inches with his weight. There was enough space to climb through. Bishop led the way into the apartment with his gun at eye level. Doyle followed just behind him with his pistol drawn. There was a heavy reclining chair propped up against the front door. Bishop kicked it further away when he entered. The hallway was long and dark. He could see two rooms off it, one on either side, then the kitchen area straight ahead. He looked at Doyle and pointed right. They both rushed forward and charged into the opposite rooms with guns waving. Both found the rooms empty and came out seconds later. Bishop led the way into the kitchen, which was empty and quickly walked through the adjoining living room. He walked back into the kitchen and peeked outside to the small yard. The back door was shut, which gave him a feeling that they already left. However when he looked outside, he could see shadows moving under a porch light. He peered closer for a moment and in the dim light was able to make out Mick's frame. Mick had a gun raised and was pointing it at something or someone, Bishop couldn't see who. 'Shit' he said out loud. Doyle stood next to him and looked down. 'He's got someone down there, let's go.' Doyle said.

Doyle led the way down the back stairs quickly, then paused at the bottom. 'Oh fuck' he said. Bishop looked past him and could see Mick about twenty feet away. He followed Mick's stare across the yard to the foot of the back porch. 'Fuck' he muttered. In the dim porch light, he could see the girl and a man he presumed was her brother. The brother stood between Mick's pointed pistol and his sister. He was a slightly built kid, but at the end of his long thin arm he held a revolver and it was pointed directly at Mick. Bishop knew they were now in a jam. Any move could spook the kid, 'or Mick' he thought. He looked over at the girl. She was behind her brother, but also behind a large grill that was covered for the winter. 'Not even a good shot from here' he thought. 'What's our move?' Doyle asked.

'Fuck it Mike, we have to do something.' Bishop said. He slowly opened the back door, then tried to quietly open the second, screen door. His gun was raised as he walked forward. The screen door creaked loudly when he pushed it open, the grating metal echoing in the quiet evening. The kid turned quickly towards Bishop. Bishop could see the fear pouring out of his wide open eyes and strained jaw. 'Hang on!' Bishop yelled and put his hand up. In an instance the kid's face twitched. 'Fuck' Bishop thought and he and Doyle dove onto the porch, behind the wood railing as the kid fired. The shot was wild and didn't come close to either man as they scrambled across the porch. Mick fired once in response. Bishop couldn't see him at first but he heard a bullet ricochet off the iron grill. He looked up and saw that Mick had charged forward when the kid fired at Bishop. Mick and the kid grappled for a few seconds on the ground but it didn't last long. Mick was a tough kid with an athletic build and he overpowered the girl's brother quickly and held him down. Bishop could see Mick now had control of the kid's gun too. He and Doyle stood up slowly and descended the steps towards them. Bishop peered through the dark yard, scanning the perimeter, but he couldn't see the girl anywhere. He looked down at Mick, who had the kid pinned to the ground. Doyle walked over and picked the guns up off the ground and stuffed them into his jacket pockets. 'Get him up Mick, he's coming with us.' Bishop said.

'John, What about the girl?'

'She's gone for now Mick. Get that kid up and into the truck. Keep your fingers crossed that she'll come looking for him.'

MCNULTY

The echo in an empty church could be deafening. McNulty heard the loud sound of a door opening at the entrance. Next he heard the slow, deliberate footsteps against the marble floor. There was no need to turnaround, he could tell who it was by listening to the man's gait alone. The steps were sure footed, light and balanced. The timing of the movement indicated a slight bounce with every step. The approach took close to a minute since McNulty sat in the first set of pews at the foot of the altar. The footsteps ceased and he heard the scrape of jeans sliding across the wooden bench behind him. No immediate conversation followed. McNulty inhaled deeply and exhaled slowly. He pressed his spine against the back of the bench. He heard the man behind him shift and lean forward. 'Bless me father for I have sinned.' McNulty said. 'It's been thirty years since my last confession.'

'Fuck off Nicky' the man behind him said. McNulty laughed and turned around to the man and rested his large arm on the top of the bench. 'Oh Billy, it's you. Sorry, thought you were someone else.'

'Yeah okay, sure you did.' Billy Carson said. McNulty smiled and shrugged his shoulders. 'Thirty years since your last confession Nick huh? I'd guess you're due.'

'Maybe. Probably more like forty five years. Thirty sounded better, you know, less needy.'

'I'm sure you can just add that lie to the bottom of the list.'

'Yeah Maybe.' McNulty said and slowly nodded.

'You were missed downstairs.' Billy said. 'The meeting's over.'

'I figured. I just couldn't face it today you know . . . didn't feel like being saved today, that's all.'

'Yeah, I know the feeling Nicky. That's how it starts.'

McNulty shrugged again. 'It's one fucking meeting Billy, relax. I'll be back tomorrow.'

'It ain't me you gotta answer to big guy.'

'Seems like it is Billy. I'm a fucking grown man . . . an old man even. You come up here to give me shit, or do we have a job tonight?'

'I'm just your friend asshole, that's all. Everyone knows you're the big bad McNulty. Just remember though buddy, even giants like you can fall.'

'Don't I know it' McNulty said. 'So what do we got, anything?'

'Nothing tonight. Unless you want to get some food or something?'

'Yeah whatever.' McNulty said.

Both men stood up. McNulty zippered his leather jacket up to his chin and genuflected at the end of the row before exiting. He followed Billy Carson down the aisle towards the large swinging doors at the church entrance. Both sets of footsteps echoed loudly around the room, the sound bouncing off the tall ceilings. Outside the air was dry, but cool, with a light breeze. Both men dug their hands in coat pockets and started down the stone steps to the sidewalk. McNulty looked down at the steps as he descended. Before he reached the bottom, a shadow caught his attention as it passed his feet quickly and he paused, slightly startled. A thin young girl had charged across the sidewalk and up the first few steps before collapsing. McNulty and Billy both paused initially, then hurried down the last couple steps and caught her before she crumbled onto the concrete. They eased her down slowly. The girl was severely out of breath. Sweat had gathered across her forehead and soaked much of her hair that covered most of her face. McNulty stood back for a moment and noticed blood on his left hand. 'She's bleeding Billy.' He said.

'Where, can you tell?' Billy asked. McNulty looked closely at her face then across her torso. He noticed a dark stain on the girl's shoulder. He reached down and tore her sleeve. 'It's her shoulder. Looks like a bad scrape and it's bruising up quick. You got your phone, we should call an ambulance.' McNulty said. Billy reached in his pocket and pulled out his cell phone.

The girl's eyes opened and widened when she saw Billy pull out his phone. 'No' she said between breaths. 'Please . . . no cops, no ambulance.'

'You're in rough shape kid.' McNulty said. 'You should see a doc.' She shook her head frantically and struggled to get her breath back quickly. 'Alright alright, hang on a sec Billy.'

McNulty saw Billy's face flash with irritation, but he put the phone down for the moment. They both stood back and gave the girl a few seconds to catch her breath. She seemed to pull herself together quickly. She checked her shoulder briefly. The bleeding wasn't severe, McNulty noticed. It still looked painful, although the girl didn't seem too concerned with her wound. She rubbed away the sweat from her face with her hands, then pulled the strands of her hair back from her face and swept the ends around her ears. McNulty squinted his eyes and tilted his head slightly in recognition. She looked very tired. Her eyes were deep set and they had noticeable circles surrounding them. Her face, along with the rest of her was very thin, though it was still strikingly attractive even in her current state of dishevel. McNulty's brain churned. She looked so familiar, but he couldn't place her. Finally she spoke, 'I'm looking for someone.' She said. 'Someone named McNulty. Do you know him?'

McNulty continued staring at the girl, although he noticed in his periphery that Billy Carson was now looking at him. He felt Billy's eyes burning through him in accusation. McNulty was confused for a second. 'What the fuck?' He thought. 'Can't be me she's looking for.' Then it dawned on him. Her face, even her demeanor he recognized. The thin face and defined bone structure. 'She's a Maguire' he thought. It was obvious now. She looked just like the Maguire kid he met the night before. 'This can't be good.' He said out loud.

'You know this girl?' Billy asked McNulty. McNulty looked over at Billy, his brow was pinched together in confusion. 'Not exactly.' McNulty said.

'Wait . . . are you McNulty?' the girl asked. McNulty looked towards the girl again, then quickly back at Billy and shrugged. 'I'm a McNulty, yeah. I'm sure I'm not the only one.'

'You're him.' She said. 'You're McNulty. You knew my cousin Brendan . . . Brendan Maguire. And you met my brother Liam last night.'

McNulty didn't answer at first as he pondered the girl's motive. 'Was she out looking for the man who put a gun in her brother's hand?' He wondered. 'No, that ain't it. This girl's not angry. If anything she's scared.' He looked over at Billy again. Billy's face had an 'I told you so' look on it and he shook his head at McNulty in disappointment. 'We don't need this.' He mouthed to McNulty. McNulty just looked away from Billy then back towards the girl.

'Listen.' She said. 'I need help that's all. And I . . . I have nowhere else to turn.'

'Come on, I'm sure you'll be fine kid.' McNulty said. He didn't believe it himself. A burning sensation formed in his stomach, and started to broaden through to his torso.

'No I won't be fine. They're looking for me. They came to my house!' She said. Tears formed around her eye lids and she sniffled. 'They took Liam . . . and they killed Jeff I know it. They'll kill me too. I'm next.' She looked up at McNulty. 'You have to help me, please. Can you at least get me off the street for a few minutes so I can . . . think?'

'Woah, relax kid, just hang on.' McNulty said. 'If someone's after you like you say, we'll drop you down to the police station. If you're serious that is.'

'I am serious!' she yelled. The noise from her strained vocal chords pierced McNulty's eardrums. 'I can't go to the police.' She then whispered. 'He'll know. He's got half the police force paid off, Jeff told me.'

'At least tell me who's after you then.' McNulty said.

The girl hesitated. Her pupil's dilated. McNulty could practically see her brain churning while she considered what do to. She finally blinked away her indecision and answered. 'John Bishop.' She said. 'He's after me.'

McNulty's back straightened when she said the name. He knew it well enough to take notice. He kicked himself for not pressing her brother more on what kind of trouble he was in. 'Not in order to get involved' he thought, 'but to avoid it.' He asked her, 'John Bishop . . . from Quincy?

That John Bishop?'

'Yes!' she yelled in response. Tears welled in her eyes again and her nose was running down to the top of her mouth.

'And John Bishop has your brother? The scrawny kid I met yesterday, is that right?'

'Yes.' She answered, more subdued this time. 'Well, I'm guessing he does anyway. I ran away when the shooting started.'

'Shooting?' McNulty thought, 'Shit . . . that explains her shoulder.' 'Why was Bishop at your house anyway? What was he looking for?' He asked.

She looked up at McNulty and answered simply 'Me.'

McNulty nodded and took a step towards Billy, who had remained quiet throughout the exchange. McNulty assumed he was trying to put the pieces together from what he'd heard. 'What do you think Billy?'

Billy Carson scratched his goatee for a few seconds while he considered the question. 'I think we need to get her off the street to start with. If Bishop is looking for her, he won't be far away. But, Nicky listen . . .'

McNulty cut him off. 'I know Billy, you don't want to get involved. Just bear with me for a few on this.' Billy shrugged in response, which McNulty took for reluctant agreement. 'Come on kid' he said to the girl. 'I live close by, you can get cleaned up and we can figure out what's next.'

The girl stood up and followed closely behind in the shadow of the two men, mostly McNulty's since it engulfed much of the sidewalk. They quickly got into Billy Carson's Buick and drove the short distance to McNulty's house. Billy let them off out front, then parked around the corner. McNulty led her up the front steps into the triple decker, then upstairs to the third floor apartment. He unlocked the door and showed her in. The apartment opened into a large foyer. All the other rooms connected to that one in some way except for the main bedroom, which was down a long corridor towards the back of the apartment. 'You can get cleaned up in there' McNulty said and pointed towards his bathroom. There's some peroxide and cotton balls under the sink. I suggest you clean out that scrape on your arm. She nodded in thanks and closed the bathroom door. McNulty walked into his bedroom and opened up a hope chest that sat idle in the corner. He reached inside and dug around for what he was looking for. He found a few old t-shirts and pairs of jeans that had belonged to his daughter. In all these years he'd always known where those spare clothes were. They were basically the last remnants of any physical connection he had with his little girl. His hands found her old t-shirts. He felt the softness of the fabric between his fingers and could still smell his daughter's perfume on them, though he guessed that was his imagination after all these years. Most of the shirts were bands she liked at the time, Red Hot Chili Peppers, Green Day, bands like that. Ones that he'd heard of but never listened to or cared for at the time. He'd heard them all since then though, although some had fizzled out, others were still around. He made it a point to try and learn about them after the fact, 'little good that did' he thought. When she walked out of his life for the last time, along with her brother and mother of course, he was dead inside. He'd been drinking a lot, pretty much all the time really. So, at the time they did leave, it was at least a couple years before he actually felt the pain of their absence. When he finally did feel it, however, when he'd sobered up and found a crater-sized hole of emptiness inside himself, the hurt was poignant. What was most unbearable to him was the realization that the pain he felt now was likely only a fraction of what they dealt with for many years. And that was all thanks to him.

He struggled to push his emotions aside for a moment. He needed to think about the here and now. He was into something now but he wasn't sure what exactly. He walked out of the room and over to the bathroom door. He knocked on it and said awkwardly 'Uh, hey kid, there's some clean clothes here that might fit you if you want to change.' There was no verbal response from the bathroom, but the door slowly unlocked and the girl peeked out. She looked at the clothes and slowly put her arms out to take them. 'It's Penny.' She said through the crack of the door.

'What's that?' McNulty asked. He was avoiding looking at her while he handed the clothes through the door.

'My name. It's Penny.'

'Oh, shit. Yeah sorry, I call everyone kid. Okay Penny . . . I'll be out here whenever you're cleaned up.'

'Okay' she said. The door closed again and McNulty walked into the hallway. He heard Billy climbing the stairs and met him at the front door. McNulty led the way into the kitchen and stepped out to an enclosed porch out the back behind the kitchen. He leaned on the ledge overlooking the backyard, while Billy sat on the edge of a chair. 'Well, what do you think?' McNulty asked.

Billy let out a sigh before responding. 'I think this kid is in over her head. We both know who Bishop is. It doesn't feel like a joking matter. I think you need to drop her off at the police station and run a thousand miles away from this Nick.'

'Maybe' McNulty said and continued peering out the window. He knew Billy was right but something wouldn't let him just wash his hands of this girl and her brother.

'What do you mean maybe Nicky? You can't actually be thinking about getting involved here. You don't know these kids. This ain't your fight man.'

McNulty turned away from the window and took a seat in a chair facing Billy. 'We've been doing this shit a long time huh Bill?' He said. Billy just nodded. 'In all these years, can you name one fight that you actually chose? I mean like one time that something wasn't dropped on you without any choice? Shit, I can't, and I'm sure as shit you can't either. So, how's this any different huh? Except that maybe for once, I get to choose my own fight.'

Billy shook his head. 'I think you're making a big mistake if you get involved Nicky.'

'Yeah Billy, you've made that clear.'

'I obviously haven't if you're still considering helping these kids out.' Billy said. 'What the fuck are you gonna do? Go to war with Bishop over some pair of teenagers that you don't know from Adam and Eve? This is bullshit Nicky.'

McNulty stood back up and slowly began pacing along the length of the porch. His shoulders were slouched and he held his hands loosely in his pockets. He paused after a moment and turned back towards Billy. 'You know what my daughter said to me . . . like one of the last things . . . she asked me point blank what was so important to me that I couldn't be around for her. Her whole life, something was always more important than me being there with her. And you know what my fat fucking drunk ass responded with? I remember the exact words . . . I said, Julia, that's bullshit, I was there when it mattered. There when it mattered . . . believe that shit?' McNulty laughed to himself. 'The very last thing she said to me after that was simple . . . it was a question. She asked me . . . when did it not matter? When I think back to that conversation, which I often do these days, you know what really strikes me? It's not how fucking dumb my words were, that's obvious, it's that she could have said that it still does matter, but she didn't. She used the past tense. Everything mattered up to that point in time, but after that moment, my chance with her was over. I had gone too far.'

Billy leaned forward and rested his elbows on his knees. He put his hands up to his eyes and rubbed them. McNulty thought the gesture made Billy look young again for a split second, until he took his hands away and the salt and pepper goatee was once again exposed. 'Nick.' Billy said. 'No one understands your losses more than me. You know that's true. But this . . . man, well, these aren't your kids man. Nothing you do here and now is gonna repair your relationship with your own children. Nothing good can come from this . . . not where you're concerned anyway.'

'Billy. I guess what I'm saying is that it doesn't matter. If I don't step in, what happens here? Some punk fucking dope peddler offs a couple of innocent kids in the wrong place at the wrong time? Fuck him.'

'If you're doing this Nick, I'm sorry, but you're going it alone.'

'It's the only way I'll have it this time Billy.' McNulty

said. He heard a throat clear at the doorway and looked up to see Penny standing there. She had changed into the clean clothes McNulty gave her and washed her face and hands. She still looked tired and scared but she was at least a little more calm and appeared fresher than before. 'So . . . will you help me after all? At least to get my brother back safe?' She asked.

McNulty gave Billy one final look. He turned to Penny and answered, 'On one condition. You sit your ass down right now and tell me every last detail of what's going on. You don't want to go the cops, but you want my help, then I need to know every fucking angle here. Deal?' He asked.

Penny stepped onto the porch and took a seat in an oversized rocking chair with chipped white paint. 'Okay. Deal.' She said.

LIAM MAGUIRE

Liam could see shadows slightly through the hood that was aggressively draped over his head once the three men got him into the large SUV. He could feel his whole body shaking and could hear his teeth chattering. He tried to get control of his breathing, but it was difficult under that thick linen hood. The shaking he guessed was his body coming down off an adrenaline rush. Either that or it was just plain old fear. He was afraid, he knew that. He wasn't ashamed of it. He'd just had the first fight of his life and lost, not to mention his first gun fight. His fear wasn't for his own immediate safety however, he was worried most about Penny. She ran and seemed to have gotten away. 'But for how long?' He thought 'surely they're going after her.' The truck started moving almost before he even hit the leather seat. They drove for a short distance then stopped for a couple minutes. The men kept their mouths shut for the most part while inside the vehicle so it was difficult to tell how many were now with him. He knew there was at least two men, but it was impossible to distinguish if they were the same two people from before. After the brief initial stop the truck had been moving nonstop for what felt like hours though Liam knew he couldn't trust his perception of time while draped in a hood with his wrists tied behind his back. Realistically it could have been ten minutes or two hours, he couldn't tell the difference. However, he was nearly certain that they had driven through Boston. That was a guess based on the smell of the sea reaching him from someone's opened window followed by sounds of a city and the echo of a tunnel. 'That was a while ago.' He thought. More recently

491

there were very few sounds at all. It also seemed to get significantly darker and he could no longer see anything but black from behind the linen. The only scent from outside was the occasional waft of burning wood coming either from a fireplace or camp fire. Eventually, he felt the vehicle slow down and he began to notice several turns. He imagined they were off whatever highway they'd been on for a long time and were now weaving through back roads.

'We must be close' he thought, 'but close to what?' There was very little exchange of conversation throughout the journey and the driver seemed to know exactly where he was heading. At one point the radio was switched on but it was switched off immediately afterwards. He assumed that was a mistake by someone, since as soon as he heard the radio, he was listening for an indication of where they were. 'We could be anywhere in New England by now.' He thought. Finally, the car slowed dramatically and then came to a complete stop. For most of the journey all he wanted was for the car to stop. He was dizzy and kept thinking he'd be sick. Now that the car actually did stop, he found himself suddenly more afraid than he had been. He wasn't sure what to expect next. 'Am I a dead man or not?' He considered. He thought he likely was but emotionally, he wasn't able to accept that yet.

He heard muffled voices outside and guessed that wherever they were now, they were being greeted by people that were waiting for them 'or me?' He considered. He heard a clicking noise and felt a cold breeze sweep through the vehicle and knew the door was open. Again, he caught the scent of campfire, this time along with the sound of water in the distance. 'We're in the woods somewhere' he thought. Someone reached in and grabbed his arms. He put weight onto his feet and stood up slowly, then was pulled roughly forward so that he stumbled out and fell from the truck. He landed heavily on his feet and heard the crunch of branches underneath him. Another stronger set of hands grabbed the back of his other arm and quickly walked him forward. After a few yards his arm was pulled upwards and his foot tripped over a small staircase. He managed to stay standing again and quickly crossed over a threshold. The floor beneath him was solid tiling. He knew he was inside from the flooring and because of the change in temperature. Also, he could see a change in coloring through the linen hood as the lighting improved. 'Where am I taking this kid?' someone asked.

'Take him up to the third floor next to the rec room. Get him comfortable, he'll be here a while.'

'Yup' he heard. 'Going up junior.' Next he was dragged up several flights of stairs. At the top they reached a landing. He could hear a television in the background and it sounded like Sportscenter was on. At the top floor, he heard the creak of another door open and he was finally pulled into another room. This room was darker again and much colder than the rest of the house. He began shivering from the cold. His nerves were shot and this marching around blindly did nothing to put him at ease. The heavy arms that pulled him finally stopped. He stood waiting, for what, he didn't know. Someone grabbed the strings of the hood suddenly and he felt them close tightly around his neck. 'This is it' he thought 'the end.' A second later, the strings loosened and the hood was pulled sharply away from his face. The shock made his knees weak and he nearly crumbled. With the hood away, he saw only blur for a few seconds until his eyes focused. As they did, he heard the flick of a knife open and the ties around his wrist were cut loose, which caught him off guard. When his hands were free, he shook them by his sides and could feel them begin warming as the blood rushed to them. A large hand shoved him in the chest and he landed against a small chair. The chair was low to the ground, it was old and uncomfortable with springs coming up from the cushion on the seat. The man that had shoved him down pulled a wooden chair closer to his own, scraping it across the floor loudly. He took a seat in front of Liam. He was older, Liam guessed in his forties or fifties. His hair was greying in most places and he had a moustache. He wore dark jeans and a leather vest over a t-shirt. The vest had an emblem emblazoned over the heart, Liam couldn't really make it out in the dark. The man had tattoos lining both forearms. Liam sat there and said nothing. He was afraid to move, he thought this might be the end. He had seen this man's face, 'that couldn't be good' he thought 'they probably won't let me walk out of here.'

'Relax junior.' The man said. 'I've been paid to watch you, not to hurt you, so just settle down.' The man got up and walked over to a small lamp near the seat where Liam sat and switched it on. Then he sat back down in the wooden chair and pulled a rolled up magazine from his back pocket and flipped it open to the center.

Liam looked at him. He was confused and didn't know what he was supposed to do. After a minute, he gathered the courage to speak up. He cleared his throat first. 'Excuse me.' He said. The man looked up from his magazine with a raised eyebrow to show he was listening, but didn't say anything. 'So . . . I'm just supposed to sit here and wait?' He asked.

The man rolled the magazine back up but kept his finger in the center to keep his page. He sat back and breathed in before responding. 'Well, you could try to run.' He said. 'But, that would change our peaceful arrangement. You see, I was paid to watch you and to keep you here . . . the latter of which I would have to do by any means necessary. You understand what I'm saying?'

Liam nodded slowly. 'Yes, I understand.'

'Anymore questions?' the man asked. Liam just shook his head 'No.' 'Good.' The man said. He opened his magazine once again and continued reading.

MCNULTY

There was a bottle of Jameson whiskey that McNulty kept sitting in the center of his small kitchen table. It was an older vintage, and he'd had it for a number of years, however it remained unopened. Most alcoholics would be crazy to do such a thing, to keep booze in their constant line of sight, taunting them every second of the day. McNulty was always just a little bit crazy anyway. He kept the bottle out in the open. Even if he did have it sitting in a shelf hidden behind some canned soup, it didn't matter. Wherever it was placed on his shelf it would eat away at his mind. Not having it at all was just the same, he was fooling himself if he thought out of sight – out of mind meant a Goddamn thing to an addict. That's the point of it all, no matter how far out of sight, it's never out of mind or out of reach. Having it sitting in front of him was a test. It was a test he forced himself to take each day. McNulty didn't want his past or his demons out of sight. He needed to confront them each morning with his coffee and cereal and either overcome them each day or succumb to their pull one final time.

He stood staring at the bottle in the kitchen in the early morning hours. He slept poorly after his long talk with Penny. He felt a bead of cold sweat on his forehead and wiped it with the back of his arm. The last time he felt cold sweat across his forehead was just prior to the episode in the gym where his legs gave out forcing him to sit motionless for twenty minutes. He grew nervous thinking that another period of paralysis was on the horizon. He poured himself a glass of water from the faucet and took a seat at the table. He waited out the dizzy spell in his chair

496

and within five minutes it had passed. He cursed his body once again, angry that it was no longer the consistent high performance vehicle it had always been.

He had made Penny a bed on the couch, giving her blankets and a pillow from his closet that he didn't even know he had. Visitors, especially of the overnight variety, were a rarity. Penny had hoped he would rush out there that very night and burn the city down looking for her brother but he persuaded her otherwise for the moment. He knew Bishop's type. He was violent but he wasn't flat out crazy. Also, after everything that Penny told McNulty about her situation, which was all of it, he was certain that Bishop would not get rid of the kid until he used him to get the girl too. If he killed Liam right away, Penny would just get spooked and likely turn to the cops immediately. Personally, McNulty thought the cops were her best option anyway. She did not agree on this subject and again refused to entertain the idea. McNulty said at the very least he'd need a few hours to think about options. It was thinking about options that had him up all night and out of bed before the sun rose. Based on what the girl told him, she was doomed. She was flat out dead as soon as Bishop could track her down, which he imagined would be pretty quickly. The kid, Liam was his name, he was dead too as soon as Bishop could manage to get the girl. McNulty knew that for certain. 'No . . . he's not crazy' McNulty thought, 'he'd be crazy to let either of them walk away now if he wanted to get away with it.' Except for the drugs, Bishop's line of business was McNulty's line of business, and in that business, one did not last long by leaving loose ends. If Bishop's intention was to continue functioning outside of a cage, then both Maguire siblings had to go, along with anyone else that dared step in his way.

Stepping in Bishop's way was what McNulty was considering. He wrestled with the notion for hours. Billy Carson was right, this was not his fight in the slightest. A smarter man would walk away. A smarter man would put that girl out on the street, give her a couple bucks and let her run on her own knowing damn well she'd be caught and fed to the dogs within twenty-four hours. That's pretty much what Billy had advocated, though not in those words. Billy thought she still had a chance to go to the cops. McNulty understood the weight that Bishop had in Dorchester and Quincy, so he assumed the girl was probably close to the truth about him having one or two cops in his pocket. He guessed she'd only last slightly longer than twenty-four hours after going to them. He knew he couldn't just turn her away. 'Nope' he thought, 'can't let Bishop close the deal on these kids.' He knew he was about to go to war. The chance of Bishop being talked out of anything was unlikely. He felt he had to try anyway. He'd go to Bishop and talk. It would be quick. He'd put his own reputation on the line and just maybe Bishop would give them a pass. It was a remote chance, but he'd take it anyway.

He tapped his toes under the table and reassured himself that his legs were back. Penny walked into the kitchen. Her hair was pulled back tightly and she wore the jeans and t-shirt McNulty had given her the night before. They were slightly baggy and hung off her skinny frame in some places. She pulled a chair out across from McNulty and slid into the seat. 'Morning' she said quietly.

McNulty nodded, 'Morning kid.'

'So . . . did you decide what you're going to do?' She asked.

'Yeah.' McNulty answered. 'I did.'

'Well?' She said.

McNulty stared at Penny for a moment. Her sense of urgency, he could understand. However, her attitude towards him was troubling. 'You forget I'm the one doing the favor?' He asked. He watched her breathe in sharply and her eyes widen suddenly with surprise. He felt bad for saying it immediately after. 'She's a kid' he thought. 'Just a scared kid.'

Her voice was higher when she responded. 'I know.' She said. 'I'm sorry . . . I just . . . I'm afraid they'll do something to Liam. And . . . it's all my fault.' Her eyes began to well up with tears and her nose started running.

McNulty leaned towards her and gently placed his large hand on her forearm. 'Hey. You're upset kid, I'm sorry I said anything. Don't worry, we'll get your brother back.'

She wiped her eyes with her hands and dragged her forearm across her nose. 'You think you can? You think he's still . . . okay?'

McNulty nodded, forcing outward confidence to reassure her. He was pretty confident the kid was still alive, but for how long was the question. 'I think he's okay for now, but it's time to act. I don't think we should wait any longer. Bishop wants you, so he'll hang on to Liam to try and lure you to him. After a while though, well . . . who knows. But we're gonna do what we can to get this done fast.'

'So . . . what then? Are you gonna like, set a trap? Use me as bait?'

McNulty shook his head. 'Too dangerous kid, we need

to keep you out of sight.' He reached into his pocket and handed her a cell phone. She took it and stared at it, not sure what to make of it. 'What's this?' She asked.

'It's a throwaway cell.' He slid a piece of paper across the table. 'Program my number in. I'd have done it, but my thumbs are too damn big.'

Penny took the paper from him and started typing into the phone. McNulty watched the smallest hint of a smile form on her face. 'That's funny huh?'

'Huh?' She said. 'Oh I was laughing at something else. I put your number in under the name Porthos.'

McNulty looked at her sideways, unsure of what she meant.

'Forget it.' She said.

'Yeah okay. Alright. Next I need you to wait for me in the basement downstairs. I'll show you the way. I have a . . . workshop down there.'

'Sounds creepy. That where you store the bodies or something?'

'What? Shit, no kid. Just listen to me. It's the most secure place I can think of on short notice. No one has access to it. Only people with keys are me and Billy.'

'Okay. What about Billy? Is he gone?'

'Yeah kid, he's not involved with this. The less involved the better.'

'He . . . ah, didn't like me, did he?'

'It's not you kid don't worry about it.'

'I know who he is . . . who his son was too. I know my cousin set him up and got him killed.'

McNulty shrugged. 'You ain't your cousin though. He knows that too, so don't worry about him. I'm gonna take care of this. Billy's due to sit one out.'

'Okay' she said. 'So what's our plan then?'

'My plan you mean, well first thing's first. I'm gonna go see Bishop.'

'What!' she yelled and stood up quickly. The chair toppled behind her when she jumped up.

McNulty held a hand up to calm her. 'I think you need to relax kid. This ain't my first sleigh ride.'

'But . . . you can't reason with this guy. I'm telling you, he's not that type of guy.'

'Sit your ass down.' McNulty said sternly. Penny obeyed. She picked the chair back up off the floor and sat down in a huff. 'So what did you expect kid huh? You want me to kill him. You want that on your conscience?'

'No . . . I just . . . I want my brother back whatever it takes. Then, I don't know, we can run.'

McNulty smiled and slowly nodded his head. 'Right. But, first I talk to Bishop. I have a certain . . . reputation. This reputation can sometimes open doors for me that close quickly for others. Sometimes it even makes unreasonable men see reason. You get me?'

Penny nodded her head 'yes'. 'And, if talking doesn't work though. What if that doesn't work? Then what?'

'That's why I need you to stay in that basement and be ready for me. Have that phone next to you at all times no matter what.'

'Okay' she said. 'I will. Is that when we run?'

McNulty shook his head. 'Kid, one thing you should know about me, I might dodge from time to time, but I do not fucking run.'

'So where does that leave me? If your little conversation goes to shit, what are you gonna do then?'

'Then, I'm gonna rattle his cage ya know. Let him

know I'm serious.'

'How?'

'Only way I know how, brute fucking force. Now get down to the Goddamn basement.'

JOHN BISHOP

Bishop sat up at the edge of the bed. The sun cut across the room through the loose curtain and scantily closed blinds. Dust molecules played bumper cars in the orange rays. He reached down to the floor and picked up his jeans that lay at the foot of the bed. He pulled them on quickly, then reached for the t-shirt next to them. He stood up and stretched, then pulled the t-shirt over his head. He ran his hands through his hair afterwards to straighten it out. He licked the tips of his fingers and used the moisture to pat his cowlick down. He heard a stirring in the bed and looked over to watch the body under the sheets shift. Curly blond hair sprouted from the top of the sheet and he could see every curve of her body clearly through the thin cotton. He reached into his pocket and pulled out a fifty. 'Hey' he said loudly. A woman's face peeked out, followed by her bare shoulders. She held the top of the sheet against her breasts, so that only her cleavage showed, no further. Bishop wondered at her attempt to appear bashful, 'too late for that shit' he thought. 'It's early.' She said.

'Yeah, it is.' Bishop said and lofted the folded fifty at her thighs. 'Here, I have shit going on today. Doyle will call you a cab.'

'What's the rush? Let me stay awhile.'

'Did I stutter?' He said 'You have five fucking minutes to get lost.' He watched her climb out of the bed in a huff. She dropped the sheet and stood bare in front of him. She found her skirt on the floor and pulled it up over her thighs quickly. She threw her shirt over her head without bothering with a bra, which she stuffed into a small pocket book along with her panties. 'You're a fucking asshole John.' She said, then stormed out of the room.

'Yeah what else is new?' Bishop said to himself. He sat back down at the corner of the bed and found his socks, then pulled on his boots. He brushed his teeth next and waited another ten minutes until he was sure a taxi pulled up outside then left. When she was gone, he headed downstairs to the barroom. The bar was dark since the heavy door was shut and curtains were pulled. Mike Doyle sat at the bar reading the newspaper under a corner lamp and drinking a coffee. Bishop walked towards him and yelled, 'want to get some fucking light in here Doyle, it feels like a dungeon.'

'We ain't open for hours. I don't usually open the doors and blinds till at least twelve.'

'Yeah, well make an exception this once. It looks like you're about to raise the dead in here.'

'Alright, alright.' He said.

'Anything in the paper?' Bishop asked.

'Nah, no mention of the gun shots which is surprising.'

'It was only two I guess and it's across from the train station. The noise from the trains could've drowned it out.'

'Lucky for us.'

'Yeah, I guess. Though I wouldn't say we're lucky yet. That broad's still out there talking to God knows who.'

'What's the plan anyway? Where you want to start looking?'

'I need all hands on deck. I want eyes on every fucking ATM and coffee shop in Dorchester and Quincy.'

'That's gonna be tough to manage John. We're shorthanded remember?'

'I know that. Do what you can. Focus on the big spots. At least cover the train stations. Have eyes on Wolly T, North Quincy and Ashmont. Those are the closest. There's too many cops at Quincy Center. Plus something tells me she'll head towards Downtown, maybe try to cut town through South Station.'

'Got those spots covered already since last night. She hasn't surfaced yet. Plus I put a call in to Sullivan. He walks the Hancock Street beat through Quincy Center anyway, he'll call if there's anyone matching her description.'

'Good.' Bishop said. 'Keep on him. Reach out to our guys in BPD too. I want radar from Savin Hill to JFK.'

'Call's in. Waiting on confirmation.' Doyle answered. 'What about the kid? What do you want do with him? Mick's out there still. He's got five Tooth & Nail heads on the clock. They don't come cheap though.'

'Good. Keep Mick and the watch crew there. The kid's bait, we need him healthy and happy for the time being. Money's not an issue at the minute. Finding this fucking cunt is priority one.'

Doyle nodded. 'Got it.'

Bishop folded up the newspaper from the bar. He poured himself a cup of coffee from the pot that sat behind the bar. Keep an eye out front here. I gotta make a few calls in the office.

'No problem.' Doyle said. 'Let me know if you need something.'

'Thanks Mike.' Bishop said. He walked to the back of the bar and over to a green door that was camouflaged by the lack of light. He opened the office using his key and kept the door ajar behind him. He dropped the paper onto his desk and sat down in his chair and sipped his coffee. The office had a wall lined with CCTV screens linked to a number of cameras in the barroom and behind the bar pointed at the register. There were also screens lining both directions out front from the corner to the width of the shop front. On one screen, he watched Mike Doyle opening up the curtains of the two small windows on each wall of the bar. He watched him unhinge the large latch and pull the heavy security door open so that light and air from the outside entered the bar through a swinging set of doors. They were old and thick wood, heavy with layers of stain. They looked antique, ripped from the old west.

Bishop smiled thinking of the doors and how aptly they epitomized his pub's throwback to the lawless west. He took a final look at the screens, which showed very little movement outside, then dug his nose into the newspaper. He looked away long enough to miss a large frame pass by the outside camera. It wasn't until he heard muffled voices out front that he paused briefly, then frantically began checking the monitors. 'Who the fuck is Mike talking to?' He thought. 'No way we have visitors at this hour.' He found Doyle on one of the screens, though his figure was almost completely eclipsed by a square set of shoulders and their accompanied shadow. Bishop leaned closer to the small TV screen. He watched the man closely. Even from the back, he could sense the man's attitude by the way his body and head moved when he spoke. It was a black and white screen, but the quality was better than average, so he could make out the shape of the man fairly well. He looked to have white or almost silver hair with large shoulders and arms covered by a close cut leather jacket. Bishop's mind started making leaps trying to piece together who the visitor was and what he wanted. He was not a believer in coincidence, the visitor could only be connected with his current situation. And, considering the man wasn't immediately familiar, he was confident the guy wasn't a friendly. He watched for a few seconds as the man exchanged words with Doyle. Doyle seemed dismissive at first, but Bishop could read from his body language that the conversation was escalating. He saw Doyle visibly tense up and shift his stance to one that indicated the onset of violence. Outside, the murmured voices grew louder and clearer with every passing second. 'Fuck' Bishop muttered to himself. He stopped watching the screens and walked out of the office and back into the bar area. He shut the door behind him loud enough to warn the two men of his presence. Bishop thought the air itself felt thick with tension and could sense the conversation had indeed ratcheted up several notches. He saw Doyle look past the man and over to him. Bishop nodded and held up his hand briefly to try and calm his . . . friend. In front of Bishop was the broadest set of shoulders he'd ever laid eyes on. He guessed the man was nearly as tall laying on his side as his was standing upright. Bishop could see his eyes had been right, the man's hair was silver and his jacket was a thick leather that looked well-oiled and tough, like walrus skin.

The man didn't turn right away. His gaze remained on Doyle for close to a minute. Bishop slowed his steps and kept a safe distance behind, unwillingly to get within reach until he had a better idea of what he was dealing with. Slowly the man's boots shifted and his foot pivoted. He slid his left foot around so that both feet faced the door. That way he could keep both Bishop and Doyle in his sight line as needed. Bishop smiled when he saw the stance the man took 'a pro' he thought 'smart enough to keep his back to something solid and keep any threats in front of him.' Bishop continued towards the man slowly and began to raise his hand in greeting. He made eye contact with the man as he did. 'There's something familiar about this guy' he thought.

When he was a stretched arm's length away he said. 'I'm John.' The man held his own hand out slowly and took Bishop's. They shook briefly, keeping eye contact. 'McNulty.' The man replied. Bishop paused then for a moment before pulling away from the shake. 'McNulty . . . huh.' He thought. 'I know that name.' He said and smiled.

McNulty shrugged and gave a small smile. 'Yeah.' He said. 'I'm old. When you're around as long as me, your name starts to linger around town.'

'I guess that's one way to put it.' Bishop said.

'You're John Bishop?' McNulty asked.

Bishop nodded his head yes. McNulty continued, 'You're man here seems a little jumpy. All I did was ask if you were in. Seems he took offense.'

'He's paid to take offense.' Bishop said. 'I guess you could say I get my fair amount of unsolicited guests.'

'Only thing worse than unsolicited guests is unsolicited advice.'

'Ha . . . yet here you are one and surely to dish out the other.' Bishop thought. He made a hand motion towards the back. 'Now that we're acquainted, why don't we let Mike here get back to work and you join me in my office.'

McNulty nodded. 'Sounds good.' He said.

'You want coffee?'

McNulty nodded again. 'Thanks' he said 'Just black.'

Bishop yelled over to Doyle, 'Make a pot and bring two back Mike would ya?' Then he turned and walked towards the office. He reached out and pulled the door open and let McNulty in before him. 'Grab a seat.'

'Thanks' McNulty said. He took a seat in front of a wooden desk. Bishop walked around the desk to the other side and sat across from McNulty. He watched McNulty as his eyes scanned the office, he focused on the walls, which were bare for the most part except for one picture hanging on it of a younger Bishop and some friends, including Brian Dawson and Mike Doyle. They were posing next to a fire pit with the lake in the background. It was Bishop's favorite memory and the one human element 'or weakness' he thought, that he let into his place of work. McNulty's gaze lingered on the photo for a few moments, then scanned further, next pausing for a few seconds on the CCTV screens lining the wall. He saw McNulty's face crease into a small smile. 'Nice setup. You got your eye on things I take it.' McNulty said.

'In my line of work, I find it pays to have a pretty good watch over what's going on around me.'

McNulty nodded. He turned his head and looked at Bishop finally. 'And what line of work are you referring to . . . the pub trade?'

Bishop smiled and shrugged with his palms facing upwards.

'No . . . you're talking about one of your more lucrative lines of business I'm sure. When I played hockey we used to call it keeping your head on a swivel.'

'I'm pretty sure they still call it that.'

'Made sense, don't see why they'd stop. You play?'

'What . . . hockey? Yeah. Well, I played past tense that is.'

McNulty smiled. 'High school?'

'Yeah. North Quincy. Then a little college before I dropped out. What about you? You play North Quincy back in the day?'

'I'm from Dot.'

'That's right, sorry I forgot. Where'd you play then . . . Don Bosco, BC High? If you're from Dorchester I'm guessing you weren't in public school.'

'Ha' McNulty said and slapped a heavy hand on the desk. 'Good guess. Catholic Memorial.'

'I knew it.' Bishop said. 'Still skate?'

'Not in thirty years.'

Bishop nodded. 'Fifteen for me.' He said. He watched McNulty's face for signs of deceit but so far found none. He knew the old man was likely feeling him out a bit, maybe trying to make him more comfortable, get his guard down or something, like they're just two old friends shooting the breeze. 'It almost worked' he thought to himself. He really was starting to relax reminiscing about the old days, before the years took hold and did their dirty work. He noticed his leg was dancing since he sat down and shifted his feet to settle them. He pulled his chair in tighter to his desk and put his hand on the desk top. His gun rested just under his hand in the top drawer of the desk. When he thought of it, he felt a warm comfort float through him. Its presence so close to his hand gave him confidence and a feeling of safety. 'So . . . McNulty. Do I call you McNulty?'

'Everybody else does, you might as well.'

'I'm guessing you didn't stop by my place here for a chat about the neighborhood. Am I right?' Bishop watched him as McNulty paused before responding. Just before he did he heard a knock on the door and Mike Doyle walked in carrying two cups of coffee. He placed one in front of each man. Bishop watched McNulty nod at Doyle to thank him. 'Thanks Mike.' Bishop said. Doyle shrugged and headed out. 'Oh Mike!' Bishop yelled to him 'You hear back from Sully? He's supposed to send a couple guys by to help you with that thing' he said. Doyle looked at him questioningly for a moment. Bishop kept eye contact with Doyle, hoping that he'd get the message, which was 'get a couple guys over to follow this McNulty character from the moment he leaves here'. Doyle answered after a few seconds. 'I'll call him again now.'

'Thanks Mike' Bishop said then focused his attention back on McNulty. He watched McNulty take a tender sip of the hot coffee. McNulty raised his eyebrows at Bishop as he took a sip. 'Good coffee John. Thanks.' He said, then put the cup down on the desk. 'I think you were about to ask me something?'

Bishop followed his hand as McNulty put the cup down. The question brought his focus back. 'Yeah. Yes I was about to. Listen, it's been nice talking to you and everything . . .'

McNulty held a hand up to stop him 'but why the fuck am I here, right?'

'Well . . . yeah. Do we have business of some sort that I'm not aware of?'

'You and me? No. We don't have any business together. Unlike you, I don't deal in poison powders.'

The remark came out sharp and stopped Bishop in his tracks for a second. He felt his blood warm and an irritating shiver ran up his spine to the back of his neck. In an instant, McNulty's tone went from congenial to something completely different. 'To something hostile' Bishop thought. 'That's right' Bishop replied. 'You deal in bones and blood only. That's much more cosmopolitan.'

'Only when it pays to do so young blood.'

'Alright then old man. Since we're done with the niceties, what the fuck are you doing here?'

'I have a favor to ask you that's all.'

'You have a twisted fucking method of asking favors from people.'

'Okay don't call it a favor then. Consider it a suggestion.'

'And what's that then? What are you suggesting?'

'I want you to leave the Maguire siblings alone. Cut the kid loose and let the girl walk free.'

Bishop laughed out loud. 'Who are the Maguire siblings? Can't say I've heard of them.'

'Yeah okay Bishop. Fucking hear me again. Cut him loose and call the dogs off the girl. You have my word nothing's gonna blow back on you.'

'Oh, I have your word do I? That makes it all good then. I'm thinking your time here is up McNulty. Why don't you see yourself out?' Bishop said and stood up from his chair. He walked to the side of the desk and motioned towards the door with an open palm. He kept his distance from McNulty's reach however.

'I'm putting my word and my reputation on this. I'd like you to give it serious consideration. No one's going to the cops, no one's saying shit about anything to anyone as long as you hand me back Liam Maguire. Where is he anyway, can I see him?'

'Go fuck yourself McNulty. The kid's gone and you need to get gone now too.'

McNulty stood up and tucked his chair closer to the desk. He adjusted his leather jacket roughly when he straightened out and took a step closer to Bishop halving their distance. 'Last chance?' He said tilting his head and raising his eyebrows.

'Go' Bishop said and pointed this time with his index finger towards the door.

McNulty tapped two fingers against his forehead in mock salute and turned towards the door.

Before he walked out, Bishop watched him take a couple steps then called to him 'McNulty!' he yelled.

McNulty paused and turned back towards him 'Yeah?'

'You've been in this game a long time. You know what it takes to last. You think I'd last much longer if I started handing out free passes. I wouldn't make it through the night and you know it. I'll be Goddamned if you ever gave a pass like that, hard man like yourself.'

McNulty pursed his bottom lip upwards into a frown and squinted his eyes so that crow's feet formed in the corners 'Maybe not John. But all that means is you gave up your one chance to be a better man than I. That ain't saying much if you ask me.'

Bishop's anger kept rising. McNulty's words cut him and he was indignant because of it. 'This tough guy waltzes into my office and thinks he can guilt me into submission. The pool I swim in is full of sharks. One sign of weakness and I'm fucking dinner.' He thought.

'Who are the Maguire's to you anyway?' Bishop asked.

'Nobody special. I'm just a concerned citizen that's all. Be seeing you real soon John.'

'Fuck you McNulty. Not if I see you first.' McNulty left the office then and continued out through the barroom and towards the light coming through the swinging doors. Bishop walked a half dozen steps behind him. He was braced for any sudden jerk or movement from the older man. He never expected him to walk out without a fight. When he did, he cursed himself for letting him leave so easily. He walked quickly up to the bar where Mike Doyle stood leaning against it just watching. 'You have eyes on this fucking asshole?'

Doyle nodded. 'A CI that Sully's connected to, plus a freelancer. Told 'em to stay close and stay connected, that we'd be shortly behind them. Any attempt to pick up the girl, I gave them the okay to act.'

'Good. This fucking guy has that bitch with him or hidden somewhere I know it. Wonder who the hell he is to them? Any idea?'

'None. Don't know who the fuck that guy is.'

'What?' Bishop said. He took a step closer to Mike Doyle and said in a lower voice 'That's Nick McNulty. He's a legend around these parts. He's getting old, but take my word for it, he's dangerous and he's a fucking problem.'

'Yeah okay. What's another one?' Doyle muttered. 'How you want to handle him then.'

'Just keep eyes on him. I want to see where he goes. He's got the girl, I know it. But, he ain't stupid. He's been around too long for that. If he leads us to her without any tricks I'll eat my fucking hat.'

'We'll see.' Doyle said.

'Yeah Mike. We'll see. I'm sure of it.'

MCNULTY

The daylight was in stark contrast to the barroom's dim interior. The change in lighting blinded McNulty momentarily. He knew walking in that reasoning with Bishop was a dead end, but he knew his reputation would at least get him an audience with the man before Bishop pieced together his motive. That's exactly what he wanted. He needed to know what buttons to push. Now he knew. Also, he knew for certain that Liam Maguire wasn't being held locally. Bishop had a coolness about him that McNulty didn't expect, but then when McNulty caught a glimpse of the photo hung on the wall, the only personal item in the entire building, he knew. The shot was of Lake Winnipesaukee. McNulty knew the area well enough, plus it made sense based on the information Penny gave him. Bishop had Liam Maguire held out of town, out at the lake, it was close to a certainty. It made sense since it bought him time and leverage, especially if he assumed that Penny would surface looking for her brother before she ended up in a police station, which was correct.

The other thing McNulty knew walking out was that Bishop was smart enough and concerned enough to fly under the radar in his own backyard and that he was too tough and too confident to be threatened by words alone. As he walked back to his sedan, McNulty decided he'd try and make an impact on both things in one fell swoop. He pulled the keys from his jeans pocket and quickly scanned the streets around him. It was still early enough in the morning that not many people roamed the streets. He popped the trunk on his walk to the car and watched it open and slowly rise on its own. He walked around the car to the trunk and reached into it. Inside was a small duffle bag. Before he left, McNulty had thrown in a few tricks of the trade. He opened the bag and pulled out a nine millimeter handgun. He kept it low in the trunk as he looked at it for a moment letting his thoughts kick around which action was appropriate. He thought back to the night before. Penny had described to him exactly what she saw. It didn't spook him, but it raised his awareness about what type of man Bishop was. She watched Bishop put a gun to a man's head and pull the trigger without a second thought. That man was Bishop's friend. He then turned and gunned down a young girl, a frightened and hysterical young girl that just watched her man's head explode. 'This man understands force' he thought 'and pain . . . but not much else.' After a few seconds, he put the gun down and reached deeper into the duffle bag. When his hand came out, he held in it one of the homemade pipe bombs he had taken from his safe. He held it tight and reached up with his other arm and pulled the trunk down. He saw his own reflection in the black paint. There was no coming back from what he was about to do. 'If this is war, here's my declaration.' He thought. He walked quickly back the few yards to the front door. On his walk back, he noticed a couple of men huddled in a truck in his periphery. 'Back up's here.' He thought. 'They must have called in reinforcements or maybe they're the tail. Fuck em.' He picked up his pace towards the same swinging doors he'd just walked out from. When he was a few feet away, he didn't hustle inside. He walked up close to the small camera outside the door that fed into Bishop's CCTV screens in his office. He smiled into the camera. Then he held the pipe bomb up to the camera real close for a couple seconds gripping it tightly in his large hand. He pulled his hand away, then jammed his other hand up close to the lens with his middle finger raised. He pulled a lighter from his pocket and lit the fuse. He watched it for a second, letting the fuse burn down. Next he took a step back and threw the explosive through the small front window. He watched it bust through the glass, then turned and jogged in the direction of his car. In his first couple of steps he could still hear the glass bouncing off the floor through the other side. He braced himself a second later, throwing his arms over his head. The blast blew out the front of the bar below the window. Wood and concrete rubble rolled across the sidewalk to the street and several car alarms erupted in unison.

McNulty sped up his jog towards his car. In seconds, he was in the driver's seat turning the ignition. 'Let's see what this Taurus can do.' He said to himself. He pulled the gearstick to drive and stomped on the gas pedal. He turned quickly down the next side street, then quickly again, so that he headed towards the main street, Newport Avenue. Without hesitation he shot out to the main street with a sharp left turn heading north towards Boston. He kept his foot almost to the floor for a quarter mile, then eased off it as he drove through a business district. He needed to move fast, but knew he had to do so without getting the cops after him. He saw cop cars and a fire engine roar past him in the other direction towards the small explosion. He could see the flashing lights and hear the sirens, but the sounds were somewhat muffled by the ringing in his ears. He kept an eye on his rearview mirror for signs of a tail, which he picked up within a minute. He saw the truck that was parked out front of the bar weaving through traffic behind him. He watched it gain ground for about a minute, then level off when it was one or two cars behind him. His aim was to create a sense of urgency with Bishop and put him on the defensive. Time would tell if it worked. Just before the bridge leading to Dorchester, McNulty hit a red light. He would've ran it if he could've made past the cars in front of him. He tapped the steering wheel with his index finger as he considered his next move. 'I need to shake these assholes' he thought. He peered into the rearview mirror, considering what to do. He could see the driver and passenger clearly. The driver looked tough and old enough to have some experience. However, the guy in the passenger seat looked more nervous than anything else. He figured Bishop and his other lackey weren't far behind. 'Better to take on two now instead of four later.' He thought. When the light turned green he started moving forward, then swung off quickly into a condominium parking lot. He drove into the lot and kept the car in drive with his foot on the brake while he watched the traffic pass behind him in the rearview mirror. A few seconds later he saw the truck that followed him pull into the lot and stop, leaving about fifteen feet between his car and theirs. No one moved for about thirty seconds. McNulty didn't blink. He kept his eyes glued to the rearview mirror. He could see the two men in the truck. He could tell they were talking and that the older guy was animated about something. The argument must've ended when the driver pulled rank and motioned for the man in the passenger seat to get out. He stepped out of the car and slowly started walking towards McNulty's. McNulty put the car in park, then his hand reached over and opened the glove compartment. He picked up his loaded revolver and put it in his other hand, held low against his thigh. He reached his right hand down under the seat and slid out a small crowbar. He gripped the cold steel in his hand and continued to watch the man walking towards him. The man's steps were tentative, but he was next to the trunk in a few seconds. McNulty's eyes moved from the rearview mirror to the side mirror. He could see the man's torso clearly and his hands. The man looked to be unarmed, at least for the moment. He hit the window button once and let it roll all the way down. When it was lowered he could hear the man's feet scrape the salted pavement right next to him. McNulty waited and took in a deep breath. He saw the man's shadow shift as his hands reached down towards the driver's side window. McNulty exhaled slowly. As soon as the man's hands leaned on the door, McNulty unleashed the steel bar on top of his fingers. The man shouted in pain and stumbled several feet back. McNulty pushed the door open and jumped out quickly. He saw the driver charge around the front of the car towards him so he raised his revolver with his left hand and the man paused in his tracks. The man he'd hit regained his footing and charged McNulty wildly. McNulty kept his gun trained on the driver and let out a kick that landed directly to the man's abdomen. The man fell to the ground and McNulty raised the crowbar. He saw fear in the man's face and paused. 'Please . . .' the man asked sniffling. 'Go!' McNulty barked at him. He watched the man struggle to get up, then take off running in the other direction.

He focused his attention solely on the driver and walked

a few steps closer to the man. 'You think this ends well?' the man asked.

'For me or for you?'

The man shrugged, 'Either I guess.'

'We'll see' McNulty said. He took a step to the right for a better angle then fired two shots into each of the tires on that side of the truck. 'You got a phone?' He asked. The man put a hand up and slowly pulled a phone from his pocket. 'Toss it here.' He said. The man lobbed the phone towards McNulty. It landed a foot in front of him. He took one step forward then stomped it with his boot. The phone crunched but still looked functional. McNulty smiled and looked up at the man. 'Tough mothafucker.' The man smiled back and shrugged. McNulty pointed the gun at it and fired. He pointed it back at the man. He felt the weight of the gun change. Only one bullet remained. 'You can take off now.'

'Close call' the man said looking at the gun.

McNulty smiled. 'I've got more.'

'Bullets?'

'Guns. Now fuck off.'

The man nodded and began walking up the street. Urgency grew in McNulty's gut again as he waited for the man to put distance between them, his steps were agonizingly slow. After a minute, McNulty gave up and jumped back into the car and burned out of the parking lot. He drove over the Neponset Bridge towards Dorchester and got caught at the lights at the split for the highway. He pulled his cell phone from his jacket pocket and hit speed dial one and put the phone up to his ear. The phone rang only once before he heard it connect as someone picked up. There was silence on the other end at first, then a series of slow breaths. 'Penny.' He said. 'It's McNulty.'

'McNulty.' She said.

'Yeah, it's me listen up kid. You down the basement still?'

'Yeah, I haven't moved.'

'Good kid, that's good. Here's what I need you to do. There's a green box on top of the shelf, looks like something from the military. You see it?'

After a couple seconds, Penny responded, 'It's here yes.'

'Okay, inside it there should be a remote garage door opener and a set of car keys. When I hang up, I want you to wait exactly two minutes, count it off if you have to. Then go out the bulkhead door and run your ass off to the garage, open it and get in that car. Can you drive a stick?'

'Uh, I never have.'

'Okay don't worry. Just get in the passenger seat and have the keys ready for me. I'm hanging up now. You wait two minutes, then go. I'll be there in three minutes. Now go, count.'

'Okay.' She said. Then he heard the click of the line going dead. McNulty stuffed the phone back in his pocket as he swung through the rotary towards Neponset. He took a side street just before his own and parked up next to the curb. He left the driver's side window down and dropped the keys on the floor at the foot of the driver's seat. He jumped out and quickly grabbed his duffle bag from the trunk. He slammed it shut then took off in a sprint through a neighbor's backyard that emptied into his own. He slid his wide frame through a large opening between a wooden and wire fence that led to the back of his garage. The morning was grey, but its dullness along with the unkempt brush in his neighbor's yard kept him camouflaged. He walked around the garage and slipped in through the open door. Inside sat his old black mustang. The caking of dust gave away that it hadn't been outside in months. McNulty walked around to the driver's door and opened it. He leaned down and peaked his head in, 'Keys.' He said to Penny. She tossed them up at him. McNulty grabbed them, walked to the back and opened the trunk. He placed his duffle bag inside and shut it gently then lowered himself into the driver's seat. He fired up the engine and rolled it out of the garage down the driveway, then quickly away from his house. He jumped on the highway a minute later heading north towards the city. Penny had watched him since he got in, but neither had spoken by the time they drove through the tunnel and emptied out onto the Zakim, then around to the Tobin Bridge.

As they drove overlooking the Charles River, Penny finally spoke. 'Aren't you gonna tell me what happened?'

McNulty looked at her briefly then back towards the road. 'Yeah. Sorry, I'll tell you now. Was just focusing on getting us out of dodge. I think we're clear for now.'

'So we're running?'

'Well . . . you could put it that way I guess.'

'I thought you didn't run for any man.'

McNulty smiled. 'In the past, I may have slightly undervalued the act of running away . . . but just as a way to get some space momentarily. Plus, I'm not running from any man. I'm running because of a girl.'

'Don't break your principles on my account.'

'What principles?'

'Yeah, good point. So . . . you found Bishop?'

'I found him.'

'And . . . '

'And, I talked to him. Didn't get anywhere with it as we both probably anticipated.'

'So, he's still looking for me then?'

'You could say that.'

'I did say that.'

'Well, you're right then.'

'What about Liam?'

'Liam's not there.'

'How do you know?'

'I just know that's all. A vibe I got. He's hidden somewhere, alive and well I hope. I think you know where. That house you mentioned . . . Bishop's lake house, could you remember how to get there?'

'Is that where we're going? Bishop has Liam there?'

'Maybe and yes I'd bet my last dime on it. Only one damn thing in his whole office that showed he was even remotely human and that was an old picture of him and some other guys taken out at the lake.'

'I can get you there.'

'Good. We need to regroup first and we need some supplies. I know a place we can hide out in the meantime.'

'What else did Bishop say, anything? Anything . . . about Jeff or anything at all?'

'Afraid not kid . . . sorry.'

'Oh . . . so how did you leave it? I'm surprised you were able to walk out of there at all.'

McNulty shrugged first, then turned his head towards her. 'Well . . . I walked out just fine. But, then I sent a message. I tossed a pipe bomb through his window.'

'You did what!' Penny yelled. 'How does that help us?

What if he . . . what if he takes it out on Liam. I mean . . . what if you're wrong and Liam was in the building somewhere.'

'Believe me, your brother wasn't there. As for Bishop, he seemed a little too in control for my liking. It occurred to me, only reason your skinny ass wasn't shot on the spot in Quincy was because Bishop doesn't like drawing attention to himself in his own backyard. So I thought I'd do that for him. We needed leverage. He'll be on the run now himself, and what's more, he's rattled. That's leverage. Take my word for it.'

Penny stared at him for a few seconds, then shook her head. 'You're fucking crazy McNulty.'

'Hey kid, you came to me. You wanted help. This is me helping. Not one more fucking word about it.' He said. McNulty crossed the bridge and continued on the highway north towards New Hampshire.

'Still.' Penny said. 'A pipe bomb through a neighborhood bar's window. This isn't the wild west for Christsakes.'

McNulty smiled again. 'In retrospect . . . it might have been a hair extreme I'll give you that. But . . . fuck it. We're in it together now kid.'

LIAM MAGUIRE

Liam felt an awful pain in his neck when he shook awake in the morning. The room had grown very cold and the dampness clung to him causing him to shiver so much that he heard his teeth chattering. He was still tied back to the same chair, however the biker that was paid to keep an eye on him cut his hands free every hour or two during the night whenever they started turning purple. He was too uncomfortable to sleep at first and too nervous. Eventually fatigue took him and he nodded off a few times, each time waking up with more severe pain and cramping. When he opened his eyes, he could tell it was light outside, but much of the room was still shrouded in darkness. He looked around the room but saw no sign of the man that had stood watch during the night. He swung his chin left to right sharply to get his neck to crack, which offered momentary relief. His lips were chapped and his mouth was drier than cotton. He shifted in the chair to try and kick out the cramp that had formed in his leg. When he moved he could feel the weight and coldness of his father's small knife that he still held in his back pocket. In the struggle and subsequent urgency the night before, no one thought to check him for any more weapons once the gun was pried rather easily from his grip. 'Overlooked and underestimated again' he thought. He forgot that he even had it himself and only remembered when he was dropped into his current chair. His hands were tied at the moment, so the knife wasn't much use. Plus, even if he did cut himself loose with the small folding knife, he was pretty certain he couldn't fight his way out of the house and down the several floors with just one little blade.

'Knife to a gun fight most likely' he thought. Still, knowing it was there in his back pocket brought him some hope. He felt like if he had to use, if it was a last resort, then he probably could. A day or two ago, the thoughts of wielding a knife and swinging it at someone would have been too far-fetched to fathom. After the twenty-four hours he just had however, which included firing off a gun to protect his sister, he felt that he could use it if push came to shove. Part of him thought that anyway. Another part of him worried that someone would discover he had it and take exception to the fact he hadn't made it known earlier. That was a chance he'd have to take now. 'No way I'm telling them to take it off me.' He thought.

He heard movement from outside the room and listened intently to the murmured voices that came from the other side of the wall. He could hear multiple tones, which meant at least two people were talking, but he couldn't make out any words. After a moment, the door creaked open slowly and the man that had stood guard since he'd arrived walked in. He carried a glass of water and a plate with a couple slices of buttered toast. He walked over to Liam and put both on a small table next to his chair. He walked behind the chair and Liam heard a swish noise, which was a blade opening. The man cut the ties from Liam's wrists, then walked around and sat across from him. Liam shook is hands loose to get the blood flow started, then rubbed each wrist slowly. He was extremely thirsty, and reached first for the water and took a long gulp. Then he picked up a piece of toast and took a small bite. The strain of the last couple days had taken away his appetite and although he was hungry now, it hurt to eat, so he took it slowly. The man sat and watched Liam slowly peck away at the food. 'Something wrong with the toast?'

Liam shook his head. 'No. Just been awhile since I've eaten anything. Not sure what I can hold down.'

The man nodded. I could probably find some instant coffee or something floating around one of the cabinets too, if you want some.'

'No I'm okay.' He said. 'I'd take a cigarette though if you have any.'

The man reached into his inside pocket and pulled out a pack of Camels. He handed one across, which Liam put between his lips, then reached over with a flame on the top of his lighter. Liam leaned over and lit the cigarette. He drew in a deep breath and then let the smoke out slowly. He took another sip of the water and watched the man light his own cigarette then put the pack away. 'I didn't know you smoked kid. I could've given you one earlier.'

Liam waved some of the smoke away from his face. 'No . . . thanks that's okay.' He said. 'Can I . . . um, can I ask you something?'

'Yeah go ahead.'

'Have you heard anything? I mean, like any word on what I'm doing here, how long they're gonna hang onto me.'

The man looked at him with a raised eyebrow. 'Honestly kid, I'm not really in the know here. I'm a hired hand for all intents and purposes. But, I will say there's more people here today and there's something buzzing around this morning that has some of the newcomers on edge.'

'No idea what?'

'None. If I had to guess though, I'd say something went down today.'

Liam took a long haul from his cigarette. He could feel his heart beat pick up speed. He began to worry again. 'Something might have happened to Penny . . . they might've found her.' He thought. 'But, if they found her, well, I'd either be cut loose or dead.'

'Something worrying you kid?' the man asked.

Liam looked up towards him. He finished his smoke and dropped it to the ground, then crushed it with his foot. 'Just thinking, you know . . . about my future I guess.'

'Now let me ask you something then.'

'What's that?'

'How does a kid like you fall on the wrong side of this crowd? No offense, but I can tell you ain't no tough guy and you ain't no criminal, I know one of those when I see one. You make off with somebody's wife or something? 'Cause other than that, I'm out of fucking guesses.'

'It wasn't me they were after.' Liam said.

The man nodded. 'Let me guess, the one they were after got away and you didn't.'

Liam nodded 'Yes'.

'Tough break for you kid. Bet you're wishing they just picked up who they were looking for and left you out of it.'

Liam's eyes widened before he responded. He took a breath then answered, 'If they caught Penny, she'd be dead.'

'Penny? A chick?'

'My sister.'

'Your sister's mixed up with this crowd?'

'I guess you could say that.'

'Well kid. You don't seem like a bad guy. Hope you

and your sister can work things out with these guys.'

'Yeah, me too.'

The man reached in his back pocket and pulled out another large zip-tie. He held it up for Liam to see. 'You all done with that toast.'

'Yeah, I'm done.' He said. The man walked behind Liam's chair and pulled his wrists out. He wrapped the plastic around them, then pulled the fastener tightly. When the man finished, he sat back down across from Liam and pulled out a new magazine that he opened and began to flick through. The water, toast and cigarette caused his stomach to hurt all of a sudden. 'Took them down too fast' he thought. He sat his head back to try and focus on breathing while he let the stomach cramps pass. While he did, he heard movement again outside the room and raised voices that started penetrating the thick wall and insulation. Suddenly the door swung open. A young man walked in quickly. He was the same stocky kid that had roughed Liam up the night before outside his apartment. The others called him 'Mick' or 'Mickey' Liam remembered that. He walked in loudly and headed straight for Liam. Liam looked up and tried to brace himself. By the angry look on Mick's face he knew something was up. Liam focused in on Mick's face as he charged forward. His nostrils flared and the freckles on his cheeks stretched with his scowl. Liam saw in his periphery, the biker kick his chair back as he stood up in surprise. 'You fucking punk!' Mick yelled and shoved Liam hard at the shoulders so that he fell over backwards in the chair. With his wrists tied behind his back, he landed awkwardly and his head smacked against the floor. Liam cried out in pain when his head hit the ground, but his voice was cut short by a kick to the ribs that knocked the wind out of him.

Mick reached down and roughly pulled Liam and his chair upright. Liam fought to get his breath back. His vision was blurred and stars shone out from his periphery. The dizziness made him nauseous too and he nearly heaved his light breakfast onto his shoes. 'Who the fuck is McNulty to you?' Mick asked.

'Who?'

Mick reached back and let out a right cross that stung Liam hard and brought blood trickling from his nose. 'Fucking McNulty! You know Goddamn well who I'm talking about. He's running around blowing shit up on behalf of you and your sister, don't play fucking dumb with me!' he yelled then reached back and let another punch fly into Liam's face.

Liam's head shot back violently and tears ran into his eyes from the blast to the nose. He felt the pain from the punch somewhat, but the adrenaline rose from fear and masked much of it. Mick reached back to strike again and Liam braced himself as best he could. He shut his eyes and waited for it. The punch never came.

'That's plenty for now' he heard the biker's voice say. Liam opened his eyes slowly and saw that the biker had stepped in between him and Mick. He said a silent thanks.

'This ain't your fucking business.' Mick said. 'Wait until Bishop hears about this.'

The biker stood tall. He was at least a head taller than Mick and nearly twice his girth. He took a long step towards Mick and spoke in a low voice. 'You fucking listen to me, boy, I said enough for now. When Bishop shows, you tell him to come talk to me. I was paid to watch this kid and keep him here. I ain't heard shit about watching him get his head ripped off. You send Bishop to talk to me when he's here. Until then, get the fuck out. Now.' Mick slowly slid his foot back, then the other. He looked back to Liam 'This ain't over yet.' He said. He walked around the biker and stormed out of the room, slamming the door shut behind him when he left. Liam watched the biker bend over and pick up the chair that had fallen over. He dusted it off and put it upright in front of Liam and sat down across from him again. When he was seated, Liam said 'thanks.'

The man nodded. 'Don't worry about it. That Young Turk will get his, I have a sixth sense about these things.'

'He'll be back I'm sure.'

'Yeah, I reckon he will. And more than likely I won't be here to stop him. That'll be up to you.'

'Great.'

'Tell me something kid. He mentioned McNulty. I know you were playing dumb and all a minute ago, but I'm curious. Is that Nick McNulty? Giant of a man that swears every other word, from Dorchester?'

Liam didn't answer, but his facial expression gave him away.

'This is between me and you right now kid, that's all. See . . . I know McNulty. He's a friend to the club. If he's involved with this shit and he's going up against our business associate, well, it changes things. It creates what we call a conflict of interest.'

'As far as I can tell, we're talking about the same guy.'

'I thought so. No wonder these fuckers are on edge. How the hell does someone like you end up running with McNulty? How do you know him?'

'I don't really I guess. I mean, I've met him once. I'm telling the truth. I don't know how or why McNulty did what he did.'

'Alright then kid. I ain't gonna press you on this. Like I said, I'm curious that's all.'

The man stood up and walked over to the corner of the room. Liam watched him as he pulled out a cell phone from his pocket and held it up high, looking for service. He walked over to the dirt encrusted window, hit a few buttons on the phone and held it to his ear. Liam couldn't hear the conversation from where he was sitting, but he could tell it was brief and to the point. 'McNulty's with Penny' Liam thought, 'How? And more importantly why?' He guessed Penny must have somehow found McNulty based on what he told her about the gun. Understanding that part was easy. But how she got him enlisted to do God knows what, that part he couldn't understand. It didn't reconcile with his impression of the man he'd met briefly on two occasions. He couldn't piece it together. Regardless of the 'why', he felt different now. Something had changed in him. He was nervous before and really just waiting for doom. He was alone and Penny was helpless. It was only a matter of time before they found her and killed them both. Now though, knowing that McNulty was helping Penny, the dread that had gripped him for over twenty-four hours began to chip away. 'It might be dangerous and premature to feel it' he thought, but it was there anyway, a sliver of hope.

MCNULTY

McNulty and Penny made it out of Boston a couple hours north to New Hampshire. For the time being McNulty bypassed Lake Winnipesaukee and continued into the White Mountains an hour north. He pulled up outside of a small motel minutes away from Mount Washington. The motor lodge was a single level strip of fifteen rooms with worn down clapboard siding and chipped red paint. There was a giant statue of a stoic Native American out front that bordered on cigar shop offensive. McNulty parked out front of reception and went inside. He paid for a room in cash and was quickly back in the car. He drove around the lot to an apartment out back that was set off separately from the main strip. He knew the place and asked for it specifically at the front desk. The desk manager took his cash and handed over the key attached to a flat wooden handle that had the words White Mountains Inn stenciled on it. He led the way up the staircase into the apartment. Inside there were two rooms and a common living area. There was a double bed in one room and two singles in the other. He told Penny to take the larger bed and try to get some rest while he figured a few things out. He knew she probably couldn't sleep after all that had happened, but he insisted she try. When she did, he took the opportunity to call Billy Carson. He and Billy hadn't left on good terms the previous night, but he was in a jam and needed Billy to pick a few things up for him. Billy gave him an earful over the phone, but agreed to make the trip and pick up what he needed, which consisted of various firearms, a few throwaway cell phones and some walking around money just in case he had to take the girl on the run for a few weeks. He also got the front desk manager to get a pizza delivered so they could eat something. After about an hour, he heard movement in her room and eventually the echo of a shower running in the apartment.

Penny finished showering and threw on some of the clothes that McNulty had thrown in a bag for her. She walked into the common area and joined McNulty as he sat on the flower upholstered couch. 'Hey' she said.

McNulty turned towards her and couldn't help but smile. 'Hey. Clothes seem to fit you okay. Good.'

'Yeah, they're fine. Are they . . . a girlfriend's? Will she miss them?'

McNulty laughed, 'Ha, no. No woman would have me. Especially none that'd fit into clothes that small. They're my daughter's things.'

'Oh. Okay. Will she mind?'

'I doubt it very much kid.'

'You don't see her very often do you?'

'You a psychiatrist or something?'

'No, just making conversation I guess.'

'Maybe try another topic.'

'Okay. But . . . can I ask . . . is that why you're doing this? I mean, you're helping me for some reason, do I remind you of her?'

McNulty paused. He didn't like the line of questioning that the girl had started. 'I'm helping you. I'm gonna help you get your brother back and try to get you both out of this mess safe. Ask yourself, does it really matter why I'm helping you?'

'I . . . guess not.' Penny muttered. 'Well, no matter what, thank you.' She said and put her slim hand on his large shoulder.

McNulty smiled at her again and she smiled back. Something about the girl gave him a warm feeling in his stomach like hot broth on a cold day. For better or worse, she had her hooks in him and he knew it, though he didn't mind. He realized all of a sudden that he was enjoying this. It wasn't the violence or danger he enjoyed, but the adventure, it gave him a sense of purpose. That was something he had gone without for a least a couple of years and he didn't realize how much 'having a purpose' meant to him until then.

He heard a car pull up outside and tires crunch over leaves and pine needles. He stood up slowly and held up a hand to Penny so she'd stay put. He walked over to the window, hugging the wall as he did. He kept his body away from the window and reached over with his fingers to gently lift the curtain. It was a dim day outside with fog cover, but there was a light by a dumpster near the stairs that shone through the mist. He relaxed when he saw Billy Carson's Buick out front. He watched Billy climb out of the driver's seat and pull a large bag from the trunk. McNulty walked over to the door and unhinged the lock. He opened it cautiously until he heard Billy's steps get closer to the door. 'Come in.' He said to Billy when he reached the landing.

Billy pushed through the door and dropped the bag at McNulty's feet. He looked over at the girl and nodded in her direction. She waved back to him. McNulty turned towards her and asked, 'Give us a few minutes?'

'No problem.' She said and got up and walked into the adjoining room and closed the door.

'You want coffee or something Billy?'

'I'm all set.' He said and took a seat in a chair next to the couch.

'Thanks for doing this. I know you didn't want any part in this.'

'Don't worry about it.' He said and looked around. 'Can't believe you even remembered this place. You remember when we had the kids here and that bear was rummaging through the dumpster outside?'

McNulty laughed. 'Yeah, you tend to remember any time you come face to face with a grizzly and your life flashes before your eyes.'

'I hear ya. Don't think it was a grizzly though. Maybe a black bear.'

'Whatever it was, it scared the shit out of me. And you too if I remember. We had the kids all gathered on the bed afraid to go outside.'

'Good times.'

'Yeah they were.'

'Anyone at the front desk remember you?'

'Me? No, must be new management. The old man that ran the place must've kicked it. A young guy is working the desk and from the looks of the place, it's gone to shit.'

'I noticed.'

'So what's the word?'

'The word is that some asshole blew out a shop front all over Brook Street. There's a lot of questions being asked. Lot of cops.'

'Should I expect blow back?'

'I don't know yet. From what I've heard Bishop's playing dumb and he split town shortly after. Word on the street is it's related to his drug business. Seems to be shedding a light on his true character around town, which

I'm guessing was part of your plan.'

McNulty nodded. 'Sometimes you just have to turn the lights on to get the cockroaches to scatter.'

'Still . . . a bit extreme huh? Could've brought some collateral damage you know what I mean?'

'I know Billy. I gotta say, I lost my head for a minute. It's fucking done now though, can't take it back, shit's in motion.'

'Yeah I can see that. There's one more thing. You'll like this.'

'What's that?'

'Got a call from Tooth & Nail's VP.'

'Peterson?'

'Yeah. One of his guys was on a contract babysitting gig for Bishop. Caught wind of your name and called it in.'

'You're shitting me. TNMC's watching the kid?'

'They are. Well, they were. Peterson's gonna pull his guys off it. Says it creates too much shit and he doesn't want to be in the middle of a beef with . . . partners on opposite sides of a mud fight, which is how he put it. Got a location though.'

'Let me guess, at the lake house?'

'Yeah, shit, how'd you know?'

'A hunch that's all.'

'Good hunch.'

'Most are, how do you think I've lasted this long?'

'Of course, you're Nick McNulty, I forgot you're not always right, but you're never wrong, I get it. Anyway, wait on it until dark I'd say. I'm guessing he needs time to pull out of there while still saving face with Bishop.'

Billy stood up and brushed down his jacket. He walked over to McNulty until he was a step away. 'I still don't like this Nick.'

'I know Billy.'

'You won't reconsider?'

McNulty shook his head. 'Gotta see it through. I'll get the kid, then I'll see them off.'

'I can't do it Nick. I can't get behind this.'

'You've done enough already. I'll be in touch when it's done.'

Billy put a hand on his shoulder. 'Stay safe old man.'

McNulty nodded. He let Billy out the door then closed it quickly behind him. He walked back over to the wall next to the window and scanned the parking lot again from behind the curtain. He heard a door open and looked over at Penny as she walked back into the room.

'Gone?' She asked.

'Gone. Got confirmation, Liam's at the lake house.' He walked towards the room with the two single beds. 'Listen. This is gonna be dangerous. Shit can get out of hand ya know. I think it's best if you let me handle this.'

'If you think you're doing this without me, you really are fucking nuts. I got Liam into this. I'll be there to help get him out.'

'You could get hurt.'

'I don't give a shit.'

'I do.'

Penny didn't answer. McNulty stood staring at her. He knew convincing her to let him go there alone was a lost cause. 'Better odds of talking Bishop into letting her walk.' He thought. The truth was he was also much better off having her with him. She knew exactly where the house was and the layout of the inside. That information could prove to be the difference between staying whole or ending up as some rotting flesh at the bottom of a lake.

'I'm going with you.' She said.

'Fine.' McNulty said. 'We leave just before dark.' He turned then and walked into the bedroom with the two single beds dragging the bag Billy dropped off with him. He lifted it onto one of the beds and unzipped the top. Inside were the supplies he'd asked for. He started to pull each item out of the bag to prepare it for use. He pulled out two Kevlar vests, one very large, one very small and put them up near the pillow. Then he started arranging the firearms next to them, matching handguns with holsters and putting extra shells next to the rifle that Billy packed. He pulled out a snub-nosed revolver, checked it was loaded and attached it to a holster on his ankle. When everything was arranged on the bed, he sat down on the empty bed and stared across at what he had. He knew he was fine for ammunition but he guessed that being one man with many guns against multiple men with several still put him at a disadvantage. He wasn't sure how deep Bishop's crew went. If he had more time, he'd have researched it. Although knowing that Bishop had contracted Tooth & Nail MC for protection gave an indication that perhaps his roster was thinned these days. Also, knowing that Tooth & Nail were pulling out of the situation and confirming the kid's location were definite advantages. He knew the window of opportunity to capitalize on that information was small, so he had no choice, he was going for it tonight. He worried about the girl however. It wasn't safe having Penny with him, but it wasn't safe leaving her alone either. He struggled with which was the lesser of two evils. He stretched his arms up, locked his fingers over the top of his head and laid back across the bed.

His thoughts were racing, but they stopped short when he heard footsteps coming from the landing at the door. He sat up quickly and was momentarily lightheaded. 'Had a car pulled up? Did I miss it?' He thought. He listened again, there was nothing for a few seconds. Then he heard a knock at the door. He heard movement from the other room. 'Penny' he thought. 'Oh shit.'

'I'll get it.' She said, 'Billy must have forgotten something.'

McNulty jumped to his feet and ran out to the common area. He saw Penny half way through the room with her hand outstretched towards the door.

'Penny!' he yelled and sprinted towards her. She turned towards him and paused in fear at the strained tone of his voice. McNulty leapt towards her and tackled her to the ground, bracing her head as they both landed. As they hit the ground, he heard her grunt in pain. He kept a large arm over her body to keep her down. A loud blast rang over their heads and splintered wood flew in their direction. 'Fuck!' McNulty shouted. He looked up with squinted eyes to see two large holes in the door where grey daylight shone through. He rolled over on the ground dragging Penny with him. 'Stay low!' he yelled. He heard the door get kicked in behind him as he crawled towards the bedroom on his knees. He shoved Penny into the room. 'Stay down!' he yelled to her. He heard another blast behind him and heard footsteps. He looked up and saw a man with a shotgun charge through the door. McNulty dove down behind the couch and saw another blast penetrate the wall above his head. His heart was racing. He'd been caught off guard, something he wasn't used to. He held his breath to wait for footsteps. He heard them, they were subtle creaks on the carpet, which muffled their impact. He could sense they weren't headed towards him, instead they were directed towards the room Penny was hiding in. 'Shit' he thought, and knew he needed to draw attention to himself. He reached down and pulled the snub-nose from his boot holster. He got to his knees, then jumped up and ran across the room towards the front wall. He fired off only one shot, afraid to fire randomly with Penny protected only by flimsy drywall. He dove to the ground and flipped the coffee table over, struggling to stay behind it. Another shot rang out, which tore away the corner of the coffee table.

'Time's up McNulty.' He heard a man's voice call. 'Drop that little bitch gun or the next one takes your head off.

'This is it' McNulty thought. He kicked the coffee table away and sat up with his back against the front wall. He put the gun on the carpet and slid it a few feet away from him. He watched the man walk towards him. He recognized him. It was the same man that tailed him a few hours back, the tough one. 'Where's your partner?' McNulty asked.

'Turns out he didn't have the stomach for this line of work. Kicking yourself for not taking me out when you had the chance?'

'That's obvious. You follow Billy?'

The man nodded.

'I should've warned him.'

'He's been around. He should've expected it.'

'Maybe.'

The man raised the shotgun again and pointed it at

McNulty's chest. 'Ain't you gonna beg McNulty?'

McNulty smiled. 'Fuck you.' He said. A loud bang startled McNulty. He tensed up and shut his eyes, though after a moment he realized he wasn't hurt. He looked up and saw the man on his knees. His face was contorted in a mixture of pain and confusion. The shotgun was on the floor and a red stain grew on the man's abdomen. Over the man's head stood Penny. She held a gun tightly in her hands. McNulty could see her body was shaking and her face was pale white. McNulty jumped to his feet and picked up the snub-nose. He walked over to the man and kicked him in the chest so that he fell onto his back. 'Look away!' he yelled to Penny and waited until she lowered the gun and slowly backed into the bedroom. The man choked and spit drops of blood from his mouth. He appeared to be trying to say something. McNulty cocked the revolver, leaned down and sat the short barrel at the man's mouth. 'You talk too fucking much.' He said. Then he turned his own head and pulled the trigger.

He wiped the gun off on the dead man's pant leg and put it back into his holster. He walked into the bedroom and saw Penny sitting on the single bed across from the guns. She was still holding the gun she'd used tightly in her hands. McNulty reached out slowly and Penny handed it to him. 'Didn't know you could shoot?'

Penny looked up at him slowly. 'Me neither.'

'I'm glad you can.'

Penny nodded.

'We have to go now.' He said.

'I know. I'm ready.'

McNulty started stuffing the guns, ammo and supplies back into the large bag. 'Good.' He said. 'Let's move.'

JOHN BISHOP

The rain had picked up again and the sky turned an angry charcoal color on the drive north to Winnipesaukee. Bishop had Doyle drive the SUV. He needed to look out the window and clear his head. He was sitting in his office with the door open when he felt the blast from the pipe bomb. The noise caused his eardrums to ache though he avoided any injuries despite having glass and other debris fly into his office. He had ducked behind the desk just in time to let the wood absorb the brunt of the force. Doyle escaped unscathed also. He heard the glass break as the explosive flew through it and took cover behind the bar immediately. The mirror behind the bar had shattered and cut up some of his back but not severely. Bishop seethed at McNulty's audacity. The strength of his whole operation in Quincy was its subtlety. Many of his customers and definitely his agreement with local law enforcement depended on it. His ability to fly under the radar took a major setback as soon as the front of his barroom wall was blown out. Now there were cops swarming and the media had gotten ahold of the story, which included some speculation on terrorism but more on possible criminal ties to the bar. Bishop had no choice but to get out of town after the cops took down his and Doyle's statements. He had to let the heat run its course.

It bothered him greatly that he let McNulty get the jump on him. He'd been blindsided by the old man's visit and even more so by his apparent connection to the Maguire's. It wasn't something he had previously considered and Doyle's intel on the Maguire's didn't hint at any involvement with McNulty. It was a major oversight. If he wasn't already shorthanded, he would've considered cutting Doyle loose for the misstep, it wasn't his first. They were both guilty of underestimating the two kids however, he saw that now. He gave Doyle an earful instead and had him keep digging on the McNulty connection. After that, it didn't take long to piece together some links. It was another Maguire that was involved a few years back in a local business man being killed. The Maguire involved in that was a cousin to the two siblings he was after. The business man's father was a man named Billy Carson. Billy Carson's name was not one that people used lightly around Quincy. Bishop knew who he was and knew enough to stay clear of him. It was also common knowledge amongst those in his industry that you rarely heard Carson's name without also hearing McNulty's. As to the details explaining how Carson's right-hand man and the family of one of the men that killed his son ended up on the same side of the fence, Bishop didn't really give a shit. He knew what he needed to know now, which was purely that they were connected, it wasn't random and now he had a legitimate problem.

He also knew that in hindsight it was a huge mistake letting McNulty walk out the door. The man had a reputation for a reason. He proved that twice within ten minutes. First blowing up the barroom, then diffusing the tail Bishop had on him. The Maguire's were kids. McNulty was a warrior and a resourceful one at that. As Doyle drove him through Boston and on into New Hampshire, a forceful dread loomed over Bishop. A reckoning was coming, he could feel it. 'McNulty knew exactly what he was doing' Bishop thought 'he has me on the run and I can be damn sure he knows where I'm going.' Bishop called in all the enforcements he currently had. Although, with his recent staff turnover he knew more than half of the guys were untested, while most of the other half were just guns for hire and there was no telling how they'd react if and when the situation reached breaking point. Based on that, he was worried. Plus, Mick had called while they drove and said something was stirring with Tooth & Nail. The details were vague, but it sounded like their support was wavering. If he lost their support, he was in deep shit and he knew it. Fear burrowed into his stomach and it was stronger than any he'd felt in years. He had sent a seasoned hired gun out on his own. A man named Wilson. As soon as he figured out the Billy Carson connection, he had Wilson sit on a halfway house in Quincy thought to be where Carson stayed. Sure enough, Wilson sent word he was tailing Carson heading north. That was a couple hours ago. 'Any word in from Wilson?' Bishop asked Doyle.

Doyle shifted in the driver's seat to pull his phone from his pocket. He glanced quickly at the phone then dropped it in the center cup holder. 'Nothing on my end. You think Carson made him?'

'I don't know. Something probably went down though, otherwise we'd have heard from him. He was heading north ahead of us, he would've called in any progress.'

'Yeah, you're probably right. If he ain't at the cabin, I think it's safest to assume he ain't coming.'

'Agreed.' Bishop said. The day was cloudy and it turned much darker as sunset loomed. The truck's automatic headlights turned on as the road thinned and grew more winding. Doyle slowed the truck as he approached the unmarked turn off. He pulled the truck left down the unkempt path and they rumbled over broken gravel, dirt and potholes. They rolled in slowly through the woods and Doyle eased the truck into the narrow drive and left it behind the row of vehicles that had begun to stack up as more reinforcements were called in. 'Jesus Christ' Bishop said. 'This ain't a fucking keg party, call Mick and get some of these fucking cars out of here.'

Doyle put the truck in park. 'I'm on it.' He said and they both opened the doors and climbed down. The wet leaves and loose gravel were a hazard in the driveway and Bishop walked carefully through the mess until the path opened to a lawn and stone walkway. He looked up at the large house. In the dark he could see lights on in several rooms on each floor. He continued down the walkway towards the kitchen door. There were two Harley Davidson's lined up in front of the wooden porch. They sat in front of several cords of firewood stacked next to the open kitchen door. 'I paid for five guys, only two bikes.' Bishop muttered to himself. He felt his blood rising with every step he took. He walked through the kitchen's open doorway and looked around. The lights were on in every room, but he couldn't hear anything on the first floor. Doyle walked in behind him. 'Where the fuck is everyone?'

Bishop held his hand up for silence. He listened closely. He heard only muffled voices coming from a stairway at the other end of the kitchen. He heard a noise behind him. 'What's that?'

'It's the fucking toilet flushing.' Doyle said.

A lock shifted and the bathroom door opened. Bishop

reached behind him and pulled a gun from his belt. Doyle did the same. Both men pointed their guns at the young man that walked out of the bathroom. 'Woah!' he yelled and held his hands up. Bishop took several steps towards the man and held the gun inches from the young man's forehead. 'You supposed to be standing guard?'

'I . . . uh, yeah. I'm watching the floor.'

'Front door's wide open and me and Doyle walked in unchecked.'

'I'm sorry . . . I had to go.' He said pointing towards the bathroom.

Bishop leaned forward and tapped his gun lightly off the man's forehead. He saw beads of sweat form and drop off the edges of his brow. 'You don't have a fucking clue what's coming for you. I might as well put one in your head now, save everyone some time.'

'Puhh . . . please.' He said.

Bishop slowly lowered the gun. 'Go find me Mick.'

The man didn't move at first.

'Fucking go! Now!'

Bishop tucked his gun back into his belt. Doyle lowered his own and did the same.

'If this is the caliber of the new recruits, we're fucked.'

'Don't worry Johnny, kid's just learning.'

'Yeah, well he better learn fucking quick.'

'I'll talk to him.'

'Good.'

Bishop heard footsteps coming down the wooden steps. He walked towards the sound and took a seat at a large table in the kitchen. Mick walked down the stairs and joined him at the table. He nodded over at Doyle. Doyle walked over and joined them too.

'Any word from Wilson?' Doyle asked.

'Not in over an hour at least, probably longer.'

'Shit.' Bishop said and laid a fist down hard on the table.

'What was the latest when you spoke to him?'

'He called in after he passed through the toll to New Hampshire. He was still on Carson's car heading north.'

'I take it you tried calling his burner back?'

'Yeah, not getting through. He might've tossed it.'

'Maybe.' Bishop said, though he felt it was more serious than that. 'Okay, well. We gotta make do with what we have. It's getting dark and something tells me if McNulty's gonna make a move on this place he's gonna do it tonight. I need this place locked down.'

'Okay. I'll get everyone set up.'

'Good.'

'What happened to your hand?' Doyle asked Mick.

Bishop looked down at Mick's hand. He hadn't noticed it when he sat down. The knuckles were red raw and looked swollen.

'Nothing, I just . . . tried to get a few answers out of our friend upstairs.'

Bishop glared at him. He hadn't given any orders to start handing out beatings.

'The kid ain't hurt bad or nothing.' Mick said. 'I swear. I lost my head for a minute that's all, only hit him once or twice.'

'Who stopped it?' Doyle asked. 'I know you well enough, you don't just hit someone once or twice when you lose your head.'

Mick paused for a moment. He looked over at Doyle, then back towards Bishop. 'Well . . . that's the other thing.'

'What?'

'Fucking Lurch from Tooth & Nail decided to step in.'

'Jesus Christ.'

'Yeah. Don't worry I didn't go after him or anything.'

'You'd be hanging from the rafters right now if you did, believe me you stupid son of a bitch.'

'I'm sorry John.'

'Everyone seems to be sorry these days.' He muttered. 'What's the story with Tooth & Nail anyway? I only see two bikes out front, I paid for five guys to stick around.'

'That's the thing. After I got into it with Maguire, something happened. Three of the guys didn't say shit, they just took off. That tall motherfucker's still on the top floor though sitting with the kid. There's another one hanging around outside the room waiting on orders or something. I pressed them for reasons why the other guys took off, but neither guy seems to want to talk to me, said to send you in to talk once you got here.'

'I'll handle it. I'll head up there now. Doyle, hang down here and get the first floor locked down. Mick, you run up with me. You can send three or four guys down to help with Doyle while you're up there. Something tells me Tooth & Nail are pulling out. If they do, you're on watch. Bishop led the way up the stairs to the top floor, which opened to the game area first with a pool table and dart board. Mick followed behind him. In the first room, a few people stood around playing a game of pool. They each put the cues down when they saw Bishop at the top of the landing. Each said hello quietly as he walked past. Bishop ignored them and continued into a narrow corridor that opened into a small foyer. A man sat on a chair next to

the door for the last room. He had long hair and a beard
and wore a leather vest with a Tooth & Nail logo sewed in
above the breast. He stood up when he saw Bishop
approach. He reached over and knocked firmly on the
door next to him. A few seconds later, a much taller man
walked out of the room. He was older than the other man
by at least ten or fifteen years. Bishop turned to Mick and
nodded for him to wait back at the game room. 'Give us a
few minutes' he said.

Mick looked hurt that he was asked to wait behind,
after a brief pause, he said 'Yeah okay. I'll be out here if
you need me.' Then he turned and walked back out the
way he came. The tall biker nodded at the smaller one,
and he followed Mick out into the main room. When they
were gone, he looked down at Bishop who was a head
shorter than him and said 'Your guy. He's got a short
fuse. I would guess he's one to watch.'

'He's young that's all. A little age and experience
should settle him.'

'You think so?'

'I don't know, only time will tell really. I've seen guys
like him go either way.'

'Yeah, so have I. I guess it depends on them, you know,
their mental make-up. Depends whether they can put up
with the stress of this life.'

Bishop nodded. 'You stressed?'

'Ha! Me? I'm too old for that shit. Nowadays I'm just
easy come, easy go.'

'So . . . is that why you guys are pulling out. Don't want
the stress.'

'Something like that.'

'I wouldn't have called your crew in if I didn't need the

help. You guys pulling out isn't good for business, mine or yours. As you can see I'm shorthanded.'

'Yeah, you're shorthanded alright. And you have a problem I've gathered.'

'What's that mean? What's this little shit feeding you?'

'Kid ain't said shit to me, it was your boy coming in shouting his head off, saying a certain name that got me thinking.'

'Who Mick?'

'Yeah, your little fire starter over there.'

'Whose name is he throwing around? I can assure you, any trouble I have isn't going to impact your club.'

'No it ain't, you got that right. Cause we're done here. Once your beef with McNulty is squashed or settled, give Peterson a call. You two can figure out how to resume operations.'

'So that's it huh? You mean to tell me you guys are taking off because of McNulty. Shit, he's just one man. I never would've thought one man would scare your club off.'

'First off, I'd watch your tone John. My club ain't scared of a damn thing. The thing is we have a long-standing policy of staying out of personal beefs. Especially when that beef is between a business partner and someone who's been a friend to the club for over thirty years.'

'So McNulty's a friend to the club?'

'A good one at that.'

Bishop paused and thought for a second. The anger that nearly blinded him when he pulled up began to subside. Now that it did he was able to think more clearly about what his options might be. He was running out of them and he assumed he was under time pressure. 'If that's the case . . . maybe the club can help broker some sort of arrangement. What about that? Help to keep both your relationships intact.'

'And what . . . you're just gonna let this kid walk away. And . . . his sister? She gonna walk away too? I don't know and I don't care what this kid and his sister did or saw or whatever. That shit ain't my business and I don't want to know. But you're obviously hanging onto him for a reason. Listen, I know McNulty. The die is cast John. Be sure about this. McNulty's gonna see this thing through.' Bishop didn't respond. Whatever Mick spurted out to Maguire in front of this guy, he said too much. 'He'll pay for that . . . in due time.' He thought. 'For now, this is done, Tooth & Nail is out.'

'I paid for five guys.' Bishop said. 'In advance.'

The tall biker reached into his vest and pulled out a thick envelope. He reached over and held it out in front of Bishop. 'Your refund.'

Bishop reached out and took the envelope. He held the weight of it in his hands for a second then stuffed it inside his jacket. 'Tell Peterson I'll be in touch.'

The biker nodded slowly then walked out of the room. Bishop followed him out with his eyes while the words the man spoke echoed in his head 'McNulty's gonna see this thing through.' The more he thought about it, the more he understood it was true. McNulty blowing up the bar wasn't just a message to him. It was a foreshadowing. He understood that now. When it happened he felt rage and confusion. His rage had dissipated for the moment, but the confusion lingered. 'McNulty is a street guy.' He thought. 'He knows having a girl walking the street knowing what she knows is nonnegotiable.' Even if

McNulty was connected to the Maguire's, which he knew to be the case now, he couldn't reconcile the man's level of commitment to their cause with any rational train of thought. Not in such a short timespan anyway. 'He's not just drawing attention to me, he's drawing attention to himself. It's likely there were witnesses on that block that gave his description to the cops already.' He thought. It just didn't make sense to Bishop that McNulty would go on the offensive so quickly. It made him question his own motives. He'd been doing that since the outset. He didn't want to kill the girl or her brother. He didn't want to kill Jeff Conrad either. Lefty had it coming. Jeff on the other hand, he was in the wrong, but in retrospect he could've given it more consideration. 'Hell, Connie was a friend . . . a good friend. Too late now.' He thought. 'Is there really a need for more blood?' Bishop rubbed his eyes with his thumb and forefinger. He'd had a headache all morning that seemed to grow more intense every minute. The light shining into the hall from the game room made it worse. He turned and pushed through the door to the room where Liam Maguire was being held, the same room where he'd ended his friend Jeff Conrad's life. His growing migraine welcomed the darkness as he walked further into the room. He left the door only slightly ajar behind him so that it blocked out the light from the hall, but he could still hear if someone approached from the game room. He looked down at Liam Maguire. He had some early bruising on his face and his nose was swollen, but it didn't look like Mick had a chance to really lay into him. The kid looked up at Bishop slowly, but didn't say anything, not that Bishop expected to hear a cheerful 'hello'. He was thin and his thinness made him look young, really young. 'Too young to be tied up and beaten.' Bishop thought 'Or killed.' Bishop visibly shook his head as he thought this. He looked the kid over again. His thin frame and even the bone structure of his face seemed so familiar to him. It was strange, but the kid reminded him of his old friend, Brian Dawson. He shook the thought from his head and walked closer to where he sat.

'You doing alright?' Bishop asked.

Liam Maguire looked up at him, then averted his eyes. 'Define alright.'

'Okay, I guess I deserve that. I'm sorry Mick came after you. There was no need for that.'

'Is there . . . is there a need for any of this?'

'Unfortunately.'

'Yeah. Unfortunate for me, and for Penny.'

Bishop walked closer to Liam. He pulled the spare chair up and took a seat across from him. 'What can you tell me about McNulty?'

'Aren't you gonna beat it out of me?'

'Not if I don't have to.'

'I'll tell you the same thing I told the other guy. I met him a couple times, I don't really know him and I don't know how Penny found him or why he's with her.'

'You pulled a gun on us at your apartment. McNulty gave you that?'

'McNulty didn't give me anything. I tracked him down based on information someone gave me. I bought a gun off of him.'

'That someone . . . your cousin? Brendan Maguire, one of the gang that got Jimmy Carson killed a while back?'

Liam didn't say anything, only nodded yes.

'He did time with McNulty. I found that out recently. So I get that your cousin gave you McNulty's name. You found him, bought a hand cannon off of him. But from there you lose me.'

'That's where I lose myself. I'm sorry Mr. Bishop, but I've been with you since. I know nothing else.'

'So you do know who I am?'

'I've put it together, yes.'

'Call me John.'

'I'd rather not.'

Bishop smiled. 'I accept that.' He stood up and stretched his arms over his head. The kid seemed to have grown bolder over the hours he'd been held captive. 'Maybe it was the biker, maybe he had an influence on him. Or maybe he feels that the end is near and it doesn't matter anymore.' As Bishop sat there in Liam's presence, looking at his young face, red with swelling and bruises, he grew unsure of himself once again. As the day wore on, his resolve wavered. Everything had always been so black and white with him in the past. He had a goal, he'd focus on it and achieve it without letting anything get in his way. If someone crossed him, they had to go. If someone presented an obstacle, they had to go. It was how he operated for years. It put him where he was today. However, it was also the root of his alienation from society, from his family and his friends. Stripped bare, it was like this, his greed resulted in loss, not of money, but in friends. His loneliness had fuelled his bitterness. His bitterness fueled violence and his violence ended in remorse. The guilt then just hung over him, like a backpack full of cement it slowed him down and eventually wore him out. He'd never meant for this life.

This wasn't how he was raised, it's just what he became, independent from his intentions. 'Who am I?' He had asked himself after his best friend Brian Dawson died, when heroin that Bishop himself was responsible for distributing funneled through his emaciated friend's body and absorbed the very last remnants of his soul. 'Who am I?' He thought again now. He still struggled with the answer.

Bishop reached into an inside pocket in his jacket and dug around for a small switch blade he kept there. He pulled it out and opened it. He watched Liam's eyes widen as he saw the blade open in front of him. Bishop walked behind Liam and reached down and grabbed his wrists. They were held together with an industrial zip-tie. He stuck a finger in to pull the tie away from the skin, then cut the plastic with his blade. The plastic made a snapping noise when it was freed and fell down to the ground. Bishop watched it land next to his shoes. He walked back in front of Liam. Liam looked confused and continued sitting down though he started to rub his wrists. Bishop was just about to start talking. He had the words on the tip of his tongue. 'You can go' is what he was about to say. Before he could, the door flung open behind him and banged loudly into the wall behind it. He turned quickly. His hand automatically reached behind him for his gun, but he paused when he saw Mick standing there slightly out of breath.

'What's up?' Bishop asked.

'Doyle needs you . . . now. We think he's here, I mean, he's been spotted.'

'McNulty?'

Mick nodded. 'Yeah, it's starting. You better get down

to Doyle.'

Bishop didn't turn back to Liam. His heart began to race and his blood started racing through his body. The turmoil he'd felt moments before suddenly melted away and nerves and adrenaline took over. He started quickly towards the door.

'Stay with Maguire.' He said to Mick and then raced past him out of the room and ran towards the light in the game room.

MCNULTY

Penny wasn't exactly talkative at the best of times. Since the motel, she'd been all but silent. McNulty was worried since the beginning that she'd end up hurt, except he expected pain to come in the physical form, not mental. He watched her from his periphery as he drove south towards Lake Winnipesaukee. He found himself rambling on to her trying to keep her mind occupied with conversation instead of replaying the scene from an hour ago in her head. The fear she must've felt when the man busted through the door, those shaking hands holding a heavy gun at the end of her long thin arms, it must've overwhelmed her senses. McNulty needed her senses intact for at least the next while if they were to successfully get her brother away from Bishop and get them both out safely. After a few minutes she seemed to calm down a little. McNulty took the opportunity to go over some basics on how to drive a stick shift in case she needed to get away quickly. He explained it to her twice, knock the gear shift into neutral, turn the key, clutch, then into first, and then just punch the gas. Finding the bite was something she could learn another time, he needed to know she could blast out of there in a hurry. He quizzed her a few times on it until he was pretty confident she understood the process. Whether or not she could carry out the actual activity remained to be seen.

As they got closer to the lake, Penny snapped into form, explaining the surroundings of the house and pointing out not so obvious turns. McNulty was impressed with her memory of the area but guessed it made sense that it was stamped into her mind due to the fear that accompanied her original escape. She directed him to a hidden drive in a small lot that was about a half-mile to the house through the woods, which surrounded the area. McNulty pulled the car to a stop in the corner of the lot and pulled out his large duffle bag from the trunk. They then started on foot into the woods until the house itself was in view. McNulty used a scope meant for a rifle to scan the house and the surrounding area. It had grown dark, but he could see lights on inside the house and some movement, mainly in the upstairs rooms. He was impressed by the size and location of the large lake house. He expected more of a cabin, but what he saw could nearly pass for a very large bed & breakfast. He spotted a number of cars lined up in the wooded drive and also got there in time to watch two members of the Tooth & Nail Motorcycle Club pull away on their Harley's. 'Their reinforcements have pulled out' he said to Penny, but she seemed not to notice. She stayed crouched down on one knee like a high school football player waiting for a pep talk. She stared out at the house. McNulty asked her what she was doing. She said she was counting the cars and trying to estimate how many people were inside. McNulty was impressed and told her to try and build in a range estimating between two and three people per vehicle, guessing it was somewhere in the middle. He handed her a small Kevlar vest, which she took and held in both hands unsure what to do.

'Take your sweatshirt off and put that on underneath.'

'Okay.' She said.

When she had the vest on and pulled her sweatshirt back on over it, McNulty strapped a holster on her as well, one over her shoulder and one around her ankle. He checked two guns, and fit them into the holsters. 'These are loaded and ready to shoot.' He said. 'Be careful.'

'Do you . . . do you think I'll need to use them?'

'Jesus Christ, I fucking hope not.'

'Should I take extra bullets?'

McNulty shrugged. 'Do you know how to load them?'

'No.'

'To be honest, if you use all your bullets chances are that shit isn't going too well . . . fuck it.' He reached into his bag and found a second clip for the gun in her shoulder holster. He made sure it was loaded. 'This is what you do.' He said and showed her how to drop the clip from the gun at the handle and reload another. 'Try it.'

She took the gun and clip into her hands and repeated the steps McNulty showed her. It was clumsy, but she got it loaded.

'Good enough.' He said. Then McNulty put his own vest on and holsters. He pulled his leather jacket on over him, but left it undone in front for quicker access to his weapons. He attached the scope to his rifle and took that in his right hand. 'Let's get closer.' He said then began walking towards the house. The wet leaves swished underneath his boots as he slowly led the way forward. He stayed close to the trees, intending to keep covered wherever possible from a clear line of sight from the house. He guessed Bishop had eyes scanning the perimeter constantly. 'He's smart enough to know I'm coming.' McNulty thought. 'Especially after his man didn't check in.' He wouldn't be surprised if the news of a dead man in a motel dumpster had already hit the scanners. 'Wanted in New Hampshire now too no doubt.' He thought. After about ten minutes walking, he and Penny ducked for cover with the house in full view. He put his hand on her shoulder. She looked up at him. He could feel her body shaking, but her eyes showed confidence, or at least, determination. 'You ready for this?' He asked.

'I'm ready to get Liam back.'

'Good. Intel said he's in some hidden room on the third floor over the back of the house.'

'I know where he is.' She said. 'It's the only place Bishop holds people. It's where he does all his dirty work.'

'So you think you can find it?'

'I know where it is. There's nothing to find.'

'Do you think you can get there without being seen I mean?'

She shrugged. 'I'll try. There's a back stairway that's dark and hidden for the most part from the rest of the house. If I can make it around back undetected, I should be able to sneak up.'

'My guess is that there's at least one or two people guarding Liam.'

'At least.'

'That's where I come in. I need you to wait here. Stay hidden in these trees until you hear my signal.'

'What are you gonna do?'

'I'm gonna try to get the troops drawn down front, get everyone away from the back. Then hopefully your path will be cleared.'

'Okay, but what's your signal?'

'I guess it's not really a signal.'

'Then what is it? How will I know when to go?'

'Tell you what. Wait for shit to start blowing up. Count to ten, then run for the back.'

'That's it . . . that's your plan?'

'Hey . . . well, Billy usually has the plan. I'm what you might call the muscle. You're stuck with me, so that'll have to do.'

'If you say so.'

'Listen to me. I'm gonna draw a crowd. You get Liam and get the fuck out. Just run. Head back to the car, the keys are under the rock by the back tire. Do not wait for me.'

'What about you?'

'Don't worry about me, I'll be fine. This shit is like playtime for me. Promise me you'll just get Liam and run. Promise me that. Please.'

'Yeah sure. I promise. Once I have Liam, I'll run.'

'Alright.' He said and put his hand on her shoulder again.

She put her hand up and squeezed his. He felt her small hand grip his fingers and squeeze. Joy and pain mixed and overwhelmed his senses at once and his knees wobbled for a moment. He breathed in deeply and strengthened his footing. He smiled at her and took his hand off her shoulder then turned towards the house. He gripped the rifle tightly in his hands as he began moving forward in the brush. He walked for a minute or two before he began to see the brush clearing. His heart started beating more quickly and he felt nervous energy all of a sudden. Using the scope earlier, he had scanned the main entrance of the house. It led to the kitchen and the opening was surrounded by several cords of firewood stacked about six feet high. He was only yards away now and he guessed if anyone looked in his general direction he'd be spotted for sure. He put his eye to the scope and aimed the rifle towards a long farmer's porch that ran along the front of the house, which was the side overlooking the lake. He'd spotted his target earlier with his initial scan. There were three large propane barbeque grills lined up on the farmer's porch. They were not so close to the back room that an explosion would harm Liam he guessed, which was lucky. They were a few yards to the right of the kitchen entrance, so his hope was that any explosion would be felt near the front of the house and send people in his direction.

He settled in his crouch and lined up the largest of the three tanks in his sight and breathed slowly. He shut his eyes for a second to clear them, then opened them again. His mind raced. Flashing images moved through his head quickly, pausing for split second intervals only. Frozen photographs of his wife and kids were included in those intervals. They weren't memories of times spent with them however, they were memories of himself looking at actual photographs through tear filled eyes. A deep sorrow swept over him again suddenly, but its shadow was short-lived. He cast it away, swallowing that pain one final time and replacing those images with a vision of Penny. Her nervous smirk and questioning brow brought a smile to his face. He calmed himself finally and breathed in one last time a long deep breath. He tasted damp autumn air and firewood on his tongue. Slowly he released his breath, mouthing a silent prayer as he did. The final puff of air left his lungs, then he fired.

LIAM MAGUIRE

John Bishop's visit was odd to Liam. The man seemed unsure of himself and just plain sad. It was a strange encounter to say the least. When Liam heard Bishop's switch blade flick open he braced for the worst. He expected the next sound to be that blade slicing through his skin and shook with fear when Bishop walked behind him. He thought he'd feel a cold blade tear into him, but instead he felt a sudden release of pressure around his wrists as Bishop cut loose his ties. Liam sat there still afraid to move. He was confused, but based on Bishop's demeanor, he actually thought for a second that he would be let go. That was until Mick ran in panting. McNulty was here. That was obvious. In all likelihood Penny was somewhere with him. Liam wasn't sure if he should feel happy or nervous about this revelation. McNulty was obviously there to help rescue him, but his and Penny's lives were still in the balance until that act was completed and right now their safety was far from guaranteed. When Bishop rushed out, he yelled for Mick to stay behind and watch him. Liam saw the interaction. He watched the exchange closely. There was tension there between the two men. Also, there was no mention of Bishop cutting loose Liam's ties. Right away, Liam put his wrists behind his back to give Mick the appearance that he was still tied up. He wasn't sure what to do next, but he knew something would have to present itself. He could still feel the bronze blade in his back pocket. At this stage it was practically embedded in his upper thigh. He didn't reach for it however, not yet anyway. Mick was the same man that attacked him earlier. Liam didn't trust him an inch, but he could tell something had happened that made him quieter and less aggressive around Liam. He even pulled a chair up closer to the door and sat several yards away from Liam, which was a Godsend since it meant Liam could more easily hide the fact his hands were free.

Liam kept watching Mick. The young man sat frantically kicking his leg and chomping away at his fingernails. Liam was considering his options for escape when suddenly an explosion shook the entire house. Liam felt the ground tremble beneath him and he nearly pushed himself over backwards in his chair. He heard Mick start yelling and swearing. He watched him jump to his feet and start pacing. He ran over to the window and pulled aside the shade. A yellow light shone through the room when he did. Liam knew it was too late for daylight and guessed whatever exploded had set off a fire. He could feel heat all of sudden. Whether it was real or imagined he couldn't tell. He felt his heart start hammering in his chest as fear and adrenaline set in.

A couple minutes passed and Mick continued pacing back and forth frantically. By this time Liam could hear a commotion. There were loud continuous pops that he guessed could only be gunfire. There were yells and swears coming from what sounded like several different voices. His momentary relief at the news that McNulty had come for him was now overburdened with fear. By the sounds of it, if McNulty wanted to get him out there was an army to fight through first. A sudden loud succession of 'pops' rang out, followed by howling screams of anguish. 'Fuck!' he heard Mick yell. Finally Mick stopped pacing. He paused and looked at Liam. They made eye contact for a moment, but Liam didn't feel any communication had passed. Mick turned and ran barreling out of the door.

Suddenly, Liam was alone. 'But for how long?' He thought. The gunfire and shouting seemed to slow somewhat, though it didn't cease. It did seem to fall into the background and became white noise after a minute as Liam sat and figured what to do next. He waited for another minute before moving. He counted out the seconds. At sixty seconds, he pulled his hands back around to his front. At seventy five seconds, he slowly stood up and let the blood find its way to his feet. At ninety seconds he decided 'that's it, now's my chance' and he crept slowly towards the door. The tongue and groove flooring creaked loudly with every step, though he knew only he could hear it with the battle continuing on the floors below him. He walked up to the door, which had swung shut when Mick stormed out and slowly opened it. He heard steps outside the door suddenly and panicked. He tried to shove the door closed, but a figure plowed through it and knocked him backwards. Liam scrambled to his feet and steadied himself for a charge. But a charge never came. As he got to his feet, he looked up and saw a face similar to his own staring back. Joy filled him and he got a sudden burst of energy. 'Penny!' he yelled. She smiled and held a finger up to her lips. He rushed towards her and hugged her. He felt tears well up in his eyes.

Penny grabbed his face with her hands and looked over his bruises. 'Are you hurt?'

'I'm fine, it's nothing. Where's McNulty? Is he . . . in that?' He asked pointing down towards the gunfire that continued.

Penny nodded. 'We need to go, come on.' She said and

started towards the door. Liam followed behind her. She paused in her tracks at the same moment Liam heard the door hinges squeak. Liam looked up and saw it swing open, he could see Mick in the frame with a gun raised. 'Get down!' he yelled and shoved Penny down behind a table. Liam jumped the other way and felt the wind of a bullet whiz passed his ear. He spun around on his knees and saw Mick walk forward and turn towards Penny. Penny struggled to keep her body behind the tiny table. She had only her skinny frame to thank. Liam had no conscious thought of what came next. He hadn't even realized his knife had gone from his pocket to his hand. He jumped to his feet and charged forward. Mick attempted to turn the gun on him but Liam tackled him first.

The two young men landed on the ground. Liam landed on top. He expected a struggle, but nothing came from Mick except a gurgling noise forced from his mouth. Liam slowly pulled his hand away and stood up. He stared at the knife sticking out from Mick's chest. He barely noticed Penny stand up from behind the table. She walked over and kicked the gun out of Mick's hand. Liam watched as the remaining light seemed to pour out of Mick's eyes. He looked up at Penny slowly.

'Let's go.' She said and walked over and grabbed his hand.

Liam nodded. 'Yeah. Let's go.' He said and he let Penny lead him out the doorway.

MCNULTY

McNulty stayed low, ducking behind a large cast iron stove that took up a significant portion of the kitchen. He loved this stove. If there was no ridiculously oversized cast iron stove that miraculously was not lit and therefore did not burn the hell out of him as he leaned against it for dear life, then he would not have lasted as long as he did in the firefight's chaos. He guessed it was around five minutes since he successfully blew out the entire first floor with the exception of the kitchen. He'd been constantly engaged in a gun battle since then, so it felt more like an hour or two, but realistically he guessed it was five minutes or less. His plan was to create a diversion and live long enough to keep it going until Penny and Liam made it out and were running to safety. The downside of his plan was two-fold. One, there was no way to actually tell if they made it out of the house. Not unless he managed to kill everyone else and do a circle check of the property, which at the current stage seemed an unlikely scenario. And two, he hadn't thought through an exit strategy for himself. He was more concerned with the first issue really since on the second front he felt like he could wing it if need be.

Another array of bullets ricocheted off the stove and into the wall behind him. 'Those were close.' He figured since the vibration off the stove made it to his head causing it to ache. He turned onto his stomach and slowly peaked his head under the legs of the stove. Out into the open he could see the first floor was in shambles. He could see bodies lying around, there were definitely casualties both from the explosion and his initial onslaught of gunfire. He'd slowed the attack down as he started to conserve ammunition. His opponents seemed to take the same approach. He knew Bishop was still alive since he could hear the man shout orders at his crew, those of them that were left anyway. Plus, every so often Bishop would yell out to McNulty something like, 'ready to call it old man?' To which McNulty would respond either with a spurt of gunfire or something like 'fuck you.'

McNulty heard a noise behind him and quickly rolled onto his back and fired. He shot the man in the forehead that had tried to flank him from the kitchen door. He watched the man crumble and held his guns up waiting for more men, however none came. 'Come on now Bishop!' he yelled. 'What do you got left, one, maybe two more guys? I think it's time you stand down boy!'

No response came initially, but after a few seconds, bullets chimed off the stove. McNulty knew Bishop was down to at most one or two men besides himself. It seemed they had themselves a stalemate, but there was no walking away from this chessboard. Smoke had also begun to fill up the kitchen and McNulty's nostrils burned when he tried to breathe. The large wooden lake house was no match for the level of explosions and gunfire it had endured, he knew the place would be nothing but ash by morning. He tried to peak his head out and around. His only chance was to make it out of the kitchen door and run into the woods, though he couldn't place Bishop exactly and he didn't think his chances of outrunning a man at least twenty years his junior were very good. 'Fuck!' he yelled to himself.

Suddenly he heard a hissing noise from a few yards away. It sounded like a muffled whistle, like a person trying to get his attention. He looked around and in a dark corner, which looked like it led to a staircase, he saw them. Penny and Liam stood tightly to the wall. Smoke bellowed from the staircase forcing them outwards in order to stay breathing. 'Exit must've crumbled' he thought. 'Fuck.' McNulty held a hand up to them telling them to wait. Penny nodded that she understood. McNulty looked around for options. There was only one way out for Penny and Liam and that was through the kitchen. He knew their run across to the door was a short distance, but it meant running right into Bishop's firing line. He had to do something however, or everything he'd done so far, all the blood . . . was for nothing. He turned onto his knees. He looked at the stove and almost laughed to himself when he saw it. The oversized stove had on it an oversized cast iron door. He pulled at it and it didn't budge. He needed every ounce of his force to move it. He jumped to his feet, still keeping his head down and pulled at it. He gritted his teeth as he did and felt his leg muscles and back muscles ache as he pulled upwards. With a final grunt he felt the hinge loosen and the large door finally came free. He had to sit back down for a couple seconds to get his strength back. Then he knelt again and gripped the large iron door with his left arm. It would never cover his whole frame, but it was better than nothing. He reached down with his free hand and pulled out his last pipe bomb from his jacket pocket. He nodded to Penny. He pulled his lighter out and lit the fuse. The flame bit the wick and started burning down. He heaved the pipe towards the direction of Bishop's gunfire. At the same time he jumped to his feet and ran across to Penny and Liam holding the massive door in front of him with all his strength. They got behind him and he backed them out towards the door. He heard gunshots all around him. Some ricocheted off the door, but others came from another direction and he realized both Penny and Liam were firing across at Bishop's crew to keep cover. They reached the door and McNulty yelled for them to run. He heard Liam and Penny's footsteps as they began running. He dropped the iron at the doorway and saw Bishop and another man running towards him. In a split second, McNulty judged their distance and their pace. There was no way. They were too close. If they made it out the door Penny and Liam were dead. McNulty looked to the right of the door. The cords of firewood hovered next to it. He looked at the size of the stack and imagined the weight. It was his only hope. He raced to the edge of the stack, turned quickly and charged into the pile with every ounce of energy he possessed. The pile shook, but didn't fall. He stood back one more time and heaved himself into it. This time the pile gave and like dominoes rolled in front of the door. He heard yells from the doorway and knew Bishop and his guy didn't make it through. He stepped down to run, he could see Liam and Penny at the edge of the brush. He watched Penny turn to look back and watched her pause when she saw him. He took one step towards them, but a noise behind him made him stop. He turned and saw that the stack of wood started to move, he could see it vibrate and could tell by the angle of the fallen wood that when it tumbled, it was going to free the doorway. McNulty ran at the wood and turned leaning his back into it. He stopped it for the moment, but the weight of it was immense. His feet began slipping underneath him. He could feel his calf muscles burning and the burning made its way up to his hamstrings, then around to his thighs. His back strained at the weight. He looked up and saw Penny edge her way a few step towards him 'Go!' he yelled 'Run! Now! Liam, get her out now!' he screamed across the yard towards the brush. He could feel his whole body shaking now. He watched Liam put his arms around Penny. She fought him hard, but he managed to lift her off her feet and began carrying her, pulling her away one leap at a time. McNulty's vision faded then focused several times in a matter of seconds. His body shook violently. His head grew lighter each second and his knee's began to wobble. His vision focused one last time and he could see Penny's face, contorted in anguish, tears rolled down her cheeks and her mouth spoke in silent screams, but she was moving now. Liam was pulling her out of there whether she liked it or not and before McNulty's vision faded for the last time, before his body gave out and succumbed to the weight of over two cords of firewood, before he took the last breath that he would ever take, the Maguire siblings disappeared into the darkness of the woods and he smiled.

JOHN BISHOP

Smoke burned into Bishop's lungs as he and Doyle fought to clear the stack of firewood from the kitchen doorway. Both men pushed and pulled at the logs frantically, knowing that to fail was to die. They saw the house coming down in flames around them. Doyle even started pumping rounds into the unforgiving wood. They fought against it, but there was a strength holding the wood against the doorway unlike any he imagined a human could possess. He imagined a herculean creature on the other side of the wall of logs, half man, half God with the strength of a thousand John Bishop's pushing against it. When the logs finally did fall, when they crumbled and he and Doyle managed to crawl out from the kitchen and together gasped for air on the front yard, he realized his imagination was not far off. After a minute or two Bishop picked himself up off the ground and walked back towards the pile of logs that moments ago stood static and unrelenting against the attempted escape. Doyle followed behind him, but didn't join him when Bishop started racing to pull the logs from the pile apart, that is until Bishop screamed at him to help. The two men then dug through the firewood, now in a race against time as the flames from the house licked out at them only feet away from the structure. Finally, at the bottom of the pile Bishop found what he was looking for. As he tossed away the last couple of logs, a man's shape started to appear. He and Doyle cleared the logs away and the two men struggled to pull the giant underneath away from the logs and flames. Bishop knelt down and leaned his head on the man's chest. He heard nothing. He reached for a pulse, but again nothing. He stood up and Doyle stood beside him. Bishop looked into the dead man's face. His eyes were closed and his face held a peaceful expression. Bishop felt a wave of emotions and his eyes filled with tears, though he wouldn't allow them to drop.

Doyle looked at him with confusion. 'So, he's fucking dead Johnny. What have we been doing? If it wasn't him, it'd be us. He's an old man, fuck him.'

Bishop looked away for a second, then lashed out with a backhand to Doyle's face that stunned him. Doyle stepped back, then looked at Bishop holding his face in awe.

'Have some fucking respect Doyle. This man was a legend. You just witnessed the death of Porthos.'

'What do you mean?'

'Forget it. Get in the fucking car.' He said. They both walked through the line of cars to the end and climbed into Bishop's SUV. Bishop got in behind the wheel this time. 'Keys?' He said to Doyle and held out his hands.

Doyle handed them across to him. 'We going after those two?' He asked.

Bishop shook his head. 'For what Mike? Look at this place. It's fucking over. The kids walk. They won.'

'Okay then John. Well . . . what do we do next then?'

'I'm gonna drive back to Quincy. I need you to do some digging and get me Billy Carson's phone number. I need a sit down with him before this shit goes any further.' Bishop started the car and put the transmission into reverse. He heard a whistling noise and felt hot liquid squirt the side of his face. He blinked it from his eyes and saw blood splattered across the windshield in front of the passenger seat as Doyle's head shot forward off the dash and his body slumped down sideways.

Bishop put the SUV into park again slowly. He took a deep breath, then smiled. When he turned around he saw the round barrel from a black silencer pointed between his eyes. A man with grey hair and a salt and pepper goatee sat back holding the gun in his outstretched arm. 'I thought I'd see you sooner' Bishop said. He noticed the man's eyes had tears lining them.

'About a minute too late.' Billy Carson mumbled.

Bishop nodded then asked 'What happens now?'

'The kids live.'

'Yeah, I get that . . . what about me?'

'What the fuck do you think?'

THE END

Or is it . . . .

Visit paulgarveyauthor.com **for more information**

Reviews are welcome and needed, visit amazon.com/author/paulgarvey **or** goodreads.com **to let other readers know what you thought about** *The Carson Series*.

Also by Paul Garvey:

Blackpool Knights (March 2015)
Fixers (March 2016)

www.ingramcontent.com/pod-product-compliance
Lightning Source LLC
Chambersburg PA
CBHW020622020726
47494CB00001B/14